THE BRAZEN HEAD

Books by John Cowper Powys

WOLF SOLENT

A GLASTONBURY ROMANCE

IN SPITE OF

JOBBER SKALD

MAIDEN CASTLE

OWEN GLENDOWER

PORIUS

THE INMATES

ATLANTIS

AUTOBIOGRAPHY

THE MEANING OF CULTURE

THE PLEASURES OF LITERATURE

RABELAIS

MORWYN

VISIONS AND REVISIONS

THE BRAZEN HEAD

by

JOHN COWPER POWYS

MACDONALD : LONDON

*First published in 1956 by
Macdonald & Co. (Publishers), Ltd.
16 Maddox Street, W.1
Made and printed in Great Britain by
Purnell and Sons, Ltd.
Paulton (Somerset) and London*

Dedicated to

GILBERT TURNER, F.L.A.

CONTENTS

I

THE STONE CIRCLE

It did not take Lil-Umbra long with her fifteen-year-old legs and her slender figure to scamper down the quarter-of-a-mile avenue of over-arching elms that led due eastward from the Fortress of Roque, where she lived, to the ancient circle of Druidic stones that had come to be known as "Castrum Sanctum". Once only did she pause: and that was because something about the manner in which all the smaller twigs at the end of one of the branches clutched at each other and then let each other go arrested her attention. It made her think of a young man called Raymond de Laon: but she could not have explained to anyone, just why it did.

The avenue sloped down all the way from the Fortress of Roque to the camp, but before it reached the latter, which was a grassy enclosure littered with broken stones, the smoothness of its gradual descent was checked and impeded, or, if you were bold enough to take them in a flying leap, accelerated, by a couple of rather high and very massive marble steps.

Lil-Umbra had already made up her mind, after seeing each of her brothers come down with a disturbing if not a disastrous collapse, that such wild jumps were beyond what was expected even from a maid "of true Abyssum spirit", as she had once heard herself described by her father to her mother. So she turned half round as she clambered down each of these two steps, touching with the tips of the fingers of one hand the slippery marble and giving a little tap on the ground with the toe of the foot that first came down, to make sure she wouldn't slip or slide. Once safely on the level grass of the Castrum Sanctum she ran with a quick bounding step to three tall

9

perpendicular stones which stood side by side in the centre of the enclosure.

During the whole of that January there had scarcely been one night of thaw, and as this was the dawn of the twenty-ninth and in a couple of days it would be the first of February, the day which was her father's birthday, she had a particular reason of her own for approaching at this early hour those three upright stones.

It was Lil-Umbra's special desire to see the sun rise that morning while the waning moon was still visible in the sky, but she never would have dared to dodge both Nurse Rampant and the Nurse's assistant, old Mother Guggery, not to speak of Lady Val, her own devoted mother, if she hadn't made an appointment to meet a person, not only respected by them all, but one who was intimately lodged in Sir Mort Abyssum's trust and confidence.

This was none other than a gigantic Tartar whose life Sir Mort had saved when they both were surrounded in a half-crusading, half-plundering skirmish in Dalmatia, by an over-powering group of reckless Arab spearmen; and who in desperate gratitude had become his devoted slave for life.

Both the man's parents had been now for a long time dead. Giants of his size were very rare among Mongolian Tartars but, all the same, Peleg inherited his gigantic stature and strength from his Tartar mother, while his name Peleg showed that his father was a Jew, and indeed the original Peleg, too many thousands of years ago to be numbered in centuries, was none other than the grandson of Salah who was the grandson of Shem who was the son of Noah.

But it was certainly no thought of Noah or any other Hebrew patriarch that drew from Lil-Umbra her cry of excited delight the moment she saw Peleg crouching behind one tall Druidic stone in that broken circle. She scampered up to him at once and when she found he was asleep she had no compunction about snatching at his sleeve and jerking it up and down to waken him.

Had the rounded rim of the suddenly-risen Sun not become at that moment a living presence in the very place where, only a pulse-beat before, there had been nothing but the deepening of a wide golden glow diffused over the whole horizon, it is likely enough that Peleg might have received a bewildering shock from Lil-Umbra's leap into the enchanted pool of his dreams.

She certainly plunged in with a splash and the way she shook the giant's sleeve was enough to have jerked any ordinary mystery-loving Mongolian out of the happiest phantasmagoria of delectable dreams.

But the sight of that red rim, all the redder from the patches of snow on the slope of the ridge and the nakedness of the tree-trunks between which it appeared, conveyed to the man in a flash the whole situation. The first move he made was to alter with scrupulous care the position of the colossal iron mace which was his habitual companion and which was surmounted by a round ball as big as any ordinary man's head entirely covered by iron spikes. This weapon, which had been lying across his knees as he slept, with his back to the tallest stone of that forlorn remnant of a Druidic Circle, he now laid carefully on the frozen grass at his side and welcomed his master's daughter with a grave smile.

That little lady, delighted at having so successfully thrust her slight warmly-clad boreal body between the ancestral pillars of the mystic avenue to her friend's oriental dream-dome, didn't restrain herself in the least, now that he was awake, from pelting him with a shower of questions, confessions, declarations, and suggestions.

But it was not long before the gigantic Oriental and the young European were equally under the spell of that magnetic red orb which did not take many minutes to be half-way over the ridge that formed the eastern horizon of the Manor of Roque.

The Manor had only been in Sir Mort's hands for a little over twenty years; but that had been quite long enough for himself and Lady Val, and their sons Tilton and John who were approaching twenty and their daughter Lil-Umbra, who would be sixteen in a month, to have grown intimately familiar with the fitful moods of the seasons in this part of Wessex, and with the particular enchantments worked upon this landscape by the Sun and the Moon in their variable seasons.

All five of them, the parents equally with their children, had established between themselves and both these heavenly bodies those private, individual, and even secretive personal relations that most human beings on this earth, whether old or young, though with very different degrees of intensity, instinctively reach.

"Well, here I am, Peleg!" gasped the young girl. "And O! how red the Sun is! It's almost frighteningly red, isn't it—rather like the Sun in that window in the Priory chapel—you know the window I mean?—that they say is a picture of the Last Day, when both Sun and Moon are to be soaked in blood. What things they do tell us, Peleg! I don't believe a word of it; do you? I bet you don't, any more than I do! It's getting too much what these priests and monks tell us! Has John talked to you about what they've done to his master Friar Bacon, the learnedest man in the kingdom? Shut him up, they have, because he won't believe their lies; and when he wants books and things—things he *has* to have if he's to work at his inventions—they do their best to stop him from getting them!

"Do you know what came into my head the other day, Peleg? And it was because of that that I wanted you to show me the Moon this morning—no! wait a second——" and the girl laid her hand on the back of the tightening and stiffening fingers by which the man was preparing to heave himself up from the ground—"It came into my head that perhaps even my father didn't really believe in all the things they try to make us swallow—and I can tell you myself of one person who doesn't, and that's Raymond de Laon of Cone Castle over there"—and she waved her hand, the one that wasn't being used to prevent his getting up, in a direction to the left of the now blazing Sun—"Raymond doesn't even believe that Pontius Pilate wrote 'King of the Jews' upon the Cross—and think, Peleg, how exciting it would be if I were more like Father in my secret thoughts than like Mother or Nurse or old Guggery or Prior Bog. What do you yourself think about all these things?"

The giant Tartar evidently thought that if he could get to his feet and convey this eager sceptic to a small eminence, only about three hundred yards away, the sight of the waning Moon, which he had himself just seen from that particular vantage-ground, would turn her mind away—at least on this particular occasion—from Pontius Pilate and the Crucifixion. He therefore proceeded to heave himself to his feet, murmuring as he took Lil-Umbra's hand tenderly but firmly in his own, " 'Twere to see the Moon it was that you came, little lady, weren't it? To see the Moon from where your old Peleg do know every look of her, and every look of the belly and horns of her, aye! do know to a sliver which way her horns do point when she be rocking and floating like a ship without a mast and without a sail, a ship that's got lost in a sea of air, a ship that can do naught but watch that air change into an ocean of black darkness."

Muttering this musical monody to the Moon as if the Moon could hear every word of it, though neither Lil-Umbra nor himself could yet catch the faintest sign of her, Peleg led his companion down declivity after declivity filled with dead bracken-stalks and flowerless gorse-bushes, and across a few small rivulets that the girl could easily jump, and through one extremely unpleasant strip of boggy marshland, across which she allowed him to carry her, till they reached at last the place he had in his mind, which was a stone seat, made not by man but by nature, and a seat so prophetical that it might well have been the throne of a great paleolithic astrologer.

Upon this throne of stone they both sank down; and there was a deep silence between them. While this silence was lasting on and on, and while both these two beings, this middle-aged giant whose Jewish blood had endowed him with a more intellectual brain than people realized, and whose Mongolian instincts had from the start provided that brain with a reservoir of thick, rich, massive, sensuous impressions, and this highstrung, wrought-up, magnetically vibrant little daughter of Sir Mort and Lady Valentia, were giving themselves up, in the same absolute abandonment, to the spell thrown out by this faint, incredibly fragile waning moon, there had arrived at the Fortress of the Manor of Roque an unexpected company of visitors.

Now it happened that by some inexplicable telepathic power the gigantic Mongol became aware of this unexpected intrusion; and it was a deeply troubling question to him whether to communicate to Lil-Umbra or not this sudden interruption. It was in psychic matters of this sort that Sir Mort completely underrated Peleg. It had always been the physical tremendousness of the Tartar's strength he needed.

He had never concerned himself very much with what went on in the man's private thoughts. One curious thing just then about the feelings of Peleg and Lil-Umbra as they yielded together so utterly to the sorcery of the Moon, while the giant wondered if it would be wise or not to speak of his new knowledge, was the way they were dominated by an irresistible inhibition against turning round to look at the Sun!

They both felt in some obscure half-conscious way that it would be dangerous and unlucky to turn towards that now fully risen luminary whose warmth they could distinctly feel at the back of their necks. Naturally the warmer the air grew and the more light there was in the sky the paler became the moon at which they were staring.

And the more the presence of the young girl at his side wrought this magic effect upon Peleg's attitude to the cosmos in general and to the landscape in particular, so the more divine did the Moon appear to him.

After a quick glance sideways at his companion as if to make sure of her sympathy but also secretly to ascertain if she were sharing his weird feeling that unexpected things were happening at the Fortress, he began to address the Moon in words more intimate and personal than Lil-Umbra had ever heard before used either to the Sun or to the Moon.

"O great Goddess," he prayed, "grant us, we beseech thee, an influence, a virtue, a secret, a touch, a mystery, from the heart of that which continueth, forever! In a few years I shall be an old man. In a few years this maiden will be a proud and beautiful woman and very likely the mother of children. Out of the heart of the Unknown thou hast come upon us, O great Goddess, and into the heart of the Unknown thou wilt soon pass from us. Heal us, therefore, O Goddess, of the hurts and wounds in our souls that ache and bleed today because of the false doctrines about gods and men that have been inflicted upon us, false doctrines about all things in heaven and earth!

"Have they not taken on themselves, these priests of pain, these ministers of blood, to invent signs and tokens and symbols and sacraments out of privation and deprivation, out of suppression and frustration, out of denial and negation? Have they not thus defied the revelations made by thy blessed mystery, and turned to nothing the secret of thy holy rapture, of thy sacred madness, of thy entranced, thy transporting ecstasy? Make them give us back the pulse of our life, great Goddess, give us back the beat of our heart, give us back the dance of our blood!"

Lil-Umbra remained silent for a couple of minutes with her face uplifted and her head turned sideways towards the colossal profile of the Tartar giant. There were several rooks and a few crows above their heads, sometimes flapping their great wings in disturbed agitation, and sometimes sailing with rhythmic risings and fallings, up and down between sky and earth.

"If I look at the Sun now," cried Lil-Umbra eagerly, "it won't make the Moon angry, will it, Peleg? I can feel it on my neck and I do so want to look straight at it!"

The giant smiled gravely. "Of course, my dear child! Let's both of us have a good stare at the old Life-Sustainer!"

When they had both turned their heads an inch towards the east, Peleg said quietly: "You'd never believe, would you, that the Life-Lord could shake off all that bloodiness so quickly and be as he is now, nothing but blazing gold."

It was at this point—perhaps under the influence of the advancing Sun, perhaps under the influence of the receding Moon—that Lil-Umbra felt an overpowering necessity to pour out from her own deepest soul a torrent of youthful revolt against the whole routine of maternal restraint and the whole authority of her old Nurse Rampant and of the still older Mother Guggery, Nurse Rampant's assistant. What especially she felt impelled to rebel against was the dullness and routine of so much oatmeal and barley-bread and rye-bread and so much vegetable-pottage in place of the rich meats and the intoxicating wines enjoyed by grown-up people; and the sudden inspiration seized her to do this under cover of the rumoured wickedness of Baron Maldung and Lady Lilt and their daughter Lilith, of the Castle known as Lost Towers, which rose out of a swampy expanse of flat treeless country, due north of both the Fortress and the Forest of Roque.

"May I ask you something, Peleg, something that's been on my mind, for a long time?"

"Of course, little lady, of course! I like to hear a child's secrets; and when that child is the daughter of my master—— Go on, my dear, go on for Heaven's sake!"

And then Lil-Umbra did indeed go on. In fact she let herself go with a desperate rush of words. "Why does God allow such wicked people as that family in Lost Towers"—and she made a little gesture with her head and one of her shoulders towards the north—"to be blasphemous about such an important thing as the food we're given to eat? Mother Guggery swore to me that Sir Maldung and Lady Lilt taught their daughter Lilith that all animals were holy angels, and that all fruits and nuts and raisins, and all plants and grasses, and every kind of grain, and all trees and shrubs and bushes and hedges, and all ferns and mosses and lichens and seaweeds, were devils incarnate. I begged Mother Guggery to tell me more: and do you know what she said! She said that Lady Lilt had a special reverence for animals' mouths, and also for the two other holes that all animals, just like us human beings, have at the other end of them.

"Mother Guggery said that Lady Lilt would run screaming up and down all the stairs and through all the passages and anterooms and corridors of the entire Castle of Lost Towers whenever she saw one of Sir Maldung's dogs with its tongue hanging out. 'Someone has hurt that angel of a dog!' she would cry. And Guggery says that whenever Sir Maldung feels bad from eating too much oatmeal or barley-meal or bread-pudding, and begs her to let him kill a rabbit for a change, she refuses to go to bed with him until he has walked to the furthest northern border of the forest, where there's a marshy swamp with rushes growing so thick that they hide every sign of the water.

"When once he's there, Mother Guggery says, he has to make a vow to animals and birds and fishes and reptiles and worms and insects that he will eat nothing but what's made out of the bodies of these vegetation-demons; yes! nothing but what's made of wheat, made of barley, made of oats; yes! made of every root that exists which isn't poisonous! That's what Mother Guggery told me.

"Lady Lilt swore, that she wouldn't sleep with him till he'd uttered his vow at the forest's end that he wouldn't eat anything except this devilish vegetation.

"No! She wouldn't let him touch her till he'd sworn his faithful oath to eat nothing but grain and fruit and seeds and leaves and buds and stalks and peelings and parings and roots and bulbs and everything of that kind in the world that isn't poisonous, and that he'll bite them up and crunch them up and munch them up, and roll them round in his mouth and chew, chew, chew them, and reduce them to messy mush, till he has *taught* them, yes! taught them utterly and thoroughly, *to be what they are* and what in their effrontery they think they are, and what in their devilish violence they actually suppose they were created to be, that is to say these shrinking, stinking, crawling, sprawling, climbing, binding, twining, sprouting and outing, knotting and rotting, sliding and hiding, shivering and quivering, tangling and strangling, burrowing and billowing, racing and facing, threading and spreading and doing all this in the pure unspoilt, original paradise of the blessed inanimates and the holy elements, where men and beasts and birds and fish and reptiles and worms and insects lived happily on the sacred flesh of one another between rocks and water, and between earth and sky before this loathsome multitude—such were the words Mother Guggery told me the Lady used—of vegetation-devils with their horrible juices ensorcerized saps, skins without flesh, pulps without bones, that originally came out of some infernal crack in the floor of the ocean!

"Lady Lilt said she wouldn't sleep with him again till he'd sworn his oath by the edge of that marsh at the forest's end that he would teach these vegetable monstrosities to be what they were by grinding them between his teeth, squeezing them between his tongue and his palate, sucking and squashing them between his healthy natural animal jaws, wringing their insides out, draining their inmost juices to the last distillation—so Mother Guggery told me the Lady said—till all their demonic greenery-sap and all the devilish sappy greenery of their entire selves had been completely dissolved and disposed of in the good sound moving bodies of creatures with hungry bellies and with legs and arms and scales and fur and feathers and with the life-breathing bodies of wholesome earth-worms and the motions and melodies of exquisite insects!

"Such," concluded Lil-Umbra with a gasp, "such were the very words Mother Guggery swore Lady Lilt used."

There was something in the exhausted gasp with which the girl ended this torrent of fantastic rodomontade that made the giant at her side seriously troubled as to what he ought to do. The climax of her elaborate litany as to what Guggery said and the Lady did really seemed to have brought Lil-Umbra to the verge of a complete collapse. Her dainty little head was now resting against Peleg's side like a wood-anemone against the trunk of a solitary sycamore.

"O my dear child!" groaned the huge Mongol: "I tell you it scares me like Hell to hear you talk in that way! It gives me the feeling that some evil influence has come over you. Dear God! but I wish to Heaven you had never asked that old bitch Guggery to talk about it at all! On my life it seemed to me as I listened to you just now that you'd got the exact intonation of Lady Lilt! I hate her; and I think she hates me. She's one of those strange ladies who are up to anything in the way of dangerous magic games! Think of her considering all the grain we eat, whether wheat, barley, oats, or rye, as horrible demons! It's pure craziness, child!"

With an almost indignant jerk he pulled her to her feet. Then, as they both stood with their backs to the paleolithic throne, they had the golden blaze of the now fully risen sun irradiating both the man's enormity and the girl's delicacy.

"I like looking at the waning Moon," murmured Lil-Umbra, "a lot better than facing the rising Sun! But, Peleg, when I said I wanted you to show me both of them together, I thought I should see them side by side. Aren't they *ever* side by side, for us to compare them with each other, one so timid, so escaping, so slipping away, and the other so bursting and bubbling with blazing gold?"

The Mongolian giant looked down at her with a very queer look, a look that she recognized and in every fibre of her being wholly accepted, but which she could not have interpreted to anyone in human words, whether such words were written or spoken.

"O most dear and most simple of little ladies!" the giant burst out. "Don't you see that the whole idea of this mad world is to be found in opposites! Everything, I tell you, my dear little lady, is a Double Opposite."

They both were forced to turn their eyes away from the full blaze of the Sun; but though Peleg turned his head as well as his eyes, so that he saw—but at that moment he saw it without seeing it—a small feathery wisp of white cloud resting against one of the horns of the waning Moon, Lil-Umbra kept her head unmoved while with lowered eyes she stared at her own clasped hands.

"I don't understand," she said now, though with some hesitation, for she hated to appear stupid in this man's sight, "how a thing can be a Double Opposite."

The Tartar giant did see the Moon now, towards which his head was turned, and he saw it with his intelligence as well as with his senses; and not only so, for he felt as if with his outstretched fingers he could touch the inside edge of that fading boat-shaped rim while his head and neck, for both were bare, felt a distinctly pleasurable sensation from the warmth of the Sun's increasing radiance.

"I'll soon show you how it is, little lady of my master," he said gravely. "Take ourselves. Take me for example. The first of my two Opposites is in myself, that is to say, my greedy-grasping body on one side and my obedient, faithful and well-behaved soul on the other side. But the second of my two Opposites is my whole self, body and soul together, as opposed to entire Creation or the total universe of which I am a living part."

Lil-Umbra's head, with its light soft, silky hair bound up so tightly with broad bands of blue satin that the compact shape of the small skull beneath them, such as any imaginable head-dress would have totally disfigured, was emphasized rather than nullified, lifted itself with an abrupt jerk.

"Oh! of course I see! I see entirely! There's a bad Lil-Umbra, ready to tease things and torment things, and pinch things and pull things to bits and to eat too many pears and sing and hum and drum when Mother is nervous or Father's tired. And there's a good Lil-Umbra feeling sorry for Mother and wanting to do everything I can to please Father. And there's me in myself, both bad and good, both Opposites joined in one, who have, as my Opposite now, the entire universe! O I see, I see! I see the whole thing now! I carry two Opposites about with me wherever I go; but I myself am a perpetual living Opposite to the entire world, so that I really am, just as you said just now *everything was*, a double pair of Opposites!

"And now do tell me this, Peleg. Raymond de Laon swore to me the other day, when I went with Mother to Cone Castle and both Sir William and the Baron were away, that he had made up his mind to think out a philosophy for himself, quite different from that of the Stoics or the Epicureans, quite different from that of any of the ancient Greek thinkers, and most different of all from any of our modern theologians.

"Now, Peleg, tell me and tell me seriously, for this is very important to me, and may have an effect upon my whole life: Is Raymond educated enough, is he clever enough, does he in fact know enough, has he travelled enough, is he honest enough in questions like this, to have the right, without making an absolute fool of himself, to work out a philosophy of his own, a philosophy that could be proclaimed in one of their university theses and even be posted up, like they do, on the doors of great debating-halls to be criticized by the doctors of philosophy in Oxford and Paris?"

Peleg surveyed his youthful questioner with a very grave face. There were implications in all this that were not a little disturbing to him. Paleg wasn't ignorant of the fact that this young Raymond de Laon was a relative of Baron Boncor of Cone Castle and that the Baron had begged him to remain with him for a while to initiate his simple-minded and honest young son into the ways of the world.

The old and ailing and mentally-shaken King Henry had been persuaded by an influential group at court to try to bind to the royal cause this powerful West Country family by knighting for some superficial and conventional reason the young William Boncor, who was, in Peleg's opinion, though a thoroughly good and nice young fellow, as wholly devoid of any particularly original or outstanding quality as he was devoid of any dangerous vice.

Thus Peleg began to feel a certain nervous apprehension; for the possibility of his master's little daughter falling in love with a clever young popinjay of the new generation was a shock to him. So it was in a tone that was new to her that he now spoke.

"I had not realized," he began, "that you and young Raymond de Laon were such friends. I knew you saw a great deal of Lord and Lady Boncor of Cone, but I never guessed you or your brothers had seen much of this young relative from abroad. Your father I know has great respect for them all at Cone: but that you and young de Laon were friends I never dreamed."

He stopped and surveyed his companion with a steady stare. "If I could only be sure," he said slowly, "that this young man has had the right teachers, I would be happier about it. Tell me, little lady," he went on. "Has your young friend actually had lessons from Friar Bacon at the Priory? They say that by taking a hare or two, or a badger, or even half-a-dozen wild geese, to Prior Bog's kitchen, people can get themselves smuggled into the Friar's cell. But I reckon they have to be pretty learned people even if it's only in Greek Grammar.

"I heard someone in those kitchens say that you had to know quite a lot of the 'Sentences' of Peter Lombard, or at least be acquainted with the Commentary on them by Albertus Magnus before you'd have a chance, even if you had a hare in one pocket and a rabbit in another, of getting a lesson from the great man."

Lil-Umbra gave vent to an exultant laugh, a laugh that rang out, rich and clear and resonant, towards the point in space whence the Moon was now retreating into the recesses of interminable remoteness; while the Hebraic Tartar, puzzled at her amusement, stared helplessly into the dazzling portion of the sky where the air like a huge celestial sponge had soaked up the burning rays of the Father of Life and Light and was diffusing them over the land and water of the whole Western world.

"But, Peleg," Lil-Umbra cried, "don't forget that John has been taught by Friar Bacon since he was no older than I am. It's a terrific secret, of course, and everybody, including John himself, always speaks of his studies in Oxford at Regent's House, and of course he would again work at Oxford if Friar Bacon were back as he was before Bonaventura became

General of the Order and had the Friar removed from Oxford and shut up, first in Paris, and then at Bumset under Bog. They say in Loam village that the reason my father keeps it so secret is that Bonaventura would be angry as Hell if he knew.

"But of course Bumset Priory is in the village of Loam, which has always belonged to our Manor; so it wouldn't be easy for Prior Bog to keep John out even if he wanted to, and you know what old Bog is, ready to serve as they say every master who comes along if he brings enough French wine. Father hasn't told a soul about John's going there so often. Sometimes I think even Mother doesn't know! If she does, she's a better keeper of things dark than anyone in the whole world!

"But I *think* she does know. I can't imagine Father not telling her when he must know that John tells Tilton and me everything about it."

Lil-Umbra could see that her bold divulging of this long and intimate association between her brother John and the notorious Friar Bacon was no small shock to her companion. The Tartar jerked back his head from the Sun-ray and gave it a rather strained twist sideways, a twist that enabled him to follow, as the girl had been doing, the retreat into space of that silvery Moon, but, instead of keeping his gaze there, he now suddenly lowered his head and turned his whole attention upon the murderous spikes of that iron mace he held on his lap, hugging it almost affectionately between his thighs, while with both his hands he abstractedly toyed with those appalling spikes, pressing his thumb against their vicious points in careful and calculated succession.

What he was feeling in his mind was a black void of desperate loneliness. He had been of late congratulating himself on having a really deep and unique pact, unspoken and inarticulate, but none the less massively consolidated, with his master Sir Mort, but this revelation from the man's daughter of a secret as important as this—and a secret connected with Sir Mort's own son—gave the gigantic Mongol the feeling that he was not even yet a really intimate member of this family and that he had better take what comfort he could as he used to do as an orphan in Dalmatia by imagining himself alone in space like the star Aldebaran.

But the wheel of his fate selected that moment to touch one

of those mysterious "opposites" concerning which he had just been talking. And it was brought about, by one of those secret chains of events that are often so confounding when they emerge out of the underground mole-runs of cause and effect into the twilight of consciousness, that some small token, either the sight at such a moment of an intensely glittering gleam where a particular Sun-ray truck a special spot on the spiky ball he was holding, or the reappearance of a tiny wisp of white cloud, totally forgotten until he recalled it now, that he had seen only a minute or two ago in contact with the retreating Moon, roused in the depths of the tragic loneliness into which he had been plunged a darting flame of a possible redemption of everything.

This came like the leap of a shining fish out of a black pool, and the form it took was the form of a girl not much older than Lil-Umbra herself. But though of like age with the young creature now leaning so trustingly against him, the redemptive vision that rushed into his mind was that of a strangely appealing Jewish maid. Before the bloody day on which Sir Mort had earned his everlasting adhesion Peleg had met in this maid the ideal love of his whole life. She was certainly beautiful; but it was in a strange, very rare degree, and with a beauty that seemed perpetually re-created by some mysterious sorcery in herself. Her name was Ghosta, and on first setting eyes on her Peleg had experienced a thrill of unutterable pride at having in his own veins the blood of Israel.

Yes, this youthful virgin of his own race became from the moment he saw her the supreme light of his life. But it had been in vain that he had rushed round the battlefield and the camp trying desperately to find her again. They had met: they had looked into each other's eyes: they had loved: and then the girl had vanished. And when all was over, and he had become for life the free slave of the House of Roque, it was as if she had been carried off on a cloud.

Like himself she must, he supposed, have been willingly or unwillingly carried off by some Anglo-Norman crusader to a castle in the north of Africa or on the borders of Palestine or in Gascony or Sicily or Piedmont or somewhere in England or Ireland or Scotland or Wales or peradventure on the shores of the Bosphorus.

23

But there now shot into the heart of the smouldering crater of his desperation a weird and unaccountable hope, based on something as slight as that wisp of cloud on the Moon or that dazzling Sun-gleam on the ball of spikes, but something from whose fluttering motion, like a will-of-the-wisp crossing a death-swamp, there arose a suggestion of salvation.

The mysterious Friar Bacon, now a prisoner of Prior Bog of Bumset, possessed a queer servant who was never known by any other name than that of "Miles", an appellation which, being interpreted, might be said to mean an extremely private, reserved, original, exceptional, but also an extremely professional *soldier*: and it had recently happened that, while Peleg was delivering a message to Prior Bog of Bumset, this same Miles had made a casual allusion which for Peleg had been like the sudden appearance, above a scoriac plain and under a dull, grey, monotonous, and devitalized sky, of a miraculous waterspout.

For a second he felt as if he were himself being changed, like Lot's wife, into a pillar of salt; but at the next moment both these mirages of sensation—himself as the pillar of salt, and the wild, mad, hope-against-hope chance that Miles was referring to Ghosta—melted into each other and floated away into space like a triumphantly burst bubble.

What Miles had alluded to in passing, without attributing any especial interest to it, was the fact that one of the Priory servants who helped Master Tuck the chief cook had declared that the said Master Tuck had recently purchased at the price of ten silver Jewish shekels a Jewish woman who had been brought over among the followers of some crusader from Mesopotamia.

Of course there was only one chance in ten thousand that this Jewish woman was his lost Ghosta; but at least it was not impossible. O if she were! If she only were! Such a chance, if it really came true, would reduce to a grain of black dust every despair he'd ever felt!

"Did you groan then, Peleg?" Lil-Umbra suddenly enquired, "or did you crush down in your heart a shout of joy? I'm sure you made a very important noise. I make important noises myself sometimes when I just *have to do something* but don't want anybody else to know!"

"Little lady——" he began; but stopped abruptly.

"Yes, Peleg: were you going to tell me just then your very, very greatest secret?"

"What makes you say that, little lady?"

"Because I heard you make a noise in the bottom of your heart like Father makes when Mother asks him what's the matter with him! I know perfectly well what's the matter with him. He's got something on his mind that he wants to take out of the place where it hurts and carry away to some great desert-plain or mountain-side where he can turn it over and over and over in his mind and nobody be a bit the wiser!"

"*He*'ll be the wiser himself, won't he, little lady?"

"Oh yes! But nobody else will know! *That*'s the great thing; nobody else to know what we've got down at the very bottom of us! But tell me this, Peleg. Why do you keep twisting your head round towards the Moon? And then start staring so straight into the blaze of the Sun? And then hang your head low down and fix your eyes on a root or a stone or a mole-hill or on one of those funny clumps of grey lichen?—and then, after that, as if you wanted to end up with something more exciting than anything on earth, why do you lift your chin up and stop looking at anything but the sky, just the sky alone, as if you expected some angel to come flying down towards you?"

The Tartar giant lowered his head and gazed earnestly at the young girl.

"I'll tell you exactly, little lady, why I look at things as you say, and in such a definite order, beginning with the Sun and ending with the universal air. As I look at each of these things in turn I make the motion of my mind that I make when Sir Mort, your Dad, is worshipping and I am with him in church, or on the march, or at a sacred shrine, or at some gathering of the crusaders. All of us in the whole world, little lady, worship in our own way and as we worship do something to the Thing we're worshipping; and we do this according to our different natures. Having an animal nature what I imagine myself doing to all the Deities I worship *is eating them*."

Lil-Umbra gave a cry of delight and clapped her hands. "Of course," went on Peleg, "I don't ask you to believe that I really and truly eat the Moon or the Sun or the Earth or the

Air. I only mean that I 'make the motion' of eating each of these things, and then afterwards imagine that I'm getting the comfortable and delicious feeling of *having* eaten them! In short, to tell you the real truth, little lady, I *pretend* to myself I'm eating these things, and play at eating them as little boys play at cutting off heads and arms and legs in imaginary tournaments!

"I admit, dear heart, *when it comes to the Air* it's not easy to pretend to myself that I'm eating *it*. But a person *can pretend* almost anything: and that's all I ask, the right to pretend I'm eating air."

"O Peleg! Peleg!" cried Lil-Umbra, in a frenzy of delight. "I'll do exactly what you do when I'm sick to death of Religion. Oh yes, I will! And I'll ask John to ask Friar Bacon what *his* opinion is of this method of worshipping. But shall I tell you a great secret, Peleg? From what I've seen Father do when I've been watching him and he doesn't know anyone is watching him, I believe he has a funny way of worshipping, just as you have. But Roger Bacon thinks the best way to worship is to invent things! John says Roger Bacon is now inventing a Brazen Head, that one day when he's finished with it will utter oracles very, very helpful to us and to our country. That's an exciting way to worship, isn't it? To invent a talking Brazen Head!"

As she spoke the girl smiled radiantly at the giant; but the mention of John brought back upon Peleg all the old cloud of deadly gloom. The thought that no one had told him anything about John having become a personal pupil of Friar Bacon, and that every single one of them, including Sir Mort, Lady Val, the elder boy Tilton, John himself, and even this little Lil-Umbra, had deliberately concealed from him this important piece of news—which wasn't only family news but was also political, ecclesiastical, and international news—was a crushing blow.

What it meant was—so he told himself—that he was not the feudal retainer of the house of Abyssum that he had begun to assume he was, but just a hired man who had to fight for them, eat for them, and sleep for them, and whose sustenance was his wage. So once again his terribly imaginative desperation returned; and he felt as if this secretiveness towards him of the family he served was enough in itself to cast him into outer darkness and to turn him into one of those lost souls he was always hearing about from the pious Christians around him who loved to remind each other of the possibility for their enemies of what they called "the Second Death". That very expression "the Second Death" came back with appalling vividness at this moment; and Peleg felt as if he were clinging desperately to one of the horns of that waning Moon that was now vanishing in space, while an unspeakably horrible monster of colossal size resembling an enormous cuttlefish dragged and dragged at him to pull him down to that same bottomless chasm in the floor of the ocean out of which, according to the blasphemous notion of the Baron Maldung and Lady Lilt, the whole vegetable world and all the grain upon which we live emerged at the beginning like one multiform devil with green sap for blood.

The wretchedness of Peleg's mind at that moment and the ghastly mood into which he had fallen was revealed at this point by a positively heart-rending sigh from the very depths of his being, the sort of sigh that a prisoner who has betrayed his best friend in the hope of saving his own life might have been heard uttering when he suddenly became aware that he has been fooled by his enemies and that his betrayal of his best friend will not save his own life.

"Peleg, Peleg," whispered the little maid at his side, "your heart is crying! Tell your Lil-Umbra what is the matter! Have you suddenly thought that the Pope might decide to start a crusade to cut off all Mongolian mothers from the face of the earth?"

The giant gasped, choked, turned his head, and spat. "Not quite as bad as that, dear child," he murmured. Then he rose slowly to his feet, and taking one of her hands in one of his, as a great wafture of ocean-foam from a broken wave might enclose a little shell, that has been lying on the sand, "I'll tell it all to you another time," he murmured, "but just now we must go back; for Sir Mort's sure to be wanting me, and Lady Val will be wondering what's happened to you."

Lil-Umbra followed obediently; but she couldn't help noticing that the long shadows as she now ascended the avenue gave the trees a completely different look from what they had when she descended; nor was she unaware that those mysterious movements at the top of the branches, that had put such strange thoughts into her head before the sun rose, had now completely passed away, and that the smallest twig against the sky was now as motionless as the largest branch close to the earth.

II

THE FORTRESS OF ROQUE

The door-keeper of the Fortress of Roque was an extremely simple-minded, middle-aged man called Cortex, whose childless wife, Bundy, ten years older than her husband, but with a considerably quicker brain, helped him at his unpredictable, incalculable job. The Fortress's entrance consisted of double doors of colossal thickness that were only closed at night. For these hours of darkness they were fastened by a couple of huge iron bars, strong enough to have barricaded the Skaian Gate of Ilium itself.

These doors opened directly into an entrance-hall that could have sheltered half a hundred men-at-arms if they had been able to pile up their armour in a secluded court-yard that was available on the inner side of this vast reception room.

While Peleg and Lil-Umbra were watching the Sun advance and the Moon retreat from their nature-made throne of stone, an interesting messenger was being interviewed at the great gate of the Fortress of Roque. This was a devil-may-care soldier of fortune called Spardo, who was a bastard son of Ottocar, King of Bohemia, and who was never tired of boasting of his regal begetting.

In order to extend his own predatory explorations, which already had carried him to Byzantium and to most of the ports on the northern shores of Africa, this plausible rogue had recently constituted himself a sort of supernumerary guide, amateur factotum, and diplomatic outrider to a European group of courtly travellers, a few of whom were bound for Oxford, but the rest were wealthy pilgrims, anxious to visit the more famous shrines in all parts of these islands.

Along with the others, however, were a certain number who at the moment were following with fanatical devotion wherever he went, as the same sort of crowd undoubtedly used to follow St. Francis and probably used to follow Jesus, the saintly "general", as he was appointed to be, of the Order of Franciscan Friars, known to all Europe as Saint Bonaventura. This was the Order that Roger Bacon had rather incautiously joined when his family had completely ruined itself in its service of the King against the Barons; and it was anything but fortunate for him when Bonaventura was made the Head of the Order.

It had been no other than St. Francis himself who had given to Jean de Fidanza the name of Bonaventura, by which he was known throughout the whole world; and it was Saint Francis who had started him upon his career of notorious sanctity.

As for this Spardo, he was a tall slender person of about thirty, with a carefully trimmed red beard and large roving blue eyes. He was now holding by the bridle an odd-looking grey horse, which at first sight might have given the impression that it had two heads.

This surprising effect was due to some organic deformity in the poor creature's neck, a deformity which excited the curiosity not only of human beings but also of other animals. As this tall, slender, comical-looking Spardo advanced towards the great gates of Roque leading this equally slender grey horse by its bridle, the man's gaze seemed to be focussed on the horse's deformity, which the horse seemed to be deliberately covering with a strange self-induced film, and to be doing this with so obstinate a determination that the simple-minded Master Cortex, as he watched the two of them approaching, received the queer impression that the lean beast was desperately struggling to answer the man's gaze through the deformity at which the man was staring, just as if that repellent excrescence possessed something corresponding to an eye.

"I have come," began Spardo, addressing the bewildered gatekeeper, "to enquire whether a special group of noblemen and ladies, who feel a natural reluctance to add themselves to the crowd who are taking advantage of the hospitality of Prior Bog, especially as they will be more than ready before they depart to offer as their quota to the doubtless already rich Treasury of the Fortress such pieces of gold and shekels of silver as may fittingly commemorate the occasion, might perhaps be welcomed by this noble and ancient Fortress of Roque and allowed to rest here for a few hours?"

At this point the man stopped to take breath; and both he and the deformed animal he was leading turned their heads a little, as if to catch upon the air some faint premonition of approaching riders.

"I can see at once, master," Spardo went on, "that you've got a long experience of life in these high circles and in these difficult times, so that you must forgive me if I don't stop to explain what might bewilder any ordinary person. But this particular group of travellers, you understand, are on a journey to Oxford and London; and it would be a most blessed relief and comfort to them if your renowned Sir Mort Abyssum and your noble and beautiful Lady Valentia would allow them to rest here for a short space and be refreshed by the famous hospitality of this princely House."

The door-keeper, though anything but a quick-witted individual, was one of those mortals whose sympathy with animals is strong and instinctive, although totally inarticulate. There was therefore a wordless exchange of ideas going forward at this moment between Master Cortex and the grey horse on the absorbing topic, of intense interest to them both, of this mysterious deformity in the creature's neck.

So occupied indeed were both the door-keeper and the horse in the exchange of wordless communications about this weird growth in the latter's neck that the former soon ceased to listen to what Spardo was saying to him. It must have been after more than five minutes of this concentrated examination of the phenomenal shape which this strange growth on the horse's neck was gradually assuming, that the door-keeper suddenly leapt to his feet and began shouting: "Bundy! Bundy! Bundy! come quick! Here's a horse that's going to have two heads! For God's sake come quick, Bundy, and look! It's going to have a man's head as well as its own! Quick! Quick! Bundy! come quick!"

The fellow's appeal didn't go unanswered. He had kept it up after leaving the horse altogether and throwing all his

31

strength into pushing the great double gate of Roque wide open enough to admit half a dozen horses, when his wise old spouse emerged from her retreat and shuffling up to the animal's side began at once stroking it tenderly. "Kyre! Kyre! Kyre!" she chanted in a curious kind of gloating ecstasy, as she rubbed the knuckles of one hand up and down over the crown of the creature's forehead, above its large, blurred, weary, and far-away-staring eyes, while with the fingers of her other hand she gently stroked its thick mane.

Her repetition of the word "Kyre" had an odd effect on the man Spardo. He had been educated in a monastery where they knew a little classical Greek as well as theological Greek; so that to hear this old lady repeat these two syllables which might mean "O Lord!" and also might mean "Hail!" and to see her obvious assumption that in either case the word would please the deformed creature, impressed to the depths of his being the man who was leading it, for he handed its bridle to the doorkeeper, came round by the animal's tail and bowed low before Bundy, who was a grey-haired old woman with an extremely long face not altogether unlike the face of a horse.

"Spardo is my name, mistress," he said, "and it's Spardo who now salutes you and does homage to you, and does so more deeply than you can possibly know. I don't suppose you've ever had the son of a king as your familiar friend; but you've got one now, and if I know anything of women you'll find me even better suited to your taste than the master here."

What the lady thus addressed felt in her secret mind, as she listened to this fantastic progeny of the King of Bohemia, it would be impossible for any male chronicler to describe—but it was clear that the rogue didn't displease her; for though she didn't blot out from her attention the massive jaw, the small eyes, and the narrow, sucked-in mouth of her mate— which latter feature resembled one of those straight lines which certain melodramatic chroniclers tend to throw in between a blow and a cry, or between a cry and a crash—she drew a little closer. Soon indeed she was touching the side of the horse with a fascinated interest in the extraordinary growth in its neck. As for Spardo, his movements were spectacular.

32

He seemed as unable to keep still as a white butterfly in a vegetable garden.

What he was doing now was rolling his blue eyes so queerly in his head that while one of them seemed to be caressing with besotted unction the deformity in his horse, the other seemed to be lingering with no less maudlin tenderness on the elongated and almost equally equine countenance of the old lady.

Then quite suddenly, and with the organic outburst of that sort of irresistible impulse that creates a psychic stir in the whole surrounding atmosphere of any particular spot, he sank down on one knee in front of her, his thin red beard brushing the knee that was not on the ground like a bird's tail that goes on flicking a branch below the one on which it has settled. While the woman's husband regarded him with blank astonishment, he began deliberately imitating the tone in which she made such a natural sing-song out of the syllables that may have been either "Kyre" or "Kaire".

"O noblest of wise women!" he cried, clutching at her petticoats so that she couldn't draw away from him, "you have no idea how near the truth you are when you chant that word. Haven't you noticed what that swelling in his neck really is?"

He now leapt to his feet and touched the horse's deformity with a solemn reverence as if it were something absolutely sacred. As for Mistress Bundy, she hurriedly let both her hands fall to her sides. Then she lifted them up a little, and proceeded to wipe them very very carefully with her apron. "It's the improperly-shaped beginning of a man's head, you cleverest of all ladies! That's what it's intended to be and that's what it will be. It will be a centaur, that's to say, a horse with a man's head!"

At the sound of the word "Centaur" the compressed mouth of the door-keeper went through a faint relaxation. In his boyhood he had attended Saint Aldhelm's School at Sherborne, and there he had heard of the centaur Cheiron and of the lessons in healing which this wise being gave the son of Aesculapius.

The word "Centaur" however meant nothing to Mistress Bundy; and there was therefore not the faintest element in her interest in this creature's neck of anything save the pure

c 33

fascination of some grotesquely weird or fantastically shocking aspect of a deformity.

Both the woman and Spardo jumped back quickly enough however when the sound of trotting horses became audible. "They are coming!" Spardo cried. "Well! I'll ride and meet them and tell them—for I can see from your manner what you allow me to say—that they may expect, if they behave quietly and don't crowd in with all their armour and if they leave their horses outside, a princely welcome!"

"O yes, yes, yes!" cried Bundy in great excitement: "Go! go! go! And Cortex will hasten now to tell Lady Val you are all coming! I am sure that both she and Sir Mort would blame us terribly if we let you pass this door and proceed on your way without stopping!"

The son of the King of Bohemia obeyed Mistress Bundy without a word. He swung himself upon the creature he had long ago nicknamed Cheiron and galloped off. There was no wind at that moment moving among the green spruce-firs and the brown larches and the few majestic deeply-indented, reddish-barked pines, which were the only trees close to this main entrance to the Fortress of Roque, an entrance which faced due south and which lacked, for some technical strategic reason when it was first constructed, any smoothly-sloping approach, like the avenue of elms leading eastward from the postern door.

But if there had been such a wind, and if we were permitted to endow it with anything resembling our own impressions about people and things, it would certainly have received a shock of surprise when it noted that before Master Cortex rushed down the passage leading to the interior of the Fortress, and before Mistress Bundy shuffled back to her chamber in the rampart beside the great gate, neither of them gave the other so much as a glance, far less made any attempt to exchange views on the direction towards which events were moving.

Meanwhile within a small ante-room to their bed-chamber Lady Valentia was impatiently awaiting her husband's return from his accustomed early jaunt. Lady Val could see from where she sat both the elderly women, the upright, bony Nurse Rampant, with her formidable clear-cut Norman

34

profile and her tall muscular figure, and Mother Guggery, the nurse's help, with her short legs, well-rounded belly, and her grey curls, so fantastically trimmed with purple ribbons that her head resembled a bird's nest in an aviary full of irises. These two females were hard at work in the inner chamber, sweeping out the dust and making the bed, and while they worked they were keeping up a regular word-dance of enticing scandal which, by an infinitely crafty and long-practised skill, they exchanged in such a way as to reveal absolutely nothing to their mistress with which she wasn't already acquainted or in which either of them could specially preen herself as the revealer.

Thus it was easy enough for Lady Val to give herself up to a certain rather bitter vein of meditation, for which she only had the appropriate leisure when, as at this moment, she was waiting for Sir Mort before taking the lead in some exacting social function.

"It's no good," she told herself, "imagining at this late stage what my life might have been if I hadn't married Sir Mort and handed this place over to him with his weird Abyssum blood, for just as I never could understand his parents, so, though I love him from my heart as the father of my two boys and of our darling little Lil-Umbra, I do sometimes feel as if, being as I am the only living descendant and representative, in this ill-mannered and unruly island, of our old and civilized house of Dormequil, I might have done better had I given myself and our historic Manor of Roque to one of our cousins in Brabant, or even to one of our second cousins in Piedmont.

"But perhaps *then* I would have died childless; for with all the proud shrinking of what Mort calls my 'virginal qualms', if I'd given myself to a man of my own nervous sensitivity instead of to my old thick-skinned raper of Sabines, these dear children of mine might never have been born! But O I do wish that Mort had never let John go to that awful Regent's College, as they call it, in Oxford, where this man they call the Doctor Mirabilis got hold of him. The boy's head has been completely turned by this cunning Friar with his devilish sorceries! Thank God that Tilton has a firm head on his dear broad shoulders! He has always been the only really well-balanced, sensible one of our family, and I can only pray he'll more and more take the lead.

"It doesn't seem quite right for a young man as well-born and well-educated as Tilton to work like a mason with his own hands at that little shrine to Our Lady he's building out there: but it shows what a good, firm, steady, reliable mind the dear boy has that he is anxious to serve God in a really practical way, rather than indulge in all these crazy and immoral ideas about inventing ships to fly to the Moon and boats to dive to the bottom of the sea and Heads of Brass to utter oracles. O my little John, my little John, if I, your mother, can't get this nonsense out of your head I can only hope that when you're a man you'll find a woman who'll be able to do what your mother can't!"

At this point Lady Valentia was seized with such a spasm of frustration and with such a sense of all the weariness and disillusionment that exist in this human world, that she bowed her head over the arm of her chair, and closing her eyes uttered a piteous prayer to her guardian angel that she might go to sleep like those people in fairy-tales and not wake up till her husband was dead and John was a man and Lil-Umbra was happily married.

It was at this moment that Master Cortex, breathing heavily and gasping a little, not only by reason of the speed at which he'd come, but also from apprehension as to the effect of his news, was ushered into that little ante-chamber.

Nurse Rampant and Mother Guggery jostled each other to be the first intermediary between this Euripidean messenger of fate and the lady of the manor; and Mother Guggery being the nearer at the start won the race. With a word and a wave she dismissed the scullery-boy who had ushered Cortex into the lady's presence, and she would have dismissed Cortex too if she could have got his news out of him before doing so; but Lady Val's instinctive tact and instantaneously available domestic wisdom anticipated any such move.

"What is it, Tex?" she enquired; and her choice of the diminutive syllable which Sir Mort always used for his door-keeper so delighted the professional pride of Mistress Bundy's stolid mate that he couldn't resist giving to both Nurse Rampant and Mother Guggery a grimly sardonic glance, not even including them in one general look but giving them each a separate rebuff, as if he said to the one, "You see it's 'Tex' between your mistress and me," and to the other, "You see how well she knows the way they treat door-keepers in King's houses!"

"Did this man you're speaking of," enquired Lady Val, "I mean the one on the horse with two heads, mention how many were coming? Did he know if the saintly Bonaventura was among them?"

Having completely disposed of the two old wives, who were now so riddled with curiosity that nothing but direct dismissal by their mistress would have got rid of them, Cortex answered Lady Val's questions with the utmost honesty.

"The man didn't say how many they were, my lady, nor did he say whether Saint Bonaventura was coming with them. But he certainly said they would be at the great gate in a few minutes; so, as I knew you and Sir Mort, my lady, would wish them to have a taste of cook's good oat-cakes on this morn of morns, I told him that their men would have to take their horses round to the stables themselves, and that if his noble lords were wearing heavy armour it had better be left in the gate-room, as we hadn't——"

"Did the man tell you that Saint Bonaventura was coming with them?" interrupted Lady Val with some degree of impatience.

The Nurse and Mother Guggery looked significantly at each other as Cortex began to explain at length just when and how, in his recent conversation, the name Bonaventura had been introduced:

"Well, Tex," Lady Val announced at last, "you'd better bring them all in here, into our reception-passage. Yes! All the lot of them! It won't do to discriminate; 'In for a shepherd's crook, in for a royal sceptre!' as the proverb says. But I wish Peleg and Lil-Umbra would come back! I can't think where Lady Lil has made him carry her. Well! you'd better go back and wait for them at the gate. I must go to the kitchen at once and find out what we've got and what cook will be able to do with what we've got"—she broke off with a little cry and a gesture that might have been of exasperation or might have been of intense relief; and while Cortex with a

37

rather dissatisfied countenance stalked out of the chamber, Lady Val turned to Nurse Rampant.

"I think," she said, "that was the postern-gate. If it was, it must mean that Peleg and Lil-Umbra have come in. I expect you had better take the child to her room at once, Nurse. For I know her Father would want her to look her very best if what Cortex said is true and this company really comes straight from France. Cortex isn't one to exaggerate, and I know there's been talk of this saintly Bonaventura becoming a Cardinal, perhaps even Pope, if his glory goes on mounting up at its present rate."

Seldom have three women separated more hurriedly and with expressions more definitely divided between lively excitement, irritable anxiety, and gloating interest than these three did now. But not much time elapsed before Nurse Rampant and Lady Valentia were in sight of each other again, although surrounded now, each of them, by a closely jostling crowd of extravagantly attired lords and ladies.

III

THE HOUSE OF ABYSSUM

The reception of guests in this central portion of the Fortress of Roque always took place in a wide and spacious but low-roofed passage, half cloister, half gothic corridor, between the kitchen and the dining-hall. Of these it was the kitchen that was far the more richly decorated, and in its roof, walls, and general aspect, far the more flamboyant, and grotesquely intricate in its ornamentation. The dining-hall was of much simpler and much older construction. In fact it must have reverted to an age only a little later than the withdrawal from Britain of the Roman Legions.

Entering it you felt you were entering what might have been a giant cave in a fairy-tale; and when you were within it, it was as if it had been through primeval forests that you had to thread your way, crossing some Roman road, and losing yourself in mouldering and broken-up vestiges of shadowy romance. It was the spacious cloistered passage between these two impressive constructions, the eastward-looking pre-historic dining-hall, and the westward-looking, intimately gothic and mediaeval kitchen, that was, upon this particular February morning, in the year of grace twelve hundred and seventy-two, when the little daughter of the house accompanied by the Mongolian giant Peleg came in through the postern-gate, more crowded than it had been since the day when the Norman bride of Llewelyn the Great was entertained here by Lady Val's family.

The crowd by which Lil-Umbra and Peleg were now con-fronted was indeed a brilliant one and yet it was also an ex-tremely confused and motley one. If there were plenty of

39

lords and ladies, there were also plenty of menials and dependents; some of these latter being almost strangers to the place, such as the blue-eyed, wispy-bearded rider of the deformed horse called Cheiron, others, like the Sygerius family, who had been Bailiffs of Roque for two or three generations, being wholly local people.

It was immediately apparent to Lil-Umbra and Peleg, even before Lady Val had been able to make her way through the crowd to reach them, that the chief topic of excited talk among all these people had to do with the coming of the famous Bonaventura, and with the relation between him and the equally famous—though some would say the abominably infamous—Friar Bacon.

The names Bacon and Bonaventura kept rising and falling like a musical refrain from all parts of the crowd. The impression Lil-Umbra first got was that at any moment the philosopher in disgrace and his saintly punisher might suddenly emerge from somewhere behind the scenes and burst into a dramatic dialogue. Then she suddenly became aware that there really was a violent argument between two excitable competitors for public attention approaching them through the crowd, but that this was a dispute between her own brothers.

She could hear her mother's voice indignantly intervening as the two young men pushed their way through the astonished guests with the evident intention of going out through the door by which she and Peleg had come in.

"I know exactly what's happened," she told herself. "Tilton's had his breakfast early, in the kitchen, as he often does, and he's going out to work at his Lady Chapel." And then, as she noticed that both brothers had caught sight of her, "I pray they're not going to drag me into their dispute! If they try to I shall just say that we'd better leave theology to people who're too old for anything else!"

But though both her brothers, and her mother too, had seen her, as she stood there by Peleg's side, it was clearly not easy for them to disentangle themselves from the press of people. Lil-Umbra moved a little closer to her gigantic companion. On this particular morning, when she had seen the advancing Sun and the receding Moon exchanging some mysterious zodiacal password as they separated to pursue their different paths through space and time, it seemed to her as if some special wave of fate had swept this giant, with his Jewish father and his Tartar mother, into her life as a colossal raft, to which, if she could only cling tightly enough, all would end well.

A sharp-cutting phrase used by her brother John, as he and Tilton shook off the interference of their mother, reached her now like a high-pitched fog-bell in a storm-rocked harbour-mouth; but more agitating to her than John's wild talk was a startling vision she suddenly had of Nurse Rampant hovering behind Lady Val. Her reply to this presence in the background was to twist her fingers desperately and tightly round a fold in the Tartar's cloak; and the hard little knot made by this bird-like clutch upon the pliant silk of the man's mantle became, as Lil-Umbra kept striking her other clenched hand upon it, a sort of musical instrument of inspired resistance to constituted authority.

Nor did this quaint combination of gigantic passivity with girlish revolt prove unsuccessful; for Nurse Rampant, who knew both the character of the mother and the character of the daughter better than anyone else in the world, saw so clearly the way things were drifting that she decided to leave Lady Valentia to deal with her three children and their unsocial behaviour as best she could, and turning her back upon them all hurried off to her own quarters.

"If I'm to dress the child," she said to herself, "to please this crowd, they'll have to send her up to me. I'm not going to wait any longer in this crazy hurly-burly!"

Things were indeed getting out of control. Both her brothers were now appealing to Lil-Umbra. Tilton was already finishing what was evidently a sentence he had begun before she had begun to listen to him. "Our learned rulers," Tilton was saying, "are surely appointed by the Church, John, to direct our campaign against Satan, just as much as our secular captains are appointed by the State to organize our campaign against Saracens and Arabians and Turks and all other enemies."

"But what I say," broke in the shrill, high-pitched, rather rasping voice of John, "is that when we come to philosophy, and science, and mechanical invention, we touch a totally different aspect of life from that with which religion is concerned. If you take philosophy for instance," and here John's voice rose to such a penetrating pitch that all sorts of resplendently dressed ladies looked significantly at each other and drew nearer to listen, thinking perhaps that here was one of those dangerous heretics that the great Saint who accompanied them was on his way to suppress, "for instance, in regard to the difference between Mind and Matter, what, I ask you," cried John, beginning to gesticulate like a practised teacher of philosophy, "are we to decide about the Aristotelian view of the Higher Reality compared with Plato's system of Ideas? Or what are we to think about the nature of these immaculate 'Ideas'? Are they perhaps to be considered as Godlike Entities in Themselves, or merely as subjective symbols of——"

"Stop this nonsense, John!" The interruption came from Lady Val. It may easily be believed that Lady Val's indignant outcry had an instantaneous effect upon the already excited, jostling crowd that surrounded them. Everyone heard her words and everyone turned round to look at her; and those who were already absorbed in watching Tilton and John turned from them to their little sister, as if they felt sure that the only female among these precocious youngsters would have some opinion on "the Ideas of Plato" different from any that had ever been promulgated to a puzzled world.

The young girl began to feel as if from every little group of people round them there emanated a violent explosion of human emotion expressed in terms of intensely coloured and passionately gleaming inanimate objects. She had heard that the great "General" of the Franciscan order of preaching Friars—this Bonaventura they were all talking about—was furiously fond of preaching to vast crowds; and she seemed to see him now, as she clung to Peleg's cloak in a sort of exhausted trance, as a great wavering pillar of light broken up into glittering facets in all manner of metallic mirrors across which were moving a wild array of gesticulating reflections.

On every side she felt aware of glimpses of blue and crimson ribbons, hastily caught flashes of waving feathers, shoulders scintillating with the polished links of special chain-armour that the wearers had been reluctant to remove, jewelled clasps at the folds of carefully adjusted robes, and silver-bordered gleaming knots of satin and silk fabrics holding together the slippery waftures of waving mantles, while here and there she actually noticed, among the ornaments worn by some of the foreign ladies who had appeared, convoluted sea-shells most curiously and fantastically tinctured with weird and unearthly colours totally alien to the sea-shore from which they had been gathered.

John neither hung his head nor answered back under Lady Val's words. He just clutched his elder brother Tilton by the belt and went on sermonizing him in a murmur too low for their mother to hear. Lil-Umbra glanced up quickly at the countenance of her tall friend Peleg; and she saw that in spite of his height the Mongolian *could* follow John's words and even approved of them.

Meanwhile she noticed that Lady Val had been suddenly captured by one of the grandest of the Bonaventurian female intruders, who wore a travelling-robe of black velvet overscrawled by amazing hieroglyphics in purple and white of the most fantastic monsters to ward off all danger of bad luck; and by scrutinising this robe while its wearer's volubility absorbed her mother's attention, she derived a certain curious satisfaction which proved to herself though her brother would not have believed it that she had a real taste of her own for beautiful shapes and rare colours and artful designs.

John was now giving Tilton a long and extremely complicated discourse on the importance of never allowing his pious opinions about unusual yet perfectly natural events, such as falling stars, whirlpools, cloud-bursts, earthquakes, tidal waves, and the like, to interfere with his daily observation of the ways and characteristics of the persons with whom he had to live, or to let these same theological opinions terrify him with apprehensions about the future of the world.

"Where Science and Philosophy are concerned," John was now assuring his brother, "it is as bad for the authorities to interfere as it is for the brutal ignorance of the common herd! What I hold is——"

"How John *does* love to say 'I hold'," thought his little sister, "but I expect he's right or Peleg wouldn't look so pleased and mother wouldn't look as if she didn't even notice the exquisitely designed robe that lady's got on!"

43

"I hold," went on John, "that no vulgar prejudice and no high-placed authority has the right to meddle in any of these things."

"You are unfair, John," cried Tilton indignantly. "Isn't he, Mother? *Do* speak, Mother—— Pardon me, Lady"—this was addressed to the wearer of the pictured robe, but Tilton went steadily on addressing his mother—"Do tell him, Mother, *please do*, how unfair he is! Do make him see! What I say is really quite plain and simple. When there's a possibility of wicked and vicious undermining with clever human reason of the long-ago revealed doctrines of the Church, doctrines that God himself——"

"O do for heaven's sake shut up, Tilton!" interrupted John. "Aren't you ashamed to put all this conventional rigmarole, all this hollow superficial humbug, into the head of Lil-Umbra? *You* agree with me, don't you, Peleg? Since you've lived in this country you have seen, haven't you, the cruel harm done to original scholarship and original thinking by the blind and obstinate tyranny of self-interest? You, as a Mongol, Peleg, must have seen among Asiatics of every sort this same terrible wrong being done to enlightened and uninhibited human thought by the tyranny of custom, tradition, habit, and common usage, blindly supported by the stupid self-interest of the particular persons who happen to be in power and who use their power to suppress the least stirring of new thought. You *do* agree with me, don't you, Peleg?"

The gigantic Tartar looked so embarrassed and uncomfortable under the impact of this direct personal appeal that Lil-Umbra was unable to contain her feelings. "I'm not backing up Tilton against you, John," she cried in a clear but not shrill voice; and then, as she noticed a slight movement of Lady Val's stately figure in her direction, she dropped her hold upon Peleg's mantle, straightened her figure, held her head high, and surveyed her excited brothers with an almost judicial impartiality.

The press of people pushing and hustling as they jostled one another in the two streams of outgoers and incomers within those great carved doors between kitchen and dining-hall, seemed, at least to the mind of the super-sensitized young John, actually to be pausing at that moment in the swirl of their movement to listen to the words of the young girl who was holding her head so high. "No, I'm not taking the side of either of you," she went on, "but I feel ever so strongly, John, that this mental argument you're using now doesn't altogether— I know there's a great deal in it: don't misunderstand me, I implore you!—but I also know that there are things to be remembered and thought of, that you, John, neither remember nor think of! There's a great deal in what you say, John dear; more, I expect, than I realize myself: but there's also a lot to be said on the other side—O! a terrible lot!—and this other side is so appallingly mixed up with our feelings that it's oddly painful, John dear, yes! oddly and queerly painful, to bring it out fully enough to be able to defend it. It's because they're such hard things to say and so mixed up with all our deepest feelings, John, that it's difficult for Tilton to express all that he has in his mind—whereas it's easy for you to express all you have in your mind—because, don't you see, dear John, the things you're talking about are clear and definite? They are supposed to be much harder to understand than our emotions and feelings; but in reality they are—and I *know* I am right in this!—*ever so much easier!* For in real truth, John, my brother, the ideas we make up in our minds can be followed by our minds; the feelings we have in our hearts are put there by Nature and they begin and end in darkness and mystery. It's not that I don't know very well where it is that you have picked up your view of things, John, and I know it is a fount of true wisdom. But there are things that a saintly great man like this Bonaventura—and you must remember that Bonaventura was consecrated for his work by Saint Francis himself who must have thought highly of him and must have predicted for him a wonderful future. So we have to remember when we are——"

"Be a good girl now," broke in her mother, who by this time had escaped from the lady with the hieroglyphic gown, "and go upstairs to Nurse. Your dear Father may be back any minute; and he'll want to see you at your best at breakfast because I have invited the whole lot of these good people to this meal with us. I have just now been talking to the Countess of Corbière-Cantorac of Caen and she tells me that the Blessed Bonaventura himself has sworn he will be here if his horses don't fail him; though at the moment he's visiting a leper's hamlet near Ilchester. If your Father's late, we'll have to keep all these people entertained and amused as best we can. He wouldn't like it for us to begin before he came."

Any sagacious onlooker who had the intelligence to ponder on the under-currents of this scene would have already decided that Lady Val, in spite of the competent appearance of worldly poise that she managed to display, was not far from some kind of nervous collapse. Nor would that onlooker have been mistaken. The poor woman actually was on the verge of such a breakdown.

"O why, why, why," she kept asking herself in the depths of her soul, "did our ancient family of Dormaquil ever allow itself to be betrayed by a romantic idiot like me into handing over Roque to a crazy breed like these Abyssums?"

What particularly disturbed her at this moment was the awkward and unconventional isolation of her three children along with that Tartar-Jew, Peleg. They are simply, she told herself, showing off their clever theories to each other, and totally forgetting their duty to the immemorial hospitality and prestige of the Manor of Roque. They ought to be moving about among this crowd with the graciousness of a proper family; whereas Tilton, I can see, is longing to go straight out to his half-built shrine and Lil only wants to put John in his place and show herself as clever as he is!

She turned away from the three of them for a moment and hurriedly examined the faces of the crowd. She soon realized that there were, sprinkled among the visitors or pilgrims from the other side of the channel, several of the richest freemen of the Manor; and she even fancied she saw a couple of serfs in their Sunday clothes. She had already noticed among the Manor officials what looked to her like the whole Sygerius family, except the old grandfather who was no doubt, as he always was, polishing and sharpening and cleaning the weapons in the armoury. This old gentleman had been the Reeve or Bailiff of the Manor for a quarter of a century, and his name was Heber, while the name of his son and successor was Randolph. Old Heber's wife had died years ago, but the wife of Randolph, whose name was Madge, was full of youthful liveliness and daring, as was indeed the whole Sygerius family including both Toby, Randolph's eldest son, and Toby's wife, an extremely pretty girl whose name was Kate, but who from childhood had had the nickname of Crumb.

"That silly girl of mine," thought Lady Val, "must be got away from all these staring people! She *must* go to Nurse and change her clothes and do her hair and be ready to sit down at table when Sir Mort appears. O why, in God's name, *doesn't* he appear? He *said* he'd be back in half-an-hour. He *said* it was only to make sure about that dammed-up mill-pool that he went out like this. He always goes out for a breath of air before breakfast, but not for as long as this! I do *so* hate it when he disappears like this just when I want him most. O there's Madge and Crumb by themselves! Randolph must have taken Toby off to help with all the horses. I must go and find out if they're going to help me at this frightful breakfast. They ought to. They *both* ought to."

Lady Val was no sooner lost to sight among the crowd than her eldest child, Tilton, after watching her vanish in pursuit of the middle-aged Madge and of Madge's laughter-loving daughter-in-law, rose quickly and caught hold of John by his belt. Tilton was a loyal adherent of the New Testament, but in a practical, not an occult or mystical, sense.

He was a tall, muscular, athletic young man, with a candid, open face, straight fair hair, and large honest blue eyes. He had a free, high-spirited, frank integrity of manner that people found very appealing. He now caught his younger brother John round the shoulder and dragged him off towards that same small postern through which Peleg and Lil-Umbra had just come in.

As he thus possessed himself of his brother, he poured out a stream of words. "But you'll see for yourself! You'll see the expression I'm carving on Our Lady's face. You needn't worry about it being cold in my little chapel. I left a good brazier of red coals in there. Besides, the Sun will be shining through the window. Don't be scared. I won't keep you more than a second!"

Lil-Umbra couldn't resist turning her head towards them and she was rewarded for her interest; for Tilton was so eager to explain to his younger brother exactly the point he had reached in his architectural and sculptural undertaking that, with his hand on the door-bar, he went on eagerly with what he was saying.

"What I want particularly to show you, Johnny, my boy, is a smile I've carved on Our Lady's face. It's a smile; and yet it's more than a smile. It's a look of worship; and yet it's a look of What's being worshipped. I won't keep you more than a second; so don't speak till I've shown you! No! No! I don't want to hear another word about reason and science! Wait till you've seen the look I've put on Our Lady's face! Of course I couldn't with only a chisel and hammer show all she was feeling; and of course anyway it would be absurd, even if I were a saint like this Bonaventura who annoys you and your miracle-working Doctor so much, to pretend that I could tell what the Mother of God was thinking. But it's funny how far a person, if he feels anything of the sort at all, can go when he's got a hammer and chisel in his hands! But it's no good talking. You'll see what I mean when we——"

At this point Tilton dislodged the door-bar and pushed the door open; and both boys, with a mutual gasp of pleasure at the bright sunshine and the smell of fir-trees, disappeared into the air. It may have been the shock of the open door—held ajar by Tilton till he finished his sentence—with its lively inrush of sun and air, or it may have been one of those apparently causeless stirrings of motivation that happen so inexplicably to us all, but the second her brothers were gone Lil-Umbra, with a quick glance at the crowd to make sure her mother was still engrossed with the Sygerian family, whispered to Peleg that, if there were any serious trouble over her disappearance, he'd better tell them that she could be found in the armoury, talking to old Heber Sygerius.

With this she left him, and forcing a path for herself through the thickest of the press, went off towards the open courtyard in the centre of the Fortress, where were the privy-retreats for both sexes, as well as storing-places for fuel and food and wine, and where there was even a miniature tournament-ground for knightly competition of every kind.

While Lil-Umbra, with a certain quickening of both heart and pulses, was making her way to the armoury, Nurse Rampant, always more anxious about her elder nurseling—that is to say Lady Val herself—than about that lady's daughter, had found it impossible to get absorbed in her needlework upstairs, and had hurriedly, though rather surreptitiously, made her way back to the scene of action. And this she had only done just in time: for Lady Val, having heard what she felt sure was the sound of her husband's horn, had left Madge, and Madge's daughter-in-law, Crumb, and had rushed to the postern-door.

The long-drawn, world-weary sigh of the solitary wind, as it passed over the roofs and entered the windows and doors of the Fortress of Roque, intensified the wild romantic prayer of Lil-Umbra that she might find by the armoury hearth, along with old Heber, no less a person than young Raymond de Laon himself. Because she had found him there once, she never entered the place without expecting to find him there again.

It was this same wind that brought what Lady Val felt sure was the sound of her husband's horn. She had hardly realized that her eldest boy had only a second ago dragged his brother away to visit the little shrine he was building due west of the Fortress. Lady Val felt certain she had really heard the unmistakable series of defiant notes which her husband loved to play on the great hunting horn that he always carried in his belt whether he was hunting or not, whether he was armed for battle or not, whether he was on horseback or on foot.

The notes of Sir Mort's horn were indeed unmistakable when heard; but had she, Lady Val asked herself, really heard them? She stood still listening. Not a sound came now from that sunlit forest. She made an impatient movement with her hands and shoulders and rushed boldly to the door. Once there she seized the massive brazen ring into which the iron rod, that made this entrance impregnable, fitted with what was to a particular vein in her nature an obliging and delectable exactitude, and jerked that iron bar to and fro sideways with a violence that required all the strength she possessed in her long slender arms, while she vaguely wondered what her two sons would feel if, instead of opening the door to listen to their father's horn, she barred it against their re-entrance.

It had become now, and she herself knew that there was something unusual in her mood, an absolute necessity, or at any rate an angry and desperate one, to hear the sound of Sir Mort's horn; and although her neck was bare and although the wind that blew past her into that crowded entrance made her shiver, the craving she felt for that sound was stronger than her natural shrinking. Wider and wider she pushed the door open, and in an impulse of sheer frenzy she was on the point of rushing out, when a figure and a voice were upon her, and the powerful hands of the old nurse dragged her back into the hall and closed the door upon both the Sun and the wind.

"Did Lil-Umbra go to her room?" whispered Lady Val to the nurse as they moved back together towards the crowd. "Not to my knowledge," returned the other. "But I may have missed her on the way. It would be an easy thing to do."

Lady Val looked at that moment as if she would have liked to have struck the woman; but the wise old nurse, though she released the arm she was holding, showed no sign of having realized the amount of indignant passion which she had aroused. Indeed she knew the lady so well that every course and twist and tangent of the feelings that showed themselves at this dangerous moment were an old story to her.

An onlooker at the scene might even have caught a faint trace of affectionate amusement in the quick look she threw upon Lady Val's nervous fingers, which were now clasping and unclasping each other as if engaged in some convulsive dance.

"So be it, my dear," she said quietly. "I'll go and find our runaway, if you go back to your visitors."

Slowly, stride by stride, holding his long spear just below its shining point, which now gleamed in the Sun in the way certain objects seem to have a special power of gleaming, as if they are consciously holding and reflecting the rays they catch, Sir Mort returned from his stroll to the small pool which in former days had been a crowded fish-pond, but which now only contained a solitary pike and a solitary perch, who, having divided the place between them, and devoured everything, were now watching each other with eyes that were both hungry and apprehensive.

Sir Mort was a tall and slender, but a broad-shouldered man, of about sixty, whose most striking physical characteristic was the shape of his skull, which was very long and very narrow and was perched like the skull of a vulture on the top of a long neck. The length and narrowness of Sir Mort's head was emphasized by his deep hollow eye-sockets, out of which his eyes, dark-green in colour, glared forth with a very peculiar effect; for it was as if they had no connection with each other at all, but were, each of them, the solitary eye of a saurian creature whose eye was at the top of its scaly head.

He had obviously snatched at the warmest and smallest jerkin to hand as he went out and at the smallest and lightest iron headpiece, which was scarcely more indeed than a band of metal round his head, a band into which had been fastened a black-and-white feather.

As he approached his Manor-Fortress he soon recognized that both its material and psychic atmosphere were wholly different from what they had been when he set out an hour ago. There was now an intermittent hum of human voices, steps, cries, exclamations, agitations, conversations; and the cold east wind that was blowing across the forest, and rustling through the spruces and the still bare larches and pines, carried upon its breath and whirled up and down, and back and forth, and round and round, what might have been an invisible emanation from that startling and surprising conglomeration of human voices, human bodies, human gestures, human cries, along with sounds of all sorts rising from weapons of iron and brass and bronze and silver and gold.

"Is our land invaded from France?" was the first thought that rushed through that vulturine skull. But the next was a more rational one. "Fool that I am!" he muttered. "It's that thrice-damnable son of a bitch they've made into a Saint who must be upon us with all his bloody followers! Poor darling care-driven Valentia! How agitated you must be! I pray John is still in the place and Tilton in not too architectural a mood! And I hope to the devil that our lusty old Jew Peleg has brought Lil-Umbra safe back! They can't, surely, all this huge crowd, expect us to feed them?"

Instead of quickening his pace, as he made his way towards the postern door, the Lord of the Manor of Roque began to walk with unusual slowness, pressing the long handle of his spear heavily against the ground at each step.

"I've got to face the fact," he told himself, "that whether I like it or don't like it, and whether poor dear Valentia likes it or doesn't like it, all this whole blasted crew will have to be fed this morning. I hope to God there's enough in our kitchen to fill their damned bellies!"

The tall lean Master of Roque who, as the sole survivor, save for his own offspring, of the incorrigibly eccentric family of Abyssum, ceased now to take even the slowest steps towards his destination. In the downright language he would have used himself, he stopped dead. "My birthday come round again!" he thought, "and poor little Valentia, with all her values and valuations, will be fifty next August! Twenty years more, according to Holy Scripture, and we shall be an aged pair, and the place swarming with grandchildren! Well, well, well."

He turned the glittering point of his spear earthward, and using both his powerful forearms, he forced it down so deeply into the earth that he soon was able to lean with the full weight of the pit of his stomach upon the large bronze knob that terminated the handle.

In this position, leaning on the handle of the spear that belonged to him and pressing its point into the ground that belonged to him, Sir Mort couldn't resist indulging in a queer mental performance that he prayed to God he had been crafty enough to keep entirely to himself—namely an almost ritualistic trick of his, which from the days of his extremely weird childhood he had been led by the deepest thing in him to practise.

The deepest thing in Sir Mort was without doubt the intense egoism of his own soul, in other words his absolutely abnormal self-centredness. None of his offspring approached him in his awareness of his interior self or ego, or in his power of isolating it and of enjoying its isolation. Sir Mort imaged this soul of his in a curiously original and indeed a very erratic way. He saw it in the shape of a particular kind of spear, the kind whose spear-head grows wider and wider for several inches, then proceeds to narrow itself for the same number of inches before it reaches its sharp and piercing spear-point.

He saw it however as made, not of iron or bronze, but of flint. He saw it indeed as a spear with a flint arrow-head for its point, a point enlarged to about a dozen times the size of an ordinary arrow-head. This spiritual spear with a super arrow-head became to Sir Mort the ultimate hieroglyph of himself; and in all his private and secret thoughts, which were often extremely fantastic, he actually saw himself as this same flint-headed spear.

He had got into the habit of imagining his inmost self in the shape of this spear with its flint super arrow-head driving its way through the mossy surface of the earth, while he forced himself to think of it as possessed of every one of his five senses.

Unknown to another soul—for Lady Val was the last person in the world to draw out of him such a secret—Sir Mort, who would have been regarded by his wife and by his sons and by all his neighbours, especially by his pious friend, Prior Bog of Bumset, as simply insane, had they known of these practices, imagined himself seeing the roots and the earth-worms and the cracks in the stones and the variously coloured veins of the different geological strata upon which his soul impinged as it descended deeper and deeper into the hole it was making!

He also forced himself to touch, to smell, and to taste, all these animal, vegetable and mineral entities into whose dwelling he was descending; and finally, so that his spiritual pilgrimage should miss nothing, he imagined himself listening, as he headed downwards, to the intercourse, in some sort of earth-mould language, which these roots and cracks and crevices, these worms in their subterranean dwellings indulged in among themselves, so that he could compare their mental reactions to life with his own.

But this was only the first "move", so to speak, in Sir Mort's intercourse with the cosmic multiplicity. The next thing this crazy owner of Roque must needs do was to pull himself out of the hole into which he had descended with such persistence and proceed to shoot himself through the air! On this air-borne quest he was careful to avoid every conceivable collision. He avoided the Moon and he avoided every planet. He avoided all the falling stars.

And then, when he had got clear of all impediments in his aerial flight, he set himself to enjoy the pure touch of nothing-ness, the ineffable taste of nothingness, the indescribable smell of nothingness, the god-like sight of the immeasurable recesses of nothingness, and finally, pervading his pilgrim-soul with the most exquisite pleasure of all, the unutterable symphonies of the music of nothingness.

And then he would force his spear-head soul to make a great dive out of the depths of the air into the depths of the sea, and it can well be believed how the touch, smell, taste, sight and sound of the swirling, the water-spouting, the whirlpooling, the towering and lowering, the roaring and soaring, the rumbling and grumbling, of the everlasting ocean, with both its eternal motion and its eternal identity, would satisfy to the full the insane void of his unending quest: and, finally and at last, into the hot fire of the Sun and the cold fire of the Moon; and from these into the incredible fires of all the living stars, until, out of earth, out of water, out of air, and out of fire, he wrested what his spear-head of a soul required for its imperishable nourishment. For the only thing in the world that Sir Mort feared was death—the thought of being *non-est*, of being as if he had never been.

He always felt, if only a shred of him remained—only a nail-paring, only a scab, only a tiny bone, only a handful of ashes—as long as this speck of the matter which had once belonged to his body remained, so that his unconquerable soul could hover over it, he would be still Sir Mort, he would not be dead yet.

He now raised himself up and pulled his spear out of the earth and stared in front of him into a great alder-bush from the heart of which, it suddenly had struck him, somebody was watching him. And then, in one quick beat of his pulse, he knew who it was. It was none other than his neighbour, Sir Maldung of Lost Towers. Not only was Sir Maldung watching him, but he held a drawn bow in his hand whose arrow was aimed straight at Sir Mort's heart.

Sir Mort had never been calmer, stronger, quieter, more entirely collected, more absolutely poised in his mind than he was at that instant. He didn't feel in the faintest degree afraid. It was a peculiarity of his that, as long as he had his wits about him, and saw clearly what his enemy was aiming at, not a flicker of apprehension crossed his mind.

"I shall know by his expression," he said to himself, "when

he lets that arrow fly and I shall be perfectly able to dodge it before it touches me! I am myself a drawn bow and a pointed arrow! And when you are yourself both arrow and bow, it is fine sport to watch your enemy's face!"

And certainly Sir Maldung's face was something to watch at that moment. It was positively convulsed with the ultimate ecstasy of killing. His mouth was open and twisted awry; his eyes stared so intently that they seemed as if at any second they might flow or drip or sweat or soak into the alder-bush. His whole face was crumpled and wrung and knotted and sucked inwards.

And then in a second it relaxed like the bursting of a boil, and became, as far as any human expression was concerned, blurred and blotted out. Sir Mort dived to the ground; and the arrow skimmed over his back and quivered into the trunk of a fir-tree.

Sir Mort straightened his body and uttered a queer little laugh. But it did not occur to him to pursue the figure that was now in full flight. "Silly old devil!" he muttered; and strolled, as slowly as he had been doing before, towards the postern entrance of the Fortress of Roque.

IV

LIL-UMBRA

"I'll go," thought Lil-Umbra, "as if Mother had sent me with an important message. I will not speak to a soul: and when anyone speaks to me I'll pretend not to hear, or to be so occupied in delivering my message that though they see I can't help hearing I need not take any notice of what people say. It *was*, after all, not only once but twice that I found Raymond de Laon there! Of course the first time he was there he couldn't have had the faintest idea that I should be likely to come in. But that second time he didn't seem surprised to see me. He seemed glad: very glad in fact, but he didn't seem at all surprised.

"O! I do wonder what he feels about me! It's so teasing never to know! That's the worst of it with a grown-up boy. If it were John now, it would all be so easy! But of course *he* would have let it out to everybody and I'd have had all I could do to make him keep his mouth shut! I suppose I'll never know with Raymond till he suddenly bursts out with it. He looks at me all the time: and that day we were alone at Cone Castle, when Baron Boncor had taken Will with him to London and I was turning the pages with him of one after another of those old books he is always finding in some secret recess in one of those lovely turrets of Cone Castle, I noticed how for some reason or other the hand I wasn't using, to turn a page or to point at a picture, was held in his hand.

"But, O dear! I am afraid I'm just being silly! Plenty of girls much handsomer, cleverer, and more important than me, must have been attracted to him and tried to win his favour. And there's that time he had—and he told me him-

56

self how much he enjoyed it!—when he was studying philosophy in Paris. He must have been a guést at all sorts of grand houses, and met lots of wonderful women! O why aren't girls like me allowed to attend the lectures of these great Doctors? It is all *so* unfair! People don't realize how lucky young men are in these clever modern days to be allowed to hear really important thinkers explaining the nature of——"

It was at this point that Lil-Umbra had to extricate herself from an extremely formidable group of crusaders from the south of Anjou who looked at her in the way—so she told herself—that such comrades-in-arms must have looked at every unravished maid they encountered in their holy campaign. "O why can't we find out the real true nature," so Lil-Umbra's thoughts ran on, and they were rendered more rebellious still by contact with these consecrated warriors, "of such mysteries as God the Father, God the Son, and God the Holy Ghost, and, let's hope, put an end once for all to all the stuff the priests"—and here her thoughts were again intensified in their revolt by yet another body of guests, for she was now squeezing herself between a sculptured procession of angels in Purbeck marble and a group of excited persons who, although freemen of the Manor of Roque, were nevertheless, as far as their habits of thought went, on no higher level than the humblest serfs—"all the stuff the priests keep putting into our heads."

It was soon after she had safely squeezed her way along this succession of marble angels, which must have been a strip of masonry left intact during the Fortress's renovation a century earlier, that Lil-Umbra came upon a narrow window, especially adapted for defence by arrow-shooting, out of which, though she had to stand on tip-toe to do so, she couldn't resist taking a peep into the surrounding forest. The Fortress was such an erratic and rambling erection, and it had been added to during so many experiments in castellated building throughout the years, that to Lil-Umbra's surprise she found herself peering into a portion of the forest almost directly opposite the small unfinished shrine to Our Lady of the Holy Ass, now being so devotedly built by the two hands of Tilton alone, though Lil-Umbra had not failed to guess that it had been under the influence of some impious brain, possibly young John's, that

Tilton had given his work that grotesque name: but at this moment it wasn't of an ass or of a horse that she was thinking, as she pressed her chin upon her eight white knuckles in order to peer out of the arrow-slit in the ancient wall.

She was indeed experiencing a moment of heart-wrung disturbance such as any ordinary onlooker would have felt to be beyond all proportion to its cause, when she saw the figure of a young girl, of about her own height and slenderness, but dressed with a most subtle and most deliberate aim, in that unusually warm February sunshine, of making herself exquisitely provocative to masculine senses, lying sideways on a mantle which she had spread out on a mossy bank bordering on the well-trodden path that led—and didn't Lil-Umbra know that path by heart!—from the postern-gate to the unfinished shrine of Our Lady of the Holy Ass.

It may easily be imagined that it was not only about the quick return to breakfast of her two brothers along that familiar forest-track that Lil-Umbra was now troubled. What if Raymond de Laon had taken into his head—O he too too easily might!—to pay a visit to the shrine Tilton was raising to Our Lady?

It was sufficiently unusual for the eldest son of the lord of a Manor as large as Roque, which everybody knew was more thickly populated than any other in the West Country, to design and plan such a shrine with his own brain and to build it and to carve it with his own hands, to have already started queer rumours in that part of England, without the half-naked daughter of the adjoining castle waylaying him between his new shrine and his parents' dwelling!

For as the agitated, and indeed the now thoroughly upset, Lil-Umbra hurried on towards the armoury, she could not keep her mind from pondering on every aspect of the fact that she had herself seen Lilith, the only child of the wicked Baron Maldung and his half-mad lady of Lost Towers, stretched on the bank by the path as if tomorrow were the first of August rather than the first of February!

O it was impossible for the infatuated Lil-Umbra not to play with the tormenting idea that there already might exist God only knew what depraved understanding between Raymond de Laon and this terribly licentious girl. "I must certainly ask him outright," she decided, "the very next time we're alone whether he is on speaking terms with this shameless girl! But till I have a chance of asking him that, I certainly mustn't let him hold my hand again. O! I just can't bear to think about it—Lilith Maldung waiting for him half-undressed outside our very gate!"

But like most of us when we are still under twenty, Lil-Umbra hadn't acquired the difficult art of putting painful possibilities out of her mind and the vision of Lilith by the wayside continued to obsess her thoughts with one horrible imagination after another. She felt ready to welcome any excuse that offered itself for not going straight into the armoury to talk to the ex-bailiff. She decided that it might be a timely occasion in the interest of her own physical comfort to visit the women's corner of the retiring-yard, and this with slow and leisurely steps she proceeded to do, finding the spot less frequented than might have been expected under existing circumstances.

When, however, returning from this retreat with that vision of Lilith still biting like a rat at her tenderest nerve—for she still felt a curious desire to put off any possible encounter with Raymond de Laon till this image from Lost Towers had faded a little—she took the more roundabout of the alternative ways to the armoury, she found herself again following a passage along the outside wall of the Fortress, a passage which was once more in full view of her brother Tilton's cheerful shrine.

And so once more, urged by the insatiable demon of curiosity, she found herself standing on tiptoe at a similar arrow-slit-window and staring out as desperately as before into the dazzling afternoon sunshine. What she now saw caused her to gasp with the same kind of choking in her gullet that a female blackbird might suffer who suddenly perceives in her lonely nest a solitary cuckoo's egg.

Another girl was now rapidly approaching that provocative figure lying stretched out on the grassy bank by the edge of the path, and Lil-Umbra was as startled by the strangeness of the new girl's look and her queer attire as by her astonishing beauty.

"She must be a Spanish maiden," Lil-Umbra told herself, "or a Jewish girl straight from Palestine! Who on earth brought her here and what does she want with us?"

59

This time it happened that Lil-Umbra's arrow-slit was so close to the alluring figure down there beneath her on the grass that she felt a faint uneasiness lest one or other of the two girls should look up and see her. "They wouldn't see much," she told herself, "in this blazing Sun and against all this grey stone; but they might see enough of my forehead and hair to realize that they're being watched!"

Lil-Umbra lowered her insteps by a fraction of an inch, thus bringing down her ivory-white forehead to a position only just above the support of that row of equally white knuckles; and it was from this position that she saw the new-comer pause by the side of the half-naked girl on the grass, evidently wishing to ask her a question.

"What question is she going to ask?" Lil-Umbra said to herself. "She may be in attendance upon one of these noble-women from France, or she may have come from the Priory."

And then she suddenly became aware that by some chance-sent miracle the wind, which in that glowing sunshine had been blowing from the east, suddenly shifted to the north, with the result that she could hear with perfect clearness every word the two were speaking.

"I was only asking you," she heard the stranger say, "where would be the best entrance into this Fortress-Castle for a serving-girl like me? I have only just come to this part of the world and I am working at present in the Priory kitchen, but they told me that the best thing to do if I wanted to meet anyone of my own race round here was to get an entrance 'by hook or by crook', as we used to say in the crusaders' camp, into the Fortress of Roque."

"The best thing for you to do, my good girl," replied Lilith of Lost Towers, without moving to change her position or to wrap her garments more closely round her, "is to go right back to the Priory the way you came! Everybody round here knows perfectly well that Prior Bog is no man to cater for the tribal pretensions of a ship-wrecked, tossed-up slave-girl such as you! Get back to the Priory the way you came, my woman. That's the road for you to take!"

Then it was that our young watcher through the arrow-slit saw an unexpected sight. For the new-comer deliberately moved forward and stood quite calmly by the side of the girl lying on that grassy bank. Luckily for our observer, the stranger stood now looking directly westward towards Tilton's shrine, and with her back not only to the Priory from which she had come, but also to the old Druidic stone-circle from which our friend that very morning had watched the Sun rise. And so it was possible for Lil-Umbra to see her profile clearly outlined against the trunk of a naked larch.

And there was such power as well as beauty in the profile she saw that she felt no surprise when the girl on the ground hurriedly got up and began re-assuming in haste every garment she had removed, and finally, apparently entirely under the psychic compulsion and the silent authority of the wanderer, began wrapping about her the ancestral cloak she had spread so carefully on the grass.

And now this mysterious foreign woman was answering the Lost Towers girl in language quite as formidable as her own but much more dignified and compelling.

"I am unknown to you," Lil-Umbra heard her say, "while you are not unknown to me; but we are both face to face with all those frightful difficulties, and appalling choices among so many completely different courses of action such as afflict all women. Listen to me, then, Lilith of Lost Towers; and I will tell you what you had better do if you want to avoid a dreadful quarrel with your mother and father, a quarrel that might bring down your whole house in ruins."

"What are you talking about, your poor slave from Byzantium? You say we're both women. Don't you see that the only important thing in our life *as* women is how to satisfy our love in the one direction and our hate in the other?"

The stranger made two or three short steps backward as Lilith said this and then made the same number forward again; and this rhythm she repeated as she went on speaking, while the tiptoe watcher, with her white chin pressed against her white knuckles, actually found her toes tapping the stone slab beneath her feet as if she were watching, or by some mysterious compulsion actually joining, some weird ritualistic performance.

And Lil-Umbra was unable to resist the curious feeling that the woman, who thus kept advancing and retiring in a sort of thaumaturgic sorcerer's dance, was actually drawing into her body as she did so the rays of this burning Sun and turning them into a protection against their chemical opposite, that is to say against some cold, dark, wet, hostile element from which emanated the very chill of death.

And all the while she was walking thus rhythmically backwards and forwards, she was chanting to Lilith of the Lost Towers what sounded as if it were the undying echo of some prehistoric war-challenge, the challenge of one long-extinct race to another extinct race, a challenge that had survived as an indestructible cry out of the heart of the earth itself, and issued forth from the earth in the form of dust and dew and spray and mist and vapour.

"The white skin and sweet flesh of a young girl like you," she chanted, "if they be offered up as a living sacrifice to the powers of destruction, will recoil not only on those who offer them up, but on her to whom they belong!"

Lil-Umbra was more astonished than she would have considered it possible for her ever to have been in the house of her birth by what happened then. For Lilith of the Lost Towers seemed suddenly seized by a great panic. She clutched nervously and frantically at a few objects of attire that she had as yet, while putting on her clothes, neglected to reassume, and holding these against her navel, she swung round, and with head down and her eyes on nothing but the path she was following, she bolted into the forest with the blind rush of a small animal desperate to escape.

V

HEBER SYGERIUS

With nothing of Lilith's desperation but with hardly less haste, Lil-Umbra now left her observation-post at that memorable arrow-slit and hurried by the nearest passage to the armoury. She was so agitated by what she had just heard and seen that the chance she might encounter Raymond de Laon had grown a bit blurred, more like the heavenly end to a complicated fairy-tale than something that might occur in a few minutes.

The armoury of the Fortress of Roque was, as anyone would have anticipated, considering the reputation for reckless violence of the ancestors of Lady Val, and considering the peculiar character of its new master, Sir Mort, as capacious and crowded a chamber as any in the place. At the very time when Lady Val, still making her heroic effort to recover from her fit of weakness and to be worthy of her grandmother when that lady entertained the rather difficult bride of Llewelyn the Great, was listening with especially gracious interest to the chatter of the new bailiff's wife and her lively daughter-in-law "the Crumb", her own errant daughter with very different emotions but with something of Lady Val's spirit was approaching the huge and glowing hearth of what might have been called the altar-fire of that vast collection of weapons, in a mood of chastened wistfulness.

It had been several weeks ago when she found Raymond de Laon here quite alone, and not only alone, but with the door ajar and praying that she might pass by! On this occasion she shut the door very carefully behind her as she went in; and once inside the room, the look with which she surveyed its present occupant was a very tender and subtle one. The

63

personage towards whom this look of hers was directed was a very old man, and an old man who was, as it appeared, luxuriating, in a quaint and peculiar manner, in his own old age.

He was like a certain broken and dilapidated stone pillar, Lil-Umbra thought, that had arrested her attention this very morning as she sat talking to Peleg on that massive stone seat which so closely resembled a giant's throne; but not only did that hunched-up pillar come into her head when she saw this old man, but his pose by the fire as she approached him made her think of a desiccated willow-stump, of which she had caught a glimpse while among the stones in the stone-circle where they had watched the sunrise.

Heber Sygerius was a short bony man with very broad shoulders. He had no hair at all on his face, which he shaved much more carefully than most elderly men, and he was almost entirely bald. His skull was large and on both sides of it were two very curious discolourations of a tint almost as impossible to describe as it would have been to describe the colour of the grey and brown mist which that very afternoon, when their late breakfast-lunch was over, would swallow up the Sun.

Full of golden light that Sun had been when Lil-Umbra had watched its first rising. Full of its light had the forest-path been she had just watched; but after this long meal their kitchen had to provide its glory would be gone. But this old man was assuredly enjoying himself before that blazing fire, into which at intervals he kept flinging a small piece of wood from a heap at his side.

What surrounded this old figure with a special aura of attraction for Lil-Umbra was that it had been to meet this man, who had only recently handed over his reeveship of the Manor of Roque to his middle-aged son, that Raymond de Laon—at least that was what he had said—had been here the last time she had come.

As we have already noted, the two latrines of Roque Fortress had finally come to be placed side by side adjacent to the interior courtyard. It is simply use-and-wont and the gradual adjustments of custom that create what historians of human decency might well be justified in calling the "epochal fashion" in excremental convenience. There were several antiquated hieroglyphs, that might well have reverted to the days of Constantine, scrawled over a low arch leading from that inner court to the left of this armoury; and another set of syllables of the same debased and deteriorated Latinity carved on a block of stone over that similar small arch under which Lil-Umbra had recently passed.

On this latter, among other syllables, was engraved the abbreviation "Fem"; and on the former the syllable "Mas". It was indeed of his own meditated retreat to the masculine one of these two retiring places that the old Heber Sygerius had been thinking before Lil-Umbra appeared, for although he was aware that neither his bladder nor his bowels needed immediate easement, he had already arrived at that stage in the progress of old age when men, and in some cases women too, grow over-conscious, though sometimes with only too good reason, of their urinal and excremental evacuations. But fortunately he was at this moment in no hurry to obey the particular bodily call of which he felt a vague premonition, so that when he became aware of the light step of the girlish intruder, he was quite ready to turn upon her his peculiarly magnetic smile full of a more than natural kindliness.

It was this curious magnetism in the old ex-bailiff that had warded off many an insurrection of the over-wrought serfs of the Manor of Roque, and had even been effective, a smile in this case being equal to the authority of the most aristocratic of stewards, in persuading various rich free-men not to take away their thrice-precious coins of the realm from the confines of this populous Manor to squander them on a last desperate crusade that would probably only land them in some French or Italian or German prison.

What was going on in the excited consciousness of Lil-Umbra as she entered the armoury and confronted the extraordinarily shaped hairless skull of this kindly-crafty grandfather-curator of the Manor of Roque? Whatever it was, it was obviously only partially revealed in the quick, gasping sigh she gave as she yielded to his welcoming gesture and sat herself down on a four-legged stool to the left of those burning logs.

When once the two of them were seated quietly together, the exchange of feelings between this girl in her teens and this

E

old man of eighty resolved itself quickly enough into pure gratitude, each to each, for the unembarrassed silence which that good moment permitted to both of them.

The thoughts that in a little while began to filter through the old man's hairless skull were curiously characteristic of the dominant temper of his mind throughout his whole life. Raymond de Laon used to say of Heber Sygerius that he had always served the Manor of Roque rather than the Manor's Lord or Lady at any special epoch. He certainly had always been, from every point of view, the ideal administrator of an exquisitely adjustable miniature kingdom, nourished from its roots up by the fruits of the earth and the beasts of the field, and dominated by a traditional routine never broken save to humour the caprices of the elements.

But old Heber's way of managing the manor was over now for good and ill. His wife was long dead, and his son and his son's wife were administrators of a totally different type. In all the spontaneous and instinctive motions of his mind Heber was still, as he had been all his days, at once profoundly kind and profoundly cunning.

There was not a serf on the manor who didn't feel towards him, in all the minutest details of their communal life, as if he really were a wise and understanding, though somewhat inscrutable and secretive, elderly relative. Like many another indulgent grand-dad, he was cruelly missed by all who suffered under less considerate successors.

What none of his own family had ever realized in the least, and what even Raymond de Laon and young Sir William Boncor among the aristocracy of that district had never properly understood, was the disturbing effect upon Heber's peculiar nature of what he had picked up and imbibed of the teachings of Friar Bacon. The Friar's ideas had not reached him directly from the philosopher's own mouth; but indirectly and, as may well be imagined, in a distorted form from various persons, male and female, employed in all sorts of capacities, within and without both Bumset Priory and Fenawl Convent, whose pastures, enclosures, fallows, and forest-tracks, together with their well-appointed tithe-barns and their movable sheep-folds, offered extensive if not specifically trained employment.

The sequestration of Friar Bacon under conditions of semi-condemnation and semi-imprisonment so close to Roque Manor had naturally a disturbing, exciting, and agitating effect upon others beside Heber; but of all who were affected by the Friar's presence in that neighbourhood the old ex-bailiff was undoubtedly the one who gave himself up to pondering on the subject with the most serious and the most simple concentration.

Such was the power of the imprisoned Friar's mind that the first difficulty the old man had encountered, and he had pondered on this for a pathetically long while, was whether these exciting new ideas belonged to the realm of religion, or of science, or of philosophy. By his using his shrewd native commonsense he decided in favour of philosophy. He felt that it was certainly easier to include both religion and science under philosophy than it would be to squeeze philosophy into the murderous arsenals of the fanatics of religion on one hand or of science on the other.

As the grandfather of this little manorial realm, to which both the Priory and the Convent might well have looked with daughter-like piety, for they were, in a real historic sense, its offspring, Heber Sygerius never let himself forget what his son and successor was only too apt to do—that the thrice-precious manorial threshing-floor and grind-stone, upon which the lives of the whole little community depended, were actually within the purlieus of the Priory; and that therefore when the serfs, who came to thresh and to grind the corn, which, when, once ground, was the bread of their life and the whole basis of their mortal existence, talked as they were bound to do with the servants of the Priory and the Convent, there was no escape from the contagion of the Friar's dangerous ideas.

For revolutionary indeed these ideas were! In fact some of them led directly to the sort of peasant-revolts against the owners of manors which were beginning to be frequent on the continent of Europe. Some of them led to the serfs of Roque Manor for instance asking themselves point-blank whether, if the Lord of the Manor could make them pay for threshing on his threshing-floor and grinding with his grind-stone, he might suddenly exact payment—in fact wasn't this what he *was* doing?—for the privilege of living on the earth at all? Then there were all those innumerable magic sayings of the Friar in his role of race-sorcerer or tribal soothsayer; most especially those sayings connected with the most notorious of all his achievements, his construction of a Brazen Head that uttered oracles on behalf of Britain against the world.

The armoury of Roque Manor was indeed what might literally have been called, as Lil-Umbra had always called it, a magic room, for this was by no means the first time that a most strangely procreative and pregnant set of thoughts had been engendered here. But none had ever been born in this place stranger or more vibrant with eventful consequence than the thought-child now created by this casual and accidental contact between a precocious young girl and an unbelievably shrewd-witted old man.

There was something about this occasion, when Lil-Umbra's mind was dallying with the hope that at any second Raymond de Laon might appear, and when old Heber's mind was full of a difficult adjustment between the four points of the compass and the geography of the Manor, that gave to the warmth of that particular fire the power of so affecting the sympathetic silence in which they both were enveloped that there actually did come into existence by a sort of spontaneous generation a thought-child of the most significant kind, an offspring for which they were alone responsible.

Indeed they both felt in a weird and rather frightening manner that between the two of them, on this special day of this special month of the year of grace twelve hundred and seventy-two, an extremely formidable thought-child had been born, a thought-child, or rather a fate-child, for whose growth in power and for whose increase in stature a moment was as a day and a day was as a year; so that before a few months were over something would happen that would make their coming together on this particular morning a fearful and memorable milestone, not merely in the history of Roque Manor but in the history of the planet Earth.

As with so many other fatal events that have become inaugural turning-points in the story of our race, the chief actors in this divine or devilish drama only felt in the dimmest, faintest, indirectest, obliquest, shadowiest manner the generative importance of their encounter. In so far as they did apprehend it they attributed it—and indeed where else could they have looked for a cause?—to the effect of the warmth of a burning fire upon an absolute silence. The old man would no doubt have defended himself from any charge of spiritual rape by emphasizing the extreme fragility, not to mention the quivering evasiveness, of a girl-child's maidenhood; while Lil-Umbra would unquestionably have sworn that her whole being was entirely dominated by one sense alone, namely by the sense of hearing. Indeed she might well have argued that all the while the spirit of Fire in this magic armoury of Roque was satisfying its desire upon the spirit of Silence, she herself was completely absorbed in listening for any sound outside the door that could possibly mean the approach of the youth who filled her thoughts.

As for old Heber Sygerius, with this sylph-like figure crouching at his side, he really had begun to permit to his natural impulses certain liberties of imagination, such as would never have been allowed to lift their heads above the ground in the mind of her Mongol friend with his Hebraic conscience. "How strange it is," the old man was pondering now to himself, "that the traditional separation between my lord's daughter and my lord's bailiff should totally stop, not only the faintest attempt on my part to meddle with this exquisite little creature, but also should prevent my explaining to her any of my private ideas about life in general, ideas that I worked out in my own head years and years before Friar Bacon was forced to leave Oxford and come among us as a half-condemned and half-imprisoned heretic.

"O! how I'd love to tell this sweet child everything I've worked out for myself about the wisest, cunningest, craftiest ways of enjoying life and holding our own against our enemies! And yet I'm not allowed by our absurd conventions to utter a single word to her as a man of the same race and the same village, face to face, an old man to a young woman, a wise grand-dad to a hasty child! O how I'd like to describe to you, you darling little creature, exactly what can be picked up of subtle wisdom from these half-burnt logs that are warming us both at this second!"

Lil-Umbra's eyes were now fixed upon the door of the room, through which there undoubtedly did come at this moment a stir and a murmur as of a noisy and rather excited crowd. Glancing from her profile to the fire the old man couldn't help noticing a perfect little blue flame that was leaping up and down on the segment of a log that still carried minute patches of greyish lichen upon its crumbling bark.

Then he looked back again at her exquisite profile. How could he, he asked himself, describe to her the very curious elation which he had felt a second ago through all his senses, an elation that gave him now a delicious aftermath of satisfaction, like a wave drawing back over a bank of pebbles? O how he longed to describe to this lovely young girl just what he had felt, and to ask her if she herself a minute ago, when that blue flame was flickering up and down between those logs, had felt anything in the least resembling it! Why was she staring so at the door at this moment? Expecting to be called by her nurse?

"No! I warrant she's listening intently for the step of some particular young man! Well, if that's the case," thought the old man, "she certainly isn't in the right mood to listen to an elaborate discussion centring round blue flames and burning logs."

And then it struck the old man that, quite apart from the difficulties of sex, it was a shame that he couldn't talk to this intelligent and sympathetic young woman about the life-philosophy he had worked out for himself. Since he had handed over the reeveship to his sturdy son, he had had a grand opportunity to work out the whole logical basis of a real life-philosophy that was entirely original and entirely his own.

And what he felt now was that he could make this girl understand things that neither of her brothers, nor Raymond de Laon nor young Sir William Boncor, would be able to apprehend, discoursed he to them never so wisely! O! why couldn't he now boldly tell this clever little lady that there was such a thing as a subtle trick of so manipulating our nerves and our senses by our mind and our will that we could render ourselves completely independent of the fate that had made us a man, or a woman, or young, or old, or well-born or self-born, or strong, or weak, or naturally courageous, or naturally full of fear?

Why couldn't he tell her about this discovery of his and

about its connection with a power he had recently begun to develop in himself, old as he was, the power of getting into touch with something that was almost like consciousness in things that are considered completely inanimate.

It was at this moment that he gave a violent start and looked at Lil-Umbra in such a way that it came near to seriously scaring her.

"Didn't you feel something then, little lady," he cried, "something you never felt before in your whole life, no! not till a minute or two ago? I felt it; and though I've lived more than ten times as long as you, I've never felt anything like it! It was as if our thoughts, your beautiful young thoughts and my ugly old thoughts, had, for a second, yes! for half the beat of the pulse of a second, become one. No doubt it had to do with our sitting in silence by these dancing flames—and then we saw something, something that was standing between us, standing between you on your stool and me in this chair, something that was like that statue of Our Lady in Prior Bog's private refectory—the one that's so dark—dark as a gipsy, dark as a Jewess!"

Not a syllable of all this had been missed by Lil-Umbra, and it had its effect. The thoughts in that preposterously bare skull and in that delicate girlish head *had* in some mysterious unique manner become one, and "Something," as old Heber had put it, had entered the room, had stayed in the room, and had stood or sat or crouched or planted itself between them.

And the thing that had done this *was*, as the young girl knew quite as fully and distinctly as the old man, nothing less than an image, or what the ancient Greeks called an "Eidolon", of that dark and terribly beautiful woman, whom she had recently seen encountering Lilith of Lost Towers!

What the old man hadn't sufficiently remembered during this whole interview was that they were waiting for the appearance of Lil-Umbra's father, under whose authority they would both go to take their places at the first meal of the day. He himself had already swallowed a substantial bowl of barley-meal washed down by a good draught of ale, whereas Lil-Umbra, though she had got up so early and been with Peleg to the Stone Circle, had not tasted a thing. Her nervous agitation at this moment was certainly accentuated by this fasting.

It may even have. had something to do with the nervous leap to her feet and the irrepressible cry, almost a little scream, with which she now greeted the opening of the door and the sudden appearance of the very person she was hoping for, namely young Raymond de Laon, accompanied by none other than her recent companion, the Tartar-Jew Peleg.

Polite and friendly, if extremely airy and casual, were the greetings with which young Raymond de Laon saluted the ex-bailiff as he carried off the girl, who herself was so excited that she even forgot to turn her head to nod to the old man till her curls were hidden by young De Laon's broad shoulders. Peleg however closed the door quietly behind them and came straight up to Heber's side.

"Has Sir Mort come back?" the old man enquired. Peleg nodded.

"And is this confounded Bonaventura, this 'General', if that's what they call him, of the Friars come too?"

"He's here now anyway," answered Peleg, "but you never know with these clerical almighties! He'll probably stroll round the kitchen first to see what sort of feast there's going to be! Some say he's one for fasting. But I doubt if he can practise that little game when he's travelling! He won't want to get so light that his horse will shake him off like a dead leaf."

Heber smiled his most endearing smile at the tall Mongol.

"Lend me a hand, my boy, will you, to help me up? And, maybe, you'll give me your arm to the dung-house next door, and then help me down to the hall?"

The Jewish Mongol obeyed and gravely helped him to his feet, and while he did so the eyes of both of them were drawn to the fire by a curious dance which a couple of lively blue flames took upon themselves to perform, for the special benefit, it might almost seem, of these two men.

We say "it might almost seem", but as a matter of fact it was a completely different set of impressions that the middle-aged man and the old man derived from that dance. If there really were any sub-human and sub-conscious psychic impulse behind the motion of those two blue flames as they raced up and down that thin strip of pine-wood between a large spruce-log and a small larch-log, both logs having their own par-ticular reaction of this performance, and if this psychic impulse had been interpreted by some new technical machine invented by Friar Bacon, it would at any rate have been made clear that such an impulse was a sub-sexual as well as a sub-human one.

"If Sir Mort," thought Peleg, "supposes that my gratitude is such a slavish thing that I'm going to take passively whatever happens, he really will have to give more attention to my character as a person. I'm ready to serve him in every possible way, but I'm a born fighter and to be nothing but a guiding-dog to a drooling old fellow like this, and nothing but a schoolmaster-nurse to a little Lady First-Love like that pretty child, is not enough. Besides—O hell's damnation take it all!"

This last outcry was due to the fact that the giant suddenly realized for the first time that he'd forgotten to leave his iron mace in its usual hiding-place and had carried it along with him. Its awkward presence in his hand at this moment set him upon imagining a terrific attack upon the fortress by a band of formidable enemies, among whom he now felt himself wildly rushing, in full fighting ecstasy for the House of Abyssum, swinging his club with its iron spikes and converting a crowd of living men into a ghastly heaving mass of bones and hair and flesh and swirling blood.

Whether an invisible spirit, reading the thoughts of Peleg at this moment, would have been shocked at the pictorial images the mind of the giant conjured up, would doubtless depend on the nature of the spirit; but these enemies twisting and jerking, scriggling and wriggling, as Peleg certainly saw them groaning and moaning, weltering and sweltering, howling and mowling, in a blood-red palpitating swirl of bodies and bones and hair and teeth and eyes and entrails, over which, with his free thumb testing the spikes of his weapon, he could stride in triumph while what *had* been living and beautiful bodies fouled his legs with filth, would certainly have disturbed some spirits.

What old Heber saw as that dance of blue flame kept repeating itself in his mind as the Mongol led him away, was nothing less than Friar Bacon's manufactured Brazen Head, enormous in size, hideous beyond all human imagination, and uttering words in a completely unknown tongue, but a tongue that was felt by all who heard it to be a multitudinous voice out of the Infinite.

By the time however that Peleg had got the old man out of the dung-house and back into the passage leading towards the dining-hall, the weird vision or revelation, which proximity to the excited heart of little Lil-Umbra had conjured into the ex-bailiff's hairless skull, had given place to something completely different. But the thing to which it had given place was still quite sufficiently interesting to the old man to compel him to stand still himself and to make the unfortunate Peleg who guided him not only stand still also, but stare along with him at the dusky smoke-begrimed wall of the passage down which they were shuffling.

"Look, look, my good friend, look, I beseech you! Do you see these hieroglyphs on the wall? Shall I tell you what they mean? I know you pass these by, as most people do on their way to the dung-yard, like queer meaningless senseless marks, figures of some sort, mathematical figures, not human ones of course. But what they really are is an oracular announcement, yes! an announcement to the whole world that the idea of there being only three Gods, as the niggardly theologians teach, is a grievous error. There are Four Gods! That is what the great ancient thinker, Pythagoras, taught to his Greek colony in Italy; and that is what I, Heber Sygerius, am now teaching you, Peleg, the Jewish Mongol! Yes! there are Four Gods. But the strange thing that I now understand as I stare at those marks—No! Please, Peleg! Please wait here a minute longer! —is that we have to go to some especial and quite different spot to worship each of these Four Gods!"

Peleg gave vent to a hopeless sigh. "Has the old dotard," he thought, "forgotten that our breakfast is waiting for us?"

Peleg looked desperately up and down the passage that led to the sleeping-rooms of Sir Mort and his lady and the sleeping-rooms of their two sons. He looked at the floor. He looked at the withered knuckles of the old man clutching his arm with the intensity of an aged hawk.

"What in Hell's name can I do?" he asked himself. "Sir Mort will curse me like the devil. He is sure to see us coming in at the bottom of the table. Besides, this old fool's son Randolph will be keeping a place for him, you bet your life, near

74

to the top! Not that *he* won't be as pleased as Pilate for me to get cursed for not dragging the old fool along more quickly! But, O Jehovah, hear me just this one single time in my life! Let me meet the whole blasted Sygerius family except this poor old doddipole for whom I've got some sort of crazy fondness, and I'll scatter their brains with my iron club on that pretty patch of green grass they're all so proud of, outside their damned front door!"

His vows of vengeance were interrupted by yet more astonishing behaviour on the part of the old man. He was now turning round in violent jerks and stamping on the ground at each spot, as he faced what he considered the four quarters of the compass.

"*North!*" he muttered in a hoarse and even frightened voice. "That's the forest of course and Lost Towers. All the worst devils in the whole world come from the north!"

He jerked himself to the right. "*East!*" he cried in an exultant tone. "*That*'s where the miraculous Doctor Bacon is constructing the Brazen Head! *That*'s where the Fourth God will speak one day!" Again he jerked himself round. "*South!*" he cried. "And *that*'s Boncor Castle and all those noble and righteous people!"

And then with a final hop and skip and a fierce clutch from Peleg to keep him from falling: "*South!*" he shouted, "where our Tilton is erecting with spade and hammer and chisel and nails a shrine of his own to Our Blessed Lady!"

"That *must* be the end," groaned Peleg to himself.

But the old man went on, still keeping them both rooted to that place in front of the wretched blotches on that dark and filthy wall. "Do you know how I discovered that there are Four Gods, Peleg, my friend? I discovered it by the help of another discovery: in fact by finding out that there is a faint dim vague obscure consciousness in everything made by the hands of men! I have found that out for myself, Peleg, my boy! And do you know what else I've found out, my good friend?"

"If this goes on much longer," thought the desperate Mongol, "I'll pick you up, Master Heber, carry you into the dining-hall and lay you down at Sir Mort's feet!"

"I've found out," went on the old man, "that on any piece

75

of earth where old rituals have been going on for six or seven or eight centuries, the actual essence of the substance of the earth begins to stir in its sleep, craving it doesn't know what! Friar Bacon teaches this—did you know that? And he calls this craving by a very curious metaphysical name. He calls it *Privation*—yes, the 'Privation of Matter'."

Peleg groaned. "O he calls it 'Privation', does he?" he murmured hoarsely; and then getting desperate he made a reckless plunge. "I am sorry to hurry you, Master Heber," he began, speaking heavily and with as much effort as if he were forcing the handles of a wooden plough through frozen mind, "but we must hasten to the hall! Tonight after supper it will be most gracious of you if you'll explain to us about the thoughts of sticks and stones and the 'Privation' they suffer when the Blessed Trinity mismanages matters and how the Fourth God eases things up."

His voice was low, but Heber caught quickly enough the new tone in it and yielded without a struggle. But move his feet as fast as he could, it was physically impossible for him to quicken to a run, and while he had breath to walk he had breath to talk.

"Of course," he said, "we needn't believe all those tales about Lost Towers. But there must be something in them. They say that when the bishop laid his hand in blessing on the head of the daughter of that house, drops of such foul-smelling blood followed his fingers when he took them away that everybody else had to leave the church or the chapel or wherever it was, so perfectly appalling was the smell! And of course you've heard how poor old King Henry, who is sick to death while the Lord Edward is crusading nobody knows where, knighted young Will Boncor of Cone the other day in Westminster? The reason for that of course was to keep young Raymond de Laon from going back to France. Young men of his age aren't happy without a comrade. They *have* to go about in pairs or they just die of tedium."

"Tedium, do you call it," cried the Jewish Tartar. "I call it by a different name! But let *that* go! . . . The point is he's come back, and Cone Castle is stronger than it's ever been in the memory of man! But so also, Master Heber, is the Barony of Lost Towers! Very, very, very strong *that* also has become! And I tell you, Master Heber, I wouldn't like to make my way against that castle, with its forest and its swamp, and its bottomless black moat where the waters go straight down to Gehenna!"

It was at that moment that a flickering torch became suddenly visible, carried round a sharp corner of the passage they were following, and the long, narrow, cadaverous countenance of Sir Mort Abyssum, Lord of the Manor of Roque, made its appearance.

"What in the name of all the angels and of all the devils has been happening to you two?" cried the apparition, as it advanced towards them entirely alone and holding in one hand the torch, now quite useless for there were plenty of lights in the passage now, and in the other a naked sword.

There sometimes arise moments in the lives of men upon earth when there is no human power or human art or human skill, whether of painter or sculptor or musician or poet or tale-teller, that could possibly do what Aristotle called "imitate nature", or what Goethe called "realize the intention of nature", or what Shakespeare and Rubens did without thinking of what they were doing.

On these occasions certain human figures make their appearance where and when there is no onlooker, no observer, no audience, no witness that is possessed of the faintest or remotest understanding of what is being presented to its attention. Its own nature has rendered this awareness as oblivious as fire to water, even when it is about to be put out by it, and as earth to air even when it is about to be dissolved into it. The human figures who thus appear and make not the smallest, faintest, weakest, slightest impression might be described as appearing in a complete void. There is for them, when they appear, a total absence of every conceivable recording and of every possible reflection or memorial.

It was in such a void that the long, narrow, hollow-eyed, hollow-cheeked, ghastly-white visage of the Lord of the Manor of Roque manifested itself on this occasion. But all the same had there been any truth—and perhaps there was some truth —in the discovery by the ex-bailiff of Roque of the semi-consciousness of certain inanimate elements, these walls of the passage between the dung-yard and the dining-hall of that place would have recorded the appearance of a human figure and a human face that seemed to be crying out to the whole universe, from the deepest pit of Hell to the highest peak of Heaven, a protest against life having been created, or having created itself, or having been brought about by chance, after the accursed manner we all know so well.

VI

ROGER BACON

A few days after the departure of those disturbing visitors to the Fortress heralded by Spardo and his deformed horse, Roger Bacon in his attic prison in the Priory of Bumset was at work on his *Opus Tertium*. He was seated on a high-backed chair with a well-stuffed black cushion under his buttocks and all his writing materials conveniently before him. These included some specially adaptable pages of parchment cut carefully into folio size and studiously covered with straight lines to guide the writer's pen, save where at certain pre-meditated places on the page these lines came to an end in order to admit of the insertion of large illuminated capital letters in every shade of colour and designed with every sort of fanciful decoration.

The famous Friar, a beardless, clean-shaved man, gave the impression at first sight of a sedentary person of high rank who might easily have been himself the Prior of Bumset, or rather perhaps, for his air and manners were not entirely ecclesiastical, some highly placed secular lawyer from old King Henry's court in London. Although beardless, Roger was the reverse of bald, and a second glance at his appearance might even have given a stranger the impression, not in this case altogether erroneous, of a man endowed with a certain fastidious self-respect in regard to the appearance and the cleanliness of his own hair and skin.

Roger Bacon always looked a good deal younger than he really was; and very likely it was this dainty youthfulness, both in his look and in his manner, that excited no small part of the almost morbid severity with which he had been treated for some time by the ecclesiastical authorities; that is to say by all except one. This one was Guido Fulcode, who had only taken orders after the death of his wife and who, as a skilful lawyer, had been the lay adviser of Louis IX of France long before, as a cardinal, he became Papal Legate in England in 1263 and was elected Pope in 1265 under the name of Clement IV.

It was only three years ago that this wise ruler of the western world's religion had himself received its last rites; but before he died both Raymond de Laon, and even Raymond's friend, the then extremely youthful John of the Fortress of Roque, had played their part as devoted adherents of Bacon and sometimes even as intermediaries between him and this briefly reigning Pope.

But this interlude of hope and harmony was now over forever; and the incorrigible Friar was left to fight for himself. From the present Pope, Gregory X, a friend of the saintly Bonaventura, he could hope for nothing. The authorities who hated him had in fact got him where they wanted. His revolt had been suppressed; and the influence of his revolutionary metaphysic, allowing such dangerous scope both to experience and to experiment, would now, so his enemies hoped and prayed, die away as quickly as the same sort of curiosity such as the study of astrology, and the same sort of scholarship such as the study of Greek and Hebrew, died away after the death of that over-clever Grosseteste, Bishop of Lincoln, nearly twenty years ago.

The Friar now pushed back his table an inch or two with both hands and jerked back his chair a little. It had suddenly occurred to him that this was certainly the day, and probably the hour too, for the return of his faithful servant whom everybody called "Miles", or just simply "Master Soldier", from an important errand. He had sent him to meet someone on board a ship arriving at the London docks who had been a pupil of the great student of magnetism, Master Peter Peregrinus of Maricourt in Picardy, for he was very anxious to learn if Master Peter had ever, among his many experiments, invented anything in the least resembling a mechanical Head capable of uttering oracles. Roger knew that the pupils of this Petrus Peregrinus were generally as reticent as to what they had learnt from him, as the man himself, save to a very few, was reticent about what he taught; but the Friar hoped the astute Miles would have been able to get from this particular voyager the information he so greatly desired.

Smoothing out a couple of little wrinkly excrescences from the manuscript before him, Roger Bacon now leant back in his chair and contemplated the curtained alcove near his bed where stood his now almost finished Brazen Head, the boldest as well as the most intricate of all his world-changing inventions.

"What it now needs," he told himself, "is something—something I mean in my own peculiar way of thinking—to play the part for it that the priests assure us is played for us in Baptism. And, I know very well the kind of Baptism that my Head wants. O I know so well!"

And lifting one of his hands from the manuscript before him he rubbed the back of his knuckles against his forehead. "What it wants is the inspiration of Virginity. The best Baptism of all for it would be from an old maid, for old maids—O and don't I know it!—are the ones who have the Secret. For who in Iscalis taught me the rudiments of Latin, and more than the rudiments of the Lingua Franca, but great-aunt Katharina? And who but Aunt Katharina collected for me what scraps of learning came blowing across the roofs of Iscalis and whirling like drifting leaves through its market-place? One day when they elect a Pope again as interested in learning as Fulcode was, I must write a treatise on all the prophetesses and oracular teachers in human history from the beginning of the world, who have been old maids. I begin to think there is something in the loss of virginity, especially when followed by pregnancy, that destroys the power in a woman to become a medium for that 'Secretum Secretorum', that 'Secret of Secrets', through which the ultimate Mystery of Life is revealed."

At this point in his exciting thoughts Friar Bacon rose from his seat at the table and began walking up and down that small room. Any intelligent onlooker peering in upon him through some crack in that chamber's wall would have noted that the excitement within him was not worrying him or troubling him or making him anxious or distressed. It was filling him with elation.

At last he stopped before the black curtain that concealed this thing of brass which he had created out of nothing. "O Head of all my Labour," he cried in his heart with a sudden desperate outburst of long-suppressed feeling. "O child of the *essence* as well as of *the being* of my deepest soul! O thou only son of *both* the energies of my soul! If only I could baptize thee with the living spirit of a true Virgin, whether she were an old maid or a young maid, I would be content!"

Suddenly there arose a most extraordinary sound from behind the black curtain which covered that alcove near the head of his bed. "It's beginning! It's beginning!" cried the especial self within the Friar that he was so anxious to establish once for all as a soul much more complicated than any of his contemporaries could imagine. And it certainly would have seemed, to any invisible reader of human thoughts, that mingled with this exultation there was a throb of something very like pure unmitigated terror.

"Have I, plain man as I am," the Friar evidently couldn't help thinking, "just by my obstinate perseverance in dissecting, as they say Democritus did, every nerve and sinew and fibre in the skulls of the dead, actually played the part, without knowing it, of God? Have I actually created a *rational soul*, above and beyond those others that are engendered out of the substance of Matter? Have I flung this new soul into the machinery of my entirely artificial and purely material Head of Brass, so that it has *come to life*? Have I created an angelic superhuman creature, to be my living oracle for the rest of my days?"

He listened intently for any recurrence of the strange sound he had heard. Was this newly-created Being, he asked himself, going through a period parallel to human babyhood? Was it even now uttering unintelligible and inarticulate babblings?

Yes! By God and Christ! There was that sound again! "I *must* take a look at it!" And although he caught himself in an actual shiver of fear, he rushed to the alcove and pulled the curtain aside! The Brazen Image regarded him with a cold, callous, indifferent, non-human stare. It was a figure constructed to be about the height of a man, but it looked larger than human owing to the fact that it was without legs or arms. It was in fact what in ancient Greek cities used to be called a "Herm"—that is to say, a four-square milestone or miniature obelisk, like the formal pedestal of a classic bust, the bust of an emperor if it were Roman, and of a philosopher if it were Greek.

In the case of this angelic or demonic creation of his, the Brazen Head itself, whose massive base was of marble, rose from this short column as a head might rise from a square neck on narrow shoulders and, as their eyes met, the Head's creator fancied he heard his creation mutter these queer Latin-sounding words: *"Birginis, Sirginis, Flirginis, Virginis."*

Roger Bacon behaved now as if he were indeed so excited by the result of his creative power that he felt an emotion filling him at one and the same moment with joy and fear. Hurriedly he pulled back the black curtain over the Brazen Head. And it was then that any crafty spy peering in at him— *not* from the window where the sweet-scented twilight hovered over the tops of the forest-trees and through which a lovely air was blowing, but through a crack in one of the other three walls—would have heard him give an exultant little cry: "By Christ, I'd forgotten! Didn't a voice wake me in the night with the word 'ghosta'?"

And then such a spy would have seen him rush with the excitement of a boy in his teens to a small square of wood set among the bare boards of that attic-chamber and marked with the letter "A". This piece of wood the excited Friar extracted neatly from its fixed position, using his nails to achieve this result, and bending down above the orifice, stared at a vellum-covered volume that lay hidden there, on the outside of which was written in bold purple letters the words *Fons Vitae Avicebron*, "You are my master and teacher." He thought as he stared at these words, "You, you, *you*, more than anyone else in the world!"

And as he bent and stared at that title *Fons Vitae* and at that name *Avicebron*, he made one of the greatest efforts he had ever made in his life to visualize, as if they really could be apprehended by our ordinary senses, that plurality of separate souls within us, of which he had finally decided that what we generally call, and feel too often enough, to be our normal human soul, actually is composed.

Intensely he struggled, as he stared at the name of his admired Jewish thinker, actually to visualize the primal elements in these souls of ours that he had come to the conclusion arise automatically within the body by the potentiality of matter itself and have no connection with the *rational soul* which is created directly, immediately, and instantaneously, by God Himself, and created ready and prepared to be joined with the body, as soon as the infant, already possessed of the primal elements of its soul, is born into this world.

At this moment as he stared at that square hole in the floor, at the title *Fons Vitae*, only just visible in the growing twilight, and at the name *Avicebron*, whose darkened letters he had to supply from his own head, he saw the first evolution of the primal soul within the womb as a wave of incurving, in-gathering, insatiable water, desperately craving nourishment and rushing furiously through the solidest as well as through the softest substances, and possessed of the swallowing mouth of a hungry fish. And he saw the second evolution of this same primal soul as a wave of quivering vapour, rushing also through everything, but endowing the matter out of which it springs, the matter that is from the start able to engender it, with all the reactions of our human senses.

And at that intense moment he actually saw the *rational soul* which he had admitted must be directly created by God, saw it as a flame of something more than ordinary fire, saw it indeed as a flame created in the shape of a man-god, a flame that could wholly possess the body and yet according to its own will and pleasure could reach out from the body to which it has been joined and inspire other bodies.

"O, if I could only decide," the Friar cried in his excited heart, "what to think about the embryo of an infant, within a pregnant mother, before it is born into this world at all and before it is given its God-created *rational soul*! O I must think and think how you, our Jewish Master of all Masters, would have dealt with this problem of the embryo had you been called upon to consider it!"

With this question in his mind Roger Bacon bent down and replaced the square piece of wood and rose to his full height. "A Jewish Maid," he thought triumphantly, "after a Jewish Sage! That's the way I'll give new life to the Brazen one!

84

Yes! you've been yourself a ghost for years, *Avicebron*, and it was your teaching about the pluralism of the soul that set me thinking first—just *why* I have no notion: it is all a mystery—of creating our Brazen one, even as God creates the *rational soul* within us! And now that I've looked at your book I know that it was you who put it into my mind in the night to cry out the name Ghosta!"

Friar Bacon now went back happily and quietly to his chair and table and to that piece of foolscap parchment half-covered with his quite legible but by no means very elegant hand-writing. But he soon had to put down his pen again, for he was interrupted by the familiar sound, not of any Master Miles returning from London, but of the heavy steps of lay-brother Tuck, ascending the narrow turret-stairs to his low-roofed chamber, bringing him his supper.

It was a beautifully tranquil and by no means a very cold twilight that had by this time diffused itself over all the western provinces of our Island, and pleasant pine-wood scents mingled with the nutty waftures from the well-spiced apple-pasty that Brother Tuck, the moment he entered, carefully set down in the middle of the empty square space on the table from which Roger Bacon had hurriedly cleared all his papers.

In the depths of his pluralistic soul the Friar was now repeating over and over to himself the name "Ghosta", but he said, "Sit down, Brother," in the particular tone of a person who murmurs almost mechanically, "And now we come back to real life."

And when Brother Tuck had jerked into position a chair of the same shape as the one occupied by the Friar and containing a cushion of identically the same colour and size, the latter added the words: "And you might, if you don't mind, get the bottle and glasses"; a suggestion that was taken with the quickest alacrity. From a small shelf in an open recess near the door was extracted a beautifully heavy and almost opaque cut-glass container half-full of the reddest Burgundian wine from which, when it stood between them on the table, the Brother filled both their glasses.

Then followed, but with the same matter-of-fact, mechanical inevitability, a very curious gesture, traditional in Bumset Priory—a gesture that Raymond de Laon was wont to declare he had heard from none other than the Papal Legate to this country who subsequently became Clement IV, was prehistoric and pre-Christian, and went back to the days of Homer and Hesiod, when, before touching any wine, you had to sprinkle drops of it on the ground and on the air. What in fact both the men did now was to dip their longest finger into their glass and lightly flip a few drops of the wine they were about to drink towards each other.

"Here's news for you, my friend and God's friend," Brother Tuck began. "The Mother Superior next door, you know, has now got a really extraordinary Jewish girl to help the old nun who cooks for them. That poor old bitch—if you'll excuse me, sir—has never had time enough to cook properly; to cook, I mean, things that she herself enjoys. She spends half her time carrying dishes around to sick nuns. But now, with this new girl there, things are going, Prior Bog assures me, so marvellously well that Sister Mandrake, the nun who cooks for them, is happy again, and poor old Serga Kathalorum has found time to look round her a bit and enjoy life a little—found time to feel that being a Mother Superior isn't quite the worst fate that could have befallen a god-fearing elderly respectable lady. Pardon me, Master Friar, but has any new devil entered your mind, like that one that made you say, 'Time is Past' over and over, just as if it were 'et cum Spiritum tuum'?"

Brother Tuck emptied his glass, holding it to his lips in order that its last drops—drops that were no doubt called "the dregs" in countries where certain accumulations of stronglysmelling residue could always be drained from the bottom of wine-glasses—and then, having allowed his uplifted eye-balls—and while he did this his expression resembled that of a frog, with its chin on a lily-leaf, searching the empyrean for thunder—to scour the discoloured interior of the glass he was holding, he repeated "cum Spiritum tuum" in a dying fall of unction that resolved itself, ere it passed wholly away, into a diffused question.

VII

THE INVOCATION

Brother Tuck was still gazing with an uneasy relaxed interrogatory stare into the abstracted eyes before him, and across the empty glass and the full glass, when to his startled and rather shocked surprise he saw the Friar rise slowly to his feet.

"Please answer me, Brother Tuck, my old friend," said the risen man gravely. "No! Stay as you are. Don't get up. Here, drink my glass. I can have another later. But it's necessary for me to ask you rather an important question. What's this new girl's name? I mean this one you're talking about, who is such a help to Serga Kathalorum at the Convent, and to the old nun—Sister Mandrake they call her, don't they?—who does their cooking?

"No, don't get up, old friend. Stay where you are. It's for the person who is asking the questions to stand. But it's important to me and important purely for myself. Yes, you must understand *that*, Brother Tuck. You mustn't think I am asking you for any reason except a special peculiar, and quite definite one of my own. But to me this matter is of extreme importance; for it has to do with the particular thing I'm working on just now, namely—though I don't want to bother you, old friend, with these peculiarly difficult matters—the question as to how far at any definite point in the passing of time—you can see roughly, old friend, can't you, what I'm talking about?—our natural human apparatus for looking ahead can be used for purposes of prediction and how far it must hopelessly collapse; and why I asked you about this person, Tuck, my friend, was because——"

87

At this moment not only did a sudden gust of wind from the north cause the wooden framework of the small window to shake, but an agitated yellowhammer, with wings and feathers ruffled and with nerves and brain confused and befuddled to such a degree by an airy panic emanating from a whirling flock of frightened starlings, that everything in the world except that little, low-roofed philosophic chamber seemed all beak and claws, burst into the room, and aware of Brother Tuck's square shoulders stooping over two glasses and Friar Bacon's bottle-neck shoulders erect over nothing, flung itself in a wild panic against the three walls in front of it, and fell dead on the floor before reverting to the fourth.

Both men went to pick up the bird, and there was something almost like a boyish scuffle between them as to which should reach it first. In the event, attained in two seconds, it was Friar Bacon who got the motionless creature into his hands and smoothed down its feathers and let its head fall limp across his thumb.

"Well! tell me now, Tuck, old friend; has this new girl at the convent got a name that suggests death or anything to do with death?" As he spoke the Friar lifted the bird's head from the back of his thumb just about an eighth of an inch and then let it sink down again. "Anything to do with Death, old friend, that's the question. And when you've answered I'll tell you exactly why I put this question to you. But sit down again, and I'll sit down too. It's queer, isn't it, how much more tiring it is to stand than to walk?"

Both the men were silent, looking at each other across the table, the Friar mechanically caressing the dead bird on his lap and the Lay-Brother mechanically running his finger round the edge of the wine-glass that was nearest to him. If only one among Friar Bacon's unrealized inventions had been present then that had the power, the moment you touched a particular knob, of uttering in a strong firm voice the thoughts of each person in turn, towards whose cranium, whether hairy or bald, the spear-point of its machinery had been directed, what a moment this would have been for a perfect proof as to how the most unorthodox, improper, shameless, outrageous thoughts flit through the heads of upright, honest, and thoroughly good men busy with entirely blameless activities!

For Brother Tuck wondered how soon Prior Bog would detect something amiss if he, Tuck of Abbotsbury, fried his own excrement for the Priory supper; and Roger of Ilchester wondered whether it would be possible for a female yellow-hammer to lay eggs if she were impregnated by a dead mate who had been galvanized into momentary sexual excitement by a thunderstorm.

"Please tell me, Tuck," enquired Bacon earnestly, "whether any idea, even the very remotest idea of Death entered the mind of the baptizer when he was baptizing this new girl at work in the convent?"

It was then that it happened to Lay-Brother Tuck, that calm, well-balanced, and practical person upon whose competence all Bumset Priory depended, to leap up from that perilous round table and from a mouth as wide open as a water-rat's hole in a river-bank to utter an astounded "O! O! O! O!" For it was one thing to give poor Prior Bog the only pleasure he got from life in the form of at least one more delicious meal before the sun went down again in the phantom waves of the sea of time, but it was quite a different thing to find that a weird Friar, doing penance among them for heaven alone could say what mysterious sins, could actually know by some magic power what other people had to find out by long years of seeing and hearing and feeling.

"You don't mean to say that you knew her name was Ghosta before I told you!"

Roger Bacon rose from his seat using self-conscious deliberation, where the other used thoughtless haste.

"Certainly I knew *the sort of name* she had. I can't swear I ever actually uttered the word 'Ghosta' to myself; but now that you've uttered it it seems curiously natural to me, almost as if I'd known it all my life."

There was now between the two men on their feet almost as significant a silence as there had been when they were seated. Of this the Friar was fully and completely aware. It is indeed quite possible that in the whole of the west country from Poole to Penzance there was then no living man who was more self-conscious than Roger Bacon. He had been born so, and from his earliest boyhood he had deliberately developed this birthright.

It had been from the start his daily habit to tell himself exciting stories; and the essence of these stories, their burden and the secret of their enchantment, was the fact that young Roger was always imagining himself, or better say discovering himself, to be surrounded by a motley multiplicity of objects, belonging to the four levels of existence, namely of human beings, of sub-human beings, of vegetable beings, and of mineral substances.

And as Roger Bacon grew older and began his studies at the Universities of Oxford and Paris, this intense consciousness of the various existences, whether animate, or inanimate, that surrounded him at any given moment, including his own self-consciousness, came to be the supreme interest of his whole life. His temperament and general nervous sensibility were such that he could not help feeling a special and quite personal "rapport" with each one of these various existences: and for good and ill each of them affected him profoundly.

Thus at this moment our morbidly self-conscious Friar was aware of a curious contest in his soul, between a desire to lie down in delicious relaxation and deep peace within the pale light-green eyes of the honest Tuck and a desire to go on gazing at the dead yellowhammer, until, through its body, he was able to pursue its soul till he found it re-incarnated in a tiny snow-white hair-like fungus, wherein it would have to await the mating-moment of a new pair of yellowhammers.

This latter desire of the insatiable scholar having thus been gratified, he was suddenly seized with a pang of remorse for not having already thrown the bird's little feathered corpse out of the window so that the first-born of the innumerable little worms that were bound to be engendered out of the putrefying corpse beneath those tender feathers might not perish in being thus separated from the elements.

"I'll run down with it presently," he thought, "and put it somewhere, where——" And then he remembered what in following in his mind that small corpse's corruption he'd entirely forgotten—that he was, save for certain appointed hours each day, a prisoner in this chamber.

"Do you know, my friend, from what race or from what country," Friar Bacon now enquired of Tuck, "this Ghosta-girl comes?"

90

It was always a great comfort to brother Tuck to be asked any direct and simple question by the Priory's illustrious captive and he brightened up enormously at this.

"Yes, indeed I do," he hurriedly replied. "Ghosta's a Jewess from Mesopotamia or Dalmatia or somewhere not very far from the Red Sea; in fact I daresay quite near to the River Jordan."

He spoke with profound satisfaction. And indeed it was wonderful to him that he, Brother Tuck, chief cook to Prior Bog of Bumset, could teach their learned captive something of which he was entirely ignorant.

Roger Bacon let his massive head sink heavily down, letting it fall in front of him till his chin seemed to rest upon the centre of his chest, midway between his breast-bones. While he did this, he closed his eyes, and fell into a momentary trance of deep thinking. But no wrinkle, no frown, no furrow, appeared on the broad expanse of his forehead, nor were his arched eyebrows drawn together.

Tuck watched him with absorbed reverence; for the cook felt exactly as he felt sometimes when a thin film of exquisitely delicate yellow-brown, which faintly resembled pure gold, yet wasn't really like pure gold, began to appear on the surface of what he was cooking.

Then Roger raised his head with a jerk, while Tuck noticed, and not for the first time either, that when the Friar was excited by some daring or original idea, it was not so much that his eyes shone as that an intense inner flame, like a magic candle burning in his very midriff, suddenly revealed itself *through his eyes.*

"Listen, my friend," Roger Bacon exclaimed, bending forward a little, and while with the exterior portion of his eyes he stared through the body of his interlocutor, and, as it seemed, through the wall of his cell, and even across the swaying tops of the forest-trees, he was unable to stop the gleaming flame of his new idea from magnetizing the amazed Tuck.

"Listen," he repeated. And then, in a perfectly calm and easy tone, while he re-possessed himself once more of the corpse of the yellowhammer. "What I want you to do, my faithful one, is to bring this Jewish maid up here to me so that I can ask her a few important questions. No! You needn't look so scared. You'll be here all the time she's here! I haven't the faintest wish to enjoy her, far less ravish her. All I want is to talk to her. But I want to be absolutely frank and open with you, old friend, and there is, I confess, one other thing I want with her—no! don't look like that! It's nothing whatever to do with sex. It's only that being a virgin—for I know from my own experience that the Jews are very particular about the virginity of their maids—she'll have it in her to give the final touch to the Brazen Head over there!"

Thus speaking, he pointed with the hand that held the feathered body towards a large alcove at the foot of his small bed—an alcove which at that moment was covered by a heavy velvet curtain hanging from a cord. Intimately well-known to every living soul in both the Priory and Convent of Bumset was that alcove in the cell of their inventive prisoner; for, of all the magical creations of this extraordinary person, his Brazen Head with the power of speech—and indeed, so it seemed to some among them, with the power of thought too— was the most astounding.

"O! of course, Doctor of all Doctors," murmured Brother Tuck with low-breathed obeisance, "anything I can do or this Hebrew Virgin can do to help with your Head of Brass *must* be done; since the Head, as we all know, is what alone can save our country and our king from destruction."

"Nothing," thought Roger Bacon, "that I have ever done in the interest of my life's work was more effective with the populace than when I told Fulcode, before he was Cardinal or Legate, that I was trying to make an Ark of the Tabernacle for the Nameless One of Israel that should protect us from our enemies as the Jewish Ark protected the Chosen People from the Philistines. Fulcode scattered that story about the Brazen Head being Britain's peculiar and special magical Protector. It is Fulcode's spreading of that tale that has protected my work from Bonaventura's hatred more than anything else! Well! while it protects my inventions it *does* protect my king and my country. The Legate could have soon found out, if he made any enquiries, how completely my family ruined itself by helping the King against the Barons. Anyone who knows anything at all knows how much more liberty there has been under poor old Henry than there's ever been under the Barons and their accurst house of De Montford!"

"Listen to me, Tuck, my dear friend," he said aloud. "The practical question for us now is how to get this girl through the entrance-hall and all those passages and up the stairs to this room. And what I've thought of is this. You know how often great fish are found stranded on Weymouth sands and on Chesil Beach? Well then! Why shouldn't I have developed a mania for trying to bring to life dolphins and porpoises and other large fish by various secret methods of my own? And why shouldn't you explain all this to the girl and persuade her to let you carry her—wrapped up of course so that nothing of her is visible—through those front passages and up these stairs? If you did it after the evening meal, there wouldn't be many people about, and those you did meet would be sufficiently dazed with meat and drink as not to be very observant or very astute in explanation of what they *did* see! Do you think you could manage to do this tomorrow night, Tuck? It would be a good night for it, because, if it's not cloudy, this new Moon will be having a steady influence by then."

The artful cook of Bumset Priory nodded knowingly, made a hurried sign of the cross upon the air in the direction of the small window, and had already turned to go, when Bacon exclaimed:

"O please take this, will you, Tuck, and bury it somewhere? Bury it *just* underground, not more than an inch or two deep—you can make a hole with a stick, or anything you find under your hand: it needn't be deep down—but I want it to be quickly and properly eaten by worms, not flown away with by carrion-crows, or lugged off down a rat-hole! See what I mean, Tuck, my old friend? And bring——"

It was at this moment before the cook departed, and in the dead silence between them created by a simple instruction on one side and unquestioning obedience on the other, that a faint tap upon the door of the cell became audible. Being quite close to it, the departing Tuck opened it immediately, but the figure standing on the threshold surprised him so much that he hurriedly drew back to let it enter, and then, with what was clearly a strong feeling that the more closely confined to the chief participants concerned this encounter was, the better for all it would be, he cautiously and very

93

secretively closed the door behind the intruding figure and returned into the room.

The new-comer was obviously, and both men saw it at once, of the female sex, although she was well muffled in a black mantle. But the slope of the shoulders and what was visible of the ankles and feet would have betrayed her, even if, though her hair was hidden, the delicate whiteness of her face and the size of her dark liquid eyes had not revealed a most magnetic femininity.

Roger Bacon walked straight up to her and taking off her cloak handed it to the somewhat disturbed Tuck, who kept muttering, half audibly and half inaudibly, what the Friar, and probably the girl too, recognized as the opening words of a familiar Latin collect; but who now, dragging a chair from beneath the table and carrying it to the wall near the foot of the bed, sat down with an air of patient submission to inexplicable proceedings and covered his knees with the girl's cloak.

"I came my lord Doctor, because I had one of my presentiments that you would be glad to talk to me. As Brother Tuck may have told you, I've come to help in the Convent; but being—as perhaps you can see from my appearance—of foreign extraction, in fact of Palestinian Hebrew blood, I am at present without friends. But I've heard that there's an armour-bearer, or whatever the name for that office may be in your country, in the Fortress of Roque, whom I once met in the East and whom I would most dearly love to meet again. He is easy to describe to you, my lord Doctor, as he resembles Goliath of Gath or Samson of Israel, being in fact what all over the world is called a giant. His lord and master here, they tell me, finds him——"

At this point Friar Bacon firmly, though very gently, interrupted her and led her to his bed, upon which, almost within arm's length of where Brother Tuck's chair stood against the wall, he made her seat herself.

"What did you mean just now," the scholar enquired, standing over her with a certain judicial authority, although still very gently and kindly, "by your presentiment? Oh yes! And may I ask you at once whether I am right in calling you Ghosta? I don't at all want, my dear daughter, to be rudely inquisitive, but would it be ill-mannered of me to ask you whether your parents gave you this unusual name?"

The girl gave him a confiding, responsive, and grateful smile. "It's rather a long story," she began, "and I don't like, O most admirable Doctor, keeping you standing while I tell it."

"O it's good for me," said the Friar quickly. "I've been sitting all day—so please go on."

The girl took him at his word, and glancing quickly round, as if to make sure she was only keeping the learned Friar, and not the Priory cook too, in a standing position, she permitted herself to indulge in quite a long biographical narrative.

"I expect it's Jewish ancestry," she began, "that really explains these queer *presentiments*. I call them that; but I've been told in the Convent that I ought to give them a different name. But never mind the name! *You* will know, O most admirable Doctor, much better, I expect, than I do, what these things are. But you see my grandfather was a Rabbi. Both my parents"—here the girl arranged herself more comfortably on the Friar's bed, evidently reassured a great deal by the way he was standing at ease and listening with what looked like most attentive interest—"were murdered in a crusading massacre soon after I was born. It was my great-aunt Rebecca who took care of me. She gave me my name to bear witness to her conversion to the Christian Faith; for she always believed that it was a special intervention by the Holy Ghost that led to her acceptance of Christ as her God. Great-aunt Rebecca's belief in this has struck many people as both presumptuous and blasphemous. But knowing Aunt Rebecca so well, and having lost in her when she died the only person in the world I've ever understood, or indeed have wanted to understand, until I met the man they now swear to me is armour-bearer at the Fortress, it's impossible for me to feel that her name for me was blasphemous. As for these 'presentiments', as I call them, though there's a nun where I work who swears to me that 'intimations' would be a better word, I put *them* down, myself, entirely to my Jewishness. Aunt Rebecca taught me to read Hebrew, and my favourite reading all my life has always been the Books of Moses; and Moses was always being told what to do directly out of the mouth

95

of the Nameless One who was the God of Israel, known only by the Four Mystic Letters '*Y.H.W.H.*'

"And it's no doubt from reading the Books of Moses so much that there come moments—not in sleep you must understand, but in reveries or trances or wanderings of thought, when I seem to hear the voice of the God of Israel speaking to me and telling me to do something. And three times lately this voice has come to me and said: 'Go to the cell of the Admirable Doctor and talk to him'——

"But, O most admirable lord Doctor, I see that Brother Tuck here whom"—and she turned her lustrous eyes to the still uneasy cook sitting awkwardly against the wall with her cloak across his knees—"whom I already know quite well by sight, has brought you your supper," and she made a gesture with one of her hands towards the great apple-pasty on the table, "so I oughtn't to stay any longer."

At this point she gave a quaintly reckless little laugh. "But the truth is, O most admirable Doctor, I keep hearing—it's very faint, you know, but I've learnt from experience to catch it—the far-off voice of the Nameless One of Israel telling me that there's some way in which I can help you with something that's very much on your mind. Of course you may feel from your worship of a Trinity, where Jesus Christ is the centre if not the circumference, that this Voice of the Nameless One, speaking to me in the same Voice wherein it spoke to Miriam the sister of Moses, means little, or as far as a christian is concerned, nothing at all; but my voice tells me you don't and cannot treat it so lightly. O my Lord, O most admirable Doctor, I do beg and beseech you to tell me——" Here the girl leapt up from the Friar's bed and stood erect before him with her back to the disturbed and agitated cook—"to tell me what it is that the Voice keeps commanding me to do for you!"

Very calmly and quietly Friar Bacon took the situation into his own hands. He showed himself as skilful at the stage-management of human puppets as he did at the invention of automatic and mechanical ones. He was indeed soon standing with his left hand on the sleeve of brother Tuck and his right on the elbow of Ghosta.

He had already induced the former to hide the corpse of the yellowhammer in his tunic-pocket, and the latter to take the mantle the man had been holding and place it on the bed; and now they were, all three, in unencumbered freedom of action confronting the mysterious black curtain behind which was the Brazen Head.

Releasing Ghosta's arm, but retaining his hold on Tuck's sleeve, the Friar now drew aside this curtain from the most renowned shrine not only in Britain but, save for the Holy Sepulchre at Jerusalem, in the whole world, and as he did so he was aware of a shivering motion in the muscles and nerves of both his companions, as if they were being compelled to make an involuntary prostration before the revealed mystery.

But he did not give them time for the smallest unrehearsed gesture. "What I want *you* to do," he said to Tuck, "is to prop up the Head and to steady it and prevent it from falling while I lift our maid upon its shoulder," and to Ghosta he said, "I want *you* to arrange your garments as if you were intending to make water, so that it is from contact with your nakedness that the Head looks forth upon the world."

It was in an incredibly short space of time, after giving the man and the woman these precise instructions, that Friar Bacon got both of them, and got the Brazen Head as well, into the position he desired; and the expression on the countenance of that Brazen Head, as its powerfully moulded eyes and ears and nose and mouth looked forth from between Ghosta's thighs and from under her naked belly, was like the expression in a marble head of the god Hermes, attributed to Praxiteles, that a nameless crusade had recently brought to the King's house in London.

"Will you both, if you don't mind," the Friar murmured, "since the ancients knew, long before the Mother of God was revealed to us, the divine power of virginity, follow me in repeating the sounds of an ancient invocation, the exact meaning of which has been lost to the world for two thousand years?"

And so slowly and clearly did Roger Bacon utter these evidently latinized syllables that neither Ghosta in her extravagant position, nor Tuck using all his strength and all his intelligence to keep the Image and its Burden upright, had any difficulty in repeating them after him: *Birginis, Sirginis, Flirginis, Virginis*; and these simple sounds had hardly died away, and the curious white light which the cunning art of the inventor had caused to play over the countenance of the Bronze Head had scarcely faded, when the Friar lifted Ghosta down upon her feet and handed her her mantle. Then he removed from the foot of his bed a cloak of his own and wrapped it round Brother Tuck. "Better take her to the Convent yourself," he said gravely. "Two cloaked figures won't excite the same interest as one alone. I shall pray for you both very particularly this night. You have helped me greatly."

98

VIII

THE MAN OF GOD

"It was indeed a special act of Providence," replied the General of the Franciscan Order of Friars from his seat on the back of the deformed animal known to its owner as Cheiron, "that we met at those cross-roads. I should have had to spend the night under these pines if we hadn't; because to tell you the truth, my good Master Spardo, nothing would have made me stop hunting for this Castle of Lost Towers except falling dead in my tracks or being killed by a wolf."

The satisfaction of the General of the Grey Friars in the absoluteness of his God-Intoxication was so deep that the ground beneath Cheiron's hooves seemed to rise to meet it. Unseen by the borrower of the deformed beast, Spardo wiped a blob of bird's dropping from the back of one of his hands upon the fringe of the ecclesiastical garment dangling at the animal's side.

"How did it happen, if your reverent generalship will not take offence at the question, that you, whom we all call the Seraphic Doctor, should be wandering about alone without a single servant?"

This not altogether unexpected question helped the bubbling spring of Bonaventura's self-love to overflow again.

"I've got the best of all possible ones *now*, haven't I?" he replied to Spardo, with an ingratiating smile. "Didn't you tell me just now that you were unemployed?"

"Hitherto," replied the bastard son of the King of Bohemia, "it has been my destiny to serve laymen: lordly laymen, it is true, and persons not devoid of coins of silver and coins of gold, but people tell me that great churchmen like thyself, O most

99

Seraphic Doctor, are very particular and very exacting about the way your food is prepared and your off-scourings disposed of and your garments kept clean. I can see at this actual moment, O most saintly of doctors, several very filthy stains on your beautiful grey mantle, due no doubt—no! I'm not being rude to you, my lord doctor; I'm just indicating the absolute necessity that men like yourself who are so spiritual and so sensitive, and who so feel very, very, *very* far from the stupid unenlightened masses of men, and just as far from their stupid unenlightened authorities——"

"Silence, man! Who has taught you to talk like that? Are we not all equal before God? Are we not all equally stupid and ignorant in the presence of his holy spirit? Are we not all equally selfish and greedy and lascivious and treacherous and deceitful under the blinding fire of his eternal righteousness and the terrible thunder of his fearful truth?"

The deformed Cheiron was so agitated by this threatening voice so close to his ears that he came to a stop and began trembling from head to tail.

"To whom have you been listening?" repeated the grey-robed rider on Cheiron's back. "*You*, fresh from our religious France and our more than religious Italy, *you*, a wanderer across christian Europe from the idolatries of the East, where, I ask you, have *you* picked up this devilish talk about ignorant masses and stupid authorities? Have *you* been listening to this Satanic sorcerer who has dared to assume the dress of a Friar just because he has lost his money, this thrice-accurst Roger Bacon? Or are all the misbegotten islanders in this God-forsaken Britain of yours so savage that if anyone wants to win their favour they've got to talk to them in this unholy way? But do you really think, O most generous of all possible wanderers through haunted forests, that you can go on guiding me to Lost Towers? You seem to me, Master Spardo, a rather tired and worn-out man yourself. I can't help seeing that you drag your feet very heavily, and even kick the tree-stumps and the earth-mounds and the fallen logs as you go along; and I noticed just now that your eyes kept shutting of their own accord, as if at any moment you might fall asleep as you walked."

"We shan't be much longer now, reverend lord," replied

Spardo, "and once there I may find a place where I can sleep in their kitchen and my horse may be able to sleep in their stable, while you, being entertained by Baron Maldung and Lady Lilt, will come to your own conclusion about their daughter Lilith, of whom rumour round here says things I won't repeat to a sacred gentleman like yourself."

After that brief summary of the situation, the three of them moved on, with the saintly Bonaventura in the saddle, with Cheiron on his faithfully plodding four legs, and with Spardo's weary head and half-closed eyes drooping and nodding more and more heavily.

Spardo's thoughts, in spite of what he had just said, were by no means in any kitchen. They were in a much grander place. He was imagining himself luxuriating on heaps of soft cushions and sipping the particular kind of French wine, of a yellowish tint, which from his Bohemian childhood he had always loved best of all the wines in the world.

As for Bonaventura, he was thinking very hard, as he rode on, about his own future destiny. "If I continue," he was saying to himself, "as effectively as I have done hitherto, in dominating my lower nature by my higher nature; if, in fact, I do attain in the eyes of the world the reputation of being a real saint, will this reputation interfere with my chance, for there can be no doubt I have a very good chance, of being elected Pope?

"Of course it does satisfy me to a mighty large extent to dominate my lower nature like I do, and to feel that in me, and to feel that others feel that in me, the Will of God triumphs over the Will of Satan. But with a character like mine it isn't enough to dominate Satan in myself; I feel an imperative need to dominate Satan in others too. Yes! and not only in individuals. I feel a need to dominate Satan in groups, classes, societies, tribes, races, countries, nations, hemispheres, worlds! But my real life is my inward life. And I and God alone know the majestic secrets of my inner life.

"The wonderful thing about me, and the thing wherein I differ most from ordinary people, is that I don't want to dominate the world by action. I want to dominate it by just being what I am; by just being myself. And in this I resemble Jesus Christ. I and God alone know what a destiny-changing moment it was in the history of Christendom when Saint Francis sought me out, among all the rest, and gave me that gift of Healing which he gave to nobody else.

"But what I and God alone know is a yet deeper secret even than that; a secret that I would not have let God know if I hadn't decided he would have found it out for himself; the way my mother before I was born felt me give a leap in her womb every time God was mentioned. She even—and this deep secret nobody in the world knows but I and God— she even prayed to God all night long, while my father by her side was snoring like a Lombardy hog, that just one tiny little infinitesimal drop of God's holy ethereal spiritual and invisible seed might mingle with the substance of their earthly terrestrial and mundane seeds, when she and my father became one in my begetting.

"Yes! I and God, alone in all the world, heard that prayer of my mother; and I and God, alone in all the world, know how lovely the face of my mother was—how it was trans- formed, transfigured, illuminated, entranced, and beside itself with mystical love, when she made that prayer. For I was in you, then, God, wasn't I, and not in my mother's womb? O how can I thank you enough, God, for separating me from, and selecting me out of, and putting me above, the myriads of ordinary souls whereof the world is so full! But I must think, think, *think*, whether it would be better for me, from now on, to go forward increasing my spirituality as a saint, or to develop that other side of sanctity which is quite as deeply natural to me and implanted in me—the sort of wis- dom that Solomon had when he decided between those two women with the living baby and the dead baby. That is the sort of wisdom we need in our Pope, and if I were Pope, I would have the greatest opportunity anyone could have in the whole world to make people obey the will of God as op- posed to the will of Satan.

"Perhaps," so Bonaventura's thoughts ran on, "the in- spiration of mine about converting to God and His Church this whole outpost of Devilry they call Lost Towers does really and truly combine both the spirituality and the wisdom of a true saint. But suppose this devil of a Baron Maldung puts me to death?"

He gave a little gasp like a frog in a cave at the striking of flint and steel. "Well, in *that case* I wonder how far my——" But Bonaventura's thoughts of spiritual advancement and of everlasting felicity were now interrupted by the sound of a horn quite close to them; and he quickly turned to his companion, who was evidently, although still plodding along by Cheiron's side, so nearly asleep that he could hear nothing.

"What's that over there? Did you hear that? For God's sake, listen, man! It's just the other side of those trees!"

Spardo slowly turned his head causing his long, slender, wispy beard to brush away several flies from Cheiron's deformity. "Yes, by Holy Jesus I do hear it," he groaned, "and what's more, O most seraphic of doctors, I can tell you whose horn it is! It's the horn of Bailiff Sygerius and I expect he's calling for one of his own rascally boys! The fellow hasn't been bailiff for more than six months. His dad, old Heber Sygerius, has only just given up the job, and I rather——"

Spardo was interrupted by an inrush upon them of several persons. A broad-shouldered, obstinate-looking, middle-aged man, who obviously was the bailiff in question, pushed forward through some closely growing pine-tree trunks, and advanced into the open, making, as he did so, several rough and brutal jerks to get rid of the hold upon his sleeve of an old and extremely agitated serf, who in his turn was clutching the hand of a little girl, who, with big frightened eyes, surveyed the two men and the deformed horse as if they had been beings from another world.

The bailiff made the appropriate gesture of respect to the man on the horse, who was obviously, although in the garb of a Franciscan Friar, some sort of high-ranking ecclesiastic from abroad.

"Pardon me for disturbing you like this, reverend Father, but I must settle the affair of this troublesome fellow before I can pay my proper respects to you."

The serf's voice had a piercingly pitiful tone of appeal which arrested Spardo's critical attention at once. "You're taking our whole life, master bailiff," the old man was saying, "when you take away our horse. My daughter has a good job in the Convent's washhouse and her children are good children; but if you take away our horse, considering my son's dead, you take the bread out of all our mouths."

It would have been clear to any less self-absorbed listeners than the two men upon whom this group of people flung itself, that in the familiar pleading tone of her grand-dad's voice there was something that spread a reassuring atmosphere round the child who was holding his hand. Tragic enough though the old man's words were, there were so many use-and-wont associations aroused in her by his special tone that her eyes ceased to be so big and scared.

It even began to be exciting to her to watch this weird horse's neck, with what really looked like a human head growing out of it, while the man with the feathery beard, like the moulting tail of Granny's jackdaw, seemed to be making funny faces at her, as if he wanted her to play a game with him.

It was early afternoon by now, and the rays of the February sun were shimmering between the pine branches at an angle about midway between earth and sky.

"I tell you, master bailiff, if you take our horse it will be just simply a death-sentence to us all!"

"Pardon me, holy sir," said the bailiff, looking straight into the twitching, high-coloured face of Bonaventura, whose excited eyes, always very prominent, were now literally bulging from his head; "pardon me till I've dealt with this fellow!"

Meanwhile the little girl, whose hand her grandfather was still tightly clutching, couldn't keep the idea out of her mind that the interest of this hooded rider in what was going on was so intense that it might at any moment project those inflated eyes of his out of his head like a pair of globular puff-balls.

She was even beginning to imagine the simultaneous pop with which those two voracious peerers would strike the tree beside her and the amount of effervescent juice that would pour down the tree's trunk at their bursting, when she heard the bailiff protest to the owner of those same orbs that he would give him his full attention as soon as he had got rid of these tiresome people.

"Full attention" was the very last thing any one of the group of human bipeds flung together beneath these pines could hope for. But at least the ragged little girl, whose name was Bet, and who had been endowed by Nature with several extra drops of imagination, derived an agreeably alarming impression from the bulging eyes of the saintly General of the Franciscan Order of Friars.

But there was nothing but distress in the shock she received when she saw her grand-dad throw himself down on his knees before Master Sygerius and actually embrace his straddling pair of sturdy legs, while with head thrown back he gazed up imploringly at all that could possibly be seen from that position of the man's physiognomy, which could only have been the reddish-brown beard protruding from the obstinately square jaw.

"If you take our horse away, master," cried the old man, "it just means starvation! While my son was alive, he could plough as fast as any man on the manor. And plough he did, and sow and reap too, with the best in the land. But if after his death our only horse is to be what's called your Heriot, considering I'm too old and feeble to plough or to sow or to reap or to carry in the harvest, it's just murder you're committing! Yes, what you're doing, bailiff, is sheer murder! I tell you, here and now, it's squeezing the orange dry!"

The bailiff, evidently no less conscious of the staring eyes of the hooded man on Cheiron's back than was the ragged little Bet, stepped away so hurriedly that the old supplicant, losing his balance, fell forward with both his hands outstretched upon the red-brown earth. The spot where the old man fell was a spot strewn with several generations of pine-needles, but it was quite bare of moss and quite bare also of that particular sort of forest-grass, soft as the hair of a Dryad, which grew luxuriantly in those parts, especially in the district between the Fortress and Lost Towers.

Little Bet had so far only spent seven years upon earth but she had already noticed that, when her elders quarrelled among themselves and began to argue, something always seemed to be drawn into the contention that came from far away. Yes! she had often noticed that some unexpected bird or beast or reptile appeared at such times, or an unusual storm of wind, or a torrent of water, or even a falling star. And it now came about that as Bet's grand-dad, whose name was Dod Pole, scrambled to his feet, with the palms of his hands and the undersides of his fingers pricking viciously from the pine-needles, and commenced in unabashed indignation to express his feelings, a tiny little bird, on the look-out for the crumbs that it had come to associate with these meetings of vociferous bipeds, was so absorbed in its own private quest that it remained oblivious to the nearby hovering of a hungry hawk, who, instinctively aware that no arrows were to be feared from that preoccupied party, descended like a feathered plummet and made its fellow-citizen of the air its helpless prey.

"O you bailiffs and reeves and forest-wardens," shouted old Dod Pole, his voice growing harsher and huskier as he went on and his grip on little Bet's hand hurting the child's fingers more and more, "you are all the same in your fat-headed stupidity! You think the land belongs to the Barons whose castles on it *we* have built, or to the Church, whose barley and wheat and fruit and vegetables we have grown. O you wooden-headed coxcombs! I tell you a day will come when we shall have a King after our own hearts, a King as wise as Solomon, and as strong as Coeur-de-Lion, and as well-supported as Caesar, and with as many magic weapons as King Arthur, who will raise us up and thrust you down! Who gave your precious Barons the right to make us thresh our corn on their threshing-floors and grind it with their grind-stones? Are your Barons so many Gods? Did they create the land that *we* cultivate? Did they create the wheat and the barley that *we* sow and reap and gather in barns?

"Just because you call taking our horse a Heriot—a mighty grand lawyers' word the word Heriot, ain't it?—you think all is settled! You wait a bit, my good master bailiff, you wait a bit, my noble lord, Sir Mort! A day will come when it will be to a really great and true King chosen by *us*, yes! by us, who are now serfs and slaves, that you and your barons will have to come for the making of all the laws in the land! And I'll tell you this, too, Master Sygerius———"

The obstinate bailiff, at whom this revolutionary outburst was aimed, still stood his ground sullenly, silently, tenaciously and with an ugly purpose in his grim countenance. But the aged Dod Pole still went on. Indeed as he recklessly and desperately flung out these thoughts, he felt in his soul as if over all the countries in the world millions of serfs and slaves like himself were uttering the same thoughts, and he couldn't but believe that the God of Abraham, Isaac, and Jacob, if not the God of Jesus, was their inspiration and would avenge them upon their enemies.

But the Bastard of the King of Bohemia, whose mother had called him Spardo and whose only affection and pride in the whole universe was his concern for the deformed horse Cheiron, had at that moment—perhaps because along with his other faculties his conscience had gone to sleep—a different sort of inspiration, one that only Hermes himself, the God of thieves, could have put into his head.

He had already observed that Bonaventura possessed a deep pocket in his Friar's garb, at the bottom of which he was carrying a leather bag full of thick golden pieces. He had found this out by spying on the saintly man when the latter retired from his seat on Cheiron to relieve his bowels; and he derived no little satisfaction at this moment from discovering that the richly-filled leather bag in the flapping skirt of Cheiron's rider had somehow or other, by good chance, worked itself along the animal's side till it was close to his own caressing, stroking, toying, soothing, and encouraging left hand.

The more violent old Dod became in what he was saying, the more closely was Bonaventura absorbed in watching him; so that to a born pilferer of unguarded treasures like this offspring of the loins of a King, who had just refused a more dangerous crown than the one he wore, it was not a very difficult achievement to transfer to his own person, in fact to an interior pocket next his own skin, two of these massive golden coins stamped with this same Germanic crown that the crafty King of Bohemia had refused to assume.

"Amen, Amen, Amen, old man!" Spardo now shouted, dancing into the arena between the feverish aura of the serf's oration and the bailiff's contemptuous silence. "In the country where I come from there are shrines to the Mother of God where every farthing offered by visitors, yes! and every penny given by pilgrims, and every shekel flung down by travellers, is gathered into a special treasury for the benefit of such as labour with their hands! Pardon me, Master Sygerius, if as an ambassador from abroad, in fact from three kingdoms and a dozen Free Cities, I exchange a few words with this ancient man of resounding speech. I think there are things that I can say to him that will be of value to him and to me and to us all!"

Old Dod now permitted his voice to die away in the midst of a sentence and looked enquiringly at little Bet. The owner of Cheiron had the wit to interpret this quick glance correctly. "Like all orators," he thought, "the old fellow is hopelessly dependent on women for every practical move he makes, and as the only female here is that ragged little girl, he daren't move a step without appealing to her!"

It was at this point that Spardo, who understood small girls better than he understood either religion or revolution, exchanged a smile and a wink with little Bet that arranged it all.

"The man wants a word with you, grand-dad," she whispered to Dod Pole; and the three of them retreated beneath the pine-trunks. Once out of sight of the Friar-General and the Manor bailiff, Cheiron's owner produced one of his great gold pieces and explained its worth in relation to the coinage of Britain to old Dod.

"Won't that be enough and to spare, my friend," he said, "to keep you and your family till next winter?"

Again he caught old Dod Pole glancing at little Bet. And again it was clear to him that the child's vigorous series of emphatic nods settled the matter. "Well then," he commanded in the nearest approach to an official dismissal he could assume, "off with you! And put that piece of gold"—and here he came close to the old man and felt his sides and hips with his two hands—"in *there*!" he added, when he had discovered a secure little receptacle in Dod Pole's innermost garment, already containing a few coins; and without a glance at their retreating figures he rejoined Cheiron and the horse's two companions.

"I've been explaining to his Reverence," announced Spardo to the bailiff, "that, when he reaches Lost Towers, he'd better take no notice of what Baron Maldung may have to say, and concentrate his attention upon any definite information he can get out of Lady Lilt. I don't know, I'm sure, master bailiff, if you share my view that in all these affairs it's wisest to go straight to the woman, if there is a woman in the case."

The bailiff of Roque looked from the General of the Franciscan Friars to the horse with the growing appearance of two heads.

"You'd better," he said, "hurry your beast on, if you're going to see anything of any of the three of them tonight! It gets dark at Lost Towers, I understand, before the proper time! At least that's what they say, and I'm ready to believe anything of that awful place! For myself I'll never be caught going near it. But they do tell me your Reverence has the reputation of being a great Saint, and my missus do say every time I put head to pillow—'Randy,' she do say—that's short for Randolph you understand—'hast thee said thee's prayers straight and proper to the Blessed Saint Aldhelm?'

"And when I do say to she: 'Bain't Prior Bog of Bumset as good a church-lord as any old Saint?' she's answer to I is allus the same: 'Bog be Bog and Bumset be Bumset,' she do say, 'but when thee do pray to They Above, 'tis a very different style of Holy Man thee dost need for thee's pass to Salvation!'

"But that bain't all my missus do say when head and pillow do come together. 'Why do us pray,' her says, 'when Night be come and Dark do cover all? Because the Devil be six times nearer to we at such times! Beware of Darkness, Randy,' she do say. 'Call on Saint Aldhelm to keep 'ee calm and cosy in the lap of the Blessed Virgin, else thee may go wandering down one of they girt dark roads that go anywhere and lead nowhere for ever and ever and ever and ever!' So my advice to your Reverence, and to thee too, Master Spardo, is to hurry on as fast as may be, lest Sun be gone when Lost Towers be come!"

And with that, and a swift look upwards, as if at any moment some vast Devil's bird might carry off the sun in its beak and darken the earth with its wings, Randolph Sygerius, the new bailiff, marched off, walking like a soldier who needs all the strength of will he possesses to accept the fact that in Roque Manor day is followed by night.

The deformed Cheiron however hadn't gone on for more than twenty minutes, with Bonaventura silent on his back and Spardo silent at his side, when they came to a track that crossed the one they were following, and there, just as if he had been purposely awaiting them, astride of his tall warhorse till he had grown as sleepy as the plodding Spardo, was none other than the Baron—not the Baron of Lost Towers, but of Castle Cone, that cheerful stronghold on the southern side of Roque Fortress, inhabited by the Boncor family.

Baron Boncor was a big strong man, with a thick fair beard and as placid and friendly a cast of countenance as any pair of agitated travellers could wish to meet. Human nature is such, however, that when we have "worked ourselves up", as we say, to expect one thing, and find instead of it not only something quite different, but something that is the direct opposite of what we've expected, even if what we've found is pleasing to us beyond hope, our immediate reaction—such is our pride in the way we've mentally prepared ourselves to meet this encounter—is a curious shock of disappointment. We might just as well have never bothered to prepare for battle at all!

But Baron Boncor had in him as much commonsense as good nature. He greeted this queer-looking trinity of unusual explorers with an instinctive courtesy that set them at their ease at once.

"Welcome to our dark forests, your Eminence!" he began. "Though I fear after your sunlit Italy you'll have to be careful to keep your cloak about you. And you too, Master Spardo, for through my wife's friendship with her good neighbour Lady Val, I've heard all about you and your strange steed here! Cheiron you call him, don't you? They talk a lot about him in the Fortress stables when I take my old Basileus there for a rub down. Give Cheiron a kiss, Basileus! No, no, a real proper kiss! *That's* the boy! I warrant he's not so much younger than you are; and who can tell? You may, if you kiss each other often enough, turn into a real Centaur as he seems to be turning. But if you do——"

He was interrupted by the appearance of the most amazing human figure that any of them, man or beast, had ever seen in his life before. This personage came dancing into their midst, and not one of them could take his eyes off him for a second when once he appeared. He inhaled and sucked in and tried to drain up the essence of every living soul upon that spot, whether such a soul belonged to a man or an animal or a bird or a reptile or a toad or a worm or an insect. None of the three human beings present at that cross-track in the forest had a flicker of doubt as to who this intruder was, who thus came dancing into the midst of them.

It was Baron Maldung himself, the Lord of Lost Towers!

Well, they had come to seek him. They had come to visit him. And here he was! Beneath his tunic and his breeches Baron Maldung was clothed in only two garments; but these two garments literally covered him from head to foot—that is to say, from half-way down his neck to the soles of both his feet. The under-garment was of thick, warm, white sheep's wool; while the garment that covered it was of thin delicate coal-black satin.

Every movement the Baron made was like a step in a dance that he knew by heart: and as he fluttered from one to another of these five beings, two super-intelligent horses, and three rather unusual men, the lightly-blowing wind as it opened his tunic revealed the fact that this black satin covering he wore above his sheep's-wool under-garment was an attempt, almost a pathetic attempt, on the part of this demonic man to round off his ungainly limbs into a sort of grace, at any rate into a grace that sheep's wool alone could not give.

"O you must come, you must, you must, you must, all of you, now at once, now that you are here!" he murmured, as he and his shadow—for the sun seemed to be playing a private game with the two of them—danced their special man-and-his-shadow dance. And the wind too had a share in it; for the thin straight dusky hair of the Baron of Lost Towers was lifted up and down on his head as if by the puffs of a petulant rival of that obsequious shadow.

Probably owing to some instinctive gust of fellow-feeling for a being as much devoid of man's moral sense as he was devoid of man's self-righteous attitude towards his exploitation of animals, both horses now made an emphatic movement to follow him.

"Well, Basileus," muttered Baron Boncor, "it evidently looks as if we men must obey the oracles of creatures who probably know the will of heaven better than we do! So come along my christian friends! Let two legs follow four legs and all our eyes see what happens!"

It cannot be said that Bonaventura looked at Spardo or that Spardo nodded a reply to Bonaventura's look. It might rather be said that the man on the back of Cheiron and the man at the side of Cheiron followed Baron Maldung as un-questioningly as if they were members of the Household of Lost Towers.

As for Baron Boncor of Cone, he brought up the rear upon Basileus with an expression on his good-natured bearded face which seemed to say: "Well! as long as I've got your crazy backs *in front of me*, I'm ready for anything! From behind I can see how things go. Chance often gives a chance to those who don't mind bringing up the rear; and, if it doesn't in this case, so be it."

It was rather a startling surprise to both Spardo and Bonaventura when they found themselves completely clear of the forest, and saw in front of them, a vast reedy swamp that extended to the horizon in every direction, save the one from which they had come to the really terrifying bulk of Lost Towers.

Lost Towers looked at first sight like a ruin built entirely of black marble; but on nearer approach it showed itself to be anything but a ruin; for the vast blocks of black stone of which it was built had something Egyptian and pyramidal in their size, and although divided and broken up into many small domes and minarets and watch-towers, the general effect made a tremendous awe-inspiring impression upon everyone who had never seen it before. There was something staggering— in truth you might say almost shocking—about its antiquity. It looked as if it had been built of materials brought on barges through a network of canals from the sea-coast, a coast which had been reached by ship from Atlantis itself in pre-historic times. A very queer effect was produced upon a traveller's nerves the moment he set eyes upon it, a disturbing, troubling, and bewildering effect. The first sight of it must have always touched some long-buried race-nerve in us all that goes back to antediluvian times.

It was certainly as queer a cortège as had ever reached that weird mass of domes and towers in all its incredibly long history, this little group that now approached its portentous entrance. By reason of its own Baron being the leader of this queer band, they were received in a manner bordering upon a religious ceremony.

Lady Lilt herself came out to meet them, dressed so extravagantly that Baron Boncor assured his grey horse that the lady must have been waiting for their arrival in a wardrobe-chamber looking out their way. The retainers who assembled on the small square of cut grass in front of the high, narrow, strangely painted gates, gates that never, by night or day, seemed entirely shut or entirely open, must have amounted to a dozen men and a dozen women, all dressed so much alike and all so mingled together that it was hard to distinguish men-servants from maid-servants as they surrounded the visitors.

But the apparel they all wore was so remarkable in its colour that only a very discerning eye would have been likely to detect that the materials, whereof these richly-coloured garments were made, were a sorry draggled-tailed patch-work of odds and ends, stitched together anyhow, a motley agglomeration of woven stuffs that had only two purposes; the first, to cover—you couldn't say to warm—human bodies, and, the second, to receive the particular red-brown dye which had been the prerogative of a special family from somewhere in the far north, who, for several generations, had lived in Lost Towers, to prepare, to make, to mix, to adapt to every kind of weather, and to apply to every sort of fabric. This colour had exactly, precisely, and to the last nicety, the shade of the ground at the roots of the forest pines, and also of the narrow foot-wide paths that horsemen, and very often their dogs too, had to follow, as they made their way through the woods.

Baron Maldung himself resembled a middle-aged acrobat with a profile so startlingly like that of certain busts of the Emperor Nero that visitors to Lost Towers who had pilgrimaged to Rome wondered sometimes, especially when they observed the dictatorial manner of the Baron and the something like obsequiousness with which everyone treated him, whether he might not really be, as the man himself always maintained he was, descended from ancestors who had not come from the North at all, but from Rome itself.

There was a tall black poplar on one side of this stretch of grass, now crowded with retainers in the Lost Towers red-brown attire; and though there were few leaf-buds on it at this early season the great tree had a happy and vital look, as if its sap was already stirring. Not far from this benevolent forest-giant there grew a small thorn, and it happened that Bonaventura, whose hold on Chieron's reins was entirely negligible, now that he had so much to see and so much more to think about, allowed the horse to press so closely against this leafless bush that a perceptible tuft of the creature's skin with a patch of his fur was torn away by the bush's powerful thorns.

In a flash Baron Maldung observed this misadventure and quick as lightning leapt upon the offending thorn-bush and began hacking at it with a short sharp little war-axe which he unhooked from his belt. Lady Lilt, who had been tenderly stroking the deformity on the neck of Chieron, a deformity that to the eyes of Spardo seemed growing larger and more like a human head with every touch the lady gave it, now sprang to the side of her lord, and first with one bare arm and then with the other, though both arms were soon bleeding as the thorn-bush defended itself, held up the thing's branches towards the slashing fury of Maldung's war-axe.

The small bush was soon level with the ground; but the insanity of life-hatred in Maldung seemed to increase moment by moment with each advance in the demolition of those crumpled, twisted, wrinkled, broken little twigs, and, as can be imagined, each little drop of perspiration from the white arms that were acting like assistant executioners added to the man's frenzy.

And it was at this moment, just when the now quite horizontal stream of afternoon sunlight had turned that small square of green grass into a radiant dance-lawn, that Spardo noticed that on the very edge of the reedy swamp there grew an immensely old oak-tree by the side of a small mound, and that upon this mound a very white full-grown lamb was bleating piteously. But all eyes, including Spardo's, were now concentrated upon the exquisitely lovely and magnetically provocative daughter of the house, who now came forth to play *her* part in her parents' battle with this sub-demonic vegetation.

Her part just now seemed to be the pretence that she had rushed forth from the hands of her tirewomen, in such haste to join the fight against these appalling monsters who had invaded this innocent world of noble animals, that she had been too hurried to remember to put all her clothes on. Her haste was, however, as even Spardo could see, attended by an exquisite delicacy of choice as to just where the effect of not being fully dressed would be maddeningly tantalizing, and indeed, not only seductive, but what you might call ravishing.

And they all could see that to the human nerves of the good Baron Boncor such provocation was unendurable. In fact all that that good-natured warrior found gall enough to do under such exceptional tension was to take a dignified and simple farewell of Bonaventura and to give Spardo a definite invitation.

"Don't you forget, Master Spardo, that you'll always be welcome at Cone Castle, whenever your wanderings bring you our way!"

And then, not without some difficulty—for Basileus was showing signs in a manner not quite seemly in so warlike a steed, of being unduly attracted to Cheiron's deformity—Baron Boncor turned his horse clear round and urged him into a rather shy and not wholly polite retreat.

But to retreat from Lost Towers, when once you had discovered it, was more difficult than the discovery. Lady Lilt lifted one long white arm to direct her husband's attention to this retirement of their chief antagonist; and with her other arm she groped for the bow and quiver hanging over the shoulder of Baron Maldung. This small bow, with its arrow already notched against its extended string she thrust into Maldung's hands. "Shoot! Shoot! Shoot!" she hissed. And when the Baron of Lost Towers released the string and the feathered shaft pierced the flesh of Boncor's right shoulder and remained there quivering, the blood that dripped in big drops upon the mane of Basileus was a much brighter red than the red-brown of the Lost Towers retinue.

But, though the blood was bright enough, the hand which held the bridle-reins was reduced to helpless impotence. But Basileus leaped forward and at a gallop now; nor was there any sign before they disappeared of the Baron falling from the horse's back. It was then and only then, that Lady Lilt turned to lead their visitors past the still half-naked Lilith into the interior of Lost Towers.

IX

LOST TOWERS

The crowd of attendants, in their rich red-brown attire, seemed suddenly stricken with a weird sort of lethargy, and indeed displayed a tendency to drift and drift and drift without any purpose. But no aimless drifting disturbed the imperious though comical figure of Maldung, now busy at a job which absolutely absorbed him. This was nothing less, as Bonaventura quickly had an opportunity of realizing, than directing the covering with suitable colour of the carved mantles in the entrance-hall of Lost Towers of certain imperial Roman heads. These had been selected by the despotic Maldung—at least as far as Bonaventura was able to realize—purely for the sake of the devilish obsessions which possessed them.

But past this avenue of diabolical physiognomies the now thoroughly agitated General of the Franciscan Friars felt he had to go, if the obsequious salutation of Baron Maldung and the engaging gestures of Lady Lilt implied that at any rate tonight, whatever happened in the future, and he did begin to feel a little doubtful about converting these people, he was at least sure of a savoury supper and a comfortable bed.

It had been a comfort to him that the murderous arrow which he had seen lodged in the shoulder of Boncor hadn't brought that worthy man down: and what he must do now was to make it clear that his stately strides towards the portal of Lost Towers were not accelerated by the sight of the provocative figure of the daughter of the house, just perceptible beyond the wicked and desperately unhappy visage of Tiberius Caesar, sated with his sadistic orgies, with his sub-human obsessions, with his super-human atrocities, and looking now as if scooped

116

out, gouged out, thunder-blasted out, after years of petrifaction from the substance of an internal rock.

Lilith was still playing her perpetual game; and it was revealed to Lady Lilt, and not wholly concealed even from our friend Spardo, that the present object of the girl's felonious wiles was none other than the saintly personage, armoured in the chastity of grey cloth, wrapped in the chastity of grey vapourings, fortified in the chastity of grey theocracy, cramped in the chastity of grey idealism, who was now approaching the entrance to Lost Towers between the door-post on the left and the profile of Tiberius Caesar on the right.

More momentous to Lady Lilt than the galvanic though invisible cord, that was stretched so taut between the flitting and wavering adumbrations of her daughter's milk-white thighs and the furtive attention of Bonaventura, was a parallel psychic cord that she now caught sight of, and by no means for the first time, between those same exposed whitenesses and the eyes of the girl's father.

Aye, but O! what Spardo would have given, possibly even the remaining golden coin he had robbed him of, to know exactly what this Man in grey, this special pet of St. Francis, was thinking just then! Would the fellow have the gall to do what everybody else was far too scared to think of doing? Would he be brave enough actually to enter Lost Towers?

He himself felt glad enough to give Cheiron's bridle a gentle twist and to turn the head of the half-human animal due south—that is to say, in the direction taken by that rider upon Basileus who now rode with an arrow in his shoulder. Nobody was interested enough, either in Spardo or his deformed steed, to follow their retreat; but had anyone done so, they would have been absolutely astonished at the speed with which Cheiron could move at such a crisis.

Meanwhile every step taken by Bonaventura towards the entrance to Lost Towers was attended by an intense and meticulous process of thought. In a certain sense the man was undoubtedly acting with real courage, and might without exaggeration have been called a very brave man. But his exorbitant notion of his own importance in the eyes of the God he worshipped, his puffed up conceit as to the eternal importance of the particular kind of sanctity he cultivated, tainted this honourable courage with a less worthy tinge. "If," he now said to himself, "I obstinately refuse to look at that girl, I shall make them think I am afraid of being tempted. What I must do is to make them understand that I and God——"

However bulging the man's eyes may have been and however assiduously he kept feeling in his pocket to make certain his imperial gold pieces were still safe, it must be allowed that there was an element of childlike simplicity in this page-boy of omnipotence oddly mingled with his inordinate conceit.

Some might say that men think in words and women in images; but if in the case of Bonaventura we were to enter the slippery topic of the syntax of psychic expression and begin to quarrel with his way of saying "I and God", it is only fair to remember that in speaking of his earthly parent he always said "I and my Father" instead of "My Father and I".

"What," so the man's thoughts ran on, as he gravely advanced beneath an unusually high arch and proceeded to leave the marble Tiberius and his sadistic stare behind, "I must make them understand is that I enjoy resisting temptation too much to run away, though it is true that in the Paternoster I pray God not to lead me into it. But I must make them understand that I have so yielded myself to God that His will is now my will and my will entirely His will. It would not be for people's good for me to let them know how much I enjoy gazing at the lovely little white breasts and delicious little white limbs of young girls; for vulgar, crude, rough, brutal, stupid, ordinary men wouldn't be able to get the pleasure I get from this. It is all in my love for God and in God's love for me. We love each other so much that I feel sure God allowed me to be with him—for this past-and-present intimacy is what you get when your love for God makes you feel one with Him—when He took the rib from Adam and out of it made Eve. When anyone loves God as I do He gives you wonderful privileges. For the sake of my great love for Him, God put back Time for me and allowed me to watch those embraces of Adam and Eve that created the human race, and the pleasure I get now from looking at this young girl is part of the pleasure which God, in return for my great love, allowed me to enjoy when He let me watch Adam embracing Eve."

Bonaventura had actually been clever enough as a boy to fool Saint Francis himself in this matter; for Saint Francis had regarded it as a perpetual miracle of grace the way in which his young friend resisted temptation, when all the while his young friend was enjoying the process of temptation itself more than he could possibly have enjoyed any fruition of desire.

Bonaventura was indeed thinking at this very moment that he might derive great satisfaction from a few weeks' residence in Lost Towers, as long as he could pretend he was resisting the most maddening temptation of his life, whereas in reality he was resisting nothing. He went on trailing his grey mantle, in this crafty pretence, through corridor after corridor, followed by the growling and grimacing, the gurgling and grinning, the gallivanting and gobemouching Baron Maldung, and in reality deliciously enlivened, not at all, as they were all believing, tormented, teased, and tantalized to the last exquisite point of provocation, by lovely little Lilith.

Farther and farther, on and on, he was led, trailing his grey garment, while the fingers of his left hand never loosened their firm clutch on the leather bag under his robe. Up stairway after stairway he had to go, down passage after passage, till the guest-chamber, where he was to sleep when supper was over, was reached at last. He had been in many feudal castles and not a few royal palaces all over Europe. He had been in several Moorish and Byzantine and Coptic sanctuaries all through Mesopotamia. But he had never been before in such a luxurious room as this. It was clear at once to him, as he turned his devouringly prominent eyes on the bed that was to receive him, and on the hot and cold and lukewarm water that was to bathe him, and on the incredible varieties of ointments and balmy balsams that were to anoint him, and on all these conveniently exposed and yet daintily barred coals of fire that were to warm him, and above all on the three lovely and alluring young sylphs, all delicately wearing the transparent fabrics and red-brown dyes and exotic hieroglyphs of Lost Towers, who were so anxious to serve him that if "he and God" decided to devote a few weeks to the purification, regeneration, sanctification, of all the dwellers in, and of all the dependents upon, these Lost Towers, there would be nothing in such delay to trouble the bodily well-being or vex the spiritual peace of God's chosen servant.

But what was this? Suddenly, without warning, all his attendants vanished, and there was revealed to him a different aspect of life in this place. Borne upon winds that blew wildly through all its walls and over all its roofs, from forests that seemed to be beyond any forests of this world, and from swamps beyond any swamps of which he had ever heard, there came into that chamber the weird lamentable cry, ghastly and desperate, that had passed through every human building raised by the hand of man upon that particular spot since Britain was first divided from France by the salt sea: the cry of the wind that since the beginning of Time had made Lost Towers what it was.

Washed, anointed, oiled, combed and curled, catered for and courted by lovely attendants, and his purpose crowned by a miraculous concatenation of convenient conditions, Bonaventura's instinctive reaction, when he heard this unusual wailing in the rafters of the roof above him and this long-drawn melancholy moaning in the corridors and landings and stairways and cellars beneath him, was simply to feel peevishly annoyed with the God he worshipped. He didn't feel towards him as one heroic conspirator feels to another who has been propitiated and wheedled and fooled into betraying their cause.

What he felt was a simple irritation. God, he told himself, ought to have known better than allow the Powers of Darkness to make a saint, possessed of a piety like his piety, shiver. For shiver he did. The ministering angels who had been hovering round him must have known at the first faint stirring of these ancient black tapestries what was going to happen; for they all vanished before it happened.

There are those who might feel that, left alone with these alarming sounds, our saint's vexation with his deity was not uncalled for. All around him was black tapestry representing terrifying battles between unicorns and river-horses, the former more red than brown, and the latter more brown than red, but both of them woven against that background of black in such a way as to annihilate completely in that portion of the building all those emanations from free space, and all those blessed airs of boundless liberation, that are projected upon any atmosphere by the colours blue and green, quite apart from the objects that we are accustomed to see wearing these colours, such as blue sky and green grass. Reddish brown, and brownish red, and both of these in a peculiar and special mingling, such as Bonaventura had never seen in his life before, were diffused, not only from the tapestry in this weird place, but from rafters and ceilings and panels and doors, until a sort of atmospheric soul of that appalling colour, something that might indeed be called the mystic eidolon of that fearful and awful colour, permeated every square inch of the invisible air within these ill-fated walls.

Though of course in a sense you could only *see* it, in reality you were compelled to taste it, to swallow it, to touch it, to feel it, to absorb it, till it filled your whole body, as air fills a bubble.

Yes, those attendant sylphs must have known perfectly well what was coming, for at the first quivering ripple in the tapestry of his chamber, they were off. And then it seemed to Bonaventura that this devil in the wind had begun to cause, not only ructions in the wood-work of the room—for there were groanings and creakings everywhere—but yawning chasms in the floor of life; for gobbets of red-brownishness and globules of brown-reddishness seemed being belched forth from a pre-historic cleft in the original matter of creation itself, as if this protoplasm of all existing things were relieving itself of some obnoxious suppuration due to a primal injury.

Everybody he met in this part of Wessex, as he pursued his obstinate enquiries with regard to what he loved to call the devil-worship of Friar Bacon, had told him about this particular wind that had been felt at this particular spot since the world began; but he had never anticipated that he himself would feel it as powerfully as this. He felt disturbed, not frightened, he hastened to assure himself, but agitated. He found it impossible to walk up and down with his accustomed dignified stride. He gave way to a series of jerky impulsive movements.

Probably he would not have yielded to these nervous debouchings to north and west, to south and east, and then round the world again, if he had not been alone; for it is queer with us mortals how some of us have completely different codes of behaviour for moments in solitude and moments when others, even if it be only one other, are there.

Bonaventura's relations with God were peculiar to himself; for they were absolutely in the mind, or in the soul, that is to say, in his thoughts. He always took it for granted that God, being a Spirit, took no interest in, and had no effect upon, the movements of his body; unless points of conscience entered, which of course changed everything.

Poor Bonaventura! He hurried headlong down the passage outside his door till it ended in a door that was sealed up, as if it led to a mausoleum of the bones of lost angels. Back again he hurried, till he reached the top of the stairs that led down to the lower floors of the building; at which point he suddenly felt the curious sensation, not amounting to a nightmare-panic but belonging to the same special kind of fantastic horror, that he used to feel when his pious mother told him in his childhood how the Witch of Endor called up the prophet from the grave.

He kept sitting down on his luxurious bed and then walking again down the passage. Had there been any luckless prisoner chained in the cell at the end of that passage, the rustle of that grey robe would have sounded like a new kind of wind from the limbo-cradle of Chaos.

Not for a moment did it enter the mind of Bonaventura that God had forsaken him. What he really felt, if the truth must be told, was that it was a shame and a disgrace that he, the recognized chief saint of all the saints on earth, should have, as his all-powerful and omnipotent deity, a deity who at an important crisis like this was not alive to the necessity of impressing these absurd and childish sons of Belial with the spiritual advantage they were bound to gain from associating with so famous a saint.

Yes, if the actual truth has to be told, it was with real irritation against his Creator that Bonaventura hitched up his grey robe, made the face he always made when he was undertaking something that required a real effort of courage—that is to say, sucked his lower lip into his mouth and tried hard to rumple and fold and curl his curiously malleable lips over his teeth, till these latter resembled broken shells pinched tight within the squeezed-up remnants of a mutilated jelly-fish, and boldly began to descend the narrow winding stone steps that led to the lower stories of the building.

The only balustrade to support a person descending these winding stairs was a ship's rope fastened to the wall by large bronze rings. Instead of the usual narrow arrow-slits all the way down in the massive outer wall of this descent, there was a foot-wide barred window on every landing, and through these windows came not only the full force of the wind but just now a most curious evening light, that struck the consciousness of this continental traveller as the very incarnation of the wailing of the wind.

It was a wet white light, and it was a white light that had a way of blurring and even of deforming and disfiguring the outlines of the objects it surrounded. Our visitor after a quick glance at the dark oaken doors, which on every landing—and he passed three in his descent—faced these windows, paused for a while on each landing to stare out between the rusty window-bars.

There was something about the white light, as it lifted every object the man looked at out of its own airy ocean and presented it to his vision, as if it were particularly anxious that he should fully take in how it was isolated in its individual identity from all the other objects, each of which, if he would only continue staring through those rusty bars, should in their proper sequence be presented to his attention.

It was from the window of the last of these small landings that he caught sight of what was obviously an enormous oak-tree, by the side of which was standing a large white lamb. Both the tree and the creature by its side were presented to the saintly traveller as if they had been mystical symbols, divided from all other visible objects in this white thick encircling sea of light.

The branches of the oak-tree were creaking in this unusual wind in a peculiarly personal manner, as if they were chanting the syllables of an immemorial incantation that the tree had learnt from the low mound on which it grew, and that the mound had learnt from some unknown angelic power that had been hovering round when that horrible devilish attack had been made upon the mass of formless matter out of which the world arose.

The oak-tree was now trying to persuade the troubled creature at its side to accept the creaking and husky chant of its branches as the true oracular response to such agitated bleating on this wild night. The pleasure which Bonaventura derived from contemplating this ancient tree, and hearing its liturgical chant to its troubled year-old companion, was considerably interfered with by the annoyance he felt at God's behaviour.

Yes, there was something that scraped and scratched his nerves in the petulant irritation he felt with God for letting this wind disturb everything. It is true that something in him responded to the storm. The creaking branches of that incredibly aged oak, borne on this wild wind that seemed to be carrying some desperate message to every ghost in Britain, did certainly—let us be fair to the man—have its effect on his Italian sensibility. But all the romantic emotion Bonaventura derived from it was spoilt by something vexing, fretting, chafing, ruffling, that came with the thought that God wasn't protecting his partner in sanctity with the whole-hearted consideration which that partner's life-long devotion deserved.

And yet, in spite of what he regarded as justifiable annoyance with God, Bonaventura couldn't resist pressing his head against those rusty bars; and, like many other watchers from stone towers at that epoch—like young Lil-Umbra, for instance, as she watched, not many days ago, the encounter between Ghosta and Lilith—he was rewarded for his instinctive curiosity by a very unexpected event.

This was indeed nothing less than the appearance beside that oak-tree of none other than the bearded Baron Boncor of Cone, mounted on his war-horse, Basileus, and still writhing in pain from Maldung's arrow stuck fast in his shoulder.

Bonaventura was very rarely driven to action by more than one strong emotion at the same time; and it would have been extremely unlike him to do anything but remain absolutely passive, when the instinct to cry out a warning to the rulers of Lost Towers strove in his breast with an instinct to do something to get that arrow out of Boncor's shoulder. For to do Bonaventura justice, there was not a speck or grain of sadism in him—that is to say, of delight in cruelty purely for its own sake.

What he would really have liked to do, secretly, quietly, unheard of by the people of the place, was to slip out of the house, extract that arrow from the man's shoulder, and command him, in the name of the Pope, to gallop off.

What he now saw however reduced both instinctive impulses to nothing; and he just watched, in petrified fascination. For the bearded man suddenly leapt from the saddle and advanced between the trunk of the oak and the bleating young motherless sheep with the obvious intention of caressing it, if it allowed him to approach. But above the creaking of the oak's branches and the disconsolate moaning of the wind rose that lamb's cry, as it bounded off with its heavy tail swinging between its legs.

But at that very second the movement forward of the bearded Lord of Cone brought the arrow in his shoulder close to the mouth of his war-horse, who promptly, quietly, neatly and expeditiously seized it with his teeth, and plucking it forth with one quick backward jerk of his head, bit it in half and let it fall against the roots of the tree, from which position both its bloody point and its agitated feathers were whirled away on the wind towards the reeds of the swamp.

It was clear that the loss of blood following the arrow's extraction left the genial Lord of Cone too weak to remount his saviour, for even with his arm round the animal's neck when he tried to lead it away, he kept tottering so unsteadily that finally he evidently resolved to take very daring measures, for he lengthened the horse's bridle by tying to it the long leather strap he was in the habit of using to tether him, so that he could eat grass or anything else he fancied while he was left alone, and proceeded to fasten these elongated reins round his own waist. Then shouting to the animal a brief and clear command in a familiar phrase well known to them both—a phrase that suggested hastening straight home to stable and straw and a well-filled bin—he folded his cloak about him and rolled over on his stomach with both arms outspread and his head thrown back.

Over the soft forest-grass, that was a special kind of grass and as delicate and tenuous as a mermaid's hair, and over the brown floor of the pine-needles Basileus now dragged his master, and did this so effectively that it wasn't very long before Bonaventura's eyes could follow them no further. Then and only then and not till then, he left the window, and calmly descending the remaining flight of stairs, directed his steps to where the sounds and smells and wavering lights and shadows made the locality of the supper-chamber discoverable.

He was clearly expected, although nobody had suggested waiting for him. But he was no sooner within the dining-hall than agitation upon agitation shook him. Why hadn't these people sent somebody to fetch him, to accompany him into this dining-hall, to tell him where he was supposed to sit? They had waited on him, bathed him, anointed him, and then just left him to find his way alone to his seat at this important meal! That wasn't the way to treat a person who, in the depth of his noble, heroic, spiritual, intellectual, and absolutely unique nature, was struggling at this very moment with the Greatest Temptation possible to a Great Man—namely whether to decide at this turning-point in his life to aim at acquiring the appearance of possessing the sort of statesmanlike sagacity which a man must appear to have if he is to be elected Pope, or simply to go on, as he was doing at present, emphasizing the unusual perfection of his spiritual purity as a real saint.

Something about the vision of the horse Basileus, pulling the arrow from the shoulder of that fair-bearded man and dragging him as if he'd been a load of hay over both brown earth and green earth, remained vivid in Bonaventura's mind. He had the uncomfortable sensation that his own fate was being pulled along by a Power over which he himself had only partial control.

And yet he kept telling himself that this feeling could not possibly represent the truth. No one in the whole world, he kept telling himself, had as close and intimate a relation with God as he had. Of that he was absolutely certain. It was his life, his destiny, his whole being! It was what made Bonaventura *to be* Bonaventura; and all the world knew it!

Nobody who had ever lived understood God and the Will of God as thoroughly as he did! Nobody who had ever lived, except Jesus Christ—and of course you couldn't bring Him into such a calculation—talked to God as he did, and was talked to by God as he was. There could be no question; there could be no doubt about it. He and God understood each other in and out, up and down, body and soul, back and front!

As he moved slowly round that great square table with patient dignity and unflagging self-respect, he told himself that he and God must consider more carefully than they had done before, whether it would be better for the world if the cardinals in conclave decided, when the present Pope died, to elect him as his successor, or better for the world that they should nominate that one among them that he, Bonaventura, decided possessed the cleverest and the most practical brain.

"O God, my beloved companion," he prayed desperately, as his staring eyes caught sight of a red stain on the edge of the table where Lady Lilt was seated, "I implore you to give me the power tonight, so to impress this evil woman and this evil man and this evil daughter, that it is resounded all over Christendom from the Thames to the Danube that Saint Bonaventura has snatched Lost Towers out of the jaws of Hell!"

It was then that he noticed that there was a large empty throne near where Baron Maldung was sitting, made of the sort of wood and of the sort of woven fabric covering the wood that lent themselves best to receiving the red-brown dye, and that next to this throne Lilith was resting, her entrancing white thighs exposed in such a manner that a man seated in that chair would naturally and inevitably, as he poured out his wine, rest his free hand upon one of those perfect limbs and lightly slide his caressing fingers between it and its mate.

He also noticed that the young girl herself was looking intently at him as he advanced towards where she sat. The air must have been full of strangely contradictory currents of thought as the saintly man approached that empty throne; for the intensity of these airy battles caused a deep hush to fall upon that whole assembly of revellers.

It was at this point that Bonaventura commanded in a clear voice one of the attendants to tie a white napkin securely round his eyes, "Lest I should forget for a moment before you all," he said aloud, "the vows of purity I have made."

The motives that led him to this move were subtler than he could himself have explained; but to one among them, had his conscience prodded him, he would have shamelessly confessed—namely, a fear that it might be supposed he was so hungry and so greedy that the nakedness of Lilith was no temptation to him at all, in fact that he didn't give her presence a thought. He even went so far as to repeat these words about his vow of purity as he allowed himself, still in the same dead silence, and taking exaggerated precautions not to stumble over any obstacle in the way, to be helped to reach his throne, and to be aided in seating himself there in close proximity to Lilith.

When, however, his hand fell, as fate beyond all human control compelled it to fall, upon that soft bare thigh, a shock of unmitigated lust so overpowered him as to change every plan he had made. Lust quivered through him with a compulsion so convulsive as to drive him into unexpected action. With something like a savage bound he leapt to his feet.

"I must beg you all," he cried in a hoarse voice, a voice that was almost like an animal's growl, "to—to pardon me": and then in a second, while they all stared at him in amazement, he had recovered his self-possession.

"The truth is," he went on, addressing them all easily and quietly, as if in some senatorial or ecclesiastical assembly, "the truth is, it is a privilege that I have been allowed by the Most High, to have illuminations or revelations direct from Himself. Such an illumination I have just had, bidding me leave you tonight and bidding me to ask you for a few important favours so as to make my departure easier, and my reception—for that is where my revelation tells me I must spend this coming night—at the Fortress of Roque more friendly and gracious.

"What my revelation commands me to beg from you is simply this, that you put at my disposal a very quiet horse, preferably an old and good-tempered horse, such as I shall be able myself to ride, and, in addition to this, put me in the care of a small party of well-armed horsemen, who will hand me over in safety to the gatekeeper of Roque Fortress and then return to you at once without demanding anything for themselves, anything except"—here Bonaventura's voice rose to something that resembled the clanging of a great cracked bell—"except what I am now going to make plain to you all."

That the man was sincere in the emotion he displayed must at any rate have been plain to all. One undeniable manifestation of it was the fact that as he spoke he wept, and as he wept his mouth and cheeks assumed the only too familiar screwed-up grimace of a small child in a fit of crying, and there was something weirdly and grotesquely impressive about the ringing and yet broken words with which this emotional saint, who had the power of weeping without sobbing, began to make his point clear.

"As you know only too well, you people of Lost Towers, there is a conspiracy against you through this whole district, based on the absurd idea that you are—what of course we *all* are, for it is the unusual condition of the children of men— more evil than good.

"Now this is what I propose to do on your behalf, my dear friends, and it is extremely simple. I *had* thought that the conclave of cardinals intended—at least that is what I imagined my angel of revelation hinted to me—to elect me Pope; but I no longer think that this is their intention. What I believe now to be the purpose of God is that I am to watch very carefully the whole array of ecclesiastical leaders, and when I have decided which particular one would make the ablest Pope, that I should pray night and day for the welfare of that good and wise man; and then, when the present Pope dies, I can name as his successor the man I have been observing and praying for all these days.

"Yes, I can name him at the conclave of cardinals; and I think, without serious opposition, get him elected Pope. And this is what I can do for you, my friends of Lost Towers, in return for your kindness to me. When I and God—I mean of course when God and I—have appointed the next Pope, and he is firmly seated in the Chair of Saint Peter, he will naturally wish to reward his heavenly Helper who is God, as well as his earthly Helper who is I.

"It is then that I shall make it clear to the Holy Father how he can reward us *both at the same time.* I shall tell him how he may spend on behalf of Lost Towers a good round sum of Saint Peter's shekels. I shall tell him that Lost Towers has been for centuries like those cities in Palestine that God told Moses to build for the runaways from justice, who wanted to cling to the horns of the altars of the Levites and there to escape being slain by the avengers of blood. I shall tell him that he had better build an Alms-House for the aged of both sexes, in the immediate vicinity of Lost Towers, with six small independent houses for women, and a larger house of two stories for the Master of the establishment. I shall tell the Pope that the inmates had better be called 'Tower Canons' and 'Tower Canonesses', and that he had better pay the Master of the place a good large income yearly, so as to render him completely independent of all influence from outside. The name of the Holy Father, whether that name be Leo or Pius or Gregory or Martin or Nicholas or Clement or Urban, shall be, I shall assure him, inscribed over the gateway to the Master's Lodge, where it shall remain forever and forever.

"And now there remains only one thing more I must ask of you all, namely, that none of you will conceal from the world, but rather will reveal to the world in all directions, that it is purely and simply by the sudden appearance among you of me and God—I mean of course of God and me—that you have all been so absolutely and entirely turned from the error of your ways as to call upon the Pope and God—I mean of course upon God and the Pope—to raise up in your midst such a monument of your conversion as this Lost Towers Alms-House for aged runaways from the justice of the king-doms of subsequent generations. This having been built, your remotest descendants will fall upon their knees on this spot, and tap the very ground where Lost Towers stands, in reverence and worship for evermore!

"And do *you* ask me, my lovely Daughter of the house—and do *you* ask me, my gracious Lady of the house—and do *you* ask me, O great Baron of Lost Towers!—what your evermore loyal and devoted pair of friends, I and God, are going to do next, when you have escorted us to the Fortress of Roque and have left us with the Gate-Keeper of Roque and have returned in peace to your own place?

"Well, I will tell you in a moment what I and God intend to do next. But, before telling you, I must let you know that the instinct in me which orders every smallest move I make, and half-creates everything I hear, see, touch, feel, or even smell, compels me to insist once again, as I always do, and always must do, wherever I go upon the surface of this earth, that the whole secret of the ultimate mystery of life is contained in those precious, holy, sweet, delectable, celestial, angelic, cherubic, seraphic, ineffable four letters composing the word Love!

"Love is simply all there is! And it is more than that. It is all there was and all there will ever be! Love is like water and air and fire; and it goes flowing, floating, flaming, round the earth, penetrating the earth, proliferating the earth, perforating the earth, and one day swallowing up the earth!

"And yet you ask what I and God are going to do next, when you, my loving friends, have left me at Roque. I will tell you in simple language. We, that is to say the All-powerful whose essence is Love, and I his humble, his negligible, his self-obliterating, self-negating, self-annihilating servant, whose essence is obedience and who has made *his* will *my* will to a degree bewildering to the whole human race, have decided that the Devil has incarnated Himself in the personality of this notorious magician, Roger Bacon, who devotes his time, his money, his leisure, his learning, wholly, entirely, and absolutely to inventing and constructing a Head of Brass that shall think as a man, and speak as a man, and even utter opinions on how the country should be ruled, like a man.

"Well, my dear friends, you who are now announcing to the entire world that you yourselves, by the mediation of his less than nothing servant, who is your do-nothing, tittle-nothing, scrap-nothing, flip-nothing, pip-nothing of a beggarly Bonaventura, are about to accept the pardon and peace of a stately Alms-House from the Holy Father, may now learn that the great God of Love and I, his disciple in Love, are about to punish, punish, punish, punish this thrice-accurst Roger Bacon, till not only his Brazen Head but his own worse than brazen skull will split into atoms.

"Yes, my beloved friends, who have today begun telling the whole world how dearly I, who am His most loving lover since the time when John of Love his very self lay in His bosom, do verily and utterly love you and how I have shown it with regard to the Holy Father, I am going to tell you now how God through me and I through God will punish this abomination of desolation who calls himself Friar Bacon!"

Here he paused to observe the effect of his words upon his hearers, and it was clear to Lilith, who by this time had stolen round to the bottom of the table with a long black mantle wrapt hastily round her and was gazing intently at him with quivering lips and ghastly-white cheeks, that he was well-satisfied with the depth, the gulf, the abyss of silence into which his audience had been precipitated. "No," he proceeded, in a very curious voice, the sort of voice a vulture might use who was holding in its claws, before the hungry beaks of its young, a dying lamb, from whose body, at each gasp of its breath, that is to say from each place where a claw entered its flesh, there ran a stream of blood, "no! no!" he went on, "and I am sure you will all understand exactly what I mean. For a man like this, who knows enough Greek to read the heathen philosophers, and enough Hebrew to pervert and twist the words of Jehovah to Moses, there is only one punishment. What I and God, I mean what God and I, have decided to do with him is to keep him in prison on bread and water, and take all his books and all the paraphernalia he uses in his inventions away from him, and thus compel him to live the life of a real Grey Friar—in other words compel this arch-devil to live the life of a saint! His work is an open insult to the Order to which I who speak to you belong. What made him join us then, do you ask? Purely and simply to support himself while he went on with his devilish inventions! His family were ruined. He was without the means of subsistence. And so he became a Franciscan Friar. He must have said to himself: 'I will go on with the inventions with which I shall eventually destroy both their worship and themselves,'—do you catch the devilry of his idea, beloved friends?—'And meanwhile I shall live at their expense.'"

No sooner had Bonaventura finished speaking than Lady Lilt and Sir Maldung, as well as Lilith, whose long black mantle now trailed after her as she moved, made a circle round him, all three of them talking excitedly and at the same time.

It was not, however, as may easily be imagined, until after a prolonged and delicious supper at this same table—without the need for any blindfolding, and after a prolonged and undisturbed sleep in that luxurious bed on the top floor, without the need for any attendant sylphs, and without even knowing whether the wind was blowing or not—that the General of the Franciscan Friars, on just the sort of horse he had asked for, and with just the sort of escort he wanted, set out in the morning for the Fortress of Roque.

X

THE JEW FROM TARTARY

Peleg took swift decisive measures, precipitate measures they might be called, to ascertain that it really and truly was, without any doubt or question, his true love of that wild night when his life was saved by Sir Mort on those crusader-battled borders between East and West, and when he made that vow of devoted fidelity to him into which he threw at one drastic fling all his Jewish intensity and all his Mongolian strength of will. And though his feeling about her was so absolute that there were moments when it actually rendered him as limp as a bending reed, he was aware at the same time of a strange shyness at the thought of their facing each other.

It was with something of a double motive, therefore, partly in order to put off for a little while longer the actual moment of this overwhelming encounter, and partly to make sure he was doing nothing treacherous to his sworn lord and master, Sir Mort, that well before noon on a fine February day, Peleg set out, when all his domestic tasks were over, to make sure of meeting this eccentric head of the House of Abyssum.

It was the very morning of the unexpected arrival of Bonaventura at the great gates of the Fortress and the morning also of the instantaneous departure, the moment the gate-keeper appeared, of a band of curious riders in ramshackle armour and motley patches of red-brown cloth.

What Peleg did to make sure of catching Sir Mort as he came out of the Fortress—for he knew enough of Lady Valentia's weakness for distinguished foreigners to be quite certain that her husband, whatever feeling he might have for or against the General of the Franciscan Friars, wouldn't stay long as a partner to their talk—was to run at full speed across the piece

134

of ground that separated the point at which the big gates were visible from the point at which the postern-entrance was visible, a distance which he could cover in time enough to catch Sir Mort departing from either of the two exits.

He took care to carry with him his mace with the iron spikes round its heavy circular head, for he had vivid memories of certain occasions when Sir Mort was all for carrying him off on a sudden foray and he had to insist on returning for his favourite weapon.

It was outside the postern that he finally caught his man, and the dialogue that followed was eminently characteristic of them both.

"That fellow with the staring eyes is after my John's friend, Friar Bacon. Holy Jesus, but he's the devil of a wizard-hunter! Do you know what he wants? But of course I'll do nothing of the kind; though Lady Val thinks I ought to! He wants me to swear to Bog of Bumset that the Pope has told him I must take a few muscular serfs with me and haul the Brazen Head down from Bacon's cell and lug the confounded thing here; so that *here*, if you please, *here* in our own grounds, *here* in this very strip of forest, the best piece of hunting-ground in the Manor, I can have this curst Brazen Head of his smashed to bits—*to bits*, mind you, and *here*, within a bow-shot, *here*, in less than a bow-shot, of this shrine Tilton's so keen on building; and very well he's building it too!

"If I'm a good fighter, Peleg, my Gim-crack Jew, Tilton's a good designer, a good builder, a good carver, and a good one, I shouldn't wonder too, at getting rid of smoke and soot. And here's this staring-eyed fellow, who thinks his grey mantle's as grand as Caesar's purple, wants us to hammer to bits in front of my boy's shrine a wizard-oracle, to whose funeral will come no doubt twenty devils far worse than any Brazen Head, who, when they see Tilton's shrine to the Mother of God, you can bet your big Tartar soul, they'll all come huddling into our house, and scenting out quick enough where my bed is, hug each other under it till midnight, and then——No, by God! I'm not going to have any Brazen Head hammered to bits in front of my door!"

Peleg had wisely held his peace during this indignant outburst; but as it went on he discovered that, without having said to himself anything resembling, "Now, my good friend, it's your business to think out carefully where your interest lies in all this," he had perceived, in a flash, in a pulse-beat, in the whirl of a swallow's wings, just what he must say.

"O you are so right, dear my lord!" he murmured, leaning in such a manner upon the handle of his iron mace as not to tower above the man who had saved him and whom he served forever, "and I have just by good chance discovered something that will make it possible, I really do think, for me to be of more real use to you than alas! considering I owe everything to you, I can often be."

"Aye? What's that? What are you saying, big man? Have you caught this staring-eyed Pontifex-Cockolorum *in flagrante delicto*? Have you found him raping our Abbess?"

"May I speak quite freely, my lord?"

"Of course! Don't we always? I to thee and thou to me's the tune! So out with it, my Lion of Judah and Behemoth of Karakorum!"

"But, my dear lord, it goes back a long way and concerns my own private life very deeply. It is indeed, if you will allow me to say so, my dear lord, my chief *secretum secretorum*, and it is only because it was a thing of despair rather than of hope that I kept it to myself."

A peculiar tone in the giant's voice quieted Sir Mort's wrought-up nerves. He fumbled at the leather belt round his waist that kept his hunting horn in a convenient position.

"Tell me straight out, Peleg, old friend, what you're talking about."

"About a woman, my lord."

"Ah! Ah! And what a double-dyed fool I was not to think of that before! Here have you been, a proud, handsome, majestic, powerful man, and, just because you're such a giant and outside the category of common men, I let myself—fool that I was!—assume that you lacked the natural feelings of every man born into the world who isn't a sodomite! Well, old friend, tell me her name quick, and where she's to be found, and by God! I'll get her for you even if she lives in Karakorum!"

Peleg did not hesitate. "She is a girl I made friends with just before that bloody fight, where, save for you, my lord, I should now be under the earth. Her name is Ghosta. She is a

Jewess from Mesopotamia and she is now working in the Abbess's kitchen here. Lay-Brother Tuck from Prior Bog's kitchen told me about her. He told Friar Bacon too about her and the Friar wished to see her, and she went to see him, unknown to her nuns and unknown to the Prior."

"So that's it!" chuckled Sir Mort with a friendly grimace. "Kitchen to kitchen, eh? And do you want to marry this ghost of a girl from Mesopotamia? If that's the idea, you old Jewish Goliath, you'll have to go to Lady Val. She's the one who arranges our matrimonial affairs. But I daresay I could— but what's the matter, Peleg? Do you feel ill? You're not going to faint are you? You look as if you'd seen something worse than a ghost-girl!"

"I—haven't—seen—her—yet," stammered the agitated giant.

Sir Mort looked at him intently. "You're bewitched, old friend. There's no doubt about it. I see you're feeling exactly the sort of thing that I felt myself when I fell in love with Lady Val a quarter of a century ago, when I'd only caught one glimpse of her at the Winchester tourney. Well, the best thing *you* can do, Peleg my lad, is to go straight away now and find your girl and have a good talk, a long talk with her, and discover what she wants to do! She may be so happy with those nuns and made such a pet of, that she won't want to consider moving to the Fortress kitchen, even if Lady Val had room for her here. On the other hand she may—Holy Jesus, take care! What *is* the matter with you? Are you ill, Peleg?"

The giant would indeed have fallen prone on his face if Sir Mort hadn't caught him in his arms. He hadn't lost consciousness however; and when his master propt him up in a sitting-posture with his broad back against the trunk of a pine, he still had the wit left to grope for his iron mace, and when he'd got it in his grasp, to prop it up between his knees, the round bronze ball of its handle, about the size of an apple, pressing against his chin.

Sir Mort laid a hand on his head. "What *you* want, my boy, is a sip of that strong water Nurse used to give Tilton when he got one of his fainting-fits. If I weren't afraid of those damned red devils from Lost Towers, who brought that Bonaventura here, lighting on you and slaughtering you or carrying

137

you off, I'd leave you here and get a drop of that stuff from Nurse. Look up, big sonny! Let a man see your face. If you're bewitched to this tune, before you've even seen the wench, what'll you be when you meet her face to face?"

At this the giant did raise his head, and the two men stared gravely for a moment into each other's eyes. Then Sir Mort hesitated no longer. "By the wounds of Jesus, I'll risk it! Don't you dare to move! And if any of those red-jerkin'd villains come along, you just pretend to be dying till they get near and then give them what for with your iron mace! If you threaten one of the sods with it, the rest will bolt!"

And with a nod and a grim shadow of a smile, he took himself off; and Peleg was left alone, propt up against that pine. His feelings grew queerer and queerer as he waited. "Am I really bewitched?" he thought, "and is it possibly that she's always been some kind of a demon and not a real girl at all? Well; I'll be damned if I care if she *is* a demon. She's my true love, demon or no demon. I'd sooner go down to Hell with her than to the highest Heaven with anybody else!

"But it's all very well for *me* to think like that! The point is: what does *she* think? It's no good for me to go on telling myself these crazy stories about her, while she, maybe, doesn't give me a thought, or, if she does, has lost all wish to see me again! Besides I must remember that by this time she's older, and no doubt wiser, and may not at all be in a mood to be carried away by the great love of a hulking monster like me. She's probably decided that all this business of having children and taking care of children, and having a man and taking care of a man, is simply slavery; whereas if she retains her maidenhood and finds some work for herself that suits her and that doesn't tax her strength beyond a certain point, she may go on being absolutely independent.

"Of course her danger in *that* direction would be the risk of becoming a nun with holy Jesus in the offing and the Holy Ghost—Ghost for Ghosta!—on the horizon. And this sort of life must in many ways, when you really come to think of it in detail, be *no independence at all*! O Ghosta, Ghosta, what are *you*, now at this very moment, thinking about? Does the faintest thought of your lover ever cross your mind?"

138

At this point Peleg's cogitations were interrupted by the reappearance of Sir Mort accompanied by both his sons; nor did our Mongolian fail to notice that, as usually happened in their father's company, the two lads were in a state of quiet fraternal expectation, ready for anything to happen, and interested in anything that did happen, but not engaged in an angry argument, as they had such a tendency to be when with their mother or their sister.

"You're sure your mother said it was pure Neapolitan, that white wine, and not some crazy drink that Tuck of Bumset has concocted and that's been smuggled into our kitchen from theirs?"

Sir Mort's words were addressed to Tilton, who held in his hands with exemplary care a four-sided bottle of colourless liquid closed with a glass stopper of an emerald tint.

"O yes, Father," Tilton replied, quietly enough, but with obvious eagerness to see what effect upon the gigantic patient this particular beverage would have, and excitedly ready to be the one called upon to administer this cure for over-excitement.

"Mother said she'd just given a glass of it to Nurse when Nurse was so upset by Lil-Umbra's taking John's side—wasn't she, John?—that her hands shook till she dropped a plate on the stone floor and it broke into three pieces; and John said —didn't you, John?—that one piece was Lil-Umbra and one was himself and one was me. Here it is! Shall I give it to Peleg?"

Sir Mort gravely nodded; and Peleg taking it from the boy's hand, and removing the stopper, poured the whole contents of the bottle down his throat in three long gulps. The effect on the big man was instantaneous. He handed back the phial that had contained this saving grace to Tilton; and quite calmly and naturally squared his shoulders, grasped his great mace by the middle, and bending his head automatically towards his master, and deliberately and with great dignity towards the two lads, went off with long and rapid strides in the direction of the Priory and the Convent.

As he went, the strangest feelings swept through him, affecting his attitude to everything in the world. He felt perfectly calm, but prepared to fight to the death, for two inexhaustible causes, each of which he saw at that moment in close connection with a separate aspect of the scenery through which he was hurrying, the first with a long line of stately pines and the second with a distant hill-top upon which at that moment rested a large white cloud.

His first cause was to win Ghosta against all the world, and his second was, when once he had won her, to fight on behalf of her people, her tribe, her ideas, her religion—yes, on behalf of everything that belonged to her, of everything she loved and represented, of everything she had set her heart upon, whether to do or to enjoy.

There was even a third cause that came to him as he passed a dark avenue descending into a mossy gully; and this was to fight to the death against all the things and people and customs and ways and systems and institutions, which she loathed and hated! It was just when he was passing this sombre declivity, which the Sun himself, even at the high hour of noon, seemed to hesitate to enter, that he heard behind him the sound of running feet and the quick panting breath of the runner.

He stopped and swung round, tightening his hold on his mace. And there, behold, was young John! John never looked his age. He was over eighteen; but any stranger seeing him as he looked at that moment would have taken him for sixteen or seventeen. John's eyes were hazel in colour, and were large and full of spirit; in fact they gave the impression that his soul was much nearer the surface of his skin than is usual with young men; and as Peleg waited till the lad got his breath, he told himself that it was no wonder this learned Friar, whom everyone talked about, enjoyed teaching a boy like this.

"Father sent me," John said, "because he thought it might help if I were to go into the Convent and say that mother was very anxious to see her and had sent me to fetch her; and then, of course, after we three were out of their sight, I could come home alone. Father said it would seem quite all right for you to take her back later, and that mother would really be very glad to see her at the Fortress."

Peleg stared down at him for a second in silence. Then he said slowly, "Your Father is extremely wise in these things. And of course when my friend and I are once safe in the Fortress, we can find out whether Lady Val would really like to see her or not. Yes, come on Master John, and we'll see what happens!"

But as they threaded their way together between the trunks of the pines, that seemed to grow especially tall in this particular corner of the Manor, Peleg cursed the hour he had decided to take his master into his confidence. "It's always unsafe to get their help," he told himself. "They are so different from us. They do everything quicker, and yet, in a manner, more sideways, than we do things. But I expect I'm silly in not being overjoyed at this young master's help. And yet I don't know! How can I be glad to have anyone else, anybody at all, present when I first see Ghosta again? O but I've been a prize fool to let them into my secret! And yet on the other hand what would I have done with Ghosta if I hadn't had this help? Where, in the name of all the devils, would I have taken her? As it is *now*, Lady Val *may* give her a place in their Fortress kitchen? But will she want that to happen? Girls are queer cattle! They live their own life quite apart from us. *That's* what these damned Nordic crusaders never have, and never will, understand!"

Peleg was so moved by this psychic discovery that he broke his silence. "What is your opinion of girls, Master John?"

John's eyes became absolutely brilliant, like two lamps lit by a divine flame in the Holy Tabernacle of the Ark of the Covenant.

"O I adore them! I worship them! I embrace—in my mind of course, or in my imagination—every single one of them I meet! Off, off, off, off I slip their pretty clothes! And oh! so quickly I'm hugging them! But that's the worst of it, for it's the whole of the best of it, and the end of it! For I have an ecstasy at once, and all my soul rushes out, and all my seed is gone, in a minute, and I've no strength left to ravish them and take their divine maidenheads!

"That's my trouble, Peleg; and I don't see how I can get over it! I don't see how I'm ever to enjoy a woman properly, or ever to have a child, or ever to become a grandfather and a great-grandfather and a great-great-grandfather and a real proper ancestor! Tilton's quite different. I *think*—only it's a great secret, of course, between you and me—but I *think* Tilton's already got a girl who lives round here. She's a very, very slim girl, and she goes about with a little child, her niece I think it is, called Bet, who's a very nice kid.

141

"Bet and I made great friends when we were waiting for Tilton. Tilton doesn't like girls—he says they don't understand architecture. His girl's name is Oona and her Father or Grandfather is that rebellious serf, you know the one I mean? The one who got on so well with old Heber; but then Heber has the trick of propitiating everybody; whereas this Dod Pole—I expect you know him—is now in perpetual trouble with Randy."

Having finished his discourse John flung upwards a quick glance from his lustrous eyes to see whether the giant at his side had taken it all in, or had allowed his mind to wander; for with an intense interest in particular aspects of life, and a tendency to philosophise at some length on these aspects, young John frequently caught people's attention wandering from what he was saying; and this made him intermittently cautious, though he hated to have to stop and scrutinize his listener.

But just then he had to be content with a hurried nod, for they had arrived at the door of the Convent. "Father said for me to go straight in," the lad now whispered to Peleg who was bending down to hear his instructions, "and not to come out with the girl—her name is Ghosta, isn't it?—but to wait inside till you've gone off with her: but I expect I'll be seeing you later, and maybe her too, so I'll only say 'good-luck' and not 'good night', Peleg"; and with these last syllables vibrating round his youthful figure, he advanced boldly to the great loose chain which was hanging from an aperture in the top part of the massive black door, and this he pulled three times, and Peleg could distinctly catch the reverberation of its echoing resonance from inside the building.

The ringer hadn't to wait. The door opened almost at once, making an aperture of about six inches, and after a brief parley with a dim, white-coifed figure, like a pale kernel in a cracked nut, the lad went inside and the door was closed. There was only one tree near this closed entrance and that was an ancient birch with a remarkably mottled trunk and only two branches, which branches, being very high up, were like the arms of a crucified queen who guarded the place by day and night and threatened every intruder.

Calmly and deliberately the huge Hebraic Mongol settled himself on the ground with his back against this solitary tree and awaited his fate. He had to wait a long time; but the curious thing was that while he waited now he felt himself to be entirely free from that sickening lethargy which had so loosened his knees and which required a whole bottle of Neapolitan white wine to remove from his midriff.

And then the closed doors opened, opened more quietly than when they had shut, and there she was! He automatically clutched his iron mace, as if the building behind her and the tree behind him had been a host of enemies, and with it in his hand he leapt up from the ground and bounded towards her.

When he reached that tall, stately, slender figure, in a black mantle with a black hood—who gazed straight into his face with eyes as dark and beautiful, and, to his feelings, just then, as terrifyingly prophetic, as must have been the eyes of Deborah, the wife of Heber the Kenite, or of Miriam, the sister of Moses —Peleg allowed his mace with its terrible spikes to fall to the ground. He could do nothing but just stand helplessly in front of her, muttering over and over again the blind words: "Ghosta! So you've really and truly come! Ghosta! So you've really and truly come!"

But she, with a gesture like that of a warrior-queen, whose lightest word was obeyed by thousands, lifted both her arms towards him, took his bare head in her bare hands, and, drawing it down towards her breast, kissed him on the forehead.

Peleg felt this to be a momentous kiss, a sacramental kiss, a kiss belonging to a ritual for the union of a man and a woman that was older than Sodom and Gomorrha, older than Tyre and Sidon, older than Babylon and Nineveh.

For a moment he stood with his eyes closed; and then, with a deep gasp for breath, as if he had just defeated an army of rivals, he bent down and picked up his iron weapon. This he now grasped tightly in his right hand, and taking Ghosta's right hand in his own left, he led her away, up a mossy slope between scattered yellow stalks of last autumn's bracken and a few dead clumps of last summer's heather, till, completely hidden from any possible onlookers from either Convent or Priory, he led her into the entrance chamber of the cave of Manawyddan, which had been a favourite resort of his since he first followed Sir Mort to that district of Wessex.

The cave was indeed so completely hidden by a grove of alders and willows that it was by no means universally known even to natives of those parts. The two of them had no sooner entered it than Ghosta's whole attitude changed. The maternal heart in her was at once touched to the quick by the various little semi-domestic arrangements that this gigantic lover of hers had made in this secret hermitage of his, such as the strewings of dry reeds that covered the floor, such as a couple of great iron trivets, one of which was carrying a deep copper basin and the other supporting a kind of extempore frying-pan which had clearly served its purpose extremely well not so very long ago. In one corner of the cave there was a large earthenware bowl of water and by the side of it a little jug with a handle that looked more Greek than Roman for ladling the water into other receptacles.

As Peleg noticed the deeply amused, and intensely practical interest that Ghosta took in all these objects, he told himself that he had been wise to keep the existence of this cave, which had originally been shown to him by a travelling tinker from Wales, entirely to himself. This Welsh tinker had told him about certain ancient Welsh gods, who had travelled through the land like himself doing work in leather and in various metals. He had explained that he himself, in every district he visited, selected some special spot where he could labour unmolested at his job and fulfil the various professional orders he obtained in that neighbourhood; and he swore that it had been in a vision of one of these old tribal deities, a being who called himself Manawyddan fab-Llyr, that he had learnt of this cave and been assured, that if he kept the secret to himself, nobody would disturb him there.

It was too early for more than a few tiny leaf-buds to have appeared on the willow and alder boughs that in a confused mass hid the mouth of the cave; but at about ten yards distance outside this half-circle of entangled trunks, and closely twisted twigs, grew an immense pine.

The rough bark of this tree, for it was a tree that stood with its back, so to speak, to the cave and to the cave's body-guard of entwined branches and twigs, had become for Peleg a token of the precise hour; for its colour darkened and lightened, flickered and shadowed, according to the advancing and retreating, the self-concealing and self-revealing, of Sun and Moon and the intermittent rising and falling of the wind.

Though he had only once or twice actually passed a night in this cave, he had of late amused himself by making careful preparations for a winter night there. He had prepared a tall barrier of wooden bars that exactly fitted the mouth of the cave, but was easily lifted up and could be deposited, after use, beneath one of the interior walls, a barrier that he could render proof against wind and snow and rain by covering it with the skins of cattle and sheep.

What he felt especially proud of, as he showed the cave's domestic conveniences to his beautiful Hebrew friend, was a tightly wedged mass of clean and dry hay, with which he had packed from floor to ceiling a rocky recess in one of the cave's corners, towards which the ground sloped upwards a little.

He studied every flicker of her expression with boyish solemnity, as he now proceeded to strew on the ground at the back of the cave a thick sprinkling of this pleasantly-scented summer-hay for their February siesta. It seemed to him that she whitened a little at the first glance she threw upon this lover's bed, then reddened a little, but she continued to watch his every movement with an expression that it would have been totally impossible for him to interpret; but which revealed in reality something of that infinitely maternal and desperately romantic tenderness that young Tilton was struggling now so intensely, day after day, with his hammer and chisel, to convey to his carved image of the Virgin as he imagined her uttering her immemorial "Magnificat".

And quite suddenly, and as it may well be imagined, to Peleg's wonder and delight, Ghosta took the whole situation into her own hands. "Let's make a good fire," she cried, "and warm the whole place before we lie down! And let's heat some water and have a good drink of hot red wine!"

Such had been his secret meticulous preparations for a situation exactly like this one, only built up entirely in his imagination, that few lovers would believe, however deeply they trusted their tale-bearers, how small was the lapse of time before a blazing fire of sticks and logs, unattended by any great volume of smoke, was burning triumphantly, and before they were exchanging with each other deep draughts of red wine mixed with bubbling water.

The effect of these timely preparations were enhanced by the noon-day sunshine, which poured down upon them past the great pine-tree outside, one of whose two big boughs lay on the ground, while the other was extended wide, with a gesture as comprehensive as that with which Jacob, after wrestling all night with the angel, must have greeted the hills and valleys and rivers of the Promised Land.

Then as they replaced the goblets, from which they had been drinking, on the wide shelf that ran round the cave, Ghosta uttered the most astonishing words that her companion had ever heard issuing from human lips.

"Now is the moment, O my friend, when you and I must strip ourselves of all. For a man knoweth not the woman he loves, nor does a woman know the man she loves, until each is as naked as the other."

The words struck him like a ritual, mystical and solemn, but the natural, half-laughing way she came close up to him and proceeded to loosen the buckle of his belt, and then, drawing back a few paces, began with incredible rapidity, but with gay and laughing interjections, and indeed with half-humorous and almost mischievous smiles at certain particularly crucial moments, to fling off every stitch of her clothing, made him feel at ease with the whole universe.

Peleg imitated her as fast as he could; but perhaps it was significant of the double stream of blood in his veins that, before they lay down together on that sweet-scented bed of hay, he lifted his wooden screen across the entrance to their amorous hermitage and hung over it a large bull's hide.

As he did so he couldn't help being struck by the sun-warmth which reached his fingers from this same skin, for he had snatched it up from the top of a pile that ever since dawn had been in reach of the Sun. Nor did the gigantic amorist, while the Sun above the bull's-hide screen caressed his own swarthy neck, fail to note with something like philosophical vanity that he was not so absorbed by the passion of love as to be unable to get, even at this moment of moments, a quite definite sensuous pleasure from the touch of the Lord of Life.

But when once those two lay down together, all other

thoughts, impressions, experiences, sensations were absorbed and engulfed in the blind intermingling of two bodies, two souls, two spirits; so much so that the shock and the blood of her ravishment by him, and the furious onslaught of his possession of her, were both swept into a whirling vortex of rainbow-irradiated bubbles, tossed into space, as the confluent torrents of their two life-streams became one terrific river.

Calling up these blinding moments in calmer blood, our Mongolian giant could not help being struck by the fact that it was Ghosta, and not he, who fell into a sleep of blissful exhaustion when their ecstasy was over. This, he decided after long and delicate ponderings, was due to the fact that, in *her* case, body, soul, and spirit were much more intimately united than in his; so that when their union had been fully achieved, there was no residual reservoir left, of "energeia akinesis", or "unruffled force", such as could keep her consciousness alert and observant: while in *his* case, whether due to his masculinity or to his stature, there remained a definite level of mental awareness that was completely unaffected by what senses, or soul, or spirit, were feeling or had felt.

And this awareness was closely allied to action. What Peleg did, therefore, when the trance of their beatitude had ebbed and she was asleep, was to slip noiselessly from Ghosta's side, and—with the stealthy movements of a male panther arranging the fragments of his half-devoured prey before distributing them to its little ones while their mother slept—to re-assume his garments one by one, till he was completely clad. Then, with a fond but not lingering glance at his sleeping mate, he stole into the interior of the cave and began completing, as far as it was possible to do such a thing without the usual accompanying sounds, all the preparations upon which of late he had been secretly engaged, so that he might be in a position to offer his re-discovered bride, when the moment came, the sort of romantic, but deliciously tasting and completely satisfying meal, that was worthy of such a never-to-be-repeated occasion.

Perhaps nothing since they had found each other again—for their supreme embrace just now had been to them something outside time and space—struck Ghosta's Hebrew-girlish mind more poignantly than what she saw when, fully awake at last and with her clothes on again, she entered that inner chamber of the cave and beheld her lover's quaint preparations for what might have been called their consummation feast.

But she kept her feelings to herself, for it was a deeply congenital characteristic of Ghosta's nature to avoid above everything the quick exclamations and exuberant outcries with which it seems irresistible to some of the nicest ladies in the world to express, or at least to convey the impression that they're expressing, the feelings of the heart.

But her smile told a lot; and as far as the preparation for their love-feast went, which he had so quaintly and crudely set in motion, her quick and competent hands soon had them seated side by side on a bench of pine-wood opposite a big round shield on a tall brazen tripod, covered with a white cloth and a couple of large earthenware plates.

Peleg was soon explaining that, when they had finished their meal, he was anxious to take her to the Fortress, where he hoped she would be able by her beauty and the power of her personality to persuade Lady Val to let her join the large-kitchen-establishment of Roque, which, though situated, as he explained, within the confines of the Fortress, was really an independent organization by whose methods of procedure the whole Manor benefited.

He was so eager and voluble about this idea of his that she should find a place for herself, and so certain that such a place would be pretty near the top, that for a long while he never saw how little she was responding to the picture he was so vigorously painting of their future at the Fortress.

When at last he paused, however, he was not only startled but shocked and hurt. He had stopped in mid-flow, so to speak, with the idea of clearing the channel-bed of his torrent of exultant prediction, so that *her* stream of consciousness might join and mingle absolutely with his own, and he was stunned and confounded by the way she replied.

"No, no, my darling Peleg!" she cried. "I can't imagine myself working in the midst of this great manorial kitchen! I know too well all it takes to prepare meals for those who plough and sow and plant and reap and bind and clear the ground of weeds! And as for having to be polite to this presumptuous and insolent bailiff of theirs, this brutal Randolph

148

Sygerius—Heavens! I wouldn't consider it for a second. But don't look sad, my precious Peleg; for I wouldn't mind coming across to the Fortress now and again, whenever Lady Val was short-handed or had any special visitors to cater for.

"But to work as a rule and every day in your manorial kitchen, the Lord God of Israel forbid! No, my dearest one! No, no, no! I'll go with you to Rome. I'll go with you to Jerusalem. I'll go with you to Sicily. I'll go with you to Constantinople. I'll go with you to Corinth. I'll go with you to Samarcand or to Trebizond or to Jericho. But even for you, my first and my last true love, I will not work in an English manorial kitchen!"

Peleg turned round and laid his great hands on her shoulders and stared at her. They were sitting side by side with their backs to a wall of wet dark stone. Down this wall dripped continually small trickles of water; while the wall itself was broken here and there by deep greenish-black clefts of incredible depth. In fact these cracks in the wall gave the impression that, were they enlarged so that a small person could worm himself into them, they might be found to lead, if the explorer had the courage to persevere and follow one of them to the bitter end, right to the very centre of the whole planet, where such an explorer would be liable to be devoured by that fabulous creature called the Horm, the legends about whom were evidently so appalling, and so likely to be disclosing a horrible reality, that, long before any written chronicler existed, they must have been deliberately suppressed by the self-preservative consciousness of the human race.

When Peleg turned towards her in his startled surprise and clutched her shoulders, they both had their backs to these sinister cracks in the wall and their faces towards the ponderous arch under which they had made their bed; and beyond that arch, outside the cave altogether, they could see, outlined against the sky, that huge mystical pine-tree, which stretched out its branch-arm for, or against, the frequenters of that ancient cave, in a gesture as wholly inscrutable as it seemed to be wholly indestructible.

"Do you realize what you're saying, child?" Peleg groaned, as he shook the girl slowly forward and slowly backward, while his large hands, had any wandering progeny of that subterranean

Horm been peering at them from behind, would have hidden completely beneath their knuckles and veins and wrinkles and creases of loose pendulous skin all the lovely rondures of the girl's feminine shoulders.

"Don't you understand," he muttered, "that I am for ever committed, body and soul, to the service of Sir Mort Abyssum? I could no more leave the Fortress than that old tree out there could leave the place where it grows, unless a hurricane uprooted it, or lightning struck it, or a savage tree-hater cut it down with a murderous axe!"

He let her shoulders go and dropped his arms; and for some time they just stared at each other, both angry, but both afraid of what they might say or do in their anger. Peleg had learnt in his world, just as Ghosta had learnt in hers, that it is wiser not to quarrel with a creature who instinctively gathers itself together before hitting back, so that, when it does strike, the blow shall be a deadly one.

At last, very quitely, Ghosta spoke: "I am ready to agree, my friend," she said, "if you are anxious for me to go with you to the Fortress and have an interview with your Lady Val; but I can tell you this in advance, and you'll see for yourself the truth of my prediction, if you accompany me into the presence of this lady: Lady Val will loathe the sight of me, and will command Sir Mort to have nothing to do with me! I don't say for a moment that he'll obey her in this, but she'll no more want to have me working in the manorial kitchen than I want to work there. It's this ancient hatred of us Jews which all the races in Europe feel, and which a certain class of men and women in this country especially suffers from.

"I've thought about it a lot lately; and I think it is purely due to our superior intelligence. They feel instinctively that they're not our equals in intelligence and that makes them hate us, and their hatred is continually being intensified by contempt every time they see how, in archery and hunting and tournaments and in all manly sports and in all athletic contests and public games, the simplest and stupidest among them can play a part, whereas we Hebrews—just as did the great Avicebron when he was a child, Avicebron for whom Friar Bacon has such a passion—have always thought that our mighty men of battle, our Samsons and Sauls and Joshuas and Abners and Joabs, were of far less account than our prophets and priests and men of God."

"But Ghosta, my Ghosta! What are you saying? Aren't our Scriptures full of the victories of Judah and Israel over their enemies? Wasn't the Lord of Hosts always giving his chosen people triumphant victories over Syrians and the Assyrians and Babylonians and Philistines?"

Ghosta gave him a most peculiar look, a look that seemed to say: "I shall have to consider this very carefully. You are a man. I am a woman. I shall have to consider whether I can talk to you about these things, and tell you all that I've thought about them for a long time. Don't 'ee look like that, Peleg darling—as if I'd slapped you across the cheek. I shall always tell you the important things of my life, and you'll always tell me the important things of your life. These political and religious questions aren't the true reality of any actual life of a man and a woman who love each other. You might be very interested in them and might be totally indifferent to them, and we could live out our life in perfect contentment.

"Everybody's life's like a star with at least forty points branching out in all directions, and every one of these points can turn eventually into a life-long road of unending interest. But at the heart of that star the real Peleg and the real Ghosta can sit at their hearth over their crock of pottage, and watch the shadows on the wall, and hear the wind in the chimney and the rain on the roof, and take to themselves the mystery of everything.

"Well, my dear, you tidy up the room and get it into the shape you like to leave it in when you go out into the world; and I'll deal with the remains of our meal and clean the things."

Peleg obeyed her; and until the horizontal rays of the descending Sun thrust the angular shadow of the pine-tree's elbow almost as far as the cracks in the wet dark wall, out of which the elfin faces of the dumb progeny of the awful Horm could be imagined peering at them, the two of them kept an almost religious silence.

Nor was it only silence they shared: for as they went to and fro about their homely tasks the same thought hovered in their minds; the thought that they were both, save for this miracle of a life together which had only begun today, strangers and pilgrims in a foreign land. And this thought of theirs, as he went on tidying up and arranging, according to his ideas of a proper chamber, the whole appearance of their cave, and as she emptied and washed and dried and polished their pots and pans and dishes, did not only hover about them; it also grew deeper and more definite.

Indeed they had both decided, before they left the cave, she with her black mantle and white hood wrapt round her body and head, and her right hand held tightly in his left, and he with his great iron mace swinging its terrific spikes through the withered stalks of last autumn's grasses, as if to scare them out of the path of the over-cautiously sprouting new ones, that there was nothing as yet in this new worship of the Trinity, with its Father and Son and Holy Spirit, so closely linked with the Assumption into Heaven of the Blessed Virgin, to compel them, by any spontaneous recognition of a deeper truth, to relinquish their old ancestral faith in Jehovah as their one invisible God, or to bow themselves on the ground before the Crucified Jesus.

That this spiritual decision, by a telepathic interchange of thought that is rare even among lovers, had been accepted by them both, was proved by the murmured exclamations they uttered as they left that glade among the rocks in a wood even more dominated by their union than that cave was dominated by its pine-tree, or those cracks in its wall at the back by that appalling Horm.

XI

EBB AND FLOW

It would almost seem as if, over every measurable geographical square of the planetary surface of the earth—and this would apply whether our earth were flat or round, or neither the one nor the other—there vibrates a special and particular amount of magnetic receptivity, by means of which each individual creature is attracted to or repelled by all the other creatures who are dwelling in or are passing through the same arena, an attraction or repulsion which is obviously stronger or weaker in proportion to the type of creature who is exerting it or feeling it.

If this theory has any truth, it was under the influence of something beyond mere accident or chance that, when this terribly-armed adherent of the House of Abyssum, holding by the hand his cloaked and flashing-eyed bride, just as the Sun was sinking behind them on that perfect February day in the year of Grace twelve hundred and seventy two, came to be within measurable distance of Spardo filius Regis Bohemiensis, along with his deformed horse known as Cheiron, the two pairs moved hurriedly to their encounter.

Peleg had met Spardo several times already, and himself was well known to Spardo; but Peleg was at this moment not a little disturbed by such a meeting and was extremely disinclined to allow it to be a cause of delay in the important business of introducing Ghosta to the interior of the Fortress of Roque. But Ghosta was, as may well be imagined, fascinated at once by the sight of this extraordinary horse, with what under the horizontal rays of the setting Sun did really look like a human head beginning to thrust itself forth through that horribly swollen neck.

153

Spardo himself treated the gigantic Mongol as he treated everybody with whom he had any contact in that part of Wessex. Without disregarding him, he behaved as if the giant had been some inanimate object, a chair perhaps, or a bench, or a ladder, or a door, or a stone outside a door, or a mat in front of the fire where his supper was being prepared, or the hand-rail beside the steps leading up to the chamber where he was to sleep, or even the barrel of oats near the comfortable manger, he would presently leave Cheiron when he had replenished his bin.

The huge Tartar managed to restrain his impatience for the space of about five minutes while Ghosta's black robe and white hood, and Spardo's flapping beard, mud-stained jerkin, and motley-coloured leather breeches, kept circling round and round that impassive horse, whose own gaze, with its far-away inscrutable stare, seemed to be fixed upon some invisible landscape where events were taking place that hadn't the faintest connection with all this fuss about that unfortunate swelling in his own neck.

When however for the third time Ghosta bent in absorbed concentration above that weird deformity, Peleg could bear it no longer. "Pardon me, Master Spardo," he cried, "but I've got an appointment for this lady at the Fortress, and it won't do to keep Lady Val waiting!"

With these words he flung his left arm round his obsessed girl, administered to Cheiron's flank a friendly tap with the knuckle of the hand from which the great mace was swinging, gave Cheiron's master an affable nod, and muttering something in Hebrew, that might have meant, as far as Spardo could follow it, "Goodbye till we meet in Hell!" he strode off with the lady on his left and the mace on his right.

Whether to their eventual advantage or disadvantage, it is curious that no instinct warned Peleg just then that the worst possible moment for winning the favour of the Lady of Roque was during the particular hour she was accustomed to move to and fro between the manorial kitchen and the dining hall, with occasional interruptions from Nurse Rampant and Mother Guggery, and intermittent debouchings up and down the steps leading to her daughter's chamber. If it hadn't been that his nerves were so strung-up by his possession of Ghosta that all life's ordinary routine seemed projected to a distance, rather like that unknown vision upon which Cheiron's gaze seemed to be fixed, he would certainly have realized this fact.

Indeed it may easily be that he did realize it, only not with sufficient intensity to allow it to influence his action. In any case, with a massive recklessness that was a deep element in his nature, though it was a rare event for him to draw upon it, Peleg led Ghosta to the great gate of the Fortress, where as a quite natural event the gate-keeper admitted them without even glancing up at his wife's window to see if their entrance aroused her more shrewd attention.

Once inside the Fortress, the worthy Cortex straightway escorted them, without stopping to obtain the mediation of any of the servants, to the familiar corridor between the dining-hall and the kitchen, where at this hour Lady Val was almost always to be found. And there indeed they found her. And if we are to assume—though at these mysterious and fatal moments in human lives, where so many paths into the unknown future seem to offer themselves, it is a doubtful wisdom to assume anything—that happy relations between Sir Mort's lady and Peleg's lady was a desirable occurrence, it was unlucky that neither Nurse Rampant nor old mother Guggery happened to be present at this encounter; for both these women had the gift, refined upon by age-long practice, of softening and modifying the impact upon the touchy and susceptible Lady Val, of any troublesome intruder.

The Tartar giant saw in a moment how completely his attempt to establish a happy understanding between these two women was doomed to absolute failure. But it was too late to retreat now; and so he blundered on.

"Pardon my intrusion, my lady, but this is an old friend of mine who comes from that so much fought-over strip of land between the Tigris and the Euphrates, where so many of your own renowned ancestors won their glory. I have already told my friend here many of those heroic stories that your revered children love to relate. Your son Tilton, for instance, has often told us about that amazing encounter between your great-grandfather, Sir Stephen Dormaquil, and that monstrous Tartar with three arms who fought with six sharp-pointed elephants' tusks, one in each of his six hands; and who, after being chopped into sixteen pieces by your noble ancestor, was carried off to the top of Mount Carmel by eagles, and there was so completely disposed of that not a bone of his own nor the splinter of his ivory weapons was ever seen again. My friend here, my Lady, has thought of nothing else, since I told her about Sir Stephen and the other Dormaquils, and she begged me to bring her here just to see, if only for a moment, the living descendant of such heroic people."

Peleg was so pleased with the whole situation, so proud of himself in Ghosta's presence for his tactful speech, and so proud of himself in Lady Val's presence for making it so easy for Ghosta to keep a discreet silence, that Sir Mort would have thought him pathetically childish not to have detected what was going on, all the while he was speaking, between the two women.

But then Sir Mort knew the mother of his three children better than the wisest of his henchmen could possibly know the lady of his house. Besides, Peleg was not only a foreigner and an oriental; he was also a giant, and looking down upon that pair of feminine brows and eyebrows, each of them quivering with implacable hostility, he was so impervious to the wordless, and you might almost say to the mindless, aura of antagonism, automatically generated between them, that he stept backwards as if to avoid a blow at the tone in Lady Val's voice as she remarked to Ghosta:

"You want employment here, I take it? Are you prepared to do any kind of work? Or do you want something special? We've no opening just now for a new hand indoors, but it's quite possible, if you apply to our bailiff, Master Randolph Sygerius, that he'll be able to find you work in the garden. We depend a lot on green food and we gather it all the year round; so if you——"

"I happen to be quite satisfied with what I'm doing in the Convent just at present, Lady, I thank you. Indeed so far I've never been driven to work out-of-doors, but if ever——"

"Where, if I may enquire," interrupted Lady Val, her voice growing shrill, "were you brought up? My family here have given work I know, in past times, to black females. In fact if I remember correctly, my grandfather's bailiff employed a family of Ethiopians. Of course this particular family may have been the slaves of some trader who died over here when he was selling leopards' skins; but if you wait in the scullery till after dinner, you'll be able, or Peleg here will be able on your behalf, to catch Master Randy, our present bailiff. Do you help, may I ask, in the Convent latrine? I remember there was——"

"My lady, my lady——" broke in Peleg at this point. "My friend here is a learned Jewess, who has worked with Doctors and with Rabbis of our ancient faith, copying, for instance, with pencils and brushes certain faded pages in the Hebrew scriptures. And so, no doubt, though the Convent kitchen must already have come to depend on her delicate touch with their food, we can hardly expect——"

"Be quiet, Peleg!" almost screamed Lady Val. "Since you brought this woman here to stare at me with her bold, black, impertinent eyes, perhaps you'll tell me whether she wants to be allowed to prepare for me some of those Jewish spells with her pencils and her brushes, such as I can use on my enemies in this place? If so, you can tell her that, though she may have bewitched you and some of those simple nuns, who in such things are no wiser than children, I won't have her bewitching me or my young daughter! But take her into the scullery, Peleg, and find a corner there for her till after dinner and then take her back to the convent. I don't want any Jewish sorceress in my house or garden or kitchen! And what's more—" This was added, when, without any other retort, Ghosta had wrapt her mantle more tightly round her shoulders and pulled her hood more closely round her face and had turned her dark eyes with a mute interrogation towards Peleg—"And what's more," announced Lady Val, "I shall have to have a very serious talk with Sir Mort about this whole subject of your making friends with women of this kind. But let that go now."

This "let that go" was uttered in the confident tone of a person for whom victory in a battle implies the power to be generous.

"You must tell Cook, Peleg," she went on, "to give your friend what supper she has time to scrape together while she's dishing up dinner. I can see she hasn't been taught in her childhood, and hasn't had an opportunity to learn since, how a well-brought-up maiden, of any race in the world, behaves when she enters anyone's house; but I'm sure she didn't mean to be rude, just standing there and staring. I don't know anything about Pharisees and Sadducees, and not much about Solomon and the Queen of Sheba; but I do know that because Queen Jezabel worshipped idols, she was thrown out of a window to be eaten by dogs. So you can, both of you, see that I am not quite ignorant of the Hebrew scriptures——"

With the sort of inclination of a half-veiled head that the mighty Sisera might have received in the entrance to the tent of Heber the Kenite, Ghosta turned away, and, followed submissively by Peleg, began to move off, not, however, towards the kitchen, but towards the door by which they entered.

They hadn't gone many paces, however, towards this door, when they were met by an extremely youthful personage, tricked out in the very latest armorial fashion for budding warriors, and before they could stand aside to let him pass, Lady Val was greeting him, and he was greeting Peleg and gazing respectfully and admiringly at Ghosta.

"Why, if it isn't our dear Sir William!" cried Lady Val—delighted, so Ghosta's giant lover told himself, at so good an excuse for smoothing over the biting sting of Ghosta's dignity under her crude abuse. "How nice you look, my darling boy, in that breast-plate and that scarf and that belt! Where is Raymond de Laon? Oh, of course I know! You men mustn't give each other away! He's with Lil-Umbra, of course. Oh yes! This is a great friend of our Peleg! I've just been discussing with him what place we can find for her in our little barony. Why, how very nicely you did that, my dear boy!"

This final remark was involuntarily drawn from the lady by the really perfect alacrity with which the slender little Sir William, after skipping up to her side, knelt down on one knee and kissed the knuckles of the hand she held out to him.

It was clear to Peleg, as she began talking rapidly to the young newly-made knight, and after every sentence shot a quick glance in their direction to see if they were still there, that her desire to have this lad to herself was intense. "She's wishing that her Tilton and her John were more like this elegant young man," the Tartar told himself. And then he thought: "I know Ghosta wants me to go off with her and that we ought to go; but I would like to see how this little elf-knight wins favour before we leave them!"

Young William Bancor of Cone was certainly what the doting old King Henry had called him at first sight—the liveliest and sprightliest little "Knave of Hearts" in the whole kingdom. His self-confidence and aplomb and his humorous enjoyment of his own attractive presence gave a zest to every moment which anyone spent in his company. Everybody could see at a glance how conceited he was. But he had no pride at all; and was prepared to throw his whole body, soul, and spirit into showing off before the poorest and meanest beggar he met. He "made love," so to speak, to every man, woman, and child, who crossed his path.

And not only to them. To horses, dogs and cats, to birds in cages, to pigs in sties, to sheep in folds, to cattle in stalls—to them all he sang his song and danced his dance! When he was eating out-of-doors he would pay court to the nearest toad or frog or blind-worm. When he was sucking an orange before going to bed, he would make overtures to a spider.

He had no pride, and he had very little vanity. He was as conceited of his eyes, nose, mouth, ears, hair, legs, ankles, feet, as he was of his voice, his manners, and his knowledge of the world. It was enough that the quality, the feature, the member was *his* quality, *his* feature, *his* member, for it to be the most remarkable quality, feature, member in the world!

His self-admiration was wholly indiscriminate. He wasn't vain of his hair, or of his eyes or his figure, or of his skill in riding or fencing, compared with other people's hair and so forth. He compared them with nothing. They were his; and *that* alone made them incomparable.

Sir William never spent, as some young men do, considerable time at the mirror, arranging his hair, his expression, his pose, his dress, his gestures. He never wasted his own or other people's time by explaining and justifying his opinions. They were his: that was enough. When asked for them he handed them to the asker, as a pilgrim might hand out pebbles from a sacred shore, or an exorcizer might sprinkle holy water on the walls of a haunted chamber.

He was younger than John, and a good deal younger than Tilton; whereas Raymond de Laon was over twenty-five.

Sir William enjoyed life so intensely that it was a pleasure to everybody who knew him to be with him. So absolutely lacking in pride was he that he seemed to be as tickled by his own blunders, by his own foolishness, by his own cowardice, by his own weakness, by his own superstition, as were his friends in their affectionate entertainment and as were his enemies in their malicious amusement.

It must have been this gift of being all things to all men, on the strength of a conceit so immeasurable, that had enabled this singular boy at a yet earlier age to be actually able, under the wise encouragement of his father, to act in collusion with young John as one of the intermediaries between Roger Bacon and Pope Clement IV.

"How is your father's injury from those Lost Towers devils?" enquired Lady Val of the lad, just as he was launching forth, for the benefit of Ghosta and her Tartar, upon a tale he had heard about a miraculous and terraqueous crusade of sea-eagles, who conveyed in their beaks from Chesil-Beach to the Holy Land enough pebble-stones of carnelian to enable the walls of Jerusalem to rival the hanging gardens of Babylon.

"O he's healing up quick and easy, Lady," replied Sir William: "the great difficulty at home just now is mother's quarrel with both Raymond and Friar Bacon. She tells father he ought never to have invited Raymond here at all, because somebody younger, somebody more like me, she says, would look better going about with Lil-Umbra."

These words caused even Ghosta to awake from a trance that had already made her lover recall the expression in the eyes of the horse Cheiron. But it can be imagined how they roused in Lady Val's soul a sharp-pointed, outward-whirling arrow-head of flame-like fury. The idea of her only female offspring, the only daughter she would ever have—and do we not know that the closest association possible between human personalities is between a mother and a daughter?—becoming the official lady-love of this popinjay of a nursery-antic struck her on the quick.

She had had a good many more day-dreams about Lil-Umbra's future than Lil-Umbra ever had herself. For just as her father did, Lil-Umbra lived in the four elements, and one of the reasons why she had such a special partiality for

Heber Sygerius was that the old ex-bailiff had, like Sir Mort, only in a different way, unusual awareness of the less palpable and more mysterious qualities of earth, air, fire and water.

Thus it was that when young Sir William blurted this out about his mother's attitude to Raymond de Laon, who, after all, was himself only a young man, an intense and violent surge of emotion rose in Lady Val's deepest being, swept up from the pit of her stomach into both her breasts, whirled up dizzily from there into her brain, and finally exploded in an outburst, the essence of which was irrepressible fury with fate because her secret, wild, ideal dreams about her daughter's future had been blighted forever; but, odd though it may sound, the form this fury took was nothing more or less than a desperate curiosity.

"Do, O please do, my dear William, tell me what that wise, clever, deep-seeing mother of yours finds wrong with Raymond de Laon! I expect she has a hundred times more insight than I shall ever have, and knows the world a hundred times better than I shall ever know it. Does your dear intellectual mother feel that something is wrong with Raymond's religion, or with his morals, or with his manners, or with his proper wish to get on in the world and to give his wife, when he has a wife, a proper position in the world? Or does your deep-searching mother—come a bit nearer, my boy, for I don't want to be overheard—feel that Raymond is perhaps not quite, not alto-gether, not wholly and entirely—I see you know what I mean, so I can speak quite simply—right in his mind? I *have* seen Lil-Umbra look strangely at him once or twice when they've been talking, as if he were saying something rather, you know what I mean, my dear boy, rather wild and—and funny?"

The youngest of all the knights on whom the aged and ailing son of the brother of Richard Coeur-de-Lion had bestowed the accolade shut his open mouth, half-closed his roving eyes, and frowned. He was evidently thinking hard: not pretending to think, but really thinking.

Then, with an upward leap of his whole slender little person and a metallic tinkling of the hilt of his dagger against the hilt of his sword as his excitable hands rushed to his belt, Sir William Boncor exclaimed eagerly: "Yes! oh yes! I heard him say once, when someone was talking about the Day of Judgment and the Last Day: 'In my Philosophy,' he said, 'there is no Day of Judgment nor any Last Day. There is only *Now*. We are born. We grow up: we have children: we die. And then the next generation is born; grows up; and dies. That's my Philosophy as to the way things go."

Sir William's flickering little frame subsided upon its heels with a gasp of ineffable self-satisfaction. The confident smile of generations of just men condemning a crazy aberration broadened upon his triumphant face. With a faint shrug of his shoulders he seemed to be saying to every doubting devil in the universe, "I am righteous, I am!" It was at this well-timed moment that the wily Mogol took advantage of the long, half-amused, half-puzzled, but by no means disarmed look, that Lady Val fixed upon the self-satisfied young knight, and without asking permission, or letting his companion make the slightest parting obeisance, took Ghosta's arm and led her out of that vortex of crazy foam by the way they had entered it.

"Mother thinks," Sir William began again, "that you don't realize half of what Raymond puts into Lil-Umbra's head. Mother even told father yesterday, when she was angry with him because he wouldn't shave off his beard, that Raymond will soon be dressing up Lil-Umbra in boy's clothes and taking her with him to Paris."

The unction with which this youngest of all the newly-dubbed knights at the court of the doting old man, who had reigned longer than any living monarch in Christendom, let these words fall upon Lady Val's tense nerves, was like the squeezing of a gobbet of spikenard upon an itching skin. As the ointment oozed forth upon the inflamed place, the fever behind it was driven in, not drawn out.

Lady Val's whole face twitched and her fingers clasped and unclasped the brooch at her waist. And then, as she gazed at this tricked-out image of youthful conceit, who was talking to her about the vindictiveness—and didn't she know intricacies of that underground stream well enough!—of her rival at Cone, there suddenly whirled up within her the blindest and most desperate wave of emotion she had ever felt in her life.

Her own mind, as it grew aware of what she felt, interpreted it as pure unmitigated and entirely justifiable indignation with Lady Ulanda of Cone, but in reality it was far more complicated. It was compounded of an intense revolt against the way fate had been treating her of late, mingled with a wild longing that her children's Dormaquil blood might suddenly assert itself and turn the whole tide of events in a completely new direction. Under the pressure of this surge of emotion, in the flood of which so many long pent-up feelings were breaking loose, she felt as though at any moment she might easily do something unexpectedly violent. It was an emotion too general, as well as too blind, to be fully interpreted by the simple definition "hatred of Lady Ulanda", but as the thing uncoiled itself from the deepest centre of her being she began to be afraid of what she might do.

Lady Val had very rarely been as conscious of her personal inner life as she was at this moment. The sudden loosening within her of this long dammed up reservoir of suppressed fury forced the torrent of emotion into a psychic channel that so far had been left high and dry. She very rarely thought of herself at all when she was angry with Sir Mort or with Tilton or John; and in Lil-Umbra's case she was so used to associating her daughter's personality with her own that, when she got angry with her, it was like her right hand getting angry with her left hand.

Anger with Lil-Umbra was indeed a unique feeling, too deep-rooted to be easily articulated. But what she felt at this particular moment was a wild identification of herself with the very substance of the great house in which she lived. She felt as if she herself *were* the Fortress of Roque, and that every stone, every carving, every buttress, every arrow-slit, every stair, every tower, every wall, every rafter, every gate, every door, every threshold to every door, of this whole old place was calling out from within herself to herself, and reminding her that they and she together were a living part and portion of the diffused presence of the spirits of all her ancestors.

She suddenly felt that the whole place, which was herself and yet much more than herself, was being threatened by her and her children with a ghastly doom, a doom irretrievable, inescapable, and final. She told herself that it was she and none other who had brought this doom upon them all; and that she had done it by yielding to her love for Sir Mort and letting him be the father of her children.

As with most of us at some desperate climax of our lives, the wild passion of anger, which had driven this tragic awareness into an inner chamber of her consciousness, changed its own nature when it had achieved this end. It was a strange sadness that now filled Lady Val's soul, as she thought of this fatal name "Abyssum" drifting and floating and flowing across every surface and through every crevice and crack of the massive stones whereof the Fortress of Roque was built.

"He is too queer, too eccentric, too remote from real life," she told herself, "to be able to save this place and to guard our name from oblivion."

It was as if the agitated lady's soul had been whirling round the outside of the Fortress as violently as it had whirled round the inside, for it happened at that moment that a single dead alder-leaf, stirred up from the bank of a small stream in the direction of Cone Castle, and wafted through one of the arrow-slit windows in some higher portion of the Fortress, came floating down to the floor of that ante-room.

Where the dead leaf fell, there did it rest; and it rested on the ground almost mid-way between the comically pretentious young knight and the desperately agitated lady of the house. Whether either of them noticed this wrinkled symbol of the passing generations, as it fell between them, neither of them later would have been able to say. Very likely they both did, but without any reaction capable of being recalled.

Situations like this, when two human beings are brought together by fate, one of them in a state of feverish mental activity and the other in a state of complacent quiescence, one of them with nerves quivering and senses vibrant, and the other with both nerves and senses lulled into a trance of self-satisfaction, have the effect sometimes of putting very queer thoughts into the mind of one or other of the pair.

What came into the head of Lady Val at that moment was a fantastic theory of her husband's about which he was in the habit of expatiating at great length and upon the most inopportune occasions. Sir Mort's theory was—and though he would swear to her and to the children that it was based on his own experience, she never could see, however excited he got about it, that it was possible for one man's experience to cover such an immense field—that there was what he was pleased to describe as an invisible Dimension that existed over the whole surface of land and sea; and that into this Dimension rushed all the thoughts and feelings and passions and even sensations of everything that was subject to these things.

His theory culminated in the amazing dogma that everything that existed had such feelings, not even excluding rocks and stones and earth-mould. And he further held that this invisible Dimension was much more crowded and much more active at certain geographical points round the surface of land and water than at others. Even where there are no human beings, this spiritual atmosphere would, he maintained, be there just the same. For not only must there be, universally emanating from the whole body of our planet, feelings that we must think of as the feelings of our Mother the Earth herself, but there must also be the feelings—or semi-conscious vibrations corresponding to feelings—of all the separate material elements whereof the substance of the planet is composed.

In fact Sir Mort insisted that all the feelings of all the things in the world are to be found in this invisible Dimension, and the fact that the earth *as* the earth has universal feelings does not mean that the separate parts and diverse substances of which she is composed are lacking in individual feelings. In fact he insisted that this invisible Dimension, or atmospheric sounding-board, of the planet upon which we live, while predominant in it are the feelings of all living men, women, and children, includes also the feelings of all beasts, birds, fishes, reptiles, insects and worms as well as of trees, plants, mosses, funguses, grasses and all vegetation.

And when we thus speak of the projected thoughts and feelings and emotions of all things, it must be remembered that we are not suggesting the existence of any actual souls that can survive the death of their bodily presence. When we are dead, Sir Mort maintained, we are absolutely dead. But while we live we are all, including the myriads of sub-human lives in air, on land, and in water, from whales to earth-worms and the tiniest gnats, in constant contact with an invisible over-shadowing atmospheric mist, crowded with feelings and dreams and emotions and what might be called sense-emanations and thought-eidola issuing from all that exists, whether super-human, human, or sub-human, whether organic or inorganic. This atmospheric dimension does not, Sir Mort argued, contain the sort of entities we are in the habit of thinking of as souls; for these perish when we perish, but it contains the thoughts and feelings and intimations and sensations which, though they grow fainter with time, do not cease to exist when the body and soul which projected them have both come to an end.

While we are still struggling, enduring, enjoying, as we move or rest in the earth, air, or water, of our terraqueous globe, there will always be this atmospheric aura about us where the psychic reactions engendered by the attractions and repulsions, the devourings and escapings, that go on in life mount up and remain, drifting and floating here and there in a curious chaotic mixture of the pleasant and the unpleasant.

And it is because of this atmospheric arena always about us, whether indoors or out-of-doors, whether on the surface of plains or mountains, whether in earth-mines or undersea-caverns, whether in any level of the air, or above any fiery crater or tumultuous sea, that those among us—and Sir Mort obviously included himself in this select category—who are alive to these rarefied visitations, are frequently exhilarated or saddened without any apparent inward or outward cause.

These sudden variations of mood without apparent cause are—Sir Mort would explain, though he assumed that his wife knew nothing of such subtle emotions—extremely puzzling phenomena. But they can, he would point out, be made less mysterious if we think of this atmospheric dimension of psychic reactions as composed not only of the sensations of all living things from the cleverest human beings and the most intelligent animals, birds, fishes and reptiles, to the most simple-minded tadpoles, jelly-fish, star-fish, earth-worms, and insects, together with the vast mass of all the vegetable growth in the world, but of such sensations as they occur in the strain and stress of cosmogonic chance.

It was all in a second curiously enough, as this tidal memory of her husband's ten-thousand times repeated harangue swept over her, that she actually found herself wondering whether there might not really be a grain of truth in all this craziness. Dimension or no dimension, there must be a reason for this ebbing and flowing of our feelings, and for our being sometimes so mysteriously happy, and sometimes so unutterably sad.

"Well," she thought, "I can't stand here staring at little Popinjay all night! I must get rid of the boy somehow." And as she raised her hands to feel whether her hair was in proper order, she became half conscious of that alder-leaf on the floor between herself, the self-questioning Lady Val, and her visitor, the quiescent and self-approving Sir William.

"She," Sir William was thinking, "must be suffering a lot. Poor, poor woman! She must know, after all I've said, that she has given her daughter to the wrong man! So I really must be kind to her in her unhappiness."

But what the unhappy lady was thinking was this: "I'll tell Ulanda what we all feel about Baron Boncor's beard, for I think that will trouble her arrogant mind more than anything else."

And what, we might wonder, was that alder-leaf's parent-tree thinking in its nakedness as it bowed before the wind? Was it thinking, "If only I could stretch a quarter of an inch nearer the water I would tell this blind, stupid, silly, deaf, dumb, idiotic stream in what direction it ought to flow if it wants to reach the sea."

And if no thought of that leaf on the floor crossed the furthest fringe of its parent-tree's cogitations, you may be sure that neither Sir William nor Lady Val gave the slightest attention to its fate; and there it would have lain for the rest of that evening and the whole of that night had not old Mother Guggery been sent from the kitchen to ask some important semi-culinary, semi-social question of the Lady of the Manor.

Mother Guggery always used a massive ebony stick when she walked, though physically she had not the least need of such support, and she showed now by the way she came stumping up between the young knight and Lady Val that the moment her curiosity was satisfied as to what they were talking about, or being silent about, she would turn her back upon the young man and concentrate on her mission to the lady.

But in a household as turbulent with new starts and old upshots, with new conspiracies and old frustrations, as was this Fortress of Roque, it was impossible, especially at the close of a sunny day at this time of the year, and upon such a central and crucial debating-ground as this particular spot, for any discussion to be long confined to its originators.

Thus before Mother Guggery had got down to the business of her message, who must come drifting in but Lady Val's younger son, the intellectual young John, who was often called "John of London" at the Priory, because of his frequent visits to the King's court on behalf of Friar Bacon. He now came loitering and drifting towards his mother with the air of one who had been using his wits all day long to such exhaustive effect among the high problems of metaphysic and theology that he has earned the right, now that the day is over and darkness is falling, to forget these high matters—yes! to forget this difficult super-world with its niceties of the human conscience, its nuances of Trinitarian Personalities, and its dissolving facets of unfathomable Absolutes, and to give himself up to any frivolity that drifted across his path in that domestic portico between kitchen and dining-hall.

Nor does life often fail us under such conditions; for there is Something in life that is at once different from Chance and yet not quite identical with all that we mean by the word Fate; and it is this Something that almost always provides us with some spontaneous motive when we are, so to speak, angling for an urge to pursue any available flibbertigibbet.

And thus it now happened with the younger son of Sir Mort Abyssum. Mother Guggery, having assumed by her lady's look that more was in the air than she could cope with just then, came bolt out with the message from the kitchen, and, as she turned to go, her eyes fell on that last year's alder-leaf lying on the floor. With the end of her ebony stick the old woman endeavoured, by obstinately poking at it, to get the leaf near enough to her feet to be able to stoop and pick it up. This whole picture, the ebony stick, the thin bent back, the patient motionless leaf, was enough, when taken in at a glance,

168

to cause young John to rush forward and snatch up the leaf himself.

And then, all in a second, an airy connection struck him between this whole small event and the teaching of Friar Bacon, who had always instructed him to save such vegetable waifs from bonfires, and to cast them, loose and free, as near their birthplace as possible. So into the young man's most intimate pocket went this lucky leaf to be disposed of later.

XII

THE HERESY HUNT

It was more than a surprise to the simpler dwellers in that portion of Wessex dominated by the traditional Manors of Roque and of Cone, and perpetually being interfered with by the unprecedented and incalculable domain of Lost Towers, when the holy, the thrice-blessed, the miraculously learned representative of the Holy Father himself in Rome, Bonaventura, the most famous of all Franciscans since Saint Francis, began, in that early spring of the year of grace 1272, searching the district for heretics and unbelievers, and using as his band of retainers nothing less than a regular cohort of brown-vested bandits from the swamps of Lost Towers.

And this singular heresy-hunt, led by a reputed saint commanding a body-guard of reputed devils, was an incredible event even to the good-natured Baron of Cone himself, whom it disturbed not a little. He finally made up his mind to accept it at its face-value; but since his youth, when serving under King Henry at the battle of Lewes, he had beheld the triumph of Simon de Montfort, he had never had such a spiritual shock.

When in the course of chronicling these events we seek to understand this shock, we are driven to conclude that it came from a certain inherent simplicity in Baron Boncor's nature, which instinctively accepted without question all those natural assumptions about good and evil, which like the biblical "charity" are only too apt to "cover a multitude of sins."

In spite of the rapid healing of the serious hurt he had received from the arrow, shot at him by Baron Maldung, he felt convinced that it would be a case of taking the side of the Devil against God if he gave any aid, shelter, refreshment, hospitality, information, comfort, encouragement or welcome to Bonaventura and his brown-jerkin'd band.

It was quite another thing with Lady Ulanda, Baron Boncor's wife. Lady Ulanda had recently abandoned herself to a savage campaign against Friar Bacon and all his works. Ulanda was anything but a religious lady. Her whole nature was practical. She was in the fullest sense a woman of action. She was suspicious of all thought, of all art, of all mental analysis. She wasn't a vicious woman, but she was what is called a possessive woman, to a degree that was a danger to everybody round her and especially to the object of this possessiveness.

The object of it in this case was no child in her domestic world and no lover in the world outside. It was simply and solely her husband. And it was because of several very curious reasons, some physical, some mental, and some the result of occurrences in the early days of her marriage, that this dominant element in her nature had never from the beginning asserted itself in any perceptible degree in regard to her son. Her attitude to young Sir William was more like that of an affectionate aunt than a mother. She doted on him as a fanciful old maid might dote on a favourite pet; and it was a real blow to her when destiny brought it about that she was compelled to witness, day by day, the rapidly growing love-affair between her husband's friend and cousin, Raymond de Laon, and the daughter of Lady Val of the Fortress.

Ulanda's almost frantic hostility to Friar Bacon was intimately connected with Baron Boncor's affection for his relative Raymond. It had been pain and poison to her from the start—the interest Baron Boncor took in Raymond. She had hated his coming to be an inmate of their castle from the very first, but Boncor was so set upon it that, without a greater quarrel than she dared to embark on, she had to accept it.

At the bottom of it was her simple recognition that her husband's regard for Raymond de Laon was not unconnected with the young man's exceptional good looks and the magnetic charm of his whole personality. She knew only too well that she herself, though full of an intense vitality and always able to carry off with dignity the proud assumptions of high-born authority, was grotesquely lacking in that sort of tender and appealing physical beauty which wins favour wherever it goes.

Like many another high-spirited and passionate lady, Ulanda of Cone felt such an intense longing to be as beautiful in reality as she was beautiful in her inner ideal of herself, that she had actually visited Friar Bacon in that upper chamber in the Priory where he was virtually a prisoner, and made a direct personal face-to-face appeal to him to help her, by means of those mysterious arts in which she understood he was such a master, to acquire, without any drastic change in her appearance, that particular magnetic charm by which the most formidable of men can be seduced and captivated by a woman.

As any of the serious disciples and pupils of the scientific Friar could have warned her, this shameless and unblushing assumption that he was some kind of a sex-wizard annoyed Roger Bacon so much that he refused point-blank to have anything to do with her; and Lady Ulanda came down the stone staircase from the Friar's chamber resolved to have the most deadly revenge she could bring about on a man who refused so rudely—and he a sort of half-condemned heretic too—a natural and perfectly lawful request from a lady of her importance in that western district of the kingdom.

Lady Ulanda was not particularly fussy or punctilious in what might be called the heraldic or antiquarian aspects of the Barony of Cone. In fact she was a good deal less primed in such matters than were most of her contemporary ladies of title. She herself came of an old yeoman family called Dunderog entirely independent of any baronial manor, but claiming direct descent from Ralph Rorsuk, the predatory nephew of King Stephen.

When not fishing or hunting or fighting or riding between his arable-fields and his pasture-fields, or surveying his forestry, Baron Boncor was in the habit of spending his time in a spacious chamber at the top of a small round tower above the south-west ramparts of the Castle. This chamber ever since his grandfather once, on a pilgrimage to Rome, purchased some illuminated scrolls, and obtained in the same city the aid of a famous book-binder to cover them with specially prepared skins, had come to be known as the Library.

Boncor's grandfather had fastened with golden-headed nails upon an enormous oak table opposite the hearth in this room a great number of large pictorial maps of the world, adapted to the comprehension of unclassical and unscholarly persons by the appearance at certain crucial points, on both land and sea, of various land-monsters and sea-monsters, and also of various voyagers, these latter enlarged in size so as to indicate by their dresses, arms, and banners, whether they came from Christian or Heathen countries, while the ships that carried them were reduced in size in comparison with the men—and women too sometimes—whom they carried, as if to compel recognition that a Power and a Mystery, that is at once half-human and half-divine, is ruling and will always rule the Air, the Earth, the Water and the Fire.

On each side of a blazing fire of pine logs, kept in constant flame by sticks from a big pile in a capacious copper container, were two deep well-cushioned chairs, that resembled the rudder divided sterns of a couple of barges rather than baronial judgment-seats or collegiate library-benches or cathedral choir-stalls.

It was between these two seats that the huge low eight-legged table of dark oak stood that was covered with these pictures of the world. One corner of this enormously large and very low table, on the surface of which Behemoths and Leviathans and dragons and sea-serpents were disporting themselves, was devoted to the art of book-binding, an art in which the present Baron of Cone took a lively and a practical interest.

On this corner of the table adjoining the Baron's chair was a careful selection of the skins of small local wild animals, by the aid of which the Baron was wont to practise with slow and sedulous care the by no means easy art of making bindings for both sacred and profane manuscripts.

The delicate results of his devoted concentration on this unusual task could be seen meticulously arranged on various wooden stands beneath all the four walls of the chamber, including the one where a low and very narrow door opened on the stairway that led to the foot of the tower. It was not until an evening in the middle of February in that eventful christian year of 1272 that the stored-up, banked-up, piled-up fury of Lady Ulanda against Friar Bacon burst out in full enough force, as she sat in the other curiously carved and richly cushioned chair over their fire of pine logs to make that easy-going Lord of the Manor of Cone realize that the situation was serious.

"If you don't do something and do it quickly," hissed Ulanda, sitting straight up at the edge of her seat, and with her long, bare arms giving the rim of the great table, which extended its breadth and its length at their side, a series of desperate blows with her knuckles, "I shall go mad!"

Across the maps fastened with golden nails to the table and making it look like the mingling of an illustrated bestiary with an illustrated cosmography, it seemed to Baron Boncor that under these violent blows all those weird sea-monsters and land-monsters quivered into a new life and ceased to be merely pictures. But the Baron's look of bewildered concern only agitated her still more; and with a frantic artfulness she manipulated her knuckles so that her enormous signet-rings— rings that she only wore when she felt especially angry with the world, and which always made her husband think of certain pre-historic rings that had been found by one of his ploughmen near an ancient burial mound in the immediate vicinity of his castle—beat upon the table.

Ulanda's parents were both dead and she had no relatives left, but she always maintained that these two rings had belonged to Rorsuk, King Stephen's nephew, and that it was because he had forgotten to put them on at some royal banquet that he was found murdered that same night in the bed of one of the court ladies.

At any rate the sound that Ulanda's rings, one of which carried on it the semblance of a wild-boar and the other the semblance of a whale, caused to vibrate across that monster-bearing table, suggested that a sea-serpent was catching its breath as it neared the land at the sight of a Behemoth munching grass on the sea-shore.

It was at this moment, before the bewildered Baron could formulate any appeal to her enraged soul, that they both became aware of steps on the tower staircase. They looked at each other and they looked at the door. But no indignant look and no muttered curse could stop that door from opening. And there, quietly crossing the threshold, was Raymond de Laon!

Raymond was as fair-haired as Baron Boncor, but his hair was straight, not curly like the Baron's, and if he had grown a beard it would probably have been feathery and wispy in the manner of Spardo's. In figure he was tall and slender, and his face had an alert, intent, interrogating look, as if he were forever searching for something he couldn't find, and yet not at all as if this search was painful or as if he felt any touch of anger or desperation at not finding what he sought.

The first thing he did on entering the chamber was to turn half-round, even while he was in the act of making a low obeisance, and to close the door. This he did with extreme punctiliousness and almost with the air of being a confederate in an exciting conspiracy. But the door once closed and his obeisance over, it was with a most unembarrassed and easy manner that he advanced to the edge of the great table, and leaning forward across it with the tips of his long fingers just touching it, he completely, although very politely, disregarded the evident hostility on the lady's face and addressed himself entirely to Baron Boncor, who had risen with a friendly greeting and now sank down, composed and attentive, to hear what his young friend had to say.

"I came to tell you, my lord," Raymond began, "that your people in the reception room downstairs have just been considerably disturbed by the unexpected appearance among them tonight of a group of men from Lost Towers. None of my friends among your people have been able to tell me who it was who let these bandits come in. I fancy myself it was some young rogue who has been looking for an excuse to leave Cone altogether and to join these crazy followers of Lost Towers. Though evidently puzzled how they got in, your excellent Ralph Turgo, unwilling to be the one to start trouble, began at once giving them refreshments.

"Well, I took advantage of this moment of relaxation to ask a few questions of one of these Lost Towers men; and what I picked up from him was an amazing piece of news. It appears that Bonaventura, head of all the Franciscans, is lodging at Bumset Priory tonight, and that he himself, and no one else, has hired for the occasion these master-ruffians from Lost Towers with the intention of using them as his own retainers, so that he can drag Friar Bacon out of his prison there, and carry him off to a ship that's waiting on the Thames in London to take him to France where he'll never he heard of again.

"I heard them telling our Turgo—and Ralph's a crafty fellow, you know, when it comes to inducing rascals like these Brown Tunics to talk—just what they told me, that Bonaventura wants them to carry off from the Priory-prison not only the Friar himself and all his unholy and heathen books, but also this Brazen Head of his, about which we hear so much. This Brazen Head he wants them to carry into some empty space in the forest, and when once they've got it there—in some empty space, you understand, between the Fortress and Lost Towers—to hammer it to bits with stones and plough-shares and iron clubs!"

Having thus delivered his startling news with dramatic intensity straight across that curious table which now bore upon its geographical face all the most terrifying monsters, of land, sea, and air, that have ever defied man's domination of the world, the fair-haired lover of Lil-Umbra let his whole tension relax, and in an easy and quiet and apologetic way moved round the table till he reached the arm of Baron Boncor's chair over which he bent.

"I didn't want to bother you with all this, my dear Baron," he murmured, "but it struck me as such an unexpected coalition between God and the Devil that it gave me the feeling of an unpleasant conspiracy against all quiet and moderate people who dislike extremes. I can't myself quite explain the shock it gave me; but an unpleasant shock it was. I rather think it had to do with the peculiar colour of the clothes these men wear, which is almost exactly the colour of that liquid we always see between the stones in those places where they slaughter animals.

"I must have imagined the actual spectacle of these savage brown tunics doing the abominable bidding of this ferocious angel of God, who evidently would have loved to have seen hammered into unrecognizable bits not only the Friar's Brazen Head but the Friar's own human, all-too-human skull!"

"And a good thing too!" hissed Lady Ulanda, rising to her feet and confronting her husband's young friend across the outer edge of a picture of a terrifying sea, whose waves were breaking on the shores of what that primeval map called "the Land of Cathay," and on whose breaking waves a monster was riding, whose head resembled the head of a colossal lizard and its rear end the tail of a gigantic dolphin.

"Forgive her, Raymond!" murmured the Baron gently. "The poor old girl had a bit of a shock a day or two ago." Something in the tone of his voice induced Ulanda to resume her seat; though those ominous rings on her fingers jangled remorselessly still against the table's edge.

"May I tell him about your visit to the Friar?" enquired the Baron; and added hurriedly: "I think I *ought* to tell him, you know, because then he'll realize better our whole feeling about the Friar and his confounded Brazen Oracle."

Ulanda's reply to this question was only a bowing of her head still lower over her knees. But her husband firmly, though very gently, went on. "Yes, she went to see this Bacon fellow to ask him to help her in preparing some of those ointments for which our present-day ladies have such a mania—the sort of ointment, you know, that that queer tinker or whatever he is, who rides a horse with a swelling in its neck like the head of a man, is always trying to sell and swearing too—I've often heard him at it!—that it's what they used in Babylon when the whale swallowed Jonah.

"And how do you suppose this modern Simon Magus received our lady! No! I'll tell him, my precious. Don't you interrupt! You can correct me later. He burst into a fit of fury and acted to Ulanda with unpardonable discourtesy— Forgive me, Raymond! It's only my shoulder. I didn't draw back from your hand—lean against the back of my neck. I don't get the ghost of a twinge there! He's not really a good bowman, our Lost Towers rogue: and I don't myself think he's much of a catch for Satan. I mean I don't think he's half as corrupt or half as clever as his wife and daughter. What do *you* say, my dear, on that nice point?"

But Ulanda who had flung herself back in her chair, her knuckles white with the intensity with which she clutched the carved lionheads at its elbow, took no notice of this amiable request.

"Tell him at once," she ejaculated, spitting out the words in a low hoarse voice, and with as complete disregard for the presence of Raymond as if what she said had to pass no further than from one organic portion of her own person to another, "tell him at once," and it was as if the gall within her addressed itself to the midriff within her, "that it matters nothing to us by whose hand this accurst wizard is unfrocked and sent begging, as long as it is done, and all his fabrications pounded into dust! Tell him to say to Bonaventura that when the job is completed, we hope to welcome him here and do all we can to help him in his hunt for other traffickers with the Devil!"

It was difficult for Raymond to get the precise expression on that curly-bearded face, as Boncor, while slowly rising from his chair, turned towards him.

What increased the young man's uncertainty on this point was the fact that the act of rising caused a spasm of pain to pass through Boncor's wounded shoulder, and this, though largely concealed by his beard, for pain affects the mouths of certain types of men more than their eyes or foreheads, did perceptibly obscure the intimately direct look which the Baron fixed upon his friend.

"I shall go downstairs with him at once, my dear, and deal with these Red-Brown Tunics from the Towers, and have a word with Turgo. You may depend on it, my treasure, that all your rightful dignity, and all your natural lady-like feelings will be considered to the uttermost in the arrangements your old adorer makes; so don't worry! Keep the fire up and get out some wine by the time we come up again! And have a sip yourself for a while! We shan't be as long as, O I know so well how long you're now imagining we'll be! You'll see. Thanks, Raymond."

And all that Ulanda could now hear were the double thuddings of their feet, her husband's considerably heavier than his friend's, as the two men tramped down the turret stairs.

Ulanda sat still, seeing nothing but the living heart of the fire in front of her, and hearing nothing but the dark, deep, dead silence that surrounded the crackling of those burning sticks. Her thoughts were much less desperate than Raymond could possibly have imagined, as he accompanied her husband into the reception chamber on the ground floor below. To be alone always suited her; and though she knew well at the bottom of her heart that her husband would never, in spite of his encouraging words, really see to it that her longed-for revenge on Roger Bacon would be brought about, she was able, now that she was no more actually in the presence of this friendship she hated so much, to treat the whole matter, and her own feelings about it, with something approaching a philosophic mind.

And the most powerful of all the divinities with whom it is our destiny to get more acquainted the older we grow—namely, that frivolous, merciless, apparently irresponsible goddess, whose name is Tyche or Chance—did not refuse at this crisis in her life to give the passionate Ulanda the breathing-space to which any sort of humane judicial authority would have taken for granted she was entitled; for there sounded now a quite different step upon the turret stairs, a step the familiar vibration of which in place of making her sit up and prepare for action made her relax with an ineffable sense of relief.

"O Mabbernob! Do you know what has just happened to me? And for the first time too in all the days of my life? And it wasn't because I'm a real knight either, and knighted by the King himself! You'll never guess, Mabbernob darling, what it was! But try a moment: O *do* try a moment to guess, before I sit down!"

An affectionately friendly and a comfortably appreciative smile spread softly over Ulanda's whole personality. She felt— she always felt in this manner—just exactly as when, after a second's submerging under the waters of unconsciousness, she had first beheld this only offspring of her love for the Lord of Cone lying beside her. It had not been very long before she found herself translating a constantly repeated sequence of babyish babblement into the word "Mabbernob," by which the little creature was designating the womb from which it came and the paps that fed it.

"Well, well," she now replied, in an affectionately jocular tone, "Honey-Pot holy, Honey-Pot mighty, Honey-Pot washed and dressed, tell Mabbernob the whole story!"

The young knight stalked solemnly to Ulanda's side of the big table, placed the back of a hand clutching a pair of gauntlets against his left hip, tightened his bare fingers about the handle of his sword, and tilted his chin in the air. "It was," he announced, "as I went into the ante-room just now. There were half-a-dozen fellows there, all trick'd out in that funny red-brown stuff they wear at the Towers, stuff that when you see it at close quarters is all made of rags, rags patched together you know, like the clots and clouts of wandering beggars on the Icen Way: and what must they do the moment they saw me standing there, but rush forward, kneel down before me, stretch out their arms towards me, and cry in the sort of voice—do you remember, Mabbernob?—in which those play-acting masqueraders who came from Sicily cried, when they acted Sabine prisoners begging to have back their wives!

"But what these poor devils cried was—but do tell me this, Mabbernob, before I go on; has Father been hunting over there and catching these wretches for sport instead of badgers and foxes?—what, I say, they cried was:

"'Be our leader, Sir William, be our leader against this wicked, hateful, abominable hell-born Friar Bacon who has devilishly been making, with all his infernal cleverness, out of tin and iron and copper and brass a real breathing, thinking human being, just exactly as if he were God, a Being, you must understand, made of Brass, a Being who predicts the end of the world, a Being who has the power not only to predict the end of the world but—think of their believing *that*, Mabbernob!—to bring it about! So please, please, *please*, Sir William,' these poor wretches cried out, 'consent to be our leader and help us to break into little pieces this New Man invented by this New Devil! Thou art a knight, Sir William, and here is work proper to thy knightly arms!'"

"Sit down over there in your Father's chair, son of my heart, and you and I will discuss this whole matter as carefully as we can."

Ulanda's voice was so extremely quiet that her son, though he wasn't quite the well-balanced sage he fancied himself to be, received not the faintest intimation of the seething and smouldering hurricane of feverish thoughts that was whirling in her head.

"Shall I use this child?" she asked herself. "Boncor will never go as far as I want; and these wretches have nothing to lose and everything to gain by killing this devil of a Friar! Besides if Lord Edward comes home before he's expected and before Henry dies, he'll be less inclined to make a fuss if it's an excitable boy who brought about the killing of this sorcerer, and did it by the hands of this Lost Towers gang who've always been irresponsible outlaws."

Thud—thud—thud—Ah! there were the steps of her bearded husband and his handsome and diplomatic young friend! As she heard these steps there was something about the image of her husband's beard that flung new fuel on her fury. In these subtle fits of nervous rage, which most of us experience at one time or another, some particular visual image will often detach itself from its proper setting, like a scarf or a belt or a brooch or a feather from some old picture upon the wall, and fly to blend itself with the bodily target of our resentment, even partaking, though the luckless thing is in itself absolutely innocent, in the special objectionableness of the cause of our rancour.

Thus it was that several seconds before the actual appearance of the middle-aged man she loved and the young man she hated, the curly beard of the former and the clear-cut Hellenic profile of the latter rose so vividly before her mind's eye that, in a flash of mad fury, Ulanda decided that at all costs, and in spite of all her love for the man himself, Boncor's beard must be cut off.

The idea of a beardless Boncor did indeed so fulfil and so satisfy her wrath that, as she listened to what the two men were saying, she became actually aware, though she wouldn't let herself enjoy that awareness, of a relaxation in the bitterness of her feelings. Something had come into her mind now that resembled a faint reflection in a sprinkling of water, by the side of a weary and unending road, along which she was riding.

She watched with an abstracted gaze how her son settled himself more and more comfortably in his father's chair, and as she rubbed with the inside tips of the trembling fingers of one hand the white knuckles of the other, which was fiercely pressed against the edge of the maps of all the world, she vividly imagined herself stroking, with an absolutely sated satisfaction, the bare, soft, hairless chin of the man she possessed.

But at this moment, as Boncor and Raymond crossed the room, she felt as if they were both as transparent as ghosts.

"They've gone, Ulanda," Boncor announced, "and you should have seen the effect of the light they carried, as it fell on the clump of firs at our gate!"

"And then on their red-brown costumes," added Raymond de Laon.

"Is Bonaventura waiting for them?" Ulanda enquired. "Is he going boldly to lead them into the Priory and straight up the steps into that chamber where the wretch manufactures his devilish machines?" As the two of them moved up to the table they both replied at once.

"I told them plainly that I wouldn't have any killing of Friars on land that belongs to me. But when they asked: 'Will you forbid your people to meddle with them as they carry off the sorcerer?' I answered that I never interfere with private quarrels between different sections of my people. If the pious ones want to kill the impious ones, *Let the Devil look after his own!* is what I say. And if the profane ones want to kill the pious ones, *Leave it to God!* is my motto."

"You know, lady, there are some quite presentable fellows among these Lost Towers rascals! I expected them to look like a pack of thieves," added Raymond de Laon, "but, I assure you, Lady, they weren't all like that!"

It was at this point that little Sir William, who had been listening to their words like a prince in a fairy-tale, rose portentously to his feet. "Don't you think, Father, don't you think, Raymond, that it would be a good thing if I went down and talked things over with Turgo? When I discussed with him last week the question of what weapons our Cone bodyguard had better carry on important occasions, he was very impressed by what I told him I'd seen in London at King Henry's court. I noticed just now when I saw what they were carrying—I mean the ones who were going into the forest to keep watch on these brown-backed bandits—that Turgo had taken my advice. But there was just one little thing that he'd forgotten on which I had specially insisted, namely that their short Roman blades should be unsheathed before placing them in their belts; and that their belts should be furnished with leather clasps, or leather bands, all the way round their waists, so that it would be possible for each man"—Here the new-made knight clapt his hands to his own belt, which bristled with the handles of two or three gleaming blades—"for each man at any sudden attack to defend himself with desolating—no! I mean devastating—no! what I had in mind was *penetrating*, for the daggers of course must be ready to *go in*—I mean to be plunged into their enemies' bodies. I think—don't you agree, Father?—that it might be a real help to our good Master Turgo if I went more fully into this matter of the way our Cone bodyguard should be armed at this important chorus—I mean crisis—in this history of our house here, and perhaps of—of—of this hemisphere. Don't you agree with me, father?"

The belted knight's progenitor bowed his head. But having gasped and gurgled and almost choked in his effort not to laugh, he glanced appealingly at his wife, and there was a prolonged—and for Raymond de Laon—an embarrassing silence.

The truth was that Ulanda hadn't been listening. Not a single word of all that her son had so pontifically repeated about belts and daggers had "penetrated" the walls of her mind. She had known he was speaking "in character". She had known that her husband was trying not to laugh. She had known that Raymond was vaguely watching all three of them with ironic detachment, and was probably calculating in his own mind how early in the morning he would have to wake up if he were to get a glimpse of Lil-Umbra before their breakfast at the Fortress, and whether he could make himself wake up or whether he'd better get Turgo to wake him.

Ulanda knew all these things. But as at this instant she glanced under the left arm of her boastful offspring and caught a certain humorously resigned expression in the eyes of her mate, she suddenly felt such a rush of love for him that she could hardly keep herself from betraying it. But she used all her will-power to struggle against this wave of emotion; and, as she overcame it, it became clear to her that to have yielded to it at this moment would have meant the giving up for good of her sworn revenge upon Friar Bacon.

It was at this precise point in Ulanda's cogitations that wild excited cries and alarming crashing sounds were heard in the rooms below, followed by a rush of half-a-dozen feet up their staircase. Raymond ran to the door that opened on these stairs and jerked it wide open, repeating as he did so in a high-pitched voice: "What the devil is this? What on earth's happening?"

But the broad-shouldered Turgo, with half-a-dozen stalwart and extremely excited men-at-arms behind him, flung him aside, and bursting into the room, stood like a rocky waterfall of indignation in front of the three persons grouped round that map-laden table, behind which, in the absence of fresh logs, the fire was almost dead.

"It's too much to endure, my lord! It's too much for anybody to endure! There's a big lot of men from the Fortress outside there now, led, yes! actually led, by that boy John who's the younger of them two, so he ain't even the heir to Roque! He's only a young scholard, that's what he is, yes! that's all he is—just a scrap of a lad at school! And there he is outside the main gate of Cone waving God knows what sort of weapon in his hand and defying these Lost Towers men and our men and all the men of Wessex to touch his precious Friar and his Friar's bedevilments!"

At this point the formidable bailiff of Cone straightened his tremendous shoulders to a degree that might have made even the powerful lover of Ghosta take notice.

"The man we need here now," bellowed Turgo, "is Lord Edward himself—O may he soon be our lord and King!—who is already on ship-board on his way home. It's *him* we need now, in this wretched bandit-beset country! Lord Edward would soon settle this crazy confusion in our ancient forest! Why, when *he* was with the King in London, none of these curst, insurrectionary barons dared lift a cry or wave a banner in this forest of ours! No, they daren't, I tell you, my lord. They daren't, I tell you, my lady! That's what we need here today, a proper knightly prince like Lord Edward!"

"I'll come down at once, Turgo," said Boncor, giving his wife an enquiring glance and apparently taking for granted that she would confirm his decision. "You'd better stay up here with your mother, son," he added in rather a less assured tone, when he noticed how nervously and anxiously the newly-made knight was pulling out and thrusting back the various silver-handled and brass-handled daggers which protruded from his leather belt.

In a flash Ulanda rushed round the table and clutched her husband by his left wrist. She had seen in a sudden vision these Fortress adherents, urged on by this crazy young John, and full of the idea that Friar Bacon, the greatest teacher in the world, *must* be saved at all costs, striking the already-wounded Boncor a blow that would be his death; while she, bereft of the love of her life, would be doomed to abide for the rest of her mortal days listening to this swaggering son of hers and trying to make him turn his words into deeds. God in Heaven, no! that would be more than she could bear! Let all three of them perish before that happened!

"You go down with Turgo, Sonny!" she cried. "Your father's a wounded man. I can't possibly let him fight with those devils! Only for Christ's blessed sake take care of yourself, son. I don't want you wounded too!"

Only once before in all his life had the Lord of Cone been required by the fate or by the chance that governs us all to make a psychic effort comparable with the one he had to make now. But he succeeded in making it; and the apparent ease with which he accepted the issue, when he had done so, was a triumph for his personality of which not a soul present had the faintest shadow of an idea.

"All right my dear; I'll stay with you. Off you go, William! Do whatever Turgo thinks best when you're down there. That little fool John has no right to bring his Dad's men into our place. But I've heard he's the best disciple the Friar's got round here; and we know what these students are! Keep an eye on our lad, Turgo, my friend. Remember he's the youngest knight of the oldest king in Christendom! I should say we do indeed need Lord Edward here; and I warrant these confounded lands he's crusading in, whether they're Arabian or Christian, will go on in the same turmoil whether he's there or not."

By the time the Lord of Cone had completely covered up the heart-heaving moral effort he'd just made in thus remaining in the library of his Castle, both Turgo and Sir William had reached the stairs, the latter much more concerned with the arrangement of the weapons in his own belt than with the whereabouts of the son of his sovereign, and the door had been closed behind them.

Ulanda promptly pushed both her quiescent lord into his chair and sliding down upon her knee drew his head towards her own. But it was then that the goddess of chance displayed her most devilish impishness. In the impetuosity of this gesture of affection the impulsive lady had forgotten a certain most perilously explosive inhibition in her own nerves; namely her loathing of beards.

But now, as their heads met, her husband's curly beard tickled her cheek. By long practice she had acquired the art of kissing him without incurring this contact. But the truth was that she had come to be obsessed of late more than ever before by this loathing for, and intolerable disgust at, the touch of a man's beard. The Baron indeed had recently begun to grow aware of this nervous mania of hers, and he often found himself wondering why at an earlier stage in their alliance she had not protested against his refusal to shave. This refusal of his was wholly instinctive.

He was constitutionally slow-moving; and was addicted to the habit of adapting himself to existing conditions; and one of the most obvious of such conditions was the simple law of Nature that the chins of men grew beards. Thus between these two persons there inevitably existed, lodged in the physical make-up of them both, the perilous possibility of a bodily, primeval, skin-for-skin quarrel of a serious kind.

It was an unfortunate coincidence however that at the very moment when her cheek was touched by the lips she loved and the beard she hated, there should have come to her ears from outside their secluded retreat, and even from outside the Castle itself, tumultuous cries and shouts and the noise of blows mixed with resounding yells of anger and pain.

These sounds may possibly have intensified her feelings by adding to her nervous mania a shiver of anxiety, though not more than a shiver, about her son. In a mad reaction against the touch of that bushy beard, she leapt up from his knee and uttered a piercing scream of rage, that flew out into the night like a wild bird whose wings were on fire.

It might well have happened that such a scream, rising from aggravated feminine nerves, and whirling off into the darkness from a height above the tops of the tallest trees, especially when the court-yard and gateway of the place were resounding with blows and cries, would have dissolved in the air unregarded by anyone except the two persons concerned.

But either by another random hit from the wanton bow of chance or, let us hope, by some special intervention of a brave man's guardian angel, this scream from Ulanda gave to the death-pangs of young Ralph Gaulter of Evercreech the one thing needed to wholly redeem his desperation.

Gaulter had only just entered the service of the Baron of Cone, and he had only done so because of a savage tragedy, three or four generations ago, when his great-grandmother, Matilda Gaulter, had been raped by one of the Lords of Roque. But at the moment of Ulanda's piercing scream that seemed to come down from heaven, young Gaulter was on his back on the grass with one of the red-brown bandits kneeling on his chest and pressing a broad and rusty kitchen-knife deep into his neck.

From his childhood he had heard tales of this ancestress of his, her beauty, her pride and her pitiful end, and now in his death throes the idea took hold of him that he was giving up his life in some mysterious way for this dead woman's living sake, and that this cry from above actually came from Matilda Gaulter.

Thus as the pressure of that broken, broad-headed, rusty knife just below the apple of his throat made his life-blood spurt forth from beneath his chin till it drenched his distorted and desperate face, the dying youth felt absolutely convinced that he really was, in these death-gasps and under these spouts of blood, sacrificing his life for this old ancestress of his who had been so horribly wronged.

Black gulfs of death might swallow up his body and threaten his soul, but the fairy-tale Great-Granny of all the years of his life was saved forever!

XIII

THE BRAZEN HEAD

Ralph Gaulter was the only one who, in this irresponsible three-cornered hurly-burly, lost his life. Others were wounded in the confusion but none of them mortally; while in the struggle of young John and his couple of henchmen with the red-brown bandits from Lost Towers it soon became clear that it was this latter group—tipsy though half of them were, and wildly excited though all of them were—who were destined to win; though when they had carried the Brazen Head away into the forest, and so well out of reach of all possible rescue or recovery, that Bonaventura himself felt justified in returning to the Priory, young John and his two companions obstinately pursued them.

Bonaventura evidently felt sure that when his red-brown allies had grown a little more sober they would finish the job and pound the Head to pieces. What really saved this unparalleled invention from destruction was not the protective magic, whether we call it "black" or "white", of its creator. It was something, though it is impossible to say exactly what, in the Head itself, just as if by some inexplicable chance the creative energy in the Friar had overreached its proper scientific limits, and had created a being capable, not only of personifying its own identity, but of escaping altogether from the control of its creator.

By the power of his immense sacerdotal reputation over the whole of Europe, Bonaventura had finally managed so to convince the Prior that he had some special mandate from the Holy Father at Rome, that he was actually permitted to lead his bodyguard of reckless devils into the Friar's chamber. Here

188

he had made them open the sacred alcove and wrench from its recess and carry downstairs the imperturbable Head.

With the person of Bacon himself he could not meddle, for the Prior of Bumset was alone responsible for his official prisoner; but it was a startling as well as a bewildering surprise to him when the Friar made not the very faintest attempt to resist this sacrilegious and autocratic invasion of his chamber, but from an absolutely calm and wholly preoccupied absorption in what he was writing at his table, simply looked up once or twice, neither smiling nor frowning, but treating the whole incident as if the General of the Order and his piratical allies were so many negligible mice.

Of what happened later, when Bonaventura, leaving the destruction of the Brazen Head to his reckless allies, had honoured and delighted the Prior by consenting to share that epicurean ecclesiastic's evening meal and to sleep that night under the priory roof, neither the Baron of Cone nor his over-wrought lady could ever get a clear or consecutive account.

It was obviously due to the commonsense and tact—yes! and no less to the courage—of Raymond de Laon that young Sir William was spared any grievous shock, whether to his person, or to his "amour propre," or to his reputation, in the confused mêlée that accompanied the triumphant departure of the excited bandits of Lost Towers, carrying with them into the depth of the forest the Brazen Head.

They were not as numerous as they seemed to be, nor half as formidable, and they were so proud of being given "carte blanche" to be the violent executioners of the will and purpose of the Pope of Rome that they couldn't resist shouting and dancing in a wild orgy of excitement round the mysterious object they were carrying.

Many of them waved spears and javelins. Others brandished two-edged swords. A few carried torches, and some had bows and arrows with which they just amused themselves, shooting blindly into the pine-trees above their heads, as if to dislodge any living creature who might be there, whether bird or bat or squirrel or wild-cat, anything in fact that might be up there and could be hit by a random shot. It took four of them to bear the weight of the Brazen Head, which they had fastened with ropes to a couple of fir-poles, and which in the thick grey darkness looked like the head of some colossal decapitated giant whom they had caught asleep.

The confused henchmen of Baron Boncor, who were much better armed, but at the same time much less certain of the reason of their arming, or of the cause of the turmoil, than any other of the groups involved, were endeavouring, in a thinly-dispersed, widely-scattered circle, to enclose the wild men of Lost Towers till they could be assaulted from every side at once and compelled to surrender their animate-inanimate spoil. The formation of this mobile circle had been the plan of Raymond de Laon and it would have been a very good plan if the course of events had followed any sort of rational order. But at that time of night and with no less than three Baronies, each acting like the troop of a separate dominion, events were badly diverted from their logical cause-and-effect sequence.

De Laon himself, armed with a long straight sword, and with a small round shield almost exactly like some of the shields depicted on certain ancient vase-paintings, kept running at full speed round this extended circle, exhorting its human figures to draw in as steadily and resolutely as possible round this dancing and shouting crew of excited bandits.

Young John of the Fortress, who hadn't been left for long without full information of what was happening in regard to the greatest of all the inventions of his admired instructor, had soon appeared on the scene with a rather eccentric couple of Roque-Manor adherents ready to follow their leader anywhere, but really rather out for adventure than for any particular cause or principle; and all John did was to lead them blindly forward, straight towards the bandits who were carrying the Brazen Head, the appearance of which made the lad think, the moment he caught sight of it under the flickering torches, of the description in the Jewish Scriptures of the "Ark of the Covenant" containing the spiritual presence of Jehovah.

So well had all the Fortress people been trained by their lord and lady to keep an eye on Tilton and John and Lil-Umbra, while they let these young people feel they were completely free to act as they pleased, that the nearer young John—who had no weapon but a peculiar kind of axe fastened to a long pole, a weapon he had invented for himself—

approached this thing of mystery, the more closely was he hedged in by two free-men of the Manor of Roque, who were both equally eccentric, but who could at a pinch hoist John upon their shoulders and make off with him.

All might have gone well for the friends and liberators of the Brazen Head; and the madly chanting bandits of Lost Towers might have been put to headlong flight, leaving their projected victim, free from even a single hammer-blow, staring up at his rescuers in divine detachment from his bed upon the silvery-grey ground-lichen, had it not been for one of those annoying accidents that we love to call "ironical", because by the use of this classic word we endow the antics of acrobatic chance with a conscious flightiness that takes away the shame of our human frustration and defeat.

What actually happened was that at the very moment when young John and his supporters came near to advancing point-blank upon the ruffians who carried the Bronze Head, Sir William Boncor, the youngest belted knight of the longest-reigning monarch in the world, stumbled over a hole in the earth containing the offspring, a male and a female, of the common badger.

These little creatures had been well-suckled that day at noon by their mother; and as a result they crept in a sleepy manner to the mouth of their hole, thinking to themselves that the moment had come for a little independent exploration of the forest; but they felt so satisfied, and so cosy and comfortable, and also so sleepy, that they soon relinquished this desire, and curling themselves up fell into a deeper sleep than they had enjoyed for months.

And it was this happy sleep that was disturbed by the sharply-spurr'd heels of portly little Sir William. These came down on both their little heads, completely separating them from their necks and crushing them together into a pulp of flesh, bones, blood, and bloody hair, against a slab of rock-slate. It was upon this rock-slate thus plastered with a gouache of bones, blood, brains and hair that both the heels of our youthful knight slid awkwardly forward, bringing him down with a mighty crash upon his back-side and extracting from him the sort of indignant and outraged howl against the whole causal sequence of events that had led to this culminating collapse, such as an

191

infant who can run and cry but cannot yet talk naturally utters when brought low.

This event proved to be a turning point in this chaotic skirmish, for it completely brought to an end all further participation of Cone Castle in the confused mêlée. Raymond de Laon, hurrying to pick up the fallen knight, whose howl he knew half-a-mile away, was soon followed by the rest of the Cone party, which was naturally, since it was all happening at the foot of Cone Castle, more numerous than John's followers from Roque; and the result of this was that the blood-and-dirt-clad bearers of the Brazen Head, still recklessly blundering through the darkness, looking for a rock, or a heap of rocks, where they could smash the Head into smithereens, were only followed with any real obstinate determination by the eccentric couple of Fortress-men who through thick and thin stuck to young John.

John himself was agitated through his whole nature. This was the first time he had found himself engaged in a physical struggle the issue of which, whether bad or good, affected what was the main preoccupation of his life—his devotion to Friar Bacon and his work. The Lost Towers gang were still shouting and jesting and leaping and dancing through the darkness, as they swung the Brazen Head, bound with cords to a couple of poles, from one pair of bearers to another; and every now and then they banged at it with some log of wood they picked up in passing, or with some incongruous piece of culinary iron, that, like John's own axe on a pole, was in some ways more deadly than an ordinary sword or spear.

They soon had gone so far, and John had had to follow them so fast, that not only was he himself completely puzzled as to the direction in which he was being led, but his two quaint attendants seemed as much at a loss as he was. One of these was a certain red-haired freeman of the manor called Colin Catteract, whose thin body, long shanks and peculiarly malleable physiognomy, instantaneously expressive of every fantasy that came into his head, made him by the destiny of his inmost identity the sort of individual who is born to be a player, a performer, an actor, especially in such a rôle as a court-clown or king's jester.

The other was at the extremest opposite pole of human

perversity. His name was Ralph Riddel-de-Rie, and he was the best carpenter in Roque, but he had such a habit of using the expression, "clamp 'em up"—an expression that always suggested to the old ex-bailiff in the armoury the figure of some colossal demiurgic world-carpenter, fitting the Earth and the Moon into the sun's chariot, before passing on to deal with Orion or the Pleiades—that he'd got the permanent nickname of "Clamp". He was a short, squat, stumpy man, and was extremely reticent. But when he did utter any opinion, he did so in a portentous tone of grim and final decision.

The present moment however certainly lent itself better to the airy-fairy vivacity of Colin than to the heavy-weather determination of Clamp. These accurst bandits might be in a riotous mood at the moment, but they were skilled in making their way through all the regions of this locality, a locality where the densest thickets or bushes and brakes often led to morasses and pools and reedy swamps, out of which again, in still more surprising contrast, rose grassy slopes and mossy undulations, pillared by tall pines: and they could accomplish this, so completely did they know the whole district, in darkness as well as in the clearest moonlight.

Young John now began to experience real terror. Whither was he being led, he and his friends Colin and Clamp? Were they being decoyed, cunningly and artfully, by this dramatic show-off of a bacchanalian riot, round the utmost outskirts of the Manor of Roque, towards the very brink of the Lost Towers swamp?

It was extremely painful to him to watch that great dim phantasm of a Human Head go bobbing up and down in front of this mad crew; and he began to experience a strange feeling about the Head and a weird fear that *It* itself—yes! this magical construction of an inventor acting the part of God— might play Satan towards its Creator, and go over to the enemy!

The bandits, after all, weren't so numerous. There were only about a dozen of them. John had already counted them. And it was clear to him that they were moving much more slowly than at the start. He and his companions had now not the slightest difficulty in keeping up with them. The odd thing was, that though, first one, and then another, among those who were not at the moment helping with the Head, turned round to take a good look at the three men, so obstinately following them, nobody made the faintest attempt to attack them or to stop their pursuit. Could he regard it as possible that they were waiting till they reached some particular spot on the borders of Lost Towers, some spot where they had already arranged that others of their band should await them, possibly under the command of Baron Maldung himself?

John's uneasiness finally rose to such a pitch over the various terrifying possibilities his mind conjured up that he called his two friends to a halt under a massive pine-tree, and put to them the blunt and drastic question whether the three of them were, or were not, rushing madly into a grievous snare? Agitated though he was John couldn't help being struck by the quaint contrast his two supporters made as he produced his small box of flint and tinder and put a light to the unlit torch Colin was carrying.

Colin himself had already begun to laugh, as was his habitual custom under all the chances and changes of mortal life. When he laughed, which was a simple and natural return to his normal condition, his childishly excited face, with the straight, pale, yellow hair waving above it, assumed the appearance of a flickering candleflame, of which his thin flexible body was the candlestick or empty bottle, from which protruded the finger of wax which contained the burning wick.

John had grown vaguely aware as they ran, though it was too dark to make out exactly what was happening to this companion of his, that poor Colin had begun to suffer, under the stress of their effort, some queer change in his appearance; and it was a comfort to see him restored once more to his accustomed look of a wildly blown candle in a dark bottle.

The stoical Clamp, on the contrary, turned towards them both in that flickering torch-ray his usual expression of obstinate indifference to all outward circumstance, or, to be more rigidly correct, to everything that occurred, whether it occurred within the mind or outside the mind.

It was clear that what Master Clamp had been destined by nature to be, or had by sheer force of will moulded himself into being, was what you might call a *conscious inanimate*, a thing made of wood, or of leather, or of baked clay, whose whole outward and inward nature implied submission—submission to whatever it might be, nervously interior or mechanically exterior, that pushed, impelled, flung, thrust, projected, rejected, lowered, elevated, inflamed, inspired, benumbed, froze, petrified it, according to a definite purpose.

He had a store of rhyming patter which he was in the habit of using as a sort of oil, or slaver, or low-pitched humming accompaniment to this sub-human submission to fate. He would say, without the least flicker of protest, or of complaint, far less of indignation: "That's the gear; I've got it clear: I've got to climb the bank up there. I've got to swish that river through. Under those bushes I've got to go, whether the danger's from spear or bow. It may wipe me off; it may help me on. We be all born; but we bain't all gone."

At this particular moment for instance, while Colin was laughing with his hair, his eyes, his lips, his skin, his ribs, his hips, his shins, his ankles, and with the fluttering fingers of both his hands, what Clamp said was: "If them's going to kill we, them's going to kill we; and if us be going to kill they, that's how t'will be; us'll be alive and them'll be stark staring. Jesus Holy will be Jesus Holy just the same; and Uncle Satan will be Uncle Satan just the same. Yes, frost will freeze and fire will burn and water will drown just the same, whether Roque eat up Towers or Towers eat up Roque. Freeze and burn and drown them will, whether a girt wave of the sea swallows all the bloody land in this blasted world, or whether the waves of every sea on the earth dry up and turn into the sands of the Desert of Sodom; just the same will it be for me, just the same will it be for thee, and just the same for this quiet old tree."

Young John kept turning this torch that Colin had been carrying so carefully for him, and that he himself had so carefully lit, from one vista of the forest to another, and then to the trunk of the tree at their side, and then up to the misty sky. And he thought in his heart:

"How many moments like this have passed for how many men like me since the beginning of the world! Here I am with these two: one dancing and chuckling with glee simply because he doesn't know whether we're going to save the Friar's Brazen Head or not, and the other already sick to death of the whole affair, and ready to be dead rather than make the effort to go on with it! And when I think how my Friar, who is, since Archimedes, the wisest sage and subtlest inventor in history, has created this Head and has given it enough brain to think and enough language to say what it thinks, and how this band of crazy miscreants is at this moment hunting for some heap of stones whereon and wherewith they may hammer it to fragments, I feel as if—as if——"

And at this point John indeed felt so much as if he were gazing into a bottomless garbage-pit of the whole creation that he concluded his thoughts with a lamentable sigh, a sigh so deep that Colin ceased to laugh upwards and Clamp ceased to groan downwards, while the six troubled apertures which those three persons called their eyes just stared at one another.

And then, without any warning at all, a startling hullabaloo rose widely into the air from the men they were following; and a wild medley of sounds made up of cries, shouts, screams, howls, appeals, threats, curses, surged tumultuously through the forest.

"Come on, for heaven's sake!" gasped young John, brandishing his blazing torch in one hand and his grotesque axe at the end of a pole in the other, and rushing headlong towards the tumult. What they saw when they arrived was the towering figure of Peleg the Mongolian, swinging his terrifying mace with its orbicular head of iron spikes, but himself in evident danger of his life.

John shuddered when he saw what was threatening this strongest of all the supporters of his parents. For two of the Lost Towers men, each of them with one of his knees on the ground while on the other he balanced the end of his bow, were shooting arrow after arrow at him; and already the head-feathers of two arrows were sticking out of his left shoulder.

Luckily for Peleg he was wearing about his shoulders a thick leathery scarf, and so, though the points of the arrows entered his flesh and stuck there, they did not really seriously wound him. Of our three friends young John with his funny-looking weapon and his torch was in front, and queerly enough it was the humpty-dumpty figure of Clamp that was a close second, while Colin, the long-legged, flipperty-flappity antic, made a poor third. This happened, either because, in spite of all his zest for life, Colin was scared of facing the arrows of that dangerous pair, or because—but these secrets belong to those interior thoughts about which not even the boldest historian dares to be dogmatic—if he'd been in front of Clamp, he'd have missed the exquisitely comical sight of the heroic spurt in which that grim little stoic indulged himself at the final lap.

But suddenly, as young John had often in his short life noticed before, but had put it down to the spiritual atmosphere of that particular district, and had even interpreted it to his brother Tilton as the influence of some quite definite "genius loci," the whole situation reversed itself in an instant, and in a contagious rush of wild and desperate panic, the gang of bandits, with those two competent arrow-shooters taking the lead, fled as fast as it was possible for active outlaws to flee, in the general direction of Lost Towers. It was now revealed to John that Peleg with his mace had not been alone when the three of them had heard this unnatural noise in the forest and had hunted it down.

And what made the whole lot of the bandits scoot off in terror was not Peleg's giant size nor his mace, but the sudden apparition, just to the left of those two kneeling bowmen, of what struck the whole lot of them as a Supernatural Being, possibly the Mother of God Herself, come to put an end to their nonsense.

It was Ghosta. But her black robe, and her white head-covering, and also, though it was too dark to see her features, her formidable dignity of movement, evoked, at that time of night, a spasm of awe that must have resembled the bewildered panic which some prowling rascal, up to no good, would have experienced had he drifted and loafed, without knowing in the least where he was going, along a cemetery path leading to the particular tomb out of which, at the very moment he arrived, Lazarus was being called forth from the dead.

The terror produced by the appearance of Ghosta was of course accentuated by her own powerful spirit. Tough nerves and thick skins and simple minds are sometimes dominated quite unexpectedly by a particular type of formidable intelligence, an intelligence which may easily strike those affected by it as supernatural, whereas in reality it may only be the power of an inspired personality.

Young John himself was affected by the apparition of Ghosta. His heart glowed within him, as, panting for breath after his run and waving his torch in a vigorous boyish manner, he stood staring at the Brazen Head which itself at that moment in the torch-light looked quite as indifferent to all outward events as Clamp himself, whose eyes kept turning heavily from the arrows in Peleg's shoulder to Ghosta's black robe, as if both these noticeable things had only been door-handles needing professional attention.

At any rate when Ghosta, who held a small lantern in her hand, came forward and moved straight to her gigantic Mongolian friend, it was not only those two arrow-shooters, both of whom leapt to their feet in consternation, who bolted in desperate panic, but every man-jack of that whole Lost Towers crowd.

Down on the earth fell the Brazen Head along with the poles on which it was carried and the cords by which it was tied, and a strange and sudden silence fell on the whole forest. Ghosta must have already seen young John and his friends approaching, but she did not even look round as they drew near. She had gone straight up to Peleg; and by the time John was at their side she had pulled out both the arrows which indeed the young man had already surmised must have left only shallow flesh-wounds, and was already bandaging the bleeding places with strips of white linen.

Did she always carry about with her, the young man wondered, these useful medicaments, or had she torn them from her own garments as she approached the scene?

The interest of both Colin and Clamp was concentrated on the Brazen Head upon which John's torch, though only held mechanically in his hand, now flung a direct blaze of light. The violent jolt with which the Head had been dropped, in the supernatural panic produced by Ghosta's appearance, had flung it clear of the poles and had dislodged from its shoulders one of the two ropes, that bound it.

The blaze of torch-light now flung upon its indefinitely moulded features gave it a most extraordinary expression. Its gaze was fixed upon Something. But upon what? That was the question which the airy Colin, as he whirled about it in protracted circle after circle, turning, so to speak, on his own axis, as he made of it a sort of cosmogonic axis for his saraband, and the round-bellied Clamp as he picked up a broken segment of rotten wood from the ground and leant on it, pressing his chin into the moss that covered its natural handle, might well have both been pondering, for they were obviously magnetized as they stared at it, to what degree it actually had been endowed with consciousness.

Its features had been so mistily and vaguely indicated by its human creator that it would have been as impossible for the most inquisitive scrutinizer to make out any expression at all. They seemed to have been arranged by their designer to prevent the possibility of their being used as a medium for any one single human emotion.

The contemplation of them always gave young John the feeling that he was surveying a wide-spread landscape from the top of a mountain. But the Head's eyes were undeniably gazing at something. Was this something a completely different world from the one out of whose elements its human creator had fashioned it, a different world in fact from the one with which we are all familiar?

Ever since the flight of that riotous Lost Towers band it had struck both the mind and the senses of our friend John that a strange silence had fallen upon the whole forest. Was this in fact due, John asked himself, to some real mental gesture of the Brazen Head?

Was it possible that, in creating this automatic Being, Friar Bacon had really created a living actual mind different altogether from all the minds so far created by the natural processes of life and nature? If this was possible, if in fact this is exactly what *had* happened, might it not be, John couldn't help wondering, that the activity of a mind, whose power of thought was completely different from any mind that has ever existed in the world before, might have such a formidable effect upon the mysterious galvanic forces that constitute the motions of the universe that a definite change would soon become evident not only in every star and planet in the firmament but in every living creature, however small and helpless, in our own immediate earth?

With such thoughts obscurely flitting through his brain John left Ghosta and Peleg to their enjoyment of what he imagined must have been for them both one of the most important moments in their lives. Together they had vanquished the enemy; and John felt sure that after Ghosta's ministration the giant's arrow-hurts would soon heal.

What he didn't feel sure of, as he turned from the two Hebraic lovers to Colin and Clamp, who were by this time engaged in what looked like an extremely absorbing whispered argument, was what effect this shock of falling with a jerk upon the earth would have upon the Head itself.

John had now been left, by the movement, so it seemed to him, of unadulterated fate, alone with the Head. He moved up so close to it that he soon stood within an arm's reach of those inchoate and incomprehensible features.

The Head's face, though it had been emptied by the deliberate intention of its creator, of all *human* expression, was in no way a blank face. The young man couldn't help uttering an inward and entirely inarticulate prayer to that chaotic brazen physiognomy, while he made absurd attempts to rouse it to some emotion, if only to the emotion of anger, by moving the fiery gleam of the torch he held with repeated switches and twitches and flashes and dashes and whirlings and twirlings between himself and that imperturbably chaotic visage.

But the countenance of the Brazen Head remained completely unmoved. John might just as well have endeavoured to evoke an earthquake or a volcanic eruption by brandishing his torch at the floor of the forest, or to draw down flashes of lightning and torrents of rain by challenging with it what could be seen of the black sky above the tops of the dark trees!

But suddenly the young man felt impelled to stop playing this silly game, and to shift the manner of his hold upon the torch he was carrying. He now began holding it as humbly and reverently as if he were at the rear end of a long procession of worshippers who were moving towards a temple.

And he made this change at the identical moment when they all heard a familiar voice calling to them from the forest and not very far away.

"Good God!" cried John, "that's the old man! I'd know his voice anywhere! Peleg, do you hear him? It's the old bailiff! What on earth is *he* doing out there at this time of night? The family would be furious if they knew! How have they let him get out of the Fortress? Is he alone?"

But John was talking now to nobody but Ghosta; for Peleg

had at once responded to the voice, and had been followed at a mad rush by Colin, whose crazy chucklings and wild gestures had been reduced to the purposeful leapings of a high-mettled steed, and also by Clamp, who kept blurting out as he bounced and bumped along, "I know'd it! I know'd it! I know'd it! I could have told 'ee the whole tale if ye'd cuzzensented to ask it of I! Yes, I could have lighted up this whole blind, blubbered, bloated, blistered fog-patch we've gone and got lost in! Why didn't ye come to I 'stead of letting this kid of a Colin What's-a-clock show itself off?"

And indeed it now struck young John, who was standing close to Ghosta, while she calmly watched the tide of events, that it was only the special kind of darkness of this particular night that had prevented them from recognizing how close they were at this moment to that little postern-door into the Fortress, of which Tilton and he had made use all their lives.

"Here we all are, Master!" The genial voice of the Jewish Mongol carried such an implication of relief, of storms over and haven reached at last, that, as Ghosta moved forward to greet the old bailiff, John knew at once that his flash of insight was absolutely correct, and that they were now at this actual moment at the furthest end of the thick group of oaks and pines, which he had looked at since he was a child and about which, since they were first conscious of such things, they had heard their parents arguing.

Lady Val had always wanted to have those trees cut down, or at least considerably thinned out, as she regarded them as a perfect ambush both for wolves and for wolfish men; but such dense thickets of forest-growth were what, in the whole of Roque, her husband, who was a born hunter, especially loved.

Ghosta had never met the ex-bailiff before, as the old man only left the armoury for the Fortress dinner, his other meals being brought to him as he sat by the fire; so there now ensued in that wild place quite a formal and even courtly ceremonial. John felt it was incumbent upon him in the absence of both the lord and the mistress of the Manor, as well as of their elder son, to play the part of host; and the already somewhat exhausted old gentleman, who approached them leaning very heavily on Peleg's arm, was now compelled to stand as erect as he could and shake hands, not only with Ghosta, but with both Colin and Clamp, while John, constantly interrupted by each gentleman in turn, did his best, with a good deal of blundering pedantry and not a little silly facetiousness, to introduce the one as a lively court-jester and the other as a disillusioned, cynical sage.

But, before he had finished, the look of pitiful exhaustion on the ex-bailiff's face forced him to interrupt himself.

"Here, master," he murmured, "sit down on *this,* and lean your back against *this!*" And lugging off the sheep's wool neck-cloth that he had been wearing all that night, he laid it on the ground under the nearest tree-trunk and helped the old man to sit down.

Ghosta at once bent over him, while Colin and Clamp moved off. "Where—is—the—the—the Head?" murmured the old man anxiously, turning his own head this way and that.

Ghosta took the torch from John and ran to Peleg's side; and John noticed that the first thing she whispered to the giant must have had to do with the arrow-wounds he'd received, for the giant promptly uncovered the places and held the light for her while she examined them.

"So all's well?" John heard him utter in an interrogative whisper; and it was clear to him that the reply was reassuring.

As soon as she came back, still holding the torch, she asked the old man whether he wanted Peleg to bring the Brazen Head near to him, so that he could examine it. John could see that this bold question at once excited and troubled the ex-bailiff, for, snatching at Ghosta's robe, he pulled her towards him till she sank on one knee, the torch held at arm's length above her head.

After a second's hesitation the old man began a rather bewildering and long-winded rigmarole about something he wanted to ask John. With considerable difficulty, but with more tact than he knew he possessed, John now listened to an agitated and complicated account of a conversation the ex-bailiff of Roque had had earlier in the month with John's sister, Lil-Umbra.

The old gentleman seemed to have been deeply impressed not only by Lil-Umbra's beauty but by her intelligence; and, as far as her young brother could make out from what he now heard, there had come a moment in the conversation when some mysterious presence, a presence whose nature neither of them really comprehended, seemed to come between them and to hover over them.

The old man had got it lodged in his head—John could see as much as that—that there was some magic bond, or some fatal link, between this mysterious Brazen Head of Friar Bacon's invention and a beautiful young woman; and John himself was anxious to learn whether his own vague sense of something weird and unusual, and something that he couldn't describe as either good or evil, either angelic or devilish, had been felt by Lil-Umbra also.

Old Heber's hope was that Lil-Umbra may have talked to John about it; as he knew she was in the habit of discussing religious matters with both her brothers. The truth really was that Lil-Umbra's nerves were so strung-up, and her heart was in such a state of tension, as to whether Raymond de Laon would or would not come to the armoury that night, that the whole subject of Friar Bacon and his Brazen Head passed her by very lightly indeed.

But now to the complete surprise of both the young man and the old man, and somewhat to the displeasure of Peleg, who by this time was towering above the three of them, and was by no means indifferent to this thing they were discussing, Ghosta broke in. "What was wanted," she said quietly, "to the completion of Friar Bacon's creation I was myself ready to supply; and at the request of the Friar, I did supply it."

The sound of Peleg's voice above their heads had a queerly hoarse note in it at this moment. "The best thing we can do tonight," he said slowly, "is to carry the Head out of this forest and into the Fortress; and I would suggest that we straightway convey it into the armoury where it will remain under the particular protection of our friend here. I believe"— and at this point the giant laid his hand on the young man's shoulder—"that your Father, Master John, will have no objection when he learns of this having been done. I don't think our conveying the Head into the armoury need disturb anybody's night's rest. In fact I can make certain that it doesn't by carrying it there myself, while Ghosta helps you, master bailiff.

"No one can have heard you leave or they'd have come with you. No one but yourself, I expect—isn't that the case, master bailiff?—heard the noise those wretched Lost Towers men were making; and as you came out you couldn't possibly have barred the door. The whole Fortress is no doubt asleep at this moment; and we shall take care to move so silently that we shan't disturb a living soul in the place. I'll be glad enough to have a rest and a lie-down myself; but I'm not so done-in as not to be able to take this old Brazen Head into our armoury! Once there, I warrant nobody will dare to meddle with it. It'll soon become a regular shrine, and as sacred as Master Tilton's Blessed Virgin."

While her giant was addressing them above their heads, Ghosta and the old man, who still had his back against the tree and John's woollen neck-cloth under his buttocks, were exchanging some extremely curious thoughts. No scrupulous chronicler of human affairs can help being aware out of the instinctive observation of the narrating mind, of the weird manner in which, amid any group of agitated people, when one voice has been monopolizing everybody's attention for several minutes, a hollow gulf of silence is created, across which all manner of disturbing thoughts pass from one person to another.

John himself at this moment, in *his* corner of this psychic gulf created by Peleg's somewhat dictatorial and irritable monologue, felt so utterly tired, after all the energy he had spent that night, that his mind, in its exhausted state, like the mind of a person who stares vacantly at his bed-posts, began vaguely to wonder whether in this silence around them and with this hoarse voice sounding above their heads, other feelings than human ones, might be in the act of being exchanged, feelings for instance of the mosses, of the ferns, of the tree-roots even, that surrounded them on that forest-floor.

Such vegetation-feelings, John pondered, might be entangling themselves with his own human feelings at this very moment; for after all it was this group of trees and bushes which he had known since his infancy, and which, from what he had seen daily of them out of that postern-door of his birthplace, had become like the fireguard in his nursery, a malleable background to every story he told himself in his day-dreams at noon and to every story he was told by his night-dreams at midnight; and it would be only natural if, on *its* side, the background of roots and mosses and ferns and lichens and ivy and blades of grass projected obscure invisible sensations, which flitted in and out of his human ones.

But what was this? There was something else. Yes, there was something else at this moment, something that was intruding itself between the furtive and fitful feelings of mosses and roots and ferns and his own weightier cogitations.

"What the hell," he groaned, "is this confounded thing that has now come into my head?" It was certainly in accordance with the multifarious influences that flit about in our life-stream, like shadowy tadpoles beneath thin ice, that it should have been what the Brazen Head itself was thinking—those thoughts, not of a God-created man, but of a man-created machine, which now butted in, like a misty cloud in the shape of the Minotaur, between the vegetation-feelings of that forest recess and the ideas, whatever they were, that were being exchanged between Ghosta and the old man with his back against the tree.

For there is no doubt that the "something" of which John suddenly became aware was some thought from the Brazen Head. And what the chronicler of these things cannot escape calling to mind was the lack of response that the old ex-bailiff had found in John's sister Lil-Umbra when the latter, her head full of the possible appearance of Raymond de Laon in the armoury, was doing her best to be nice to him. But this lack of response was now wholly compensated for in the old bailiff's mind by Ghosta's attitude.

Young John and the old man were however both vaguely conscious that it was some mysterious connection between the Brazen Head and Ghosta that was now giving to the voice of Peleg, as it rumbled hoarsely above their heads, an irritable and dictatorial tone. The giant concluded with these words: "I'll fetch the Head now, and carry it straight to the postern; for I can see exactly where we are, torch or no torch! Better give the torch back to Master John, Ghosta, and then you all——" and he threw this out, like a handful of crumbs, in the direction of Colin and Clamp, who, conscious of not being altogether indispensable as the drama thickened, had linked themselves together in the last few minutes in a rather childish though very natural way.

Clamp had picked up a moss-grown stick from the ground that had a couple of tiny ferns growing out of the middle of it, and had poked Colin with it to show him this phenomenon, and the flickering torch had at once revealed those small ferns; and Colin had promptly seized the end of this interesting stick, and now neither of this quaint pair would be likely to relax his grasp.

It was clear that, in their uneasiness as to whether they would be allowed to follow the others into the interior of the Fortress, this mossy stick gave them some curious support, as well as uniting them on this particular occasion.

"And then you can all," Peleg concluded, "follow me to the little door. Isn't that the thing, Master John?"

John, who had begun to long for his comfortable bed in the little room that had been his own now for a couple of years, agreed at once; and Peleg, without even glancing at Ghosta, who had obediently handed the torch to John, snatched up the latter's woollen scarf upon which the old man was no longer sitting, and clapping it upon his own head like a turban, rushed over to where the Brazen Head was surveying them all with the stark indifference of a rocky landscape, and seizing it in his two hands heaved it into the air till he held it propt up on the top of his head. The effort required for this was so great that it drew from him a really terrifying sound, a sound such as Samson must have made when, with the central pillars of the Temple of Dagon in his arms, he bowed himself down and brought down with him the whole of that great building.

An outrush of blood from the two arrow-hurts in his shoulders accompanied this sound; and John, who was close to Ghosta, heard a similar sound, bursting unconsciously it would seem, from her; and it certainly was all he could do to restrain in himself a cry of amazement.

But he had the wit to see what the two of them had to do at this important juncture. He began hurriedly helping the ex-bailiff to his feet. "*You* take hold of him on *your* side," he said to Ghosta, "and I'll help him on my side!"

And then he shouted after the departing figure of their friend, who was carrying away the Brazen Head on his own head as if it were a gargoyle made of the fossilized features of some antediluvian giant, belonging to the same race, though of an earlier breed, as the man who was carrying it. "Wait for us at the postern, Peleg! We'll help you in with it!"

The thoughts and feelings of the old man as he stumbled along over the tree-roots and over the mossy stones, while John's torch flung the sort of wayward and flickering bursts of illumination that can be both angelic guides and devilish betrayers, grew more and more intense and more and more unrestrained as they drew near the postern-gate.

"I'm glad I came out," he told himself, "if only to be able to brood over the unbelievable advantage of being allowed to sit by the fire in my own chair in that faithful old armoury until I die. But—Jesus help us!—these young folk seem to think I'm half-dead already! Not one of them asked me whether I wanted to spend my days and nights with the Friar's Head of Brass! But I'm glad they didn't. For it would have been terribly hard to explain what I *do* want! And now that I come to think of it I seriously believe it was some queer understanding between the Head and me that brought me out here tonight! I wonder what time it is? About two o'clock in the morning, I wouldn't wonder! *It has that kind of feeling*. O! but this Ghosta-girl had better be careful how near to this Head her home-sickness for Palestine and Jerusalem draws her! I didn't have that queer presentiment for nothing that night when I sat with Lil-Umbra waiting for her lover Raymond!

"Sitting alone by the same fire, day in, day out, a person picks up a few little things about life here below, things that great giant Jews dream not of! And when I watched that little sister of yours, Master John, and talked of this same Head, I knew all of a sudden, and for a certainty, that this Thing, created not by God but by Friar Roger, *needed*, to make it complete, to make it its real self, to make it a true oracle of life's hidden secrets, to be in some way connected with a maiden, who, without officially losing her maidenhead to the Head, would lose something of her inmost self, her secretest feminine self, to it, giving it that unique power of revelation, of illumination, of ultimate vision, that virgins alone possess!

"There's the Fortress! We shall be there in a minute! Whether spending the rest of my days with a living intelligence created by man and not by God will lengthen or shorten my days, I don't know and don't greatly care! But that it will make life far more interesting to me is certain. I've always hoped for something like this to happen and now it *has* happened! Maybe this will prove a moment in the history of our race of an importance second only to the creation of Adam! We shall see!

"Meanwhile what I've got to do now is clear. I must make them all take off their shoes, and not utter a word, even in a whisper! And as for this pair of antics, this Colin and Clamp, hanging on to that pathetic old stick as if it were the sceptre of Solomon, I suppose I must find a corner for them to sleep in, in the Manor kitchen. They won't do any harm, wherever they are; and I certainly can't have them in my armoury!"

XIV

FRIAR BACON'S CHAMBER

Several months had passed away into the revolving rubbish-heap of time—or, to placate our final resting-place with a grander name, into the palindromic abyss—since an abode was found for the Head in the armoury of the Fortress and under the guardianship of the old ex-bailiff.

"Why did you straddle me in my nakedness round the neck of that thing of brass?"

These startling words were the first that greeted Friar Bacon from the lips of Ghosta, when the old factotum of his prison-chamber brought her to see him.

"Sit down, my daughter," the Friar replied, laying down his pen and pushing back across the table from beneath his wrists the parchment upon which he was at work.

"There, child, sit down *there*!" And he pointed to an upright seat on the opposite side of the table, a seat which in appearance was the sort of chair that any young girl in any epoch would have associated with some sort of goblin royalty and elfin ritual. "And you may leave me," he added, turning to the lay-brother, "for a few minutes now. I shall not be doing any harm to this good maid, but I want to talk to her alone for a while if you don't mind."

Brother Tuck gave them a quick glance and a grave nod, and, shuffling to the door, took himself off.

"Well, my dear, I'll tell you exactly why, so to speak, I behaved to you as the angel, on Annunciation Day, behaved to our Lady."

"You don't mean, I hope, Father," Ghosta interrupted earnestly, "that you did really marry me to the Head, because

o   209

if you did I must, with all the power I have, beg you to divorce me at once; for the truth is, Father, I want to marry a man of my own faith and my own race, which, as I expect you already know, is the Jewish faith and the Hebrew race. Yes, Father, I belong and always shall belong to the House of Israel; and it is as impossible for me to enter into such a covenant with any Christian as it would be for a sea-gull to swear fidelity to a barn-door fowl!"

"Listen, dear child," said the Friar, speaking very slowly and in a voice that was as grave as if he were reciting a pardon on a scaffold. "There are moments in all our lives when it is necessary for us to act in a way that makes use of both good and evil. In actual reality—for we need not drag in that treacherous word 'truth', which can cover and justify a thousand abominations—in actual living reality we are compelled—and if you ask me 'compelled by whom or by what?' I can only say I do not know—but we are compelled by a force, that may be as much outside the Devil as it is outside God, to do something which is clearly contrary to goodness and righteousness and morality and sanctity and holiness and virtue.

"You must understand, my dear child, that I'm not saying we have at these moments to become one with any devilish power that is opposing God or defying all that the prophets have taught us down the ages. We must honestly recognise, however, that without becoming a part of the Evil Power that opposes itself to God, we are at this particular moment acting contrary to what we know to be the good way and the righteous way.

"The point is that we are acting thus in obedience to a force within us, which we feel by an overpowering instinct to be as much outside the Good as it is outside the Evil, and as much outside God as it is outside the Devil. What we feel, my dear child, at these moments—I mean what I, your old Friar, feels—is that I am obeying an absolutely new revelation, a revelation that may change the entire world."

Ghosta, who had been listening with concentrated attention to all this, now lifted her elbows onto the table and rested her chin upon her two hands.

"Was it a part," she enquired earnestly, "of your creation of a living soul in a Bronze Head to make me embrace that

Image as you did, straddling across its neck in my nakedness? How did you manage to read my secret thoughts and the hidden feelings of my most secret life? For you were right, Father, you were perfectly right. It had been my desire, while remaining a virgin—for I always had an absolute horror of losing my maidenhead—to experience once in my life before I died, the sensation of giving in a clinging embrace the life-drops from my innermost being to *Something* that I pressed close against me.

"It needn't have been a man! That was the queer thing about the longing I had. It was that I, Ghosta, might, in my virginity, and without losing my maidenhead, and indeed, if possible, without having any love for this Something—I didn't care what it was—which I embraced, be the creator of a completely new, new, new,—No! I was never presumptuous enough to think of it as a new world, let me call it a new form of life in the world. I was always—but you know me through and through already, Father, my Friar of Friars—fascinated by the word *Parthenogenesis*.

"It is a long word, and I have been told it is a Greek word, and that its meaning is the giving birth to a new life by a girl without losing her maidenhead or forfeiting anything of her natural virginity. So that when you hoisted me a-straddle that day round the neck of the Head of Brass, with my nakedness pressing against its brazen skin, I had an ecstasy. I said to myself: 'What is happening to me now is the very thing I have always longed for! I am not losing my maidenhead, and yet I am drawing from the inmost depths of myself a dew-drop of living creation.'"

A look of indescribable relief passed over the Friar's troubled face, and he leaned forward across the table and touched with the tips of his long fingers the head which the girl was supporting on her arms as she leant forward.

"The Lord bless thee and keep thee!" he said gravely, "and lift up the light of his countenance upon thee and give thee peace!" And then he added, withdrawing his right hand from his guest's forehead and his left hand from his own manuscript, and tilting his chair a little to the rear on its back legs, "I swear I don't know, my dear daughter, any living woman I could talk to as freely as I am now talking to you. I certainly couldn't do so to any of the ladies who rule the Manors and Castles round here! Have you, my dear child, realized why it is that I go on so steadily refusing all invitations to leave this prison-chamber and go where I'd have more freedom of movement?"

Ghosta smiled a quite whimsical smile. "Yes indeed, Father, I can answer that! This old Prior who is master here, as I know well from my life in the Convent, where the nuns always consider him and his ideas and his policy above any line they are ordered to follow by the lady who immediately rules us, has only one object in life—namely, to enjoy himself as much as he possibly can in the narrow circle into the centre of which fate has dropt him.

"What he has to consider are the hours for meals, for strolling in the grounds, for listening to the anthems and chants from his choir-pew in the chapel, for studying the particular Latin text, whether from the Priory library or from his own private shelves, which carries in its train the largest number of old memories of his far-off youth. Now when we consider this matter quite clearly and honestly, Friar, my revered Father, we find nothing less than the surprising fact that this devotion to his own personal pleasure and interest for the whole of the day, and for whatever portion of the night is at the disposal of his personal will—for we can hardly include the hours when the worthy man is asleep, for our dreams, and I'm sure you'll agree with me there, Father, are *not* under the control of our will—is identical with what thinking people like ourselves are absorbed in.

"Whereas these rulers of great manorial castles, with their Ladies and their Bailiffs, and these royal rulers of great lands with their Treasurers and Chancellors and Bishops and Captains and Princes, are occupied day and night with meddling in other people's affairs, with invading other people's territories, with taking away other people's property, with imprisoning and murdering other people's subjects and citizens. Haven't I been speaking truly, Father, in what I've just said?"

Ghosta had indeed been uttering these unpopular and unorthodox feelings in a voice not only a good deal louder than the one she generally used, but a great deal more heavily charged with emotion.

Friar Bacon brought his chair back to the table with a jerk and stretched out his right arm clear across his manuscript, upon which from the small square aperture in the roof the sun was at that moment throwing down a long straight ray, a ray more crowded with sun-motes than Ghosta, had she been in a mood to observe such things, would have had to confess she had ever seen in a sun-ray before.

In spite of the fact that they were looking straight into each other's eyes, the Friar's gesture was so unexpected that for a second she disregarded it. Then she met it with her own right hand; and, in the warm pressure that followed, the heart-felt alliance between them was sworn and sealed.

The Friar's hand rested once more on the edge of his manuscript, and hers once more clasped its fellow and propped her chin while her elbows remained on the dark, smooth-polished wood of that round table. And now both the Friar and Ghosta smiled at each other and turned their eyes away. This they both did naturally and instinctively; but having done so, the quick and lively perception they each possessed was severally attracted by the quivering and elongated sun-ray above their heads and its myriads of tiny little dancing specks.

"Isn't it queer to think," commented Ghosta, "how many historical characters such as we read about in the scriptures, and such as they lecture about in the universities, like Moses and Joshua and like Plato and Socrates and Julius Caesar and Cicero and Marcus Aurelius, must have noticed in their colleges and palaces and temples, and especially at crucial moments in their lives, these millions of dancing atoms! What did Socrates feel when these tiny atoms came dancing into his cell while he was waiting for the executioner with the Hemlock?"

"A question indeed, my dear!" echoed the Friar. "And I'd mighty well like to hear how Plato, who was so confoundedly clever at reaching that great teacher's secret thoughts, and cleverer still at giving them the particular twist that would make them fit into his own ideal system, would describe how the great self-doomed corrupter of youth would have argued with such an one, if some God had endowed one of those motes up there with the power of speech and started it off on a meta-physical protest against the claim of the human race to be the only judge amid the atomic children of the Cosmos!"

"O Father, my dear Father!" cried Ghosta in huge delight. "*Do* go on imagining what one of those tiny dots of matter would say to Socrates if it did question him!"

"Well! for one thing, my dear child," rejoined the Friar, and then he stopped abruptly.

Ghosta, who was turning from him to that descending sunfall of dancing motes, and then back again to him, had a look of reverence on her face as if he'd really been the great magician that most of his enemies and a few of his friends considered him, and as if he might, at any moment, without moving a hand or a foot, give orders to that sun-stream to alter its course, and as if the sun-ray might obey him, and after making a disconcerting circle round their chamber, might hasten to the door, and vanish down the tower-stairs.

But he went on quite calmly. "Don't you suppose, my dear, that this whole business of being one of the lucky millions of dust-specks, out of the trillions and quadrillions of less lucky ones, must be so exciting to every one of those little objects that the whole of its being would be so absorbed in what is happening to it that it wouldn't have a particle of power left to ask any question of anybody. Yes, and I would say—and wouldn't you, my dear girl, say the same?—that if it had any choice left to it, it would feel it was wiser to lavish all its power of response on that lucky moment than to ponder on suitable philosophical questions to put to——"

At this point they were interrupted by shouts and cries outside, by a clatter of feet on the stairs, and by the flinging open of the door. It was young John who now rushed in, followed by Colin and Clamp, and three or four of the Fortress's most active retainers. John was carrying a broken piece of statuary pressed against his chest; and this he hurriedly flung down on the Friar's bed in the corner, after a quick nervous glance at the despoiled alcove hard-by where once stood the Brazen Head.

"What on earth is this, Master John?" cried Ghosta, rising to her full height and hurrying to the bed to see what the young man had deposited there. But Friar Bacon remained seated with his pen still between his fingers, and the only special movement he made that Clamp and Colin, who were both observing him closely, were able to discern, was that he began to draw some sort of Euclidian figure at the bottom of the parchment in front of him, and that this Euclidian figure was an equal-sided square surrounded by a circle.

"Father! Father!" murmured Ghosta a moment later, "do, for Heaven's sake, look at this!" and, shaking off young John, who tried to hold her back, and advancing straight to the Friar's chair, from the side opposite to where Clamp had already begun to watch with mute and fascinated absorption the movements of the Friar's pen, she thrust under Roger Bacon's eyes what clearly was the broken half of a female head, elaborately chiselled out of a block of very hard stone.

But a torrent of verbal eloquence, like the sound of a breaking wave to the splashing tune of which the Friar studied what Ghosta thrust beneath his eyes, was uttered by the excitable Colin, and accompanied by such lavish gesticulation that it was like being addressed by one of those flocks of winged angels speaking with one voice, such as in religious altar-pieces often form the flying chariot of God the Father as it descends from Heaven.

"The General of the Franciscan Order, this thrice-accurst Bonaventura," cried Colin making his voice resound through every portion of the chamber, and it was as if the quivering sun-ray, which had removed itself altogether, had suddenly returned in a new incarnation of pure sound, "has now with the help of those ruffians from Lost Towers, whom he swears he has converted, and at the command of the Pope, whom he swears he represents, begun meddling with Master Tilton's statue of Our Lady in that shrine he's building!

"And do you know what this false saint has done now? He has started a shocking and wicked rumour, entirely a lie, of course, but you know how these lies spread—that Master John's sister and his brother Tilton have been found guilty of incest! And—as if *that* wasn't enough!—do you know what further lie he's invented? He swears that our Master Tilton, heir to the Manor of Roque and to the Fortress Castle, which his mother's family have held since the days of King Stephen, has an even greater sin on his conscience than incest with his sister! For—says this pretty saint, who behaves far worse than Judas—our Master Tilton has committed the supreme sacrilegious sin, of carving the face of Our Lady in the centre of this shrine so that she shall resemble his sister with whom he has sinned!"

"Has Bonaventura really had the gall, John my friend, to go to such lengths as this man says?"

The Friar's voice was as steady, and his manner as quiet and collected, as if he were referring to no more than a point of propriety in some public, metaphysical debate; but Ghosta noticed that he made a slight motion of his hand as if to wave back a little both Colin and Clamp and the two or three armed men who accompanied them.

"Yes, Master, across my heart and on my life," replied John. "That's what he's done! My mother is so upset that she has shut herself up with my sister and won't allow her to go riding with Raymond de Laon, as the two of them had arranged to do today, for fear that this wretched Bonaventura, with his Lost Towers troop, might kidnap her or imprison her, or even carry her with him in a ship to Rome, as he has already done with other ladies who have been accused of various offences of the same sort.

"As for my father, he refuses to take the thing seriously. He says that Tilton ought to be hunting wild boars in the forest instead of building shrines with his own hands and using Lil-Umbra as his model for the Mother of God. But I notice that he has remained at home since the trouble started, and that he's set a guard outside the shrine, to make sure that this mock-saint doesn't excite his cohort of 'converted' robbers to destroy the whole shrine and ruin Tilton's hard work on it for nearly a year!

"What drove me to come, most honoured Friar, to make a special appeal to you, was the fact that I chanced to hear" —young John flushed a little as he announced this, revealing the fact that he had not been able to resist the temptation to listen at his parents' door—"to hear my father tell my mother that if they attacked the shrine again, or came anywhere near the postern-gate again, he would arm all our people, both serfs and freemen, and make such an attack on that damned Lost Towers as would settle them for ever and a day! You see, most reverend Friar, this man undoubtedly was at one time the Pope's emissary or legate or ambassador or whatever the proper legal name is—round here they use a word for him that's too bawdy to repeat—and no doubt at *that* time when he had the proper seals of office he might have been able to carry off Lil-Umbra, and Tilton too, to Rome and accuse them there. But as it is, with no official credentials from the Pope, and with no proper royal support from our sick King, I don't believe he can do very much to hurt us, except start rumours and spread lies."

Friar Bacon groaned, and bowed his head for a second over his pen and paper. Then he said quietly, but without looking up:

"Sit down a moment, lad, while we consider all this as steadily as we can. What would *you* advise us to do, Ghosta? Both John and I—that's true, isn't it, lad?—hold the view that at most dangerous and ticklish crises, it's often from the feminine mind we get the best hint as to what to do."

Ghosta didn't hesitate a second. "How did the shock of this wicked accusation," she enquired, "strike your sister and brother, Master John?"

"Well, to tell you the truth—" and it was clear to everybody that young John was very glad to be asked that question, "I felt proud of the way they took it! You know it was Nurse who first told us about the dastardly fabricated tale which this devilish wretch started; and we were all together up in the nursery at the top of the house when she blurted it out. Father had come up about this attack on Tilton's shrine; and no sooner had Nurse used the word than Tilton threw his arms round Lil-Umbra's neck, and gave her a great hug and a lot of loud kisses all over her face. 'Don't you mind, my darling!' he cried. 'If I ever tried to do such wickedness to you I'm sure the good God would strike me dead before it was done!'"

Roger Bacon's face lit up with satisfaction, and with a certain humorous amusement too, young John thought, as he eagerly watched him; but the Friar's words when he spoke were anything but final or conclusive:

"But now listen to me, my children both, and you two also my kind friends," and he made a double gesture with the hand that held his pen, one in the direction of Colin, and the other in the direction of Clamp, "what we've got to do now is to think of some way of out-witting this self-appointed representative of the Holy Father, supported—and the thing's not without precedent in the history of our mad purblind human race—by this local nest of rapscallions. If any better idea comes into your head, Ghosta, while I'm explaining my scheme, let's hear it at once, and don't mind interrupting me if you're afraid of forgetting what you suddenly thought of!

"But this is what has just come into my mind as a good plan. A week ago I had a communication from my friend Peter Peregrinus, who is now lecturing in France, to tell me that the famous master in philosophy, Albert of Cologne—who belongs to the Dominican order, and indeed is such a loyal Dominican that, when he speaks in the University of Paris, he defends his view of Aristotle against both all the Arabian and all the Latin Averroists and completely demolishes them—is at this very moment visiting Oxford! This is an astonishing piece of news to me. I *had* heard that he was interested in the *Summa Theologicae* of Alexander of Hales, but I never thought I'd live to hear that the great Albert of Cologne should actually be in this island, still less that he should be visiting Oxford!

"I have exchanged letters with him a good many times, as I suppose all disciples of Aristotle have done, and he and I have always agreed that the science of life didn't end with Plato or with Aristotle or even with Grosseteste or with any other student of philosophy. But, my dears, the reputation of Albert of Cologne all over the world is terrific, greater than that of any other modern master. Every man who can read and write in this whole west country, whether they're Franciscans or Dominicans, Monks, or Friars, Abbots, or Priors or parish priests, have heard nothing but praise of him since they first began their A.B.C.! When you come to metaphysics he's the top boy, so to speak, of the whole *schola mundi*, if you leave out Israel and India and China! Now if we could send to Albertus some wise and diplomatic representative of our side, in this quarrel with Bonaventura, it strikes me that it's not at all impossible that the great teacher from Cologne might be persuaded to come, as the most famous Dominican, to confront this troublesome Franciscan.

"That would soon, as we used to say in Ilchester, 'settle the hash,' of our Bona, the Venturesome! I am perfectly certain that what started the whole thing was the fact that your excellent parents, John, gave shelter in the Fortress to my Brazen Head.

It was this that kindled all this obstinate rage in our ex-legate's mind. He's somehow got it lodged in his one-track sanctified midriff that the Holy Trinity we all worship has received a staggering blow from my having dared to create in the person of my Brazen Head a rival creation to Adam and Eve. I tell you, my good friends, I tell you, John dear, if we could only hit upon the right person to send as an ambassador to the great Albert now in Oxford, a person who would be in a position to escort him down here, with him as the chief Dominican to confront this pseudo-saint of the Franciscans, the whole affair would soon be settled."

As can well be imagined, both Ghosta and John were now murmuring, each with their own special manner of emphasis and intensity, the name of Raymond de Laon; and Friar Bacon, as if to seek still further confirmation of this idea, looked first at Colin and then at Clamp. Both men came so close on getting this faintly interrogative glance that they completely hid the Friar from Ghosta and John, but a double vote of unqualified recognition of Raymond as their Ambassador to Albert of Cologne these two certainly did give; for the voice of Colin seemed to flap its wings in widening circles above every back and every head in the place; and the voice of Clamp seemed to drive in one rusty nail after another as he fastened up their decision over the Norman arch of the event.

"Well then, my friends," cried the Friar, rising from his seat and moving quickly round the two men who were bending over him, "we may take it that our Council chamber has uttered its decisive verdict, and that Raymond de Laon shall be our ambassador to the great Albert in Oxford. Will you convey our request to him, John my lad, and let us know the result as quickly as possible? And now I think I must beg you all to descend to the lower regions of this hospitable Priory; for it is really absolutely necessary for me to finish this page of what I am calling my *Opus Major* before I sleep tonight; and your arrival, gentlemen, is the cause of this necessity, and I cannot tell you how grateful I am to you all for being this same cause.

"For the real truth is that your sudden appearance and the more than startling interest of what you have announced to me, combined with the expectation of encountering, man to man, he a Dominican and myself a Franciscan, the great Albert of Cologne, has caused me to remember certain intensely important details that I had completely forgotten relating to the journey of Brother William of Rubruck to the Grand Khan at Karakorum in Tartary, where he stayed from December 1253 till July 1254.

"It was Brother William himself when I met him in Paris who told me these things; and although at this moment I was writing about the sermon he told me he preached in Constantinople on Palm Sunday 1253, I had absolutely forgotten that great congress of religions over which the Mongolian Khan presided at Karakorum, a congress of the Mohammedan, Buddhist, and Christian religions, and I really must write about it while it has come back so vividly to my mind. I am sure I would have left out Brother William's description of that Karakorum congress of religions altogether if our little meeting tonight, and our decision to send an ambassador to bring the head of the Dominicans to deal with the head of the Franciscans, hadn't stirred up my memory of what the brother told me."

A universal murmur, in such low tones among themselves as almost to convey the impression that, having been thus commended for stirring up the Friar's mind, they were seized with the fear of so disturbing it by their lively discussion that the effect on his *Opus Major* would be destructive of the good they had already done, was the immediate result of this grateful appeal to their courtesy. Then without another word, and headed by Colin and Clamp, and followed by Ghosta and young John, they gave a series of quaint little good-night salutations and descended the stairs.

XV

VISITOR FROM PICARDY

Friar Bacon was left standing alone in that topmost chamber of Bumset Priory. He still held the handle-end, so to speak, of the pen he had been using when he rose to return their valedictory gestures; and now automatically began moving it to and fro, as if the talk-charged air of that recently crowded room were itself the parchment upon which it was his destiny to hand down to posterity his ideas and his discoveries. Strange and far-reaching were the thoughts that passed through his head.

"Here am I," he told himself, "one of the curious animals produced upon this planet that have come to be called men, and are now confronted by the necessity of recording for the benefit of future specimens of such creatures, what were the actual causes of our appearance upon this particular promontory of matter."

The Friar at this point ceased inditing invisible words upon the invisible air, and, after deliberately replacing his pen upon the table by the side of his unfinished parchment page, crossed over to his bed and stretched himself out on his back upon it, with his head on the pillow, and clasped his shins with his hands.

"Little did I think," he pondered, "what I should be doing in three years that night when Fontancourt showed me the letter he'd just had from our friend Petrus! Didn't Fontancourt swear to me that Petrus would never stop studying magnetism or writing about his studies? Three years ago that was! O God, O God! what things have happened since then and are still happening!

221

"Why didn't I tell those fellows just now before they went away that it was Peter Peregrinus, and not their old Roger, who first thought of using a lodestone to draw like to like; and that if it hadn't been for that divine inspiration of his I could never have invented my Brazen Head? How we damnable inventors do love to hug our inventions and get drunk on the glory of them! And now I must needs defend my precious discoveries by setting this Dominican wolf upon our Franciscan fox!"

At this point the Friar let his thin legs sink down side by side on his bed, and lifting his clasped hands as high above his head as they could reach began murmuring—not in Latin, far less in Hebrew, but in the Wessex dialect of his native Ilchester—a homely and natural prayer: "O Everlasting God, who lookest down from far outside all this curst universe of matter which thou hast created"—and here he couldn't resist using, with a wry touch of the incorrigible humour which not only characterized all his intercourse with others, but displayed itself even in his secretest thoughts about himself, and about the whole confused arena of contemporary speculation, as a little private joke between God and himself, the quaint, precise, technical, academic and metaphysical phrase for "outside our whole system of things", namely the phrase "*ab exstrinsico*", which, as he now muttered it aloud with a sort of chuckle in that slowly darkening room, would have had a queer effect upon any eavesdropper—"and *ab exstrinsico* save me!"

But after making this appeal to the Mystery at the back of all life, Roger Bacon closed his eyes with such a peaceful sigh that it was clear that he himself felt perfectly satisfied with his little private interview with his creator.

The Friar's descent, or ascent shall we say, into the blessed land of oblivion, now gently and deliciously invaded by the feathered dreams of sleep, was soon disturbed however by a resolutely firm and yet cautiously light knocking at the door, a knocking which did not wake him at first, but mingled with his dreams, and mingled with them in such a curiously prophetic manner that he became vividly aware, even before he awoke, of the personality of the intruder, who was none other than his faithful friend and devoted adherent of a great many years, his servant Miles.

Miles and he had indeed been young men when their association first began, and Miles always absolutely refused to be known by any other name than this Roman word for a soldier. Miles came from the old Roman town of Durnovaria, a town which the people of Wessex had already begun to call Dorchester, just as the older name of Friar Roger's own ancient market-town had recently come to be changed into Ilchester.

Yes! His waking dream had not misled him. There, in the fading, late-afternoon twilight, when he went to the door and opened it, standing erect on the threshold, was his friend, his man, his devoted under-study, his partner, his disciple, his obedient slave, his servitor, his alter ego, Miles of Dorchester!

"Master!" cried Miles in an ecstasy of joy; and flinging his hawk-feather cap into the middle of the room, he fell upon his knees, clasped the Friar tightly round the waist, and pressed his forehead hard against his hero's navel.

"There, there, there!" murmured this latter reassuringly and tenderly, and very much in the tone with which a responsive dog-lover would soothe a majestic, over-emotional, over-sensitive wolf-hound; and as he spoke he raised Miles to his feet, led him across the floor incidentally picking up the man's hawk-feather cap and handing it to him as they went, and seating him in the chair recently occupied by Ghosta, sat down opposite to him and laid his two clasped fists upon his page with the air of one who has decided to substitute some different form of urgent pressure for the one associated with pens and parchment.

One remarkable peculiarity of the man Miles was the way his countenance altered in a moment from a majestic, monumental, and commanding reserve, not unmixed with an astute alertness that had in it something of the primeval and bottomless cunning of a simple animal, into a melting abandonment to an emotion of devotion so extreme that it was almost painful to witness.

The Friar pressed his hand on the man's shoulder as he himself got up again to set before them both some wine and a couple of goblets. Then, when the Dorchester-born warrior, who, while lifting his glass, looked, with his massive neck and his clear-cut profile, distinctly like a well-known bust of Caesar Augustus, had rested and refreshed himself a little, the Friar put the straight question to him, "Well, old friend," he enquired, "and what's the news?"

"He's down there now. I left him in the lobby. They are all busy in the kitchen, and the Prior's begun his dinner. So I left him in that dark entrance on that cushioned seat. He'll be asleep, I wouldn't wonder, when I go down to him. Shall I tell them in the kitchen that you'd like him to have his supper up here with you? And that whatever they've got for you will do for him too? Shall I tell them that you'd like a bottle or so more of wine and of the best they've got? And shall I say that they'd better bring out a mattress for him into the lobby where he is now and a few coverings for it?"

Had Ghosta been there still, or indeed had any feminine being been there, she would not have failed to follow the varying expressions that crossed the Friar's face as he listened to this speech, and to follow them with growing astonishment. Friar Bacon's countenance, together with the shape of his head, represented, as any intelligent woman would have recognised at once, or any man either, who happened to be possessed of that sort of visual penetration in which most women leave most men far behind, a perfect example of the pure intellect as it struggles almost always with difficulty, and generally totally in vain, to cope with the irrational changes and chances of human life upon this planet.

The Friar had a delicate face in the precise sense in which all the way down the centuries the word "sensitive" has been used. Anyone could see at one glance that the man was abnormally porous to impressions. And it was indeed clear at this moment that the impressions which reached him from the revelations that this Durnovarian retainer of his was so calmly and relentlessly disclosing were of the most crucial intensity; for little complicated patterns of criss-cross interlinings began to appear on his forehead and under his eyes that resembled frost-marks on an exposed window.

It was only when Miles, having entirely finished what it was his business to report, had permitted his Roman features to assume that patient expectant look of an officer anxious to catch from the lips of his general every faintest nuance of the orders issued, that the Friar realized that their relative positions had been reversed, and that it was himself who was now standing in front of Miles, watching and pondering, and asking, not this unqualified fellow-man, but the inscrutable features of Fate itself, what on earth had to be done now.

What he said, when it came, was pathetic enough in its simplicity. "What do you advise me to do, Miles?"

That this typical Centurion had, from old experience of the master he loved so passionately, expected just exactly this supplication, this appeal to a knowledge of life as it went along such as had nothing to do with learning, was proved by the military decisiveness of his answer.

"I think," he replied firmly, putting down his glass, and speaking in his calmest and most Roman tone, "that you'd better send me into the kitchen to emphasize this man's importance, and yet to make it plain that it would be more considerate to Prior Bog to spare him any immediate invasion; at any rate to let us all have dinner in peace before we do anything and before he has to do anything."

A sigh of relief so deep that it seemed to come from the soles of his sandals shook Friar Bacon from head to foot.

"But you'll have to bring him up here, I suppose?"

And when Miles nodded to this his master accepted it as if it were the word of destiny, escape from which would be hopeless.

"Very well," he conceded. "Bring him up; and explain to him that you'll come up yourself a little later with his meal. We don't want anyone else up here, do we?" This last sentence the Friar added in what was almost an appealing tone. And Miles, already at the door, answered with a significant shake of his head.

The moments that followed were among the most painful in Roger Bacon's life. From his habitual loneliness as a scientific prisoner of religion, he had come to be a man of two different worlds; and since each of these worlds required, if he was to deal with it adequately, all the creative power as well as all the destructive power he possessed in his own personality, it was no easy thing to deal with both these worlds at the same time.

It was natural to him to concentrate his attention upon his private world of lonely thought and lonely experiment, and to feel a peculiar kind of nervous suffering whenever it was necessary for him to face the shocks and clashes and misunderstandings of real life.

"And now," he told himself, "I have to meet the one man in all the world with whom I find it hardest to deal."

Yes! There he was! And since the door had been deliberately left open by the departing Miles, it was inevitable that after a series of rather dragging footsteps—to which the Friar, as he stood in the centre of the room, listened with something like a suspension of breath—the man who entered made no pretence of knocking.

He was of low stature and of a thin weak body; but the extraordinary thing about him was his head. The head of Master Peter Peregrinus of Picardy was simply enormous. It made his body and legs look like those of a dwarf, though in reality they weren't quite as small as that. The skin of his face was so deadly white that, if you had come upon him asleep, you would have certainly assumed that he was a corpse. His hair was straight, not curly, and of a glossy jet-black, with each individual hair as thick as that of a horse, so that their combined weight, massed together on the top of his skull, give his whole figure at a distance the effect of a wooden post on an exposed sea-bank, with either a thick growth of dusky seaweed covering the top of it, or a big black feathery bird perched upon it.

The chief peculiarity of Master Peter's mouth was its absence of lips. It was simply a slit in smooth white marbly stone. And it seemed as if in dispensing with lips it had also decided to dispense with teeth. What did appear, and that not unfrequently, was Master Peter's tongue. This object, abnormally long, and unusually pointed, was always shooting out from that slit in its marbly home, and every time it withdrew it gave the impression of having licked up some form of life which it would shortly be digesting.

But what the most ramificating, debouching, circumnavigating, deviating, perambulating chronicler would have had to be leading up to all this while, like a slippery serpent approaching something as hard to catch off-guard as itself, are, as the simplest reader has long ago guessed, Master Peter's eyes. These were so large that when the man was excited, as he always was when not stunned by a blow or sunk into an impenetrable gulf of sleep, they conveyed the impression of being a pair of outlets for some interior volcano that if it were blocked up or barred down, would burst the cranium that contained it into a million smithereens.

It was doubtless to evade, for at least a couple of beats of the pulse of time, a glance into this explosive crater that Roger Bacon, uttering, as casually as he could, the exclamation, "Well! Well! Well!" made a deliberately slow circuit round his visitor from Picardy, and firmly, calmly, magisterially, and yet very softly, closed the door.

On returning from this breathing-space it can be believed he felt no surprise when he found Master Peter already seated at the table, not only tapping with the narrow finger-nail of his longest finger the word "vibrationem" half-way down the parchment page in front of him, but even steering a little horn-cup, with red wine-stains inside it, up and down among the oddly-patterned wood-marks of the table's edge.

Master Peter's demonic spirit did indeed so completely dominate the situation that the nervous Friar found himself seated at his own table in the visitor's seat with the visitor in the host's seat, found himself staring blindly into those two black holes, each of them a swirling Charybdisian vortex, and listening to the man's words without asking him a single question or contradicting a single statement he made.

At last the man broke into his own tricky rigmarole by asking a plain blunt question. "Can you guess what I'm doing now?"

"Doing?" echoed Bacon in puzzled bewilderment.

"Yes, yes! *Doing*! to earn my bread, of course! Doing what you yourself were forced to do when your family was ruined by those scurvy De Montforts and their bloody Barons! You put on a Friar's grey rags: and I put on sword and shield. And I'm still a man of war, Roger old friend. Get *that* into your pullulating pipkin! In Picardy, let me tell you, when once you've served your Lord in a vital campaign and given your bowels more action than they're used to, by living on hedges and in ditches, you'll soon find that the lords and prelates, who gain by the blood you lose and the sweat you're drained of and the dung you evacuate, will see to it—it's as much their interest, as it's the interest of the dear God Him-self, to have worshippers—that you don't die in an almshouse

227

but live to sit at street-corners, selling burnt almonds, singing ballads, and praising the king."

Petrus Peregrinus had arrived at the two syllables "dear God" in the rush of these words, when, moving very slowly, the door began creaking a little and swinging inwards. By lolling his black head an inch to the left of the Friar's grey shoulder he was able to envisage the appearance of a large metal tray, the rim of which, directed by the hands that held it, was itself propelling the massive weight of that huge oblong of impenetrable wood.

It was as impossible for the troubled apprehension of Roger Bacon to miss this gesture of his formidable visitor as it was for him, the second he observed it, to restrain his cry: "But, Miles, Miles! what we need now——"

Nobody will ever know for a certainty just what was in the Friar's mind at that moment; although it would be easy to imagine several things. But what happened was that the Friar at that particular moment lost consciousness. Whether he fell, chair and all, to the floor and was lifted up by both men after the tray had been deposited on the table, or whether he had himself, after losing all consciousness of what he was doing, stumbled across the room to his bed and laid himself down on it, must be left as a *blank lacuna* in any narration of these events, until either Petrus or Miles chooses to reveal what each of them must have retained very clearly in his memory.

What we do know from the consciousness of the Friar himself is that when he awoke from his trance, or whatever may be the correct name for the overwhelming mental oblivion that descended upon him, he found himself lying on his bed with the devoted Miles kneeling beside him and watching his awakening with the most intense and concentrated attention.

"Is he gone?" was the Friar's first question.

"Yes, dear Master," replied Miles. "He's gone."

"Do you know *where* he's gone?"

"I think, great Master, he's gone to the Fortress."

"Do they expect him there?"

"It is my impression, O most Admirable of all Teachers," responded Miles, "that they have been expecting him for some time."

"How did they know he was here?"

"From what I could make out from him as we went along," replied Miles, rising from his knees and standing, grave and upright, like a majestic Roman statue at the foot of the Friar's bed, "but you know, great master, what he is, and what dunghill talk he uses and how little he cares whether the person he's talking to understands one jot of what he's saying! I don't take to him, master, and that's the bone truth! He's a scholar right enough. I don't quarrel with his learning. Thee be a man of learning, thee wone self, and I admire 'ee and look up to 'ee for't, like as thee were a kind of God in 'eaven and no nonsense!

"But this bob-by-night, and I don't care who hears me say so, be the sort of Mumbo-Jumbo—Prick-and-Thumbo what they do tell I be found in them girt Fairs in London and Paris and Consinotabel, such as travelling pipshaws do visit in their carry-otteries by day and by night.

"But the man be a man of Latin and Greek, us must allow 'im that much, for all it be worth to 'in, but when I do think of thee, master of mine, and how thy girt wisdom do go along with a girt heart, and how ye do give scoops and bowls o't, yea! basinsfull o't, to all and sundry as comes to beg for a crumb of real learning, it do make my gorge to 'eave up. Thee do use thee's girt learning to give us more pottage in all our porringers; but this man thinks only of inventing magnets to draw the gold from other men's treasure-chests into his own. There! If I've not gone and done the one thing I didn't ought to 'a done—made 'ee, O master my dear, dead-tired by listening to I!"

At this pathetic self-accusation the Friar quickly opened his eyes.

"No, no!" he cried, "you've put new life into me, Miles old friend, by giving me your real and actual feeling about Petrus Peregrinus. But you were beginning to tell me why you thought they were expecting him at the Fortress."

At this the majestic Roman physiognomy of Miles dissolved into the love-ravaged confusion of a guilty hero-worshipper, and with a convulsive sob he sank on his knees.

"He ate and he drank," were the words that that crumpled visage now moaned into the edge of the prisoner's coverlet, "everything I'd brought for both of ye! And then, when he was satisfied, he just went off. He glanced at you before he went and kept muttering to himself without taking any notice of me, "O he'll come to life in a minute or two! come to life in a minute or two! He'll come to life in a minute or two!" And off the man went. But I do think I picked up from his randy chat, while I was pegging along by his side and carrying his bundles, that he had been told of your Brazen Head having been taken into the Fortress and put into the armoury; and I think myself, master, that it was with the idea of visiting your Brazen Head that he wanted to get in touch with the lord of the Fortress. At any rate we met young John, and John must have told them to expect him."

The tone in which Miles uttered this last sentence contained, in its military resonance, a finality which conveyed such an utter removal of all responsibility for what was happening from the recipients of the news it brought, that Roger Bacon, only just hoisted up from the heavenly tide of oblivious sleep, turned over on his bed and closed his eyes.

XVI

THE LODESTONE

Petrus Peregrinus had found no difficulty, when once he had descended the stairs, in persuading, by the offer of a sufficient bribe, one of the pleasant-speaking boys from the Prior's kitchen to lead him to the Fortress. Once inside the Fortress he had no difficulty on that particular evening in obtaining a leisurely and agreeable interview with the Lord of the Manor of Roque.

The Baron's curiosity in relation to this singular intruder was lively from the first moment he heard the rumours about him, but as soon as he met him face to face on this night of the man's departure from the Priory, he felt it was imperative that he should have him to himself in private for at least a quarter of an hour.

No! He couldn't deal with the fellow in the presence of the family. For here was his forever indignant, forever outraged, forever grievanced Lady Val, whom he always thought of in his own mind as "Valentia the Irreconcilable", and here was his excitable daughter Lil-Umbra, and here was his anxious, concentrated, architectural-minded elder son Tilton, and finally here was the adventurous young John, who of late had become such a fierce champion of Friar Bacon that he had rendered himself as fully liable to ecclesiastical censure as was the Friar's older friend Raymond, whom Lady Val had already accepted as Lil-Umbra's betrothed.

Here they were, all the lot of them, gathered together in high spirits after a lively evening meal, and simply waiting for some event of an exciting nature to occur. What could he do to get the fellow entirely to himself for a while? He looked first at one of them and then at another, as they all stood round him

231

while the young man from the Priory, having ushered Master Peter into their presence, made a little speech, as dignified as it was natural, emphasizing the fact that the fame of the Brazen Head, possessed of the power of speaking and perhaps even of the power of thinking was what no doubt had brought this notable visitor.

At last the Lord of the Manor of Roque got an inspiration. And it was Lil-Umbra who gave it to him. The others had already begun to talk among themselves when she spoke up boldly and clearly, addressing her father.

"Better take Maître Pierre de Maricourt"—for the traveller had evidently instructed the boy from the Priory kitchen exactly how to announce him—"upstairs to your little room, Father. And then you'll be able to tell us better and clearer about him, so that Mother, and we all, can do him the honour which we feel sure he deserves. Tilton and John and I are so keen to know all about him that we might be a bother to him. But with you to explain——" And Lil-Umbra ended with a pathetically beseeching glance at Lady Val, as much as to say, "I'll be very *very* good and do everything, yes, everything, you want me to do, if only you'll agree to this!"

But the Lord of the Fortress was so quick in taking his daughter's wise hint that Lady Val had no chance to intervene, nor had her brothers a chance to accompany the two of them, even with the politest intentions. For throwing his powerful right arm round the slim, frail, weedy little body of his guest, as if he were his uncle rather than his host, he hurried him upstairs to the "little room" to which Lil-Umbra referred.

This, as a matter of fact, was a small apartment next door to their large bed-chamber, an apartment where the Baron kept the smaller, rarer, daintier, more delicate, more breakable utensils of his hunting, fishing, spearing and arrow-shooting gear.

The Baron himself and Peter of Maricourt in Picardy would have indeed been a perfect subject for a painter in oils, had one such been there to watch them; and indeed the mere sight of them, as they sat facing each other in the Baron's "Little Room", might possibly, had Tilton been daring enough and unscrupulous enough to slip up there after them and peep at them through the half-open door, have turned him from a sculptor into a painter.

It was a characteristic of several of the rooms in the Fortress that the doors were so constructed that it was physically impossible for them to be properly shut, so that the young man could have watched them for some time with an interest that might have inspired him with a passion for portrait-painting.

Yes, if the boy had been rude enough to follow them, the effect of the extraordinary vibrations thrown off all the time from the person of Master Peter might have affected this serious-minded young man's life in a really startling manner.

But Tilton did not follow them into that little room with the door that couldn't shut. We may imagine his doing so; but he didn't and that ends it. The chance came. The chance was not taken. The particular sight that, if it *had* been taken, would have changed his whole life, was never seen by him.

Chroniclers of human history talk of Fate, or Destiny, of what Homer calls "Keer" or doom. But all the time it is the great goddess of Chance—the present chronicler shirks using her name, because to anglicize it we have to turn the Greek letter called "upsilon" into our "Y", which always tempts us to pronounce it like our "i", which spoils its beauty altogether —yes, all the time it is the great goddess of Chance who turns the scale at the supreme crises of our life.

But though the sight of their figures facing each other remained unseen, Master Peter of Maricourt in Picardy and the Lord of the Fortress of Roque certainly did not "beat", as the saying is, "about the *bush*".

"What is that fool of a Friar made of," queried Master Peter, "that he spends all his time, now that you people have got his Brazen Head, in writing long elaborate criticisms of these miserable doctors in Oxford and Paris, when he must know perfectly well that they are all tarred with the same brush and the same tar, the brush of obstruction and the tar of abstraction?

"And what a simple mind the fellow must have to make these attacks on the stupidity of the great mass of people and on the ignorance of their teachers! What does the man expect of our poor wretched human race? Hasn't it been the same from the beginning? Can you or anybody else imagine anything different? Jesus Holy! How can the fellow suppose that even the cleverest of our masters with a class of young men before him as simple as our boys are—and they weren't very different in the days of Confucius or the days of Socrates!—can bring, to what he tells these kids, inspiration and wit and insight enough to start them off looking up words in their Greek and Latin dictionaries?

"And the double-dyed idiot goes further even than that! Do you know, my lord, what I saw with my own eyes written on one of his carefully chosen parchment sheets? You would never guess! Nothing less than a passionate appeal to these teachers and to the young men who themselves want to become teachers, young men of good birth, like your own sons, to study Hebrew! Of course he's perfectly right—you and I, my lord, don't need a Grey Friar to tell us *that*—in indicating that the translations of Hebrew, all except that of the incomparable Jerome, are pretty rotten. But will these kids he's catering for find the time, find the grammars, find the god-given or devil-given wit, to correct these treacherous and dangerous mistakes?

"How much better it would be for him, my Lord, if he would do what I do—that is to say leave all this theological business alone, and concentrate on experiment and invention; on experiment first, to find out what *can* be invented so as to be in harmony with Nature; and then, *when we've got our invention*, experiment again to find how far its use can go and yet remain in harmony with Nature."

The perfectly abysmal self-satisfaction expressed at that moment in the unnaturally large face, under the alarmingly large forehead and beneath that huge crop of jet black hair, roused in the Baron of Roque more anger than he had felt for many a long year. But he succeeded in restraining himself from displaying anything but the alert interest of a polite host in the presence of a voluble guest for several seconds of expectant silence.

"Surely, O great Experimenter, surely, O great Inventor," his alert pose seemed to say, as he leant forward from the round, hard, circular, gilded seat of his small upright armchair and clasped his fingers over his right knee, letting his foot thus balanced in the air sway interrogatively, "surely a man of your calibre didn't allow a simple grey friar of the order we all know so well," the Baron's mute expectancy went on, "to reduce you to the position of a silent listener at a theological lecture?"

The invisible chronicler of all these events, which were of course both physical and psychical, cannot help noting how much more detached from any sort of egotism or self-assertion was this lord of the biggest Manor in Wessex than this plain soldier from Maricourt in Picardy.

The psychic difference between them displayed itself physically with nearly perfect propriety in the way the two men consciously or unconsciously managed their mouths. The red point of Master Peter's tongue kept darting out from between his lips, just as if it were the instantaneously deadly sting of a human-headed Goblin armed with the poison of a hornet; while behind the lips of the Baron's mouth some unspoken word seemed roaming about, testing and trying every surface of the walls of its prison-house, as if conscientiously seeking the entrance to a promised passage of escape, concerning whose existence, though it was supported by universal consent, he himself was rather doubtful.

The only light in what, throughout the whole Fortress, was known as "The Little Room" came from a large oil-lamp in which two wicks, each with its own particular flame, floated quietly, and by their light, on the thin sill of a small square window, looking out on nothing but darkness and square stone towers, a small gnat could be seen marching resolutely up and down.

The only heat in the little room—but this was quite sufficient to make it perfectly warm—came from a stately bronze receptacle containing red-hot coals, with which the Baron's retainers kept it liberally supplied both by day and by night.

What Master Peter was thinking at that moment had certainly little to do with either theology or metaphysics.

"Would it be to my advantage or to my disadvantage," he was asking himself, "to tell this patronizing English lord about the magnetic shock I gave to this fool of a friar? What's against my doing so is the fact that I don't yet know how long the shock I gave him actually lasted; indeed I don't know yet whether it knocked the breath out of him forever! I rather hope it didn't, because there is still that little point about the value of manganese as an ingredient in the making of an elixir, that I ought to ask him. God knows why I forgot."

What the Baron was thinking was: "All these confounded quacks, whether they call themselves scientists or astrologists or alchemists or metaphysicians or inventors or theologians, are only plotting to get power for themselves over other people and glory for themselves over each other! What we must realize is that life goes on exactly the same whether we're with them or without them! When Lord Edward comes home from these absurd crusades we shall all know better where we stand. These damnable Scots want to be hammered into quiescence by somebody who understands the art of war, not the art of changing metals.

"And for these Welsh thieves who keep invading this country, if once metal-changers and sorcerers really begin, as they seem to be beginning, to rule the world, it won't be long before we shall be conquered by some ancient British robber who claims to be descended from Alexander the Great or Julius Caesar.

"But I know what I must do with this rogue—for it's clear he's some sort of oriental gipsy with the devil knows what games and tricks up his sleeve—is to get that fellow Spardo to take him round the ring of all the manors about here, even if he's got to mount him on that unfortunate beast with a man's head coming out of his neck! They told me out yonder that this fellow swears he comes from Picardy and that he likes to be called Maître Pierre. Well! he can Maître-Pierre it to his heart's content with old Spardo dancing round him, and with that horse—what's its classic name?—to ride on! By God! that's what I'll do!"

At this point, in this curious dialogue between two silences, there suddenly opened one of those queer holes, or gaps, or gulfs, or chasms in the psychic-contact of two speechless persons who are watching each other like two animals, each wondering, in a sort of trance of expectation, not exactly whether it would be a good thing to leap at the other's throat, but whether the power that moves the world, whatever that power may be, will decide on their battling or embracing; and in this hollow void it was brought home to the Lord of the

Manor that this Master Peter in front of him was really and truly some kind of Medium.

For what did my lord hear, clearly and unmistakably, at that identical instant, but the familiar voice, carried up on the eddying wind from the darkened forest below, of Spardo himself addressing his weird horse and of Cheiron answering his owner's voice with one of those indescribable sounds made by a self-conscious and self-possessed animal, a sound that had grown to have its quite definite meaning in the language of their mutual understanding.

"Come out with me for a moment, Master Peter of Maricourt, will you please? I want you to meet some very old friends of mine!"

The wanderer from Picardy followed him without hesitation or demur. When they reached the ground-floor the Baron hurried his guest through the anteroom and the entrance-hall, till he got him to the main entrance of the Fortress, and once there, with nothing but a humorous nod to the gate-keeper and the exchange of a more reserved and even a slightly enigmatic quip with the gate-keeper's wife, he pushed open one of the big gates, and with a hand on Master Peter's shoulder got him into the open, where by the light of a lantern hung on the branch of a tree they found Cheiron eating a supper of oats, and his master squatting on a fir-stump beside him devouring from a bowl on his knees some sort of steaming stew which the gate-keeper's wife must have provided.

"Where are you going to sleep tonight, Spardo?" The Lord of the Fortress never for a moment lost his special and peculiar power of propitiating the oddest, queerest, and most intransigent personalities in the world, whether in the human or sub-human sphere of life.

At this moment, without ceasing to transport to his mouth as much stew as his wooden spoon could carry, Spardo didn't hesitate for a second in his reply to this question.

"With your permission, good my lord, I should like to tie up Cheiron in the horse-stall behind the Fortress; for I've got the permission of the dame at your gate, if yourself, good my lord, have no objection, to sleep in her gate-house across there."

"Could the same good lady, do you suppose," said the Lord of the Fortress, "find room on a mattress in the same retreat for my friend Maître Pierre, a foreign gentleman from Picardy?"

The said Master Peter, as may easily be imagined, did not miss one jot of the instinctive sagacity with which the Baron, upon whose good or bad, wise of foolish behaviour so many destinies in that corner of the west country depended, managed to eliminate himself completely, as the local potentate whose whim was law, and to create a half-humorous atmosphere of adventure in which they all were taking chances.

Nor did he miss the perfectly natural manner in which Spardo, who was now scraping the inside of his bowl with his spoon, entered into this game, and instead of rising from the tree-stump on which he was squatting, when he saw Cheiron straining to get some fodder that was just beyond his reach, called out to the Baron, "Kick that stuff nearer the horse, my lord, if you don't mind!"

And when the Baron obeyed this curt command, Spardo only acknowledged it with a nod. It would be almost as difficult for the most penetrating chronicler to describe the thoughts that whirled through the head of Peter of Maricourt at this juncture, as it would be to describe what Cheiron himself was thinking.

But this much might certainly be hazarded: that if Cheiron's thoughts were concentrated partly upon what Spardo had given him to eat, and partly on the question as to whence this food came and how much more of it was available in the place, wherever that place was, from which it came, Master Peter's thoughts were concentrated, first on the question as to whether he dared to make another experiment with the perilous object he kept in a velvet bag between his legs, tightly pressed against his body close to his privy parts, or whether the present moment was even less propitious for an experiment of this sort than was the recent occasion in Roger Bacon's room at Bumset Priory.

The object in that velvet bag, squeezed so scrupulously against his most hidden stretch of skin, was indeed the very centre and focus of Maître Pierre's whole life. It was a magnet of immense and so far of quite unfathomed power.

Ever since he'd been a small boy Maître Pierre had been obsessed by a passion for magnetic experiments, and for the last twenty years his whole life had been given to the study of everything he could pick up on this queer topic.

The accumulated result of this frantic quest—for in many ways it was much more like this quest for the Sangraal than any ordinary alchemistic pursuit—was, as far as the man's own secret life went, only alchemistic on the side. In its main conscious urge what Master Peter of Maricourt was after was nothing less than the deliberate manipulation of his own sexual force, by means of this powerful magnet, for the domination of the souls and wills and minds of other entities.

He was in fact at this moment absorbed in this particular game, just as he had been for the last twenty years, and it was Friar Bacon's psychic awareness of this mania in his friend that always troubled and alarmed him when they were together, although it had a tremendous interest for him. The Friar never let it invade his own experimental work; and whenever it became evident to him as uppermost in Peter's mind, it troubled him both in his nerves and in his conscience.

Yes! and in something else within him, beyond both nerves and conscience; for Friar Roger in his own spirit was always aware of the presence of an almighty force behind the whole panorama of experience, behind the animal, vegetable and mineral worlds, behind infinite space and infinite time, behind all possible suns, moons, planets and stars, in fact behind all possible, as well as all existing, universes.

It was his consciousness of this remote and ultimate power that Roger Bacon felt he needed to keep his peace of mind and keep him happy and contented in his work. Thus there was always something, in spite of his admiration for Pierre of Picardy, that frightened him about his friend's attitude, for it struck him as reducing not only his own life, as he knew it himself, but the lives of all other entities as they knew them themselves, the lives of insects, such as midges and moths, the lives of plants and trees, the lives of worms and serpents, the lives of fish in the sea, birds in the air, the lives of the beasts of forest and field; reducing in fact all these lives to the level of lonely, desperate, lost souls, clinging to each other in a boundless, godless, cavernous nothingness, in fact to what he had heard a travelling Welsh tinker call *Diddym*, " the ultimate Void".

To the original mind and autocratic humour of the Lord of the Manor of Roque there was something about this scene under the light of that suspended lantern that seemed monstrously comical as well as strangely weird and startling. What was this man up to now?

Master Peter had clearly and obviously some concentrated purpose; but who could possibly know that he was pressing that lodestone of his, in its absurd sheath of flexible velvet, against his naked organs of generation? His eyes, as he did this, were fixed on the head of the horse Cheiron, who was snorting rather indignantly and gazing rather reproachfully at his master, Spardo.

Spardo himself never moved from his seat on the tree-stump which had become for him a sort of elfin throne from which he could, though without any oracular authority, and without attempting to claim any mundane weight, play the part of a wandering goblin, who happened to be making a grave attempt to be an historian of the primitive antics of the human race.

Nor was it very long before both the eccentric Baron of Roque and the observant owner of Cheiron had something to set down in their "year-book" of manorial history. With his hands pressing more and more strongly, and with ever intenser concentration, his precious lodestone against his privy parts, Peter did really seem at that moment to be a man possessed by a fit of insane devilry. It is likely enough that what made him select Cheiron, rather than Cheiron's master, for his magnetic experiment was the passing glimpse he may have had, when the darkness was broken by some gleam from the lantern swaying in the wind, of that deformity in the horse's neck.

But whatever it was that set him off practising his tricks in this direction, the result was sufficiently unexpected. Cheiron suddenly leapt up on his hind-legs and advanced, pawing the air with his front-legs, straight upon Master Peter, who promptly scuttled behind the Lord of Roque.

And this moment really produced, if the truth had been carried over the length and breadth of his manorial domain, one of those situations in which this extraordinary owner of this by no means extraordinary strip of fir-forest had a chance of showing that it was not for nothing that the skull of his grandfather, when by some chance it was exposed to the air long after it was buried, had a twist of dark hair gathered round it, indicating, so an Assyrian astrologer who saw it declared, that its zodiacal tendency belonged to the constellation of the Ram, since there had always been known, from the beginning of history, certain rare persons born under that influence, the roots of whose hair came from a deeper level than their skin.

Instead therefore of being in the least perturbed by the towering belly and menacing hooves hovering above him, the Lord of Roque experienced the sort of exultation that Job declares Behemoth felt when he believed he could drain Jordan to the dregs of all its waters.

Spardo was so astonished at what he now beheld that he rose from his seat on the tree-stump and stood like one confounded. Master Peter whose magnetic experiment was the cause of this classic catastrophe, did what Friar Bacon's collapse had clearly *not* made him do. He carefully shifted, in a number of minute jerks, his perilous lodestone. He did this knowing the thing couldn't be lost, for its velvet container was suspended by a cord from his waist; and he adjusted it now so that while it was still in contact with his bare skin, it was at the base of his stomach and quite out of reach of his organs of generation.

But not a soul in that small lantern-lit group was more astonished than was Cheiron himself when he felt, hurled against *his* privy parts—which were, and this was no doubt an additional effect of Master Peter's experiment, unusually excited just then—the formidable skull of the Lord of Roque.

Unable now to bring his legs to the ground, the angry horse found his right hoof hanging helplessly over the man's left shoulder and his left hoof thrust out at an extremely awkward and even a painful angle over the man's right shoulder, while he himself, his whole equine shape and deformed neck, was lifted bodily off the ground!

It only lasted a second, this incredible display of human strength, a display that Hercules himself would have witnessed with amazement: but when it was over the Lord of Roque and his deformed antagonist were struggling together on the ground.

And it was then that there occurred the same total collapse of consciousness in the brain of the Lord of the Manor as had occurred some half a dozen hours earlier in the case of Friar Bacon. At one second he was saying to himself: "I am a beast. Man is no more. Your own beasthood learn to adore!" and was beginning to force himself to enjoy the strong hirsute odour of Cheiron's under-belly, when suddenly, without any warning at all, everything became dark, and he himself became as non-existent as if he had never been born.

The sharp-eyed dame of the gate-keeper had already left her less alert husband's side; and with a thick scarf round her head, and a still thicker one round her shoulders, was soon at the side of her unconscious master; and it can be imagined, with an experienced old lady of her sort at the head of affairs, and with the gate-keeper, inspired by her example, obedient to her least hint, how soon it was that the Lord of the Fortress lay stretched out on his own bed with Lady Val bending over him and his three children, along with excited emissaries from every part of the Fortress, hovering round the door.

Both Spardo and Cheiron were comfortably asleep, and also in closer proximity to each other than anyone who had witnessed the recent struggle and its surprising termination would have predicted, before Master Peter of Maricourt had succeeded in persuading the perspicacious lady of the gate-house to allow him a sleeping-place. This indeed, when she found it for him, could not be called under her roof, for it was in the back premises of the Fortress on the opposite side from the entrance, but such as it was, it was so much in the warmest part of the whole building and so surrounded by the sleeping-places of animals, that when Peter of Picardy had settled his great black head on the sack of wool that formed his substantial pillow, he found that the melancholy wailing of the wind across the forest was so comfortably animalized by the noises of the beasts in his immediate vicinity that his thoughts became so agreeable to him that he felt reluctant to fall asleep too quickly.

His present situation was indeed so harmonious with his mood that he disentangled his precious lodestone, which, it would seem, after these two murderous experiments, could scarcely be called a harmless magnet, and examined it as carefully as was possible under the light of a stable-lantern which hung from a time-darkened oak-beam several yards above his pillow.

"I have succeeded," he told himself. "I have succeeded beyond all expectation." Had there been an onlooker at this scene—say an angel or a devil crouched on that wooden beam above the lantern and endowed with a powerful enough sight —he might, or she might, have described this half-natural, half-artificial object to some acquaintance up in the roof in the following terms. "It is about half a foot long and is simply a spear-head of the particular colour which waves take when they are beginning to change from blue to green, a change which happens when the winds rise, not so much as a sign of a coming storm, as to prove that, if a storm did come, they would show themselves to be the proud-curving cohorts they were, of an approaching sea-god."

With exquisite satisfaction did Master Peter of Picardy caress his newly formulated, newly invented, newly tested magnet; and as he did so a series of the wildest fantasies raced through his mind. He saw himself dominating the rulers of all the countries of the world, and through his power over them he saw himself, although always craftily in the background, having his revenge upon the whole human race.

"O how I do hate them all!" he thought. "I hate them with my brain, with my body, and with my soul! I hate them with everything I am, everything I was, and everything I shall be!"

And then he began again to wonder, as he had so often wondered before, whether it was possible that he really was that Antichrist, prophesied of from the beginning of the world, who was destined to destroy the Kingdom of Christ.

"What I would do then," he told himself, "the moment I had got the world entirely under my control, would be to build up an absolutely different kind of world altogether. I would have no more of this hypocritical humbug about 'love' —as if it were possible for any child of the elements, born of earth, air, water and fire, to fight for anything, to achieve anything, to enjoy anything, to become anything, except by the assertion of his separate, distinctive, individual, and unique self —and what I would aim at in *my* world, in my Antichrist world, in my super-scientific world, would be to create a new race of beings altogether, creatures as superior to what mankind is now as man is superior to beasts, birds, and fishes!"

The demonic delight, which radiated in the train of these thoughts through the whole being of Master Peter, was so deliciously transporting that it carried him away altogether from his material position at that moment, and bore him aloft, as if in a chariot of air and fire, a chariot that flew upward upon the waving of two wings, one of which might have been Space and the other Time, for both together seemed to acquire a mysterious force that soon carried their voyager into a sleep, if sleep it were, where he found himself in reality, if reality it were, beyond all description by the words the human race has hitherto used.

XVII

ALBERT OF COLOGNE

Raymond de Laon was not given to moods of special exultation or to moods of special depression. He possessed an extremely well-balanced nature. He had been saved from quarrels with parents by having been made an orphan at an early age; and he was lucky now in having found a betrothed who exactly suited him. He took the shocks and accidents and mis-adventures of life with a calm, and yet, in a certain way, with an exultant commonsense, that was as much a support to Lil-Umbra as it was an authentic advantage to himself in his struggle with life. He had certainly done well in his present mission; for here by his side was none other than Albertus Magnus. At this moment with his band of armed retainers, who had been rather unwillingly provided by the authorities of Cone Castle to support him on this daring embassy, he had just reached the entrance to the convent where Ghosta was employed, and they were all now about to pass, while the Sun was at his hottest on that June day, the mysterious cave in the grove of oaks and willows, which Peleg had been assured was the abode of that tinker from Wales about whom the wildest rumours were current.

It was said for instance that he was helped in his work as a travelling tinker by several women from different parts of the country, all of whom had sold their souls to the Devil.

It was at this point that Raymond began rather nervously explaining to the great teacher from Cologne that they would be soon arriving at the main gate of the Fortress of Roque; and he went on to indicate more specifically, what he had already mentioned shyly to him before, namely that Lady Val, who was expecting him as her guest that night, was the mother of the young lady to whom he himself was betrothed, and was the wife of the most formidable boar-hunter and wolf-slayer in all that portion of England. Nor did he hesitate, though even more diffidently, to explain that they were all so weary of the violent personal quarrels between these two belligerent Franciscans, Friar Bacon and Bonaventura that they welcomed the appearance among them of a renowned Dominican whose presence alone would be sufficient to break up these vindictive quarrels.

The whole party paused at this point at the request of the visitor, to enable him to retire behind a clump of willows with a view to relieving himself. When he returned he kept them standing for a moment above the leafy declivity containing the entrance to this cave of the tinker's witch-wives, while he begged Raymond de Laon to tell him as definitely as he could what his own private and personal reaction was in regard to the quarrel between these famous men.

He had no sooner asked this question and Raymond was frowning and biting his lips and searching his mind for an adequate answer, when they all heard quite distinctly, borne up upon the wind from the depths of the leafy gully beneath them a wild husky voice singing a ditty which clearly was, whether they were able to follow all its crazy words or not, a blasphemous defiance of Providence above, of the Church below, and of all that mankind from generation to generation has been taught to hold sacred.

The day was so hot and the sky above was so blue, that the effect of this howl of defiance to everything they had all been accustomed from infancy to venerate was enhanced by the complete absence at that spot of any work of men's hands, whether of wood or stone. It was like a voice from the depths of the earth replying to a voice from uttermost space. It seemed to be addressed to the formless and shapeless rocks of granite and basalt that lay around this small group of travellers, and it seemed to be appealing desperately to earth, air, and water, not to allow the sun-rays that were so lifegiving to all, to fool them by their warmth.

It was the sort of defiance such as the ghost of a baby of a million years ago, a baby or "baban" whose skull, "penglog", had been discovered in the grave of an antediluvian giant, "gawr", might have uttered to all oracles and prophets and announcers of revelations and to all deities and pantheons of deities who were already gathering in the mists of the future to claim human worship.

> "Until I'm dust I'll enjoy my hour—
> Penglog y Baban yr Gawr!
> I'll gather my harvest and grind my flour—
> Penglog y Baban yr Gawr!
> With Holy Rood I'll have naught to do—
> Penglog y Baban yr Gawr!
> Adam am I, and Eve are you,
> And Eden's wherever we are, we two—
> Penglog y Baban yr Gawr!
> A mortal's fate is the same as a mole's—
> Penglog y Baban yr Gawr!
> The same as the fishes that leap in shoals,
> Penglog y Baban yr Gawr!
>
> Where leaf do fall—there let leaf rest—
> Where no Grail be there be no quest—
> Be'ee good, be'ee bad, be'ee damned, be'ee blest—
> Be'ee North, be'ee South, be'ee East, be'ee West
> The whole of Existence is naught but a jest—
> Penglog y Baban yr Gawr!"

The effect upon that small company, together with Raymond their leader and Albertus Magnus their visitor, of this weird ditty, a ditty followed by dead silence, save for the sound of the wind in the trees about them and the far-off cry of a buzzard high in the air above them, would have been for anyone concerned with the results of unexpected shocks upon human nerves, of no small interest.

It had an effect however that no chronicler, however sagacious, could possibly have foreseen. Every single one of those six armed men, as well as their leader and his visitor, behaved exactly in the same way. They all were so startled and shocked that they simply dared not comment on what they had heard. Every single one of them pretended—whether to himself as well as to the others who could tell?—that he had heard nothing!

The shock of what they *had* heard, for all this pretence, followed them, all the same, through the burning heat of this mid-day in June, as they pressed on, leaving the stone circle to their left, and that lonely stone seat where Lil-Umbra, on an early February morning, had asked Peleg such searching questions, on their right, till they approached, not the small postern this time, for they were too large a party, and it was too cogent an occasion, to use that entrance, but the main gate of the Fortress.

As soon as Raymond told him they were approaching their journey's end, Albertus brought their march to a halt and put to his young guide the direct question, which the voice of that cave-devil had for the time postponed.

"And what," he asked him, "is your own private attitude to these disputes?"

The Cone Castle men, who were already alert, now crowded quite close to them, and it became clear to Raymond that they felt unusually concerned. And indeed there was unquestionably something about Albertus Magnus that attracted the attention of intelligent persons wherever he went. He had already held for a couple of years an important bishopric in Germany, but this he had recently resigned together with all the influence and wealth that a bishopric gives in order to devote himself solely and entirely to the metaphysical and botanical and entomological studies that were the main interest of his days upon earth.

This absorption in the mysterious life of all the creatures of Nature and in the whole problem of mind and matter, since it was combined with a lively interest in men and women for themselves, threw a very singular aura round him, an aura which, though it rendered him separate and aloof, endowed his presence with the peculiar attraction which certain rare and evasive animals and birds and insects possess.

And not only was Albertus Magnus an unusual, indeed we might say a unique person in himself, but the particular line of philosophical investigation into which he threw his whole nature linked itself with metaphysical thoroughness to his wide natural sympathy. He himself described it as finding the *Universal* "before" all, "in" all, and "after" all. He was not only a student of plants, trees, flowers, and insects, but of human

248

beings also; and he sought to find this *Universal* of his in all its three stages of "before", "in", and "after", in every living thing he studied.

In appearance Albert of Cologne was curiously impressive. He was of medium height but very powerfully built. He always wore, day and night—for it was a weakness of his to be physically sensitive to catching cold, and it was a conviction of his that where he was especially menaced by this affliction was through his head—a curiously shaped white cap that had a remote affinity to an academic cap, and also to the metallic cap of a knight in armour, but was first suggested to him by the singular night-turban worn by an Arabian student of Aristotle with whom he had shared a lodging in early days in Swabia.

But the chief advantage of this ubiquitous protection against colds was that it was made of such soft stuff that any kind of ceremonial head-gear, from a pontifical mitre to a more secular token of authority, could be squeezed over it.

The head of Albert of Cologne was if anything not larger, but smaller, than most human heads. He had a long straight nose with wide sensitive nostrils. He had small ears close to his skull, extremely full and very attractively curved lips, a large mouth that was often open and even had a tendency to dribble, an unaggressive and retreating chin and a pair of small hazel eyes under bushy grey eyebrows, eyes that searched affectionately and longingly into every person and thing he looked at, as if seeking to trace "within" this person or thing the *Universal* in which he believed, the Universal that had been "before" it and would be "after" it. The truth was he was always aware of the contrast between the touchingly pathetic brittleness, feebleness, silliness and conceitedness of the particular small creature he was regarding and the enormous life-force which brought it to birth.

"What I would like to be able to tell you, Doctor," replied Raymond hesitatingly, fully aware that his Cone Castle friends were glancing quickly from one to another as they followed his words, "would be that I have steadily tried hard, ever since I realized the bewildering complexity of all these ultimate problems, to keep my mind entirely open and my personal conclusions undecided and hanging in the balance. But such is the weakness and such is the pride of human nature, or at any rate, great Doctor, of my nature, that I cannot resist bringing into the workings of my will and of my faith in myself all manner of obstinate prejudices and too-quickly reached conclusions."

Albert of Cologne made a quick little inclination of his head, upon which for this journey through the forest of Wessex, he wore above his white skull-cap, a traveller's variant of a Dominican cowl.

"Please give me, my dear young guide, and let me tell you I shall certainly congratulate your future parents-in-law on having secured for their daughter such a thoughtful and resourceful bridegroom, some general notion of these fixed ideas of yours before we have to separate."

"Well, master; to confess the truth," and Raymond de Laon looked nervously round him at a receding glade of sun-illumined bluebells in one direction, and at several sumptuous bunches of horse-chestnut blossoms in another direction, and finally at the illimitable gulf, of that early June's noon-deep, noon-blue infinity above them, and then, with a quiver of unquestioned sincerity in his voice: "What I feel myself, great master," he said, "is that it's wrong for the church to forbid Friar Bacon to work at his self-chosen inventions. And I also feel that it's wrong, and worse than wrong, in fact I think it is devilishly wicked in this Bonaventura, who by some pious people among us is regarded as a saint, and who at one time was the Pope's Legate, to start the rumour"—here the young man's voice became broken by a sound in his throat that was clearly a choked-down sob—"that my pure-minded young betrothed and her serious-minded elder-brother Tilton have committed the shocking sin of incest."

His voice rose stronger at this point. "This man Bonaventura knows absolutely nothing of us people in the west of England. He knows nothing of the childlike and innocent character of the young man and young girl he is attacking in this gross manner. And further, great master, you must understand that he actually went so far as to urge on a band of notorious outlaws from a castle in this neighbourhood called Lost Towers whose lord is known far and wide as an enemy of God and man, but whom this Bonaventura, for his own secret ends, pretends to have converted, to attack Friar Bacon.

It was this rabble who under his direction smashed a shrine which my betrothed's brother was building, and were on the point of destroying Friar Bacon's Brazen Head, if it hadn't been for——"

Albertus Magnus interrupted him. "You've not forgotten I hope, my young friend," cried the famous teacher, "that it was only your promise that I should be allowed to sleep in the same chamber as this Brazen Head that made me put off my return to Cologne? This particular invention interests me profoundly. To tell you the truth, Raymond de Laon, what I had been hearing from England about the experimental theories concerning physical science originated by your great Robert Grosseteste had led me to aim at something very much on Friar Roger's lines. It was when they made me a bishop that I had too much work and too much responsibility to be able to go on with such things; and I warrant it was the same with your Grosseteste who must have been both a real scientist and a real saint.

"But I can tell you this, my lad—I can tell you this, my friends—when a thinker gets an appointment all his thinking's done. We are just idiots if we imagine we can accept responsible positions in Church or State and go on thinking just the same. I tell you, my dear lad, I tell you, my excellent friends, the noble words I have already read written by this Friar Bacon have interested me greatly. He knows Aristotle through and through and few scholars have better interpreted the *secretum secretorum* of all matter, I mean the *energeia-akinesis*, or 'energy without fuss', that is at the heart of the world.

"And as for his Brazen Head, I have tried myself in my own blundering and amateurish way to invent a machine that can use what we have come to call the *agens intellectus*, or the mental driving-force, that exists in the ultimate substance of things and which we are told in the scriptures is the Spirit of God. But I seem to be saying things contrary to what you are feeling about all this, my dear son, and I beg you to tell me at once where your difficulty lies; for I can see that many of our friends here are interested in this point, and I shall perhaps have more to tell you when I have spent a night under your betrothed's roof and in company with your Friar's Brazen Head."

Raymond de Laon looked round at the faces about him, and he was forced to admit to himself that they did indeed look surprisingly interested as to what he would say in reply to all this. He made up his mind to blurt out the precise truth.

"You are quite right, master," he said, making a peculiar gurgling noise in his throat before each word he uttered, as if it had been projected out of him by squeezing his wind-pipe. "There *is* a thing that I really must ask you, master, while I have a chance, for there is no telling how long my destiny will enable me to remain at Cone Castle where already I am by no means, as my friends here could tell you, what at Oxford they call a *persona grata* with everybody. But what I want to ask you is this, for my betrothed's younger brother, whose name is John, and whose quickness in learning things has been a tremendous help to the Friar, has recently, in his talk anyway, shown a tendency to follow some of the more satirical Latin poets and to grow sceptical about our holy faith and I am not clever enough, nor is my betrothed, to refute young John's arguments; but I certainly think he goes much further in the direction of unbelief than the Friar himself does, who indeed, from what I've been able to pick up, remains an entirely orthodox Christian. My question, great doctor, is simply this: *Where*, in a world composed of matter possessed of this *energeia-akinesis*, does God come in? What place in fact is left, in a world of such self-creative energy as you describe, for any sort of Creator?"

The moment was a singularly intense one for that small group of about a dozen men. The average intelligence among the retainers of the Lord of Cone was a good deal higher than it was at the Fortress; and ever since Raymond's official betrothal to Lil-Umbra, whose young brother was known to be a reckless supporter of the Friar, there had been lively discussions in the ground-floor reception-hall, as well as in the kitchen, as to whether the Friar was inspired by God or by the Devil.

Not for nothing had Albertus been an active bishop for a couple of years. By his use-and-wont contacts under such conditions with all sorts of people he had developed, to a degree unusual in such a speculative thinker, an awareness of the thoughts and feelings of the people that surrounded him, or that at any moment accompanied him, or that happened to be listening to him.

From boyhood he had been a naturalist, and by this time he knew much more about birds and beasts and insects than any other thinker of that epoch who was proficient in Greek and Latin.

At this moment as he encountered the earnest faces round him and noted the almost distressed look in the long thin countenance of Raymond de Laon, a countenance that already bore more wrinkles between the eyebrows than seemed natural for so handsome and diplomatic a youth, he suddenly caught sight of a butterfly he had come to name a "Wood Argus" because of the markings on its wings, that now had settled, since this group of two-legged monsters seemed inclined to be quiescent, on a little poplar-twig just above a regular bed of bluebells.

A particularly brilliant ray of June sunshine was at that second turning into a shining little arrow-head of gleaming silver the white stalk of one of these flowers, and as he watched it, Albert of Cologne couldn't help wondering whether this particular "Wood-Argus" came regularly at this particular hour to this particular spot.

In a small leafy grove just outside Cologne he had frequently constituted himself a patient and watchful sentinel of whatever light-winged butterfly-emperor ruled that forest-glade, a sentinel big enough to ward off any feathered freebooter, who might come sweeping down through the fragrant air-gulfs of the noon-heat, with the deliberate intention of snapping up so divine a mouthful.

He now had the experience and the wit to see clearly that by his reference to the self-creative energy of the "Hulee", or "raw-material" or "formless timber", as Homer might have called it, out of which the world is made, he had touched an extremely ticklish subject, in fact the subject of all subjects, he now told himself, about which, in connection with Friar Roger, the intelligent minority was most hotly divided.

"I *must* be careful," he thought. "O how mixed up, how cruelly mixed up with our personal prejudices, is every exciting topic we touch!"

And then, when it must have been clear to them all that he was longing to say something that was very important to himself, but found it hard to get the right words for it, his eyes were caught by the largest of a few dark holes in the ground in front of him, obviously caused by the cloven hooves of some wandering steer or heifer, and which had been filled with water by last night's rain. Upon this small black pool, in his effort to decide what it would be best to say, he was now fixedly staring. As he stared, he suddenly grew aware that the mid-day Sun was also busy with this hand's-breadth of dark water, and that he was now staring into his own reflected visage, above which his complicated head-wear had already become among the bluebells a portentously hovering shadow.

"*What place is left for a Creator?*" was now the question which the mind behind that bulging forehead, those quivering nostrils, those small deep-set tearful eyes, had to answer; and as, aware of that attentive group of men, and of that more than attentive young lover, the great teacher from Cologne struggled with the riddle of existence, he felt as if this floating "something" that was himself, now confronted by this like-ness of a not very striking human face in the wet hoof-print of an animal, was being carried, just as that reflected face looked as if it were being carried, up, up, up, through all Space and all Time, searching for the thrice-blessed gulf of absolute nothingness that is beyond all that has a name.

At last the words came. "There are some of us," he said, speaking slowly, and beneath and against and under, so it felt to him, the warm breath of every star in the firmament, "who hold that all the ideal words that we philosophers use, such as 'matter' and 'substance' and 'form' and 'essence' and 'finite' and 'infinite' and 'transitory' and 'eternal' and 'nature' and 'super-nature' are only so many names, sounding syllables that signify nothing. Others hold that these words represent ultimate and basic realities by the use of which we recognize and interpret the *Entelecheia* of existence, that would be just meaningless smoke without them!

"Now what I hold, my dear friends, is especially difficult to make clear because it partakes of the opposite opinions of both those two camps of thought. I do hold, as strongly and as absolutely as it is possible to hold anything, that behind all the visible and intelligible phenomena of the cosmos there exists the invisible and unintelligible reality which we call God.

"According to the philosophy of the greatest of all philosophers—I speak of Aristotle—the material stuff of which the Cosmos is composed is eternal, and contains within itself the creative energy that builds the world and produces all the innumerable lives around us, such as we know and such as we are. But we Christians have been given a—a—a——"

Here he hesitated and a very queer sound came from his body as he stood there before them, like a great black rook come down from a nest that a quarter of a year ago has served its purpose to the limit and now awaits its dissolution, a sound that might have been an explosion of wind, either from mouth or from anus, but a sound that resembled the cry of an unborn child, that with the permission of nature had been engendered in the duodenum of an elderly man by deliberate impregnation from a superhuman minotaur—"have been given a—a *Revelation* that alters from top to bottom the whole situation."

Here his voice rose just as used to rise the voice of each of the Homeric heroes at some special crisis in the Trojan War. "We cannot, we dare not, we must not, lest we become the murderers of the truth that is in us, deny the integrity of our own reason. And if we accept our reason we must recognize that the deepest, wisest, completest embodiment of it, so far, and until this moment, is to be found in the works of Aristotle; and Aristotle maintains that since matter is eternal in its inherent essence and is capable, in itself and by its own secret energy, of renewing the universe, and of bringing into existence an everlasting recurrence of the multiple forms we see around us, we are driven by our reason to assume that the cosmos is eternal. But this whole assumption, this whole implication, this whole conclusion is surpassed and transcended"—Albert's voice became the voice of a trumpet— "by the *Revelation* brought by Christ, the revelation of Christ Himself and the revelation of the Holy Spirit!"

The warrior-retainers from Cone Castle were so accustomed to associate any reference, in any formal service of worship, to the Holy Ghost, as a sign that this same service had reached its termination, that now they all solemnly and mechanically, just as in some ordinary daily ceremonial, lowered one knee to the earth, and then, standing erect, murmured the word "amen".

Albert of Cologne would never have become what undoubtedly he had, by the pure power of his intrinsic personality, quite deservedly become, the best philosophical teacher in Europe, if he hadn't long ago acquired the power of not losing his temper, or the thread of his discourse, or even his own zest for the subject, when the bulk of his audience missed the whole point, as they certainly did now.

The grand trick he had acquired was a very daring one, and one whose nature would have been extremely shocking to many pious souls, namely the device of treating the words of Jesus, on almost all the well-known occasions when the Master uttered decisive and pregnant announcements, as if they contained in them, however tragic they might be, a peculiar element of sheer humour.

And the psychic trick Albertus used on this occasion was the wisest possible one he *could* have used, namely the trick of appropriating to himself and to his own feelings at such moments the bold and perhaps scandalous assumption that the Son of God was humorously aware of the sublime stupidity of the race of mortals, whose flesh he had submissively adopted for some unknown and secret purpose of his Divine Parent.

Raymond de Laon however had not bowed the knee at the reference to the Paraclete, nor had he stiffened himself in preparation for entering the Fortress. His face had indeed taken on a look of infinite relief. He had in fact been terribly afraid that Albert would at this juncture try to do what so many of the so-called Averroists did—namely, slur over the Athenian thinker's conviction as to the eternity of "Matter" or "Hulee", and insert into this unconscionable substance a nebulous and vaporous wedge of divine providence.

To Raymond it was a turning point in his whole mental life, this frank and free admission, by Albertus of Cologne, that, if a student honestly followed Aristotle, he couldn't, with any integrity of mind or any consent of reason, refuse to accept the Aristotelian conclusion as to the eternity of the world.

It was therefore with the abysmal craving of his deepest

nature that Raymond now awaited from Albert some notion of what he actually meant by the word Revelation.

"What we must do as christians," Albert of Cologne announced slowly, "is just to accept by a pure and simple act of faith the Revelation of Jesus that He was, and is, the Son of God, and that God in the beginning created the world. There are therefore," Albert went on quietly, "two accounts of the origin of all things: first the view offered us by the greatest of all human thinkers that the world never had a beginning, but has always existed, and secondly the revelation of Jesus that He and He only is the true Son of God, and that in the beginning God created the world.

"The first of these opinions is the one we hold when we follow our human reason. The second is the one we hold when we accept the view that Jesus is the Son of God, and what He tells us about the universe is the truth. Which of these two views about the beginning of things we as individuals accept will therefore depend upon how far we are ready to follow Faith, when it goes beyond Reason and even when it flatly contradicts the view derived from Reason.

"If Matter is eternal, why then the world we live in is likewise eternal, for it is made of Matter or what the Greeks called "hulee"; and, if our world is eternal, it has not been created by anyone. When Jesus talked of 'His Father in Heaven', it is quite clear that he spoke as a Jew, and that he was thinking of the God of the Jews. By the Divinity within Him on the strength of which He spoke, He was Himself convinced that He was the Son of God, and it was in the Power of this conviction that He enlarged his Father's Godhead till it went far beyond the Jewish race. The God of the Jews, though nameless, we call Jehovah; but the God whom Jesus called Father was the God of the whole world, who existed before he created all that is, and who will go on existing when all that is has ceased to exist."

Raymond de Laon had missed no syllable of this pronouncement; nor had he failed to notice how easily, naturally, and unofficially this tremendous Credo had been declared.

"Will Lady Val," he thought, "let me take Lil-Umbra for a short ride after their visitor has been properly welcomed and has gone to the armoury to rest? Will they find the old bailiff still there? Or will they have moved him elsewhere so that this man can sleep alone, as he clearly wants to do, with that awful Brazen Head? God in Heaven! I wouldn't sleep with that Thing in the room, though by so doing I were to be crowned King of Poland! What if the Thing Inside *came out* and stood by the head of my bed? I verily believe I'd go crazy with terror! O I do so long to talk to Lil-Umbra about all these things. She's got all young John's cleverness and all Tilton's soundness and good sense."

"Well, my Lord Albertus, shall we move on again? It's not more than a mile from here."

"I'm at your service, my son; and I warrant that you, my lads"—and he gave the Cone Castle group a friendly smile—"will be thankful enough to exchange our theology for a beaker of good ale or even a flagon of cider!"

258

XVIII

THE VIGIL

The silence of them all was very marked as they threaded their way between mossy fir-stumps and ferny rocks, while the hot noon-rays, hidden by one branch and revealed between two branches, and forever being broken and intercepted by the dark feathery foliage of ancestral pines, turned the endless blue-bells, upon which it seemed impossible to avoid treading, into an elfin army of some aboriginal pixy-monarch, who though confronted by a cohort of giants was by no means frustrated in his attempt to add yet another outpost to his sylvan realm. It was indeed a natural part, this speechless silence of them all, of the sweltering docility of every forest creature under the royal glare of the lord of life.

When they came in sight of the Great Gate of the Fortress a curious psychic event occurred. This was an event that, in itself without any further evidence, is a proof that all those wild and desperate feelings which reach us from every quarter of the horizon, passing from the north to the west, and from the west, through the north again, to the south, are sometimes fully justified.

For here, precisely and exactly here, where, by a superhuman and Herculean heave, such as more than the muscles of any ordinary human frame could have endured without cracking or breaking, the Lord of the Manor of Roque lifted the horse Cheiron from his four hooves and rolled him over on the ground, the appalling strain of the effort he made, and the weird desper-ation of the awareness accompanying it, had actually created a living spirit.

And at this point in their approach to this spot every single

259

one of this small company, including Raymond and Albert the Great, felt a definite stab in the region of their heart, as if an invisible spirit had struck them just there.

And if Albert of Cologne had boldly enquired: "To what tribe of spirits do you belong?" this "Genius Loci" might well have answered with the words: "I am the spirit of a supernatural effort, an effort that was not only an effort of muscles but an effort of will and an effort of mind and an effort that drew into itself a positively unlawful, insupportable, and intolerable strength from all the living things about it, from the trees, from the creatures of the earth, from the birds of the air, from the actual stones and rocks and earth-mould of this place, so that", thus might the spirit of that shock, the spirit of that superhuman strain have replied to the bold question of the sage from Cologne, "so that I am a spirit which to the end of time, yes! until ice from above, or fire from below, destroy this whole forest, will embody in a shudder of this air the effort this man made; one of the most terrific efforts ever made on this earth since Hercules lifted up the Giant Antaeus in his arms to strangle him in the air; and I, the spirit of this appalling effort, will remain here to guard this man's gate against all his enemies unto the third and fourth millennium of his descendants!"

It was about this man, the Lord of the Manor of Roque and the master of the Fortress, that Albertus Magnus enquired at once, the moment he was ushered by Raymond de Laon in to the presence of Lady Val.

"Yes, O yes!" the lady replied, "and I'll certainly tell him that your first question, reverend sir, was about his health. He strained something inside him. Gorthruk, our manor leech, who came here five years ago straight from Oxford, and is said to have studied medicine under the court physician in Paris, is of opinion that though the injury itself can never, by the nature of it, heal itself, my husband will very shortly be well enough to resume his hunting and fishing and his usual protective investigations round the outskirts of the Manor.

"Gorthruk has given us an ivory box containing three or four compartments each one of which contains several differently tasting tablets. Gorthruk says that, in his own village of Tintinhull, the blacksmith has been kept alive by just such curative pills for four and twenty years, after a strain similar to the one suffered by my husband; only *his* trouble—the blacksmith's I mean—was caused by a wrestling-match with the bailiff of the Manor of Montacute who was a very heavy man, and thus, when the blacksmith of Tintinhull picked him up in his arms and threw him into the village duck-pond, the village priest, whose name was Humph, and who came from Gloster, had to wade into the pond to get him out; for he hit his head on Gammer Grundy's bucket, which had lain there, down in the mud, since the days of Thomas à Becket.''

Raymond de Laon had never before heard his betrothed's mother talk in this free and easy way; but he told himself it must be due to the fact that all women, especially those in responsible positions and those with important households to look after, are invariably anxious to win favour with church dignitaries.

They are also, Raymond's erratic thoughts ran on, often much more interested than are their hunting and fishing and fighting husbands, in historical and philosophical subjects, in spite of the fact that their opportunities for such studies are so much less. As to the easy homeliness of Lady Val's talk, ''don't they all go on in that sort of way,'' Raymond said to himself, ''when they want to captivate us? The only alternative I suppose would be sculleries, store-cupboards, and meat-skewers, with a sagacious allusion, or even a sly glance now and again, towards bed-clothes.''

Whether sage or sly in her welcome, Lady Val soon disposed of her chief guest, and arranged for the Cone Castle contingent to dine at an earlier hour than was usual and at a special table in the dining-hall. She likewise gave her most regal and gracious permission to Raymond, as a reward for his skill as a tutelary ambassador, to take Lil-Umbra for a couple of hours' ride in the forest.

''You'd better,'' she added, as the pair went off, ''start, and come back too, by the main entrance. Your father has placed such a powerful guard at Tilton's shrine that there's no possible danger from that quarter. But as nurse always used to say, 'It's silly to shout till the Devil's gone out.'''

With a big silver tray arranged conveniently between them upon a stool made of exquisitely slender delicately twisted willow-twigs, upon which stood two glasses and a huge beaker of red wine and a few oaten cakes, the old ex-bailiff of the manor of Roque found a perfect listener to his rambling talk in the great Albert of Cologne.

Accustomed to the part of the chief talker in the presence of less experienced, less volatile, less egocentric and much younger hearers, it was an indescribable relief to Albert the Great to rest and recline in this ancient armoury and listen in peace to this old gentleman's rambling stories of an up-and-down long life full of the simple power of representative authority and of the simple piety of unquestionable conviction.

There in the background, just as if "It" also was listening to the old man's talk, stood the Brazen Head, its confused multiple-mooded expression rejecting placidly any dogmatic solution of the entangled problem of existence. It may well be believed that Albertus Magnus didn't confine himself to listening. Every now and again with the subtle wisdom of a born decipherer of difficult old documents he interpolated at certain turning-points a question by which into the unpremeditated debouch-ings of the senile narrator there was insinuated a flickering lantern, tied, as it were, round the neck of a darting bird, a lantern that might be compared to some providential fire-fly giving a celestial clarification to our dark pilgrimage through the mists of Chaos to the City of Cosmos.

But what struck Albertus Magnus most about this loquacious old gentleman was his attitude towards the Brazen Head. There was the Brazen Head, quite close to the ex-bailiff's side, in fact almost touching the old man's right shoulder; but its presence didn't seem to disturb him in the least. Nor was it as if he altogether disregarded it. It was as if *he and it* had already reached some personal understanding between themselves, by virtue of which there was no longer any necessity for both of them to speak, since, when the ex-bailiff spoke, he spoke for them both.

"The whole trouble in this Fortress," the ex-bailiff was presently murmuring, "comes from the fact that Lil-Umbra's brothers are so different from each other that they are always arguing and disputing. This makes it necessary for Lil-Umbra to keep the balance between them, sometimes taking the side of Tilton the elder one, and sometimes the side of John the younger one."

"But I should have thought," protested the great teacher from Cologne, "that just for that very reason their sister's mind would gain enormously and show signs of wonderful development."

"You see, it's like this, great Master," murmured the old man rather querulously. "The elder boy is mad about architecture and about carving, while the younger thinks of nothing but what Friar Bacon has lately written or is likely to write; and the moment the poor girl feels sympathetic towards the artist brother, the other one, the younger one, gets indignant and begins railing against God and the church; and this of course sets the elder one off upon *his* particular hobby-horse, and they argue with each other just as, we are always being told, you great doctors of divinity dispute together, about essences and qualities and aspects and substances and forms, and how powerful angels are, and how crafty devils are, and whether the world had a beginning and whether it will have an end: and the result of all this is just the very opposite of what you have just now suggested; for the dear girl—and she is, I tell you, my lord, the sweetest and loveliest creature you ever saw— begins to hate the whole subject and to wish she'd been born a Mohammedan, or a Buddhist, or anything rather than a Christian."

"You will, I hope," threw in Albert of Cologne eagerly, for he recognized at once that he was on dangerous ground; and he didn't fail to notice that this peace-loving old gentleman, who wandered a little in his mind, had a deep tenderness for this young maiden who was the betrothed of Raymond de Laon, "you will, I hope, forgive an impertinent and even a discourteous question, but I'd be very thankful if you'd tell me what it was in the relations between this maid of whom you speak and her brother Tilton, the builder and sculptor with his own hands of a shrine to Our Lady, that made it possible for Bonaventura to accuse them of the terrible sin of incest?"

To his great relief this daring, rude, and even outrageous question did not seem to trouble the old ex-bailiff in the very least.

"O *that's* easily explained, great Doctor! Searching round in the ardent spirit of a born sculptor for some living model for the figure of Our Lady that he was so anxious to carve for the shrine he was building, it naturally came into his head to make use of the perfect form and heavenly features of his chaste and beautiful sister.

"But when this accurst Bonaventura saw Master Tilton's Blessed Virgin holding the Holy Babe, he commanded those bandits from Lost Towers to hammer the whole thing to bits! You may well indeed look horrified, O greatest of all Churchly Doctors, but I haven't sat here since my retirement from office, with the lady Lil-Umbra visiting me daily, and Master Tilton and Master John, one or the other of them, coming in to see me pretty well once a week, without learning something of what goes on; learning, I mean, what historians learn by living *after the event*, only I've been learning it by watching the event closely and yet watching it from a certain distance *while it was going on.*

"And I can tell you this, great Doctor—and do you, as Master John, who has been trying to learn Greek, says Homer always says, 'and do you lay it to heart'—all persons, whether male or female, who make it the chief object of their lives to seek out and uncover sexual sins and sexual obliquities in other persons, are themselves—and you can perceive it, O most renowned Doctor, in their countenance, especially in their mouths and nostrils and eyes—are themselves just the very ones to be most easily assailed by an itching desire to enjoy the very same lecherous sensations which they are so anxious to condemn.

"Now, O mighty Sage, please accept my word. The moment I encountered this Bonaventura at close quarters, I knew at once from the man's eyes and mouth and lips and nostrils that he was the sort of person who could easily be completely obsessed by sexual lust. What sins this man has committed in his own life I have not of course, O great one from Cologne, any way of knowing. But this I can tell you and this I do know; though being a little shaky in my mind from old age, you must take what I tell you with your own reservations. This abominable legend about Lil-Umbra and Tilton is simply the outward and visible expression of the viciousness of the fellow's own nature."

These final words of the ex-bailiff were uttered with such intensity that the face of his hearer, which was as much a hieroglyph of sympathy as, according to the old man, Bonaventura's was of lechery, positively became a quivering crow's beak of concentrated attention.

"I would like to know very much indeed, O most renowned of doctors," went on the old man, "just what you feel about this matter of Roger Bacon's influence over young people, like our mutual friend Raymond de Laon and like Lady Lil-Umbra's brother John. Do you consider that this Friar, who is such an adept in all these new scientific inventions, has a good or a bad influence over our younger generation? Whether because of the presence of *That Thing*"—and the old man gave a significant jerk of his shoulder in the direction of the object indicated—"or because of this wicked lie invented by Bonaventura, or simply because I've been more impressed than ever of late by the goodness and sweetness of Lady Lil-Umbra, I've been thinking a great deal about Friar Roger and his new science; and I've come to the conclusion, mighty Doctor, that there's a change coming over the whole of Christendom—I might go so far as to say over the whole world—and I've decided that it's the duty of all of us who are believers, to think out carefully for ourselves what our position is.

"It was all very well when we were young to just repeat the lessons taught us by our parents or by our priest or in our school, but when we become men—that's what I've been thinking lately in this old armoury of ours, great master—we ought to 'put away', as holy scripture says, 'childish things'; and not only so, but we ought to examine, yes! examine down to the very bottom, all our inherited presumptions, suppositions, and beliefs, everything in fact to which we've become accustomed, everything that we now take for granted; yes, examine it all, examine it over and over again from the very start, rejecting *this* and retaining *that*, as our separate, independent, individual spirit tells us, for it is our individual spirit that, at the bottom of everything, is, and always will——"

He was interrupted in his speech, and the magnate from Cologne was interrupted in his sympathetic listening by the sudden opening of the armoury door and the entrance of none other than the gigantic Mongolian Jew, Peleg. Peleg walked with slow deliberate steps straight to where the two men were seated, and addressed himself to the ex-bailiff.

"Lady Val has sent me, sir," he said, "to convey you, if you will be good enough to allow me to help you, to my lord's Little Room. My lady wishes me to say that her first thought was to have the two young masters' beds moved there for the night, but my lord felt strongly that you would yourself prefer the Little Room to any other and feel more independent there. You will be, my lady wished me to say, quite as comfortable there, perhaps *more* comfortable than you are here in the armoury."

The relief on the face of the old man at hearing this news was so evident to Albertus Magnus, that this latter suppressed his instinctive inclination to make a polite apology for being so anxious to spend the night quite alone with the Image of Brass.

"If," he thought, "I make a fuss about any of this business, I shall be only confusing the issue. What I want is to have this armoury to myself for just one night—to myself along with this man-created man—if *that's* what you are!" and he shot at the Brazen Head a challenging and yet a pitying glance before turning his half-scouring, half-cleansing, and altogether benevolent little eyes upon the gigantic Peleg.

"The little room!" cried the old man. "Nothing in this place could please me better! And, Peleg, old friend, I am indeed perfectly ready to go there at once if you will give me your support."

Without further speech, and with one of Peleg's powerful arms round his shoulder, the old man rose stiffly to his feet, and laying his left hand with a sublime indifference to this weird entity's claim to be a living soul, upon the shoulder of the Brazen Head, as if it had been the wooden back of a negligible bench in some public hall-way, he offered his right hand to Albert of Cologne.

"We shall meet, your—your—your Eminence," he murmured, clearly regarding their visitor as a Papal Legate, or at least as a Cardinal, "and then we shall, I hope, be able to finish our conversation."

Albert of Cologne looked at him with all that humorous tenderness he liked to think he had learnt from Jesus. "I shan't forget, you may be sure," he said, "the exact point we've reached in our talk! Peleg here can well imagine," and he gave Peleg a subtly-charged smile, as if he'd known him for years rather than was now seeing him for the first time, "just what we were discussing! and perhaps you wouldn't," he added, "mind telling the Lady Valentia that I feel too exhausted to require any dinner tonight, and shall soon take advantage of the excellent bed I see ready for me. And no doubt I shall dream of all the wonderful people and of all the amazing things I shall encounter tomorrow."

With these final words he lowered himself in his chair, thrust out his heels with a somnolent leathery sound across the reed-woven rug in front of him, and closed his eyes, while Peleg in dutiful silence led the ex-bailiff from the room.

Into the deep quiet that followed their departure Albertus sank down, as if into the original ocean of silence out of which all sounds first sprang. Sleep was certainly what the man from Cologne needed, and he must have slept till not only the light of that long June afternoon was over, but its evening twilight too; for, when he awoke, the armoury was nearly dark.

As soon as he was on his feet, however, the first thing he looked at, by the light of the small uncovered oil-lamp that stood in front of it, was a tiny image of the Virgin, which had been a gift to the ex-bailiff by his grandmother in his childhood and which was very precious to him.

What, to confess the truth, made it especially precious to him was the fact that his little sister—who was his only youthful companion, for his parents had no other children—had once, in one of her moods, whether a mood of skittishness or of naughtiness, or because she had overheard it in some argument between priests, carved in big letters, clear across the base of the little image, the single word *Parthenogenesis*.

Moira had been drowned in the river Wey and her body carried out to sea before she was fourteen, and the ex-bailiff's son, Randolph, had steadily refused, probably because of some prejudice of his wife against the child's name, which is Greek for Destiny or Fate, to use it for any of his own daughters, of whom he had several. So nowhere upon earth save in her brother's heart, and in the exquisite trouble she herself had taken to form those fifteen letters, did there exist any memorial of the little carver of that big word.

It certainly was not of those significant syllables, nor of the question as to who had inscribed them upon that small image, that Albertus Magnus of Cologne was thinking as, by the help of the flame at that tiny shrine, he lit the chief light of the armoury and began making his preparations for the night. Once safe in bed, with an excellent pillow under his throbbing skull, and the armoury-light turned low, and a couple of warm blankets over him, he gazed steadily at the Brazen Head.

"If you can manage for me to spend one night entirely alone with the Head," he had told Raymond de Laon, "I will most certainly come."

Well! Here he was, alone with It, and there were four or five hours of total darkness in front of him and no apparent danger of any interruption to whatever communion of body, mind, or even spirit he could bring about between this man-created Being and himself.

Albertus had by nature an outward-working mind, and his natural urge to talk, to teach, to write, to read, to direct, to examine, to explore, to plan, to construct, to build, to organise, to reform, to originate, was so powerful that it was extremely difficult—O much worse than difficult!—extremely repulsive and even loathsome to him to indulge in any sort of introspection.

It was pain and grief to him to analyse his own thoughts, feelings, impressions, and reactions. He might have been bolder in this direction, if he had not known by instinct that there were sleeping devils in the intricate corridors of his mind that it would be dangerous to disturb. He was indeed continuously aware of a particular region in his response to life that held a dark, ultimate, indescribable horror for him.

It was in fact so horrible that it was imperative for him to avoid this region of his mind at all costs. It was a region which, if he couldn't steer his way round it, and, as far as this was humanly possible, forget it, and behave as if it didn't exist, would eventually by the pressure of its sheer horror disintegrate his whole intelligence.

It is perfectly possible for an energetic and powerfully galvanic will to win renown for its owner, while the deepest part of the personality which that towering will-power has to carry along with it, just as a swiftly driving chariot might have to carry in the belly of its body a writhing and squirming serpent, may be secretly twitching and quivering with all manner of maniacal distastes and repugnances.

"All my life," thought Albertus Magnus, "I've been escaping from myself. What I've been always secretly afraid of is neither God nor the Devil, neither man nor beast: it is simply and solely myself!"

He had grown so accustomed to make certain deeply intimate and yet automatic debouchings and deviations from the direct path in his consciousness of life, so as to dodge, and carefully circumnavigate, and craftily avoid, all those places where his most fearful personal mania and most horrified shrinking would be brought into play, that it was a dangerous shock to him to find that the presence of the Brazen Head disturbed this wise habit.

The only companion, whether male or female, to whom he had ever given a hint of this lake of horror in a secret valley of his soul, was Thomas Aquinas, with whom he had shared lodgings in more than one great seat of learning, and of whom he would retort when the others ridiculed Thomas as a dumb ox, "when this dumb ox starts bellowing, he'll make the whole world listen." But we can well believe that it would not have been easy to make a young metaphysician of Thomas's calibre realize the existence of such a background to his adored teacher's lively lessons.

But whether Thomas Aquinas realized before he died—for the master outlived the pupil by several years—all that the great Albert's benevolent energy concealed behind its absorbing and compelling instruction, there can be little doubt that this supreme teacher's frightful necessity to keep his own nervous malady in the background had something to do with the desperate fervour of his way of teaching.

The more passionately and comprehendingly he could follow and interpret the subtle distinctions in theology, the further he was able to withdraw himself from that appalling lake of horror in the secret depths of his own mind.

What he found himself wondering now—as with rather a troublesome effort he squeezed the thickest of his two pillows under the back of his own head and stared at the Head of Brass—was why the word, that he had by chance noticed inscribed in childish capital letters on that little image of the

Blessed Virgin, kept hovering on the intervening air, like faint streaks of splashed blood, between himself and the expressionless countenance of the Brazen Head.

"But surely," he thought, "in the creation of that Image and in the elaborate workmanship or exquisite machinery that he gave to it," here he jerked his own head forward almost defiantly—"yes! I'm talking of you, you new Adam, you Adam of wires and wheels and screws and scuttles, and I'm telling you now, here and now, that what your man-maker forgot when he wound you up was the touch of a Virgin!"

What happened then was a volcano-like explosion of feeling, an explosion to which both Magnus and the Brazen Head must have contributed something. The accumulation of force which burst at that moment drew from Albertus, in one whole rush, all the smouldering depths of the spirit with which he had for the best years of his life flooded the gaping arteries of his devoted pupils; while the imprisoned demonic power in the Brazen Head, which seemed only to have been waiting an opportunity to escape, burst forth to meet what the other was giving.

It was not until much later that Albertus was able to offer —to himself we must understand—some kind of an account of what happened. He felt as if the whole dark, enormous, inscrutable mass of blackish-greyish matter, which Aristotle called "Hulee", and which the philosopher and many of his disciples held was eternal, indestructible, and without beginning, was now around him on every side. He could see it, he could feel it, he could smell it, and it was bearing him up, up, up, on the titanic curves of an agglomeration of merciless substance!

Wildly and desperately Albertus realized that the material substance of his own body had begun to grow larger and larger; and as he was carried upward he became frantically and dizzily aware that in front of him was only empty Space, yes! Space absolutely empty, leading on and on and on, with no limit and without an end!

And then suddenly he spoke to himself in a still small voice. "Albert, old friend," he said to himself, "there's no need for you to be alone in Space like this. You have forgotten what all creatures ought never to forget. You have forgotten that there is also Time."

And at the thought of Time—Time that can reduce Space by measuring the segments of it, Time that can remember backwards to wherever man has been or might have been, Time that can imagine forwards to wherever man will be or could be, Time that's our friendly and customary home, Time that belonged to our fathers before us and will belong to our children after us, Time that clothes us as with familiar raiment and nourishes us as with bread and wine, Time that gives us a bed to sleep on, Time that gives us a tent to cover us and a fire to warm us—Albertus of Cologne had no sooner uttered these words in a low voice, himself speaking to himself, than lo and behold! he was back again in the armoury of the Fortress, back again with his thickest pillow squeezed under his neck, back again with the flickering blood-stained letters of the word *Parthenogenesis* hovering in the darkness between himself and the Brazen Head.

And he was only aware of being back again, for a second or two of submission to Time, the magic power which had delivered him, when he was lost, to all that was and all that might be, in a deep and dreamless sleep.

XIX

MASTER PETER PEREGRINUS

It was not until the late summer of the year of grace 1272 that Petrus Peregrinus of Picardy approached the channel between France and England with the intention of crossing to the district in this latter country, where his scientific rival Roger Bacon was still incarcerated. He had been supporting himself in his usual manner, till what he called his "experiments in magnetism" brought him serious enemies, and so discomforted the local authorities as to endanger his freedom of movement. It was then that he decided upon a bold move.

In plain words he joined, for the time being, and with an understanding that he could leave it whenever he wished, no less important a body of European soldiers than one of the divisions of the King of France. He took service in this particular body of men not from any hostility to the Swiss or the Spanish or the Portuguese or the Italians or the Germans, but purely from a desire to earn money which he could save up and spend on leisure to study magnetism and to write a treatise on it.

He had been in luck this particular summer; for though the force he chose to join had had nothing to do with any crusade, nor had been used for any important campaign, it had been posted in a part of the country where there was a constant demand for military aid in the protection of rich farmers and of their flocks and their barns from wandering bands of marauders, whose extreme destitution had made them freebooters.

Petrus had given himself up to all manner of mad dreams while his camp was moved from place to place; but in one way and another he had saved up quite a little hoard of such silver pieces as were exchangeable coins, if not current coins, in most of the countries of Europe.

It was on a hot day in late summer, and he had reached a little circular valley in Savoy, when an event occurred that was of importance in his life. He suddenly came upon a cross-road hut in the centre of this little valley, which was inhabited by a couple of persons who were so aged as to look barely human. He had been along this border of Savoy before but had never before passed through this particular valley, but it was here he was destined to receive, or here that pure chance flung upon him, an inspiration of a very curious kind.

Whether this inspiration came from an angel, and had an angelic purpose behind it, or came from a devil, and had a diabolic purpose behind it, it would be impossible to say. But either, if for the nonce we rule pure chance out of it as the arbiter of such events, was certainly possible.

An angelic power might very well have decided that, before Peter Peregrinus had continued his tortuous career for another day, it would be good for the world in general if it were cut short. On the other hand a devilish power might easily have come to the conclusion that there was nobody on earth at this hour who, if only preserved alive for a few moons longer, could work so much harm to the human race as this traveller from Picardy.

"What do you call your turnpike corner?" enquired Peter of this couple of age-stricken ones, as they sat side by side on a wooden bench, filling a big wooden bucket with a mess of sour milk and mouldy bread and bad potatoes, while a big bristling sow of a yellowish colour uplifted her snout from a hollow place scooped out of the ground before them.

"What does the lord on his feet say?" enquired the antiquity who wore male clothes, addressing the antiquity who wore female clothes.

The woman made no reply to this question. But she rose to *her* feet and held out a long skinny arm with a regular birds' claw at the end of it.

"Give silver, great lord of the highway," she murmured huskily in a queer French patois: "and me yes! even me, will give you the magic word for your long travel."

s   273

The enormous head of Peter of Maricourt moved a little, or perhaps we ought to say drooped a little forward, while from the white expanse of his face, like the sting of a creature that might have stung itself to death in the days of the father of Abraham, protruded the sharp tip of a presumably human tongue.

His black eyes seemed to the companion of the female antiquity, who still kept opening and closing her extended fingers, to flow into each other till they ceased to be two bottomless blacknesses and became one. But whether they were one or two, they evidently read in the Cretan Maze of feminine wrinkles upon which they were now concentrated that that seemingly dried up fountain of wisdom had a tap that was well worth tapping.

"Yes, by Satan," the traveller must have thought, "*I'll get something out of you!*" for he was not only nodding with his head now, but he was also searching in the lining of his jerkin.

At last he brought out a couple of silver coins, a big one and a little one. These he turned over in his fingers many times, so as to make sure the woman saw just what they were and the difference between them. Having satisfied himself that both these things had been observed, he negligently flipped the edges of the two pieces of silver together and permitted his own raptorial orbs to relapse into their respective hollows, while they took in the geographical position of this most pitiful of all possible turnpikes.

He soon became aware that the narrow road he had come by, and the three radiating roads now offering themselves as rivals for his next move, were all sloping upwards. And the queer thing was that, while there were occasional trees, some big, some small, some deciduous, some coniferous, along the edges of all these roads, the ridge or rim of the shallow grassy basin out of which they all led and over which they all vanished into the void or into the clouds, was entirely bare, bare of gorse or bracken or black-thorn, so nakedly bare that it was possible even to note the varying height of particular patches of ordinary meadow grass.

"Why is it," the man asked himself, "that to stand at the bottom of a shallow bowl like this and look up at its grassy rim, about half a mile, I suppose, from this hut, gives me such complete acceptance of my fate as I feel at this moment? If my fate had been totally different from what it is, I mean different from the fate of being the *Antichrist*, who has been prophesied of as long as the *Christ* has been prophesied of, should I, I wonder, feel this same acceptance of it simply from staring up at this rim of grass?

"If, for instance I'd been a Jewish youth like Moses and had come here straight from a vision of the burning bush, with the voice of Jehovah issuing from it and the revelation that it was my fate to lead Israel out of Egypt, should I be feeling this same calm acceptance of such a fate as I feel now when I fall into my rôle as the self-appointed antagonist of Jesus? Is there perhaps a revelation of some planetary Anangkee, or sublime Necessity, in the mere presence of a naked rondure of earth and grass like this against the whole of empty Space?"

With this thought and with this spectacle in his mind, Petrus Peregrinus returned the larger of the two silver coins to the folds of his jerkin and handed the smaller one to the woman, who clutched it, and proceeded to bite it with what were obviously the only teeth in her head that were opposite each other.

Clearly satisfied with the sensation in her mouth caused by this action, she opened with a metallic snap a small receptacle fastened to a leather belt round her waist and slipped the coin inside.

"And now," cried Petrus Peregrinus, fumbling with a bag in the lining of his jerkin adjoining the abode of his special treasure the loadstone. Presently he produced from this receptacle a small live slow-worm, at the sight of which the woman in front of him was seized with panic, and leaving her seat crouched down behind her mate, who groaned and shut his eyes.

All Petrus did however was to fling the slow-worm into the uplifted jaws of the great sow, who promptly bit off its head. Nobody but Petrus saw the pitiful flap which the tail of the slow-worm made to avoid following its head down the sow's throat. These are the things that, if they can only be seen by the right person, lead to some very curious conclusions as to the mystery of life. For as the sow lay down to digest what it had swallowed, the decapitated tail, without wriggling at all and with a final motion of infinite relaxation, as if it were thankfully joining the vast army of exhausted organisms whose reckless, desperate, and aggressive "heads" have flung them aside, stretched out to welcome eternal rest.

"And now," murmured Petrus Peregrinus, "I shall leave you, and take the road to the nearest port for the Isle of Britain where I have a greater conquest to achieve than you— or he——" and he nodded at the old man with closed eyes— "or *you* either, old lady——" and with the handle of his sheathed sword-dagger he prodded the sow's back—"could possibly understand. And *that*"—and he pointed to the continuation, over the rim of the valley, of the road by which he had come, "*that* will be the way I shall go."

With this he turned his back upon them all, upon the old man, whose whole conscious personality seemed devoted to the task of allowing nothing to make him open his eyes, upon the sow who was clearly finding the digestion of a small saurian head an occupation both peaceful and soothing, upon the absolutely motionless body of the decapitated slow-worm, against which, as against the side of a Leviathan, two small insects were already tentatively extending their minute feelers, and finally upon the old lady, who, as she watched that small dark figure—for his soldier's cap was black, his jerkin was black, a heavy velvet cloak he carried on his arm was black, his stockings and wooden shoes were black, while the blackest of all was his one single weapon, that half-sword, half-dagger, which he left in its sheath and used as a short staff to support his steps on any uphill road—uttered from the depths of her whole being the oldest of all European curses.

It wasn't till he was just not quite out of hearing that the old woman stretched out both her arms to give full expression to this malediction. With the fingers of both her hands tightly closed she repeated the word *Erre!*

"Erre! Erre!" she cried over and over again, pronouncing each syllable of the word with peculiar emphasis.

Petrus of Maricourt turned quickly enough when he caught those two syllables upon the air. In Picardy, as well as in Savoy, and of course everywhere along the shore of the Mediterranean, that phrase was used to express loathing and bitter contempt. So *there* was the magic word that he had stopped so long at that turn-pike hovel to extract from its witch-wife! *Erre!* And the word was the very same curse that had been heard in all the harbours of all the coasts and islands of the Mediterranean and Aegean since the days of Homer.

Petrus Peregrinus hadn't been a traveller in all parts of Europe for nothing, and he had often pondered on the mystery of this word with its deadly rush of execration—"Get *out* of here, you rat, you maggot, you worm, you abomination, you lump of filth!"—and he knew well that it had been allowed to remain in all the most authoritative texts of the Homeric manuscripts, and must have been passed, not only by the Athenian censors of the days of King Peisistratus of Athens, but by the far more particular censors of the Library of Alexandria and by the tremendous scholars who revised the "Codex Marcianus" in the Library of San Marco in Venice.

He made no retort to it at this moment however; but every time he pressed his scabbarded sword-dagger into the ground to support his steps over the rim of the basin-like declivity from which he was now rapidly emerging, he concentrated his whole soul upon a solemn covenant he was now making with himself.

"It has become clear to me," murmured his inmost heart communing with itself, "that my chief enemy at this moment among the righteous is Albertus of Cologne. He seems to have got some *secretus secretorum* out of the raw material of the Aristotelian "hulee", of which the universe is made, that enables him to cast some sort of spell over his pupils. He's been having with him of late, and they say they live together in the same lodging, which always gives a teacher a special personal influence over a young man, that eccentric silent youth with a big head who is called Aquinas. Yes! I know what *you* want me to do, my darling little Rod of Power!"

And the weak-legged, black-garbed, black-capped, wooden-booted climber upwards clutched, as he mounted the rim of the depression, the lodestone in the slit of his breeches.

"You want me to go straight to this great donkey of Cologne, who makes friends not with handsome young people but with great head-heavy lunatics, who think of nothing but dove-tailing fantastical dogmas, and when I'm face to face with this double-dyed idiot, you want me to let *you* loose on him, to make him skip a bit! Don't tell me that's *not* what you want, for I know very well it is! But listen to me, my precious little Baton of Power. You're the Wand of Merlin the Brython. You're the Rod of Moses the Israelite. You're the finger that Jehovah lifted when He bade the World leap up like a fish out of Nothing.

"But though you are all you are, little Push-Pin of Omnipotence, the fact remains that, if I am to win in this contest with Albertus Magnus in this arena of this amphitheatre of the universe, I must confront the fellow face to face.

"Well, little soul-prick of the world's gizzard, you think that's impossible don't you? And you think since it *is* impossible, you and I will have to find another way of getting round this beggar and outwitting him! But let me tell you now, my Magnet of Satan, it's *not* impossible. I've just heard—never you mind *how* or by whom!—that he's been invited by Roger Bacon—yes! by Friar Bacon himself, Push-Pin, my devilkin! and you take note of *that*!—to go and see for himself that Brazen Head magicked into life by Brother Bacon. So that's where you and I come in, little lovely, and so let Holy Jesus beware!"

The small dark figure with his black military boots, black military cap, and black sheathed weapon to support his weak legs, was now well across the rim of the geological earth-circle over which that Homeric "Erre! Erre!" of the old woman had hurried him.

Looking round at all he saw and at how the highway he was following was losing itself in a distance that he knew well was westward and seaward, our resolute antagonist of the Christian religion, whom many people would have described as a grotesque little idiot but whom Paul of Tarsus and Jesus of Nazareth would have taken as seriously as he took himself, plucked now from out of his garments the magic lodestone with which he hoped to frustrate the whole Revelation. Rubbing it up and down against the tight black garments that covered his emaciated flanks, just as if he were sharpening a butcher's knife, he proceeded to stretch the thing out to the full length of his arm and began working it up and down as if he were actually making a slit in some vast, invisible, planetary tent, through which when once his stabber, his prodder, his love-piercer, his hope-drainer, his life-borer, his faith-rinser, his root-sucker, his magnet of universal destruction had found its way, it might really hurt and wound and injure whatever universe or multiverse there might be outside and beyond our world.

Once clear of this whole district and aiming for the channel between France and England, our peregrinating Antichrist pursued his future movements with what really was uncommonly careful consideration. Having made straight for the channel, he followed the French coast harbour by harbour, till he hit upon the precise sort of vessel he wanted sailing direct to a Wessex port.

All went well, just as he hoped, and it was not until he had actually disembarked that any trouble came, and when trouble did come, it came from out of his own head, and not from any external event. How it came, why it came, and what made it come, Petrus had not then, and never had afterwards, any clear idea.

It came suddenly out of his memory, as he stood on the shore after waving farewell to the ship that had brought him there: and it came to him just as if somebody else were telling the story, somebody, however, who knew his thoughts and feelings with a perfectly terrible exactitude, somebody in fact who was uncomfortably like God.

What came to him was his memory of a certain occasion when, with other French soldiers, he was being conveyed in a French ship along the shores of Palestine not far from the Port of Acre. Here, because of something he had done or had not done, the ship's commander had had him thrown overboard.

He had not clung very long, however, to an overturned boat which happened to drift past him, when he suddenly found himself close under the bows of the grandest British vessel that in all his peregrinations he had ever beheld. That this vessel was English there could be no doubt, and that it carried on board some extremely important, perhaps even some royal personage seemed more than likely.

"Can it be Lord Edward's ship?" he thought; and in a shorter time than it would have taken him to consult his lode-stone, which he always treated as a familiar spirit, he found himself hauled on board this formidable vessel and confronted with its royal voyager who, as he had predicted, was indeed no other than Lord Edward himself, the heir to the British throne.

The whole interview that followed took place on the main deck of this crusading vessel.

"I thought you were right, Gunter," Lord Edward muttered, addressing the master of the vessel, a man whose most marked propensity was the power of becoming nothing, and a predilection for becoming nothing, or as near nothing as it was possible for a native of the harbour of Weymouth, near the ancient city of Durnovaria, with a handsome wife and a dozen children, to become.

"My sailor-friend here," went on the warrior-prince, addressing Petrus now, but practising as he spoke, just as if he were quite alone, some particular gesture in the difficult art of slinging, "assures me that his wife has relatives in Picardy and that he felt quite certain, from the tone of your voice just now when you answered him from the sea, that you were from that part of the world. Is that so, master? Well, in any case,"— and Edward turned a shrewd glance upon the vessel from which Petrus had been flung, and which was now making use of every inch of sail it possessed to get quickly away—"your friends aren't waiting for you! May I ask what your business is? Or are you, as seems more likely from your looks, now that I see you close, travelling to London from some foreign court? Are you perhaps from Madrid or from——"

Their conversation was interrupted by a series of piercing and painful screams, and Edward turned angrily to the ship's captain whom he had addressed as "Gunter". "Haven't I told you I won't have that man allowed to make that noise! Didn't I tell you to tie him up so that he *can't* scream? Its all in the way he's tied, I tell you! The point I insist on is that he should suffer pain; but that doesn't mean that I want to *hear* his shrieks. In fact if he's tied so that he can't shriek, he'll suffer a lot more. To shriek is a relief. That's why Nature lets us indulge in it. I trust you haven't forgotten, Gunter, quite all I ordered. I am accustomed to being obeyed at sea as promptly as on land. That man deliberately disobeyed me, and he must suffer till he has learnt his lesson!"

It was almost as if the sea itself, with the whole weight of the steel-green purple-shadowed mass of its salt water, had risen up to protest against this haughty announcement; for a terrific wave curved up out of the deep at that point and completely drowned both the screams from below and the exchange of words between the Lord Edward and Master Gunter and Peter of Maricourt.

But it may easily be believed that the last named had not missed the rough brutality with which the future ruler of England had referred to this victim of his violent temper; and as he gazed at him now while all three of them were watched rather humorously by a couple of sailors, his own bodily longing to change his clothes became far less important to him than a rush of purely emotional feeling that quivered through every nerve of his body, a rush of desperate hatred of this powerful, dominating, ruggedly handsome, battle-loving, strong-willed Lord Edward.

And under the power of this blind rush of emotional hatred which he longed to gratify by some spectacular use of his precious lodestone, he realised that this was a crisis in his life.

"Yes," he thought, "may my soul burn in hell if I don't give this great English bully something to make him remember those screams."

But as he watched him closely and dallied with the instrument pressed against his own body, it came over him with the unutterable force of a premonition totally beyond the range of his own fighting spirit, that it would be useless to try to work by magnetism the death of this particular tyrant.

"*But wait a moment*"—he felt as if these words were reaching him out of the air—"What about this hammering bully's offspring? He's the King's son. Will not *his* son be King also when the time comes? And how unlikely, how almost impossible, as the world goes, it would be for the son of a man of iron like this, a back-breaker and a skull-cracker, a master of armies and a sacker of cities, to be born like his begetter, or, if the child were a girl, for her to be a stirrer up of savagery and slaughter! So listen, Lodestone darling! Don't you agree with me, you precious little heart-breaker, life-piercer, lava-flinger, angel-slayer, blow-them-up-alive? Surely you do, my darlingest of little volcanoes? Surely you do? Very well then, my pretty one! The covenant's signed and sealed twixt thee and me. What we'll do is to lie in wait for the feeble offspring of our great shark; and when we've got him we'll fix him! We'll follow him up all his life—or if we're dead our spirits shall—and he shall die screaming!"

It was a curious thing—indeed it was what we pathetic tribes of mortals love to call "one of those things"—that almost simultaneously with Petrus's private talk with his lodestone, Master Gunter, who had gone below, came up again, and going straight up to Lord Edward, announced the death of the man who had been screaming. But that was not all, for there suddenly fell in the midst of the three of them, slam-bang upon the deck, the bleeding, mangled body of a small sea-bird that had been suddenly seized by a roving sea-hawk ready for any mouthful but not inclined to pause for a substantial meal.

The sanguinary slap that the fall of this small feathered corpse made upon the deck, and the shrill wail from the creature's mate that followed it, shook Petrus out of his diffidence to such a degree that he boldly asked Master Gunter whether he could give him a berth and have his clothes dried; and it was almost within touch of the man who had just paid the last penalty for defying the ruler not only of the land, but of the waves of the sea, that Peter of Picardy fell asleep that night hugging his lodestone.

XX

THE CERNE GIANT

It was of these events that our student of magnetism was thinking now, as he stood staring for almost five minutes at the uneven curves of the sea-tide's advances and retreats, as if he were listening to an invisible Brazen Head reporting these things to a mixed court of celestial and infernal judges. When, however, he shook off his memories, he found himself on the edge of a series of wide-stretching reedy swamps, interspersed with estuaries of salt water where wind-tossed alders and wind-swept willows led to lonely huts on flat marshy levels, only separated from the sea by desolate sand-dunes, whose human inhabitants lived on the finned and feathered natives they snared and slew.

Peter of Maricourt was in his most natural element here, for the human beings he encountered had for so many hundreds of years been accustomed to just such predatory explorers that they were as little surprised by the strange appearance of some of them as by the weird accents of others, or by the extraordinary weapons used by yet more unusual apparitions.

As may well be imagined a large portion of the retainers of Lost Towers had been supplied from dwellers in this sea-bordering marsh-land which was inserted, so to say, along that coast between high-rolling chalk hills like a wet wide-open entrance-gate between towering walls.

Lilith of Lost Towers found most of her female intimates in the human hovels sprinkled along these desolate haunts of unusual sea-birds interspersed with wild geese and wild ducks. Nor was it unnatural that this strange maiden herself should in some of her moods, when out of touch it might be with both her parents, pay lengthy visits to these intimates of her own sex in these lonely places.

"As it happened however," so the wisest chroniclers, who are also the humblest, are always being reduced to admitting, Lilith's chief confederate didn't live in the midst of these sea-marshes but on the edge of a quite different stretch of country. This was an expanse of rough, wild moorland, covered with heather, which, as long at any rate as local memory went, had been regarded as once belonging to the ancient Welsh god or king whose name was Llyr or Lear. The woman in this case was Mother Wurzel, who lived in the part of this moor and from which there was a rider's track leading to what was once the important Roman city of Durnovaria, where Lilith's friend as a practiser of both black and white magic had clients of many different sorts.

Petrus Peregrinus had visited the rather unusual abode of Mother Wurzel more than once in his expeditions through Wessex, for it was his practice, when he had too soon exhausted the money he had earned by soldiering, to make use of the innumerable tricks which his pet lodestone could play to keep him in bread and in cheese and in wine.

The habitation of Mother Wurzel was founded upon a very small circle of tall upright stones. The stones must have originally come from the isle of Portland, but they looked as if before being brought here they had stood in a much wider circle; for they had a rather uneasy expression, as if they were not receiving their due of respect in their present crowded and somewhat humiliating position.

And yet the maker of this queer habitation cannot have been totally indifferent to the elements of dignity and beauty, for great care had been taken with regard to making the super-structure harmonize with this queer base. The space within the circle had been given a smooth marble floor and a roof arched as carefully as the crypt of a cathedral, and there had been placed over that one single wooden chamber entirely built of oak. The first time Petrus entered this dwelling, which was called Deadstone, he enquired of Mother Wurzel how on earth she had got possession of it; and she explained that it really belonged to the Lord of Lost Towers, but that he, under his daughter's influence, had made it over in perpetuity to herself as his daughter's friend.

Having got safely clear of the formidable Lord Edward, it didn't take the wanderer from Picardy very long to reach Deadstone, and after an enjoyable night there, for Mother Wurzel's middled-aged daughter, whose name was Puggie-Wuggie, had more deliciously wicked little ways when once you had her by your side in bed than any feminine being Petrus had ever known, he was allowed the privilege of meeting Lilith herself.

When once these two were together, however, things moved more crucially; and everything, at least for our student of magnetism, became much more complicated. In the first place there happened to him something that had never happened to him in his life before. He became completely infatuated with this fatal young lady.

The scrupulous chronicler of these agitating events has to endeavour in his narration of them to proceed as cautiously and meticulously as the events themselves seemed to be proceeding. As always with the actual impacts of life, there were so many different currents joining our special stream of events that this same stream was constantly being thickened here and thinned there, darkened here and lightened there, rendered bluish here and greenish there, and even splashed, it might be, with horrifying drops of blood at certain other places in its course.

At least that is how it all presented itself to Peter of Maricourt; and it did so with such ever-increasing, and now and then with such overlapping, overwhelming, overpowering, and almost drowning force, that he felt as he looked at her that, whether she yielded to his obsession or whether she didn't yield to his obsession, it was now quite as important to him to remain in sight of her as it was to know that he, the gatekeeper's son in the manor of Maricourt, was really and truly the long rumoured, long predicted, long prophesied Antichrist of sacred tradition.

The little red point of Peter's tongue didn't stay quiet any longer within the inner side of its menacing port-cullis. It came out; or, as a more elegant historian would say, it issued forth. What in plain words it did, this tongue of the enemy of Christ, was to lick both its upper lip and its lower lip, a proceeding that would have been a staggering sight for Peter's only friend, his precious lodestone, if that object, now pressed so nervously against its owner's organ of generation, had possessed the power of vision.

"You are asking me, my beautiful one," he was now saying to Lilith, "what I want you to do for me at this juncture. Well! I'll tell you exactly what's in my mind. I think the thing for us to do is to go as quickly as possible to the Fortress, while this ex-bishop from Cologne is still there.

"Since I've found out how perfectly beautiful and irresistible you are, it has come over me that if I want to stop this man's interference with everybody's affairs in this part of the world— and you know how deep the gulf has already grown—down to the centre of the universe—between Bonaventura, and his dice-games with Satan, and Friar Bacon and his attempts to change the creative methods of God by getting some parcener of Eve to help him in the making of Adam. You know of course, my beautiful one, the difficulties we have to surmount if we really are to put a stop to this man's meddling? But here is my plan, my dear, if you'll help me to carry it out.

"In the first place we've got to pretend that we are horrified, beyond all expression, by this assault on Bacon's Brazen Image, which must be to us of course the work of a loyal believer in Christ; and not only so but must contain within itself a splash, a spark, a breath, a sip, a sigh, a bubble, a dewdrop of that Spirit they believe in, who, at Pentecost, descended from Heaven in the shape of a thousand flames of fire and lodged on the heads of a crazy crowd of Jewish madmen.

"Of course it was in the shape of a dove that the Thing descended on Jesus himself at his baptism in Jordan. But by the time of Pentecost Jesus was already 'ascended', and when this Ghost they call 'Holy' 'descended', it came as a sort of Substitute for Jesus to keep things going till the event they call the 'Crack of Doom' or the 'Last Day'."

While Petrus was thus lecturing her on what, if they were to be successful in destroying it all, it was necessary for them to know, he was embracing her with every portion of his mind and not a few portions of his body.

"What we've got to do, my loveliest of all possible Eves, is to remember how long these confounded doctors of the church have been confusing our brains with their absurd problems about the embryo in the womb. This poor little urchin of a formless foetus begins by being on a par with the vegetable world, and has only got what they call a 'vegetative soul'. Then, when it is a tiny bit bigger, and is being definitely fed upon the substance of its mother's life, it is promoted to share the lives of all baby-creatures of the animal world and is allowed to possess what they call a 'nutritive soul'. But just listen to this, my sweet," and, as he spoke, his amorous caresses made it clear that he would not in the least object to becoming the begetter of the kind of creature he was describing.

"What we've got to remember is that this luckless infant only possesses a real soul when it is separated from its mother. What they try to drag in is the old Jewish Jehovah as the Creator of heaven and earth. And at this point, my beautiful one, we've got to remember that the great Aristotle, whom they all regard as the wisest of thinkers, taught that there never was a beginning, but that the matter out of which our world sprang into existence contained, and still contains in its own nature, all the creative energy that is needed. You do see, don't you, my precious, how confusing these learned doctors are? You know, don't you, how they tell us that we must hate the Jews because the Jewish Priests wanted Pilate to crucify Jesus?

"And yet they are always telling us that Jesus himself was the Son of David, and a descendant of Abraham, Isaac and Jacob. The truth is, my darling, we've got to make it clear to everyone we have any influence over that this whole business of the christian religion is full of paradoxes, blunders, manias, idiocies, and ridiculous contradictions.

"Now listen, my pet; wouldn't you like to come up with me now, as they say Satan was always wanting Jesus to go up with him, to the top of some high hill near here to see the wonders of the world and the glories of them?"

The simple-minded chronicler of these events can only record at this point that the daughter of Maldung of Lost Towers gave Petrus of Picardy a very piercing look. But with this piercing look there was mingled—and no other female in the wide world could so charge a single glance—an overpowering appeal and a desperate cry, a cry that was thrown into the very heart of her seduced-seducer, a cry that sounded like: "Take me! Take me! Take me! or I shall melt into thin air!"

"What about our visiting the Cerne Giant?" she whispered. No sooner did this murmur become audible than Petrus leapt to his feet elated and transported.

"Yes! yes! yes!" he cried; and began in his excitement to make a most curious gurgling noise, a noise which, if anyone who did not know him had heard it, would have suggested the bubbling and exploding, the bursting and dissolving, of a miraculous stream of salt water that had somehow or another got into the centre of a rushing waterfall of fresh water.

Nor did it take these two very long to climb up to the Cerne Giant, which was still as it had been for thousands of years— just a figure on the summit-slope of a grassy chalk hill where the grass had been religiously, though most heathenly, prevented from invading by the least fraction of an inch the preposterous picture, in white upon green, of a monstrous giant with his sexual organ erect, awaiting, you might say, the thousand-years-postponed arrival of his female partner, with whom he might play the immemorial game in full and shameless sight of the far-off sea and the eternally receding sky.

Petrus Peregrinus had removed his hand from the magnet beneath his clothes; but he still kept using his short sword in its black scabbard to assist his steps and to play one part of a third leg. The arm and hand and fingers, however, which, like the wind-tossed branches sprouting from a tree that had the power of motion, belonged to whatever activity he chose to exert on his left hand, were entirely free during their rapid ascent to that expectant Cerne Giant.

It must indeed have been a profoundly religious, as well as a profoundly sacrilegious, instinct in more than a thousand generations of Wessex men and women, that had preserved this defiant superhuman figure, thus exposed in the chalk-grown grass on that particular hill. Never once, from beginning to end of their association, would Pierre de Maricourt, have been able to say that any movement he ever made in connection with Lilith, whether in his mind or with any portion of his body, was ever made on his own initiative. Everything he did or said or thought would have struck him, had he ever tried to recapture it, as pure and simple obedience to Lilith.

And yet, always there, close to his side, was his magic lodestone, ready to be brought into contact with every motion of his will, whether towards exertion or relaxation, whether towards attraction or repulsion, whether towards love or hate.

Plug! Plug! Plod! Plod! thudded his short black-sheathed sword-dagger into that grass-grown chalk hill. He could hear the sound of a bell tolling in the bell-tower of a monastic church at the foot of the hill behind him; and he found himself taking a queer satisfaction in mixing the sound of this monotonous bell with the feeling of pressure in the palm of his right hand from each step he took supported by his leather-covered weapon.

Wild, strange, weird, and often quite mad, are the thoughts and fancies of every one of us with regard to each other; but, when we come to face it, the most crazy and indeed the most disturbing and upsetting of all our imaginative excursions are when, as a man, we have a woman, or as a woman, we have a man at whom to let fly.

Plod! Plod! Plod! But while he ascended that hill, to the sound of the holy bell of Cerne, Peter's left hand and active fingers found time to untie every knot, loosen every tape, release every pin, disentangle every fold of the most intimate garments of the lovely creature at his side; with the result that, when their four feet and his plodding stick finally touched the chalk-white base of the Giant's throne, there was nothing for it but a mutual collapse beneath the generative tool of that gigantic figure and an unavoidable union of their two bodies then and there.

No man will ever know what thoughts, and still less what feelings, passed through the consciousness of Lilith, while Petrus wreaked upon her the full measure of his unconscionable lust; but the thoughts and feelings of our great specialist in magnetism were very definite. Although with his face buried in the disordered tangles of Lilith's hair, he could not see the sea, nor the Isle of the Slingers, nor that majestic beach of semi-precious stones that has come to be named Chesil, Petrus was in some curious and peculiar way conscious of these things.

As he merged his life with Lilith's, it seemed to him as though the whole cosmos were being cleft in twain. It seemed to him as if he were himself all the oceans and seas and lakes and channels and estuaries and rivers in the world, and as if the slender form he was clasping were all the continents and capes and promontories and islands, round which, and across which, and into the heart of which, all these waters, salter than tears, were pouring their life.

And as these desperate paroxysms of ecstatic union went on beneath that shameless symbol of primeval audacity, it seemed to Petrus as if he were something more than those wave-curves and wave-spoutings. It seemed to him as if he were at that transcendant moment a real, actual, living incarnation of all the creative semen of human life from the day of Adam, the first man.

He felt as if beneath their united bodies the whole of that haunted West Country, from the furthest promontory of the Isle of Slingers to the furthest shoals of the mist-darkened Severn, were heaving up towards the Moon.

Was it, he thought in his nerve-dazed trance, that ever since Joseph of Arimathea brought the blood of Jesus to this coast, consecrating thereby the Mystery of Virginity and throwing a strange and desecrating shadow upon the greater Mystery of Procreation, there had been a craving, a longing, a hungering and thirsting, in the whole earthy substance of this portion of the West, so that the actual soil and sand and stones and rocks and gravel and pebbles of Wessex, along with the very slime of the worms beneath and the slugs above and the spawn of the frogs and the scum of the newts, and the cuckoo-spit of the smallest insect, had been roused to revolt against this preposterous edict of unnatural purity.

And Petrus of Maricourt swore within himself that it was upon him, and upon him alone of all men living or dead, that the burden of the tremendous deliverance was laid.

"I am the one," he cried to the very tune of his embraces of Lilith, "appointed from the dawn of history to lead the revolt of all natural earthly life, whether human, animal, vegetable, or mineral, against this accurst inhibition, inspired by these mad religious teachers from Palestine. Anti-Christ! Anti-christ! Anti-christ! That is what I am. And the crazy joke of it is that this Jesus, whom they call the Second Person of this Trinity they've invented, always said that we were all the Sons of God."

At this point Petrus of Picardy scrambled to his feet, and bending down modestly and courteously over his companion arranged and tidied her disturbed garments.

It was nearly dark by the time Peter of Maricourt and Lilith of Lost Towers passed that glen of the Welsh Tinker which was so near the gate of the Convent. They were on their way to the Priory, where they hoped to waylay Albertus Magnus, who had—so local rumour informed them—been invited that night to dine with the Prior. It was in the mind of Petrus Peregrinus that they might encounter young John there too, setting off for home from his daily visit to the imprisoned Friar. This possibility however Petrus refrained from communicating to Lilith, though exactly what his motive was for this particular piece of rather curious reticence he would have been himself puzzled to say, although it might enter the head of a mean-minded chronicler that it had something to do with the good looks and youth of the person in question.

It was in any case much less of a surprise to the girl from Lost Towers than to the man from Maricourt when up from the Tinker's Cave, where these children of Israel had been stealing between their separate duties a celestial hour of delicious happiness without troubling their heads about Welsh gods or Welsh tinkers or Welsh witches, came the giant Peleg holding his Ghosta by the hand.

The path upward of the ascending pair crossed irrevocably the path of the couple who were skirting the edge of the declivity, so that an encounter was inescapable. Any aboriginal spirit at this juncture, whether that of a deity, or a tinker, or a witch, who possessed the power of reading the thoughts in alien brains, would have been fascinated, as it darted like a sand-martin from cavity to cavity in these unusual skulls, to note the absolute difference between what was going on in all four heads.

Lilith was wondering whether she lost anything by the fact that the deliciously wicked delight, which she derived from leading people into mischief while she satisfied her senses with their erotic embraces, had never been, even to the faintest wafture of such a thing, touched by the breath of romantic love. "What the devil *can* that feeling be like?" she wondered irritably.

Peleg said to himself: "This queer-looking little fellow in black stumping along with a Roman sword for a staff must be the Lost Towers' latest pick-up. From the fellow's expression I doubt if the wench has got him as completely as she thinks she has!"

Petrus thought: "Haven't I met this dark girl somewhere before round here? Or is it *you*, my pretty one," and he gave a caressing squeeze to the lodestone in his innermost garment, "who have pointed her out to me when we were going about? Whoever she is, she's a powerful person; and I'd be a prize idiot to neglect her help in my Antichrist crusade and a plain fool not to try to find what she herself feels about this damned Brazen Head?"

As for Ghosta herself; she was acquainted, by reason of her job in the Convent kitchen, with all the gossip of the neighbourhood, for the Nuns heard everything, and those among them who weren't born to be spiritual were the best authorities in the district on all that was going on, on the quarrels and alliances, on the friendships and enmities, on the misunderstandings and idiotic manias, in all the various manorial centres whose circles of authority over-lapped at this point.

"O I do hope and pray," Ghosta cried in her heart, "that Peleg's discovery of this traveller's association with Lost Towers won't start him off again on his mad suspicion of their being some sexual connection between me and the Friar!"

It was naturally enough the clever clasper of that dangerous magnetic weapon who broke the somewhat awkward silence with which the pair ascending from the cave encountered the pair skirting that tricky declivity.

"I am a visitor to your country, Master"—here Petrus bowed politely to the Jewish giant—"to your country, Mistress"— and here he did the same to Ghosta—"with the purpose of inspecting this wonderful invention of your Friar Bacon of which I have been told by this gentle lady, whom I had the good fortune to meet when I first landed on your shores, and which she tells me is to be found in a Castle called the Fortress of Roque, the Lord of which has only recently recovered from an attack made upon him by a demented animal, by a horse in fact, whom some wicked magician had tried to turn into one of those classical creatures who have men's heads on horses' necks and were called Centaurs, and one of them indeed"—here the traveller bowed graciously to both the giant and Ghosta—"as frequenters of monastic libraries, like yourselves, no doubt know, was a sort of schoolmaster to swift-footed Achilles."

"You had better take them to the main Fortress gate, Peleg," said Ghosta quickly. "I must run back to the Convent now, and I shan't have to ring that big front bell anyway, for I'll get in at the back, where there's a door close to the passage where my room is. I'll be here," she added in a lower voice, giving the great knuckles of the giant whose right hand was squeezed into his leather belt, a quick pressure, "tomorrow, wet or fine, at the same time as today!"

And with this she was off; and they all watched her tall slight figure hurry down the path towards the Convent.

"Well, Master—well, Mistress Lilith," said Peleg, "shall we go straight to the Fortress? It's inside the Fortress, you know, in fact in the armoury, that the Friar's Brazen Head has been put for safety. This Papal Legate, or whatever he calls himself, whose name has such a friendly sound—I mean Bonaventura—has been making so much trouble round here that we—but I mustn't go on like this with you, Mistress Lilith, here; for you naturally have to take the side of your dad and I naturally have to take the side of my lord—but anyway, you, sir, as an experienced traveller, will have seen many local divergencies far more extreme than any of ours and bringing with them far more risky consequences to the country concerned."

Lilith smiled at him with a quick, humorously confidential smile, as much as to say, "O my dear big man, you weren't born in the midst of our silly little dissensions, but you'll have to take us as you find us."

"Somebody told us as we came along," murmured Petrus almost wistfully, "that, if we wanted to have a word with Albert of Cologne, who has come over here to see Friar Bacon, we ought to go to the Priory where the great man has been invited tonight to dine with the reverend Prior. It would be a pity, wouldn't it, to put you to the trouble of showing us the way to the Fortress, only to find when we reach it that the man we are seeking has just left to go to the Priory?"

To this fretful commentary upon the course of events it was Lilith, not the Jewish giant, who replied.

"The obvious thing to do," she said, stepping forward quickly, and with one slender hand putting pressure on the giant's hip and with the other upon the elbow of Petrus Peregrinus, "is to get to the Fortress as quickly as we can and find out if the man has yet started for the Priory. It may well happen that we shall be allowed to accompany him there, and possibly be able to eat a crust with the Friar, while Albertus is dining with Prior Bog."

The long legs of Peleg and the short legs of Petrus found themselves obeying her, almost as if they'd been the fore-legs and the hind-legs of the same horse drawing her chariot.

"Little does this fellow guess," thought Petrus pressing his sword-staff into the rocks and the lichen and the moss and the mud and the grass, and his lodestone into his own scrotum, "that the sole reason of our desire to meet this Albertus is to put an end to his fight on behalf of Christ, and to help this self-worshipping Bonaventura to smash to atoms the Friar's Brazen Head."

But, whatever their thoughts, they all three hurried on, and had the Welsh tinker or one of his witch-wives watched them pass, they would have seemed like a giant from Palestine accompanied by a dwarf from Egypt and led by a siren from the Isles of Greece.

The truth was that Peleg and Lilith between them managed to lead the student of magnetism so rapidly, and by paths so completely unknown to him, that it was neither a surprise nor a shock when the girl stopped them with an excited gesture and pointed to a moving mass of gleaming weapons at the foot of four great dark-foliaged pines, and cried out in a thin, wavering, wispy voice, as if she'd been a frightened maiden from the convent rather than the seductive heiress of Lost Towers: "There! there! there's a lot of soldiers! Your friend from Cologne must have brought a big bodyguard with him! They're coming this way. What about waiting for them here?"

It was then that Peleg intervened. He spoke slowly and deliberately; but it was clear that he was agitated by what he saw.

"It seems to me, Master Petrus, that those are King's Men from London; and what is more, Mistress Lilith, I believe I hear some royal music. So it can't be the ecclesiastic from Germany. It must be some royal captain on his way from London to tell us all some important news. Perhaps King Henry is dying. News doesn't travel as fast in this island as it does between the Tigris and the Eu——" He stopped suddenly; and Lilith, who had been watching him, turned round, as suddenly, to her other companion.

But her other companion was behaving in a very strange manner. It appeared that Petrus Peregrinus was undergoing a kind of mental agitation so extreme that it amounted to something resembling a fit. He was holding both his hands to his ears, as if to render himself deaf to some sound that he was finding too horrible to endure; and he was doing this without losing his hold of the sheathed weapon he had been using as a staff.

Suddenly with a choking gasp he let his hands sink down till his weapon, held to his wrist by a strap, trailed in the dust. At the same time an expression of incredible relief relaxed his features and clouded with a misty haze his incredibly black eyes. Both Peleg and Lilith surveyed him with astonishment, an astonishment that was increased when they heard him talking to himself, and doing so in English though with a strong French accent.

"Thank the Devil he'll be dead soon now! And thank the Devil that he can put so much power into his voice that even in the midst of this unspeakable way they're murdering him a lot of the pain goes into his screams. O thanks be to the Devil! He's quite dead now!"

Pierre of Maricourt became silent at that point, and leant so heavily on his scabbarded weapon that it sank several inches into the marshy ground upon which, at the sight of the gleaming arms of those distant men, they had all three paused.

"What is it Sieur de Maricourt?" enquired Lilith. "Nobody is screaming here. Nobody is being killed here. What is it, Maitre Pierre?"

The reply came slowly but quite clearly, each word of it being like an enormous gobbet of human flesh, steaming with red foam and dripping with hot blood.

"No! no! this thing is not happening now. It's *going* to happen! It—is—all—in—the—future. I—am—*making it— happen*. It's going to happen to the son of—never mind that!— who is being tortured to death in a castle whose name is—whose name begins with B. But he's dead now; and with his screams went a lot of his pain—into the air! My little pretty one and I have done it . . . the prince of . . . of . . . of . . . of . . . But never mind that! But mark you . . . it *has* . . . it *has* . . . it *has* to happen! Little Pretty and I have done it already! All the rest can be left to the huge wave of natural necessity that carries us all before it. But there are certain"—and here even Lilith, the daughter of Baron Maldung of Lost Towers, was startled by the look of concentrated, merciless, indeed you might say *insane* ferocity in the two enormous black eyes, now almost become one, above the traveller's raptorial beak—"but there are certain turnpike valleys, in the future lives of us all," he went on, "in which things can be made to happen to us, either as a blessing or as a curse, by concentrated will supported by concentrated prayer addressed to Heaven or—mark you! —to Hell: certain turnpike valleys I say that this great rushing universal stream of Necessity lacks the power to touch.

"These turnpikes in our lives are so indurated, so scooped and gouged out, so chiselled and indented, so engraved, so *branded* by the intense will and the intense prayer of our worst enemy or our best friend, that this frantic *hate* or this desperate *love* works those effects that our excitable doctors of divinity, like this confounded Cologne potentate, call miracles.

"And in a popular sense they *are* miracles. But we must remember that the mass of people are so stupid, yes! so stupid and dull-witted and silly, that anything achieved by exceptional will-power or exceptional energy appears miraculous. And these accursed ecclesiastics are worse than the mob; for they are at bottom as stupid as the mob, but they have learnt the tricks of their trade and know how to appear both learned and clever."

Peleg and Lilith exchanged amused glances at this point; for it had become clear to them that this student of magnetism had already become, not only a professor, but a professor whose contempt for other professors surpassed his contempt for common humanity. His companions' thoughts must somehow have reached him, but instead of quelling his professorial desire to lecture, not so much to teach others as to get the thrill of haranguing others, these thoughts of theirs drove him on. For human beings are only surpassed in their quickness of emotional reaction to unspoken thoughts by one other animal on earth; namely by dogs; but unlike the reactions of dogs, our reactions are generally contradictory. This is proved by the way Petrus acted now.

He straightened his rounded shoulders and thin legs, and hurriedly clambered up upon a broad flat stone. Mounted on this natural rostrum he stretched out his black-sheathed sword-dagger towards the soldiers, who were now definitely marching in their direction, and cried in a shrill voice:

"And these military people too! What do any of them know of the real nature of the necessities of the country, or of the king, or of the nation? All they know is how to obey their trumpets and bugles. After the vulgar herd, and after the grotesque array of half-doting, ridiculously pontifical teachers, the most absurd body of men to be found in our crazy world are soldiers—yes! every kind of soldiers, soldiers of Kings, soldiers of Queens, soldiers of Regents, soldiers of sovereign realms who have only Dictators!

"You tell me those soldiers are English soldiers. Well, I can only tell you that I feel unutterable contempt for every soldier serving in that force and obeying a kindly King who is weak and dying, and only longing to obey a King who is strong, hard, and brutal and loves fighting for fighting's sake. I tell you there's not one single one of all these men now marching in their damned orderly ranks towards us, who has the intelligence of an ordinary dog, not one single one!"

Peter Peregrinus now descended from his stone of oration and put a straight question to the beautiful Lilith. "Well, little lady? Had we better wait their arrival here? Or shall we just go boldly on to meet them, and then enquire, of whatever captain or centurion or prince who is leading them, whether he knows *just where* Albertus of Cologne is passing the night? We could tell him that I have come from a besieger's camp in France, especially to bring him an important message."

No chronicler could describe in words the expression on the face of Petrus Peregrinus at this moment. Neither Peleg from above him nor Lilith from below him had ever seen anything like the way those black eyes, just as if they had become the one solitary eye of an antediluvian creation from the bottom of the ocean, looked with an indescribably *inward look* at what his own red tongue was doing in its own cave-like mouth, into which it seemed as if this one eye must be able to watch this unique tongue tentatively emerging from the devil knows how much deeper a cavern, and beginning its exploration of the blood-sucking meat-mill which it has entered.

But the eyes of Peter of Maricourt saw something now that drew them away from his own interior being. He saw two young men coming towards them down the slope of a hill, from a direction that was at right angles to the direct line between the place where they stood and the point now reached by the advancing soldiers. To him they were unknown; but the moment Peleg, following the obviously startled look he saw him turn in that direction, caught sight of them, their identity was revealed.

"Why! there are Master Tilton and Master John! Do you wish me, Mistress Lilith, to call to them? I don't think they have seen us yet; and to tell you the truth I don't think they are likely to see us till they get quite close! It's plain to me: indeed I can clearly hear," and he exchanged a quick glance with Lilith, "that they're arguing and disputing; and when those two begin that sort of thing, there's no use trying to make them notice anything."

It was Lilith who spoke then. "And what," she enquired gaily, "do *you* think, Master Peter?"

What Peter thought, before anything else occurred to him, was simply how queer it was to see his wicked temptress of Lost Towers act like an ordinary and natural girl. It was clear that she was delighted with this new turn to the stream of events.

Peter of Maricourt didn't openly hesitate. But in his heart he did more than hesitate. What rushed across his mind, as the girl waited for his answer, was the thought that, if he could deprive the Fortress of both its young men, it would be a better stroke in his Antichrist crusade than even if he managed to put an end to Albertus of Cologne.

He closed his mouth firmly against any premature licking of his lips; but there had come an excited note into his voice which it was impossible to miss, though he answered quietly enough.

"There are times in life, little lady," he said, "when we can only listen to the ticking of the clock of fate and wait for what is destined to happen. This is one of those times."

XXI

THE PENANCE

"But haven't you the power to see," young John was saying to his elder brother, his voice mounting up almost to a shout, "that the church has just created this whole business of the Trinity in order to catch the three in its fishing-net?"

"What three classes," enquired Tilton, "have you got in your head?"

"In my head—nothing!" cried the other indignantly, "the classes I'm talking about are with us always. They are *here* in the Fortress! They are *there* in the Priory! They are everywhere. I am talking about *first*, stupid, simple, ordinary people: *second*, artistic, imaginative people: *third*, strong ambitious people. This third class is of course the class who govern and rule us—not always on thrones or on horseback, or in chariots —very often entirely behind the scenes.

"By the idea of God the Father they catch the strong rulers who imprison and execute their enemies. By the ideas of God the Son they catch the simple, stupid mass of ordinary people who aren't tricky or clever enough to be anything but good and obedient, and who make of what they call *Love* a mystical and magical power that works miracles.

"And finally by the idea of the Holy Ghost they catch the poets, the story-tellers, the musicians, the painters, the builders and the scholars; and these are the ones who have invented Our Lady, and made Her the Mother of God, and the Fourth great Panel of the Pythagorean square!"

"I've heard enough of your fancies and theories, John," retorted his brother. "For heaven's sake let's take advantage of having the whole day to ourselves, while Mother and Father are both taken up with listening to this Dominican from Germany refuting this Franciscan from Italy."

John decided at this point that he must be more practical in talking to Tilton.

"Presently," he remarked, "they'll be having—father and mother I mean—a nice tricky job if these King's Men from London demand shelter for the night. I can't make out what the idea was in sending them down here at all. I don't believe the old King had anything to do with it. I fancy there's some 'funny business', as we say in Oxford, going on in the King's court. What we want is Lord Edward back again! Why does he go on with this ridiculous crusade? What's this city of Acre, to him, or him to it, that he should fight for it? What I think about this whole affair is——"

"*Please*, John, don't go on any more like this! And *look there*—Isn't that our Peleg? Who on earth are those two with him? Why—John! If that's not Lilith of Lost Towers! Who's that man with her? He's a foreigner of some sort. He doesn't look as if he knew his head from his tail. He's mad or something! There! He's seen us now. What the devil is he up to? He's moving about watching us with his hands pressed between his legs as if he were turning himself into a flying battering-ram."

"Never mind *him*, Tilton. *He's* nothing to us. The person for us to watch is that devilish girl! God in Heaven, but she's a beauty! I'd like to—— Listen, Tilton, why shouldn't we get hold of her? Let's carry her back to the Fortress as a prisoner-of-war!"

"John, John, what's come over you? What's the matter with you? You're looking at me as if you'd like to knock my head off. What have I done to make you so angry? Do you think I want to start fighting as to which of us should have that girl? Heaven help you John! You're getting queer. It's that confounded Brazen Head that's the trouble. Ever since that blasted thing came into the armoury you've been behaving more and more queerly. Didn't I hear you the other day tell mother that you'd like to go and visit Iscalis—or what do they teach us to call that village now—Ilchester! And why? I know the damned place. There's nothing there but a river, and a few houses by a bridge, and a lot of marshy fields! You think it's wonderful because your precious Friar's uncle or brother or somebody lives there. I tell you it's not half as exciting as Montacute, where at least there's a high pointed hill, or as Glastonbury, where King Arthur's grave is!"

"If you don't stop talking such nonsense, Tilton, I'll give you such a rap over your dull, stupid, traditional, commonplace, church-building skull that you won't be able to sleep for——"

"Stop that, you two fools!"

The sudden appearance of the utterer of these surprising words was as much of a shock to the two brothers as it was to Lilith and Maitre Pierre de Maricourt. Peleg was less startled because he had been for some while able, from the watch-tower of his own height, to detect some creature's secretive movements from alder-bush to alder-bush, scrub-oak to scrub-oak, weeping-willow to weeping-willow; but he hadn't imagined for a minute that a warrior in the rather extravagant accoutrements of a captain from the Royal Guard should be following these tactics.

But so it was. The intruder, who had interrupted not only this old familiar quarrel between the brothers that was being so craftily fomented by Master Peter and his pet lodestone, but who also had diverted from their aim that traveller's further plans, turned out to be none other than Perspicax himself, captain of these King's Men who had just arrived, and a cousin of Friar Bacon and like him a native of Ilchester.

By this time Perspicax, through his social skill in the delicate art of handling superiors and his formidable gift for inspiring respect in inferiors, had become one of the most active and important military officers that the old king possessed.

Having heard of the disturbances stirred up by Bonaventura and of the local war—for it had by now become more than a feud—between the Manor of Roque and the Barony of Lost Towers, Perspicax had persuaded the already dying Henry to let him come down to the Wessex Coast with a quite large squadron of King's Men.

With a few decisive explanations and a moderate use of his enormous powers of persuasion and domination, Perspicax soon had all the five of them, the two young men, equally with

Peleg and Lilith and Master Peter of Picardy, under his personal control.

He led them all straight back to the Fortress, and he found no difficulty in arranging with the door-keeper, or rather with the door-keeper's competent dame, exactly just where and how the whole lot of his men had best encamp that night, and what special additions to their already substantial supply of food and drink they might expect to receive. He then found no difficulty at all in smoothing the way with Lady Val and the Baron, not only for the reception of Peter Peregrinus, but even—and this made everybody in the Fortress exchange puzzled and excited comments—for the conferring of a solitary night's rest in a suitable chamber upon Lilith of Lost Towers.

Once safely alone in a small room at the back of the Fortress, a room which their nurse, in that instinctive forestalling of awkward situations which had made her what she was to all of them, had reserved as a sort of retiring-place for herself, our lonely traveller, whose magnetic power had led him to regard himself as Antichrist, decided that it would be silly to play any of his tricks with "Little Pretty" while he was only half-alive by reason of an overpowering need for sleep.

So, removing the said "Little Pretty" from its coign of vantage at the fulcrum of its owner's life-force, and placing it on a small bracket at the foot of a stone image of Our Lady that had obviously come from over-sea, for its whole style suggested North Italy, he managed with the most reverent and the most delicate care to prop it up in such a manner that "it", or "her", or "he", was supported by the droop of the Virgin's robe as it hung between her knees.

This duty having been satisfactorily performed, with a final worshipful glance at the foot-long object of his veneration, now safely if sacrilegiously propped up at the knees of the Mother of God, Petrus flung his sword on the floor, wrapped the bed-blanket round him just as he was, and sank into an impenetrable sleep.

What he would have done if there hadn't been a clear sky and a three-quarter Moon that night, together with a window through which this luminary could shine, and a particularly well-polished metallic receptacle for both solid and liquid human excreta from which its light was brilliantly reflected, is indeed a question. He would either have had to play his tricks in pitch darkness or he would have had to give them up till the arrival of dawn.

As it was, it must have been about midnight when he awoke; and awoke to find himself in full moonlight. He tossed off the blanket, picked up his sword, still in its black sheath, and hung it on the handle of the closed door, a handle very imposingly moulded and much more like the hilt of a Roman sword than was the object which he suspended from it.

Then he rushed to the base of the image against the wall, extricated his egregious darling from between the knees of Our Lady, and held it up in the moonlight. The lodestone was about seven inches in length and about one inch in diameter. Its colour was a pale pinkish grey touched here and there with blots and smears of a dim yellowish tint. But one end of the thing was a good deal thicker than the other, and this thicker end did unquestionably possess a certain remote likeness to a human head.

Nor was an obscure resemblance to a human face quite wanting either, if a person did what the thing's owner was certainly always doing, that is to say if he made a lively use of the imagination. The thing, however, never changed its expression. No imagination could make it do that.

But its expression was one which, if this dressing-room of the old nurse of the Fortress could speak, it would have described as "wicked curiosity".

With those peering eyes at such a queer angle to each other, with that almost frog-like nose and mouth, with that forehead that seemed to bulge where it ought to retreat, with those ears that looked as if in the endless process of listening to dirty sounds and yet more dirty echoes, they had been worn into filthy cracks, all these characteristics only required a little imagination to be the perfect attributes of a lodestone converted into an orectic and prurient spy.

Sitting on the edge of his bed after pressing to his lips in the moonlight the particular smear on his pet's visage that he liked to pretend was its mouth, Petrus now jigged the thing up and down in the air towards what he assumed to be the southern and eastern and western portions of the Fortress.

He vaguely took it for granted, from what seemed to him to

be the position of the Moon, that he was sitting with his back to the north; and it was one of his occult theories that it was always from the north that great magicians—and of course Antichrist must be a very great magician—always came and always summoned their devils.

The southern populations of the world might be gluttonous, lecherous, and wine-bibbing, but it was from the north, and from no other quarter of the compass, that Satan always set forth on his goings to and fro over the earth.

There is no doubt that, compared with the authentic inventive genius of Friar Bacon, Master Peter of Maricourt had only an extremely exalted imagination. For years he had used this imagination to complete in every way he could what might be called the feminization of his precious lodestone. What he had to do at this moment was not at all easy. He had to make a guess as to the particular direction, north or south or east or west of where he was now, in which a room had been found for Lilith in this ramshackle edifice. But assuming, from the outrageous tales he had listened to when with Mother Wurzel and her daughter at Deadstone, that Tilton would be far too occupied with his sister Lil-Umbra to give Lilith a thought, he forced "Little Pretty" to concentrate her dangerous attention upon young John.

In fact he went so far as to direct the whole of his own will-power, and the whole of the magnetism in "Little Pretty" that worked with this will-power, towards establishing an erotic connection between young John and Lilith.

"The time must be now," he told himself, "about half-way between midnight and one o'clock. In that case, shouldn't 'Little Pretty' draw young John to slip quietly on bare feet or in silent sandals to Lilith's room? She'll be wise enough to guess who it is if he knocks gently at her door, and once together he'll be her slave forever!

"That it's such a devil of an effort to me to do this may simply be because I'm her slave! I am, I am, I *am* her slave; I confess it. But not perhaps forever. I've enjoyed her so fully, so utterly, so completely—and from such enjoyment the male animal enjoys anyway the *sensation* of domination—that I already feel to a certain degree free from her: not altogether free of course, because I shall never to the end of my days enjoy anyone as I do her, but still a good deal more free than I ever thought would be possible before we visited the Cerne Giant. Well, Master John, you've got, you've got, you've *got* to go to Lilith's room!"

He pointed the head of the lodestone towards a certain queer stain on one of the walls, a stain that he had noticed directly he entered the room, which had by this time associated itself in his mind with a spurt of blood from some rarely affected human vein.

It was at this moment to his unspeakable surprise that he heard a knocking at his own door. He plunged his "Little Pretty" into a much more natural place than the knees of the Madonna, and scrambling across his bed, for he had been sitting with his back to his own door as he thought of young John's door, he unhooked his sword from the bronze door-handle, and holding it, still in its black sheath, in his right hand, he opened the door with his left.

It was Lilith herself who now slipped into his room, slim as a hamadryad from the Moon who has descended straight from the clouds, and arrayed in a floating white night-gown much too large for her, which she had borrowed for that one night from Lil-Umbra. This garment hung so loosely on her slender figure that, as she stretched herself upon his bed, Petrus of Picardy was compelled, for the third time in his whole life, to give himself up to such a wave of passionate adoration that he felt he could sacrifice even the pride of being Antichrist in his worship of those pearly contours of Lilith's body, now resting there like a white shell half-revealed and half-concealed beneath a wavy tangle of foam as it lies on the sand.

Although he had already enjoyed her that same day at the foot of the Cerne Giant to a degree that he supposed must have exhausted all his seminal energy, and though this day itself had followed a night of the grotesque debaucheries of Dead-stone, it suddenly came over him that, if he clutched his lode-stone tightly enough in his hand while he was enjoying her now, he would find himself endowed with a superhuman power.

And so it did, in God's truth and the Devil's truth, happen, before the two of them were asleep. And, as may be imagined, the sleep that followed this Elysian ecstasy was so deep for them both that the dawn was well advanced before Petrus realized that the light which was making his eyes blink so hopelessly as he tried to open them was the light not of the Moon but of the Sun.

"I'll wrap *this* round me," whispered Lilith hurriedly, snatching up the blanket from the bed, "and, when I'm dressed to go out, I'll come back here for you; for I want you to take me home. So don't go till I come!" And, as he kissed her, Petrus recognized that this really was a solemn league and covenant between them.

His dressing took no time at all, and he had comfortable leisure to caress his "Little Pretty", otherwise his demonic lodestone, to his heart's content, as well as to make the pillows and the extremely primitive goat-skin rug that covered the foot of the bed look as if the room had been used solely as a retiring place for relieving human bowels; and since there was no way he could empty that particular piece of furniture, all he could do was to sit on the bed and wait.

When at last Lilith returned, she looked as fresh as a wild, white convolvulus on an ivy-covered wall.

"I've found a way out," she whispered hurriedly, "and once out I know how to dodge this camp of King's Men. Just come quietly after me, step by step as quickly as you can, and we'll soon be clear of this blessed place."

Petrus obeyed, and she led him out of the Fortress by a small door among the sheds and stables, the look of which and the general atmospheric odour of that part of the establishment reminded him of the occasion when the Lord of the Manor had suffered a fall wrestling with Spardo's deformed horse, and when the idea of filling the prophetic role of the actual Antichrist had first entered his own head.

Lilith was perfectly right about her ability to dodge the camp of the King's Men. At one point they did catch the voice of Perspicax giving orders in that effective competent way that was a second nature with him. And though it can well be believed how tightly Petrus clutched his little monster to his navel at this sound, he was far too scared of throwing everything into a chaos, in which anything might happen, to take the risk of pointing the lodestone at this man from Iscala who boasted himself to be a first cousin of the maker of the Brazen Head.

But the authoritative voice of Roger Bacon's relative from Iscala had hardly died down, when lo! directly in their path through the forest, appeared a group of about a dozen men, unmistakably clothed in the red-brown attire of Lost Towers. These men were advancing with the swift, furtive, stealthy, wild-animal-like self-confidence of a perfectly trained body of woodsmen, to whom every aspect of forest life had been familiar from earliest boyhood.

Without a cry of delight or the faintest sign of surprise Lilith ran towards them; and in a pulse-beat of his agitated heart our all-too-human Antichrist began searching with the tip of his tongue the whole surface of the cavernous roof of his mouth, as if that tongue of his, which *could* be a deadly sting, had also the power of transforming itself into a divining-rod, a rod that could reveal the presence of any drop of the water of life in any portion of the skull that contained it.

But while Lilith was gliding in and out of the ranks of her red-brown adherents, like a "Wood-White" butterfly dominating a confused rabble of billowing and swirling "Meadow-Browns", there suddenly emerged, walking towards him in an extremely dignified, though somewhat dramatic manner, out of the centre of the red-brown men, no less a personage than Bonaventura himself!

This tremendous redeemer of footpads was evidently deeply impressed by the revelation that Lilith, whose entrancing body he had only resisted because God destined him to be Pope or the maker of Popes, had a man-friend.

He recognized at once the black cap Petrus was wearing as part of the uniform of one of the best troops among the soldiers of the King of France; and the wild hope rushed into his mind that this siren of a girl had just come back from crossing the Channel with a body of men as large, if not larger, than the King's Men who would shortly be waking from their sleep in the camp of this Perspicax of Iscala or Ilchester.

This descent upon Wessex of the King's Men from London had been the second startling blow that Bonaventura had received in the last few days. The first was the appearance, totally unforeseen by him, of Albertus of Cologne, for whom, as the most famous of all teachers in the Dominican order, he, as the best known Franciscan throughout the world, felt the emotions that all of us experience, though some of us are cleverer than others in hiding them, when confronted by a successful rival.

Petrus of Maricourt clutched "Little Pretty" tightly against his skin and looked his opponent full in the face. "Mistress Lilith told me," he said, "that I *might* have the proud pleasure of meeting the late legate of the Holy Father and the greatest doctor that our Holy Faith possesses in Paris and Oxford, but I never for one moment imagined that her words would come true. Your eminence knows what young ladies are, and of course I have already heard that your reverence disapproves of Friar Bacon's Brazen Head. In fact, to be quite truthful, I have answered a number of people on this point by telling them bluntly and squarely that some of Friar Bacon's inventions are under examination by the highest authorities in the Church, in case they may turn out to have no divine sanction but, on the contrary——" here Petrus bowed with his head and scraped with his foot, as he had seen his mother do when the Lord of Maricourt walked down the street—"on the contrary, are the work of the Devil."

"What, if I may enquire," asked Bonaventura, "is your name? And what, if you will absolve me of gross inquisitiveness, is your purpose in visiting these parts?"

Our traveller clutched with his left hand the body of "Little Pretty" under his clothes, and placing his right hand against the hilt of his eternally sheathed sword, he proceeded to balance his bottom upon this convenient knot of hammered metal-work and got strength and relief by so doing.

Indeed for a moment or two, as he listened to Bonaventura repeating his question with the judicial unction of an official executioner at the oriental court of Karakorum, he experienced a delicious thrill of complete irresponsibility, as if he had been an anonymous figure seated on a marble stool impervious to the goings on of mortals.

"My name, your Eminence, is Pierre de Maricourt, and I come from Picardy. My profession, as you see, is that of a soldier of the King of France. But I am also a student of the ancient tongues and I spend my wages in buying books. I know a little Greek and Latin, your Eminence, already;

and I hope, before I die, to be able to learn a little Hebrew. I came over to have an opportunity of acquiring at close quarters a few details about the kind of mistakes—in orthodox divinity I mean—which Friar Bacon has been making."

Petrus spoke slowly from more than one motive, and from more than one motive too he kept his terrific black eyes fixed as magnetically as he could upon Bonaventura's face. Beneath his clothes, as you may believe, he kept the head of Little Pretty—for he knew by touch her head from her tail—aimed straight at his interlocutor and it soon became clear that Little Pretty's effect, aided by the intensity of his own magnetic gaze was overmastering.

Bonaventura began showing signs of extreme agitation. He kept turning round and glancing anxiously at the brown-and-red jerkins and breeches of the group he had just left, as if he were afraid that the presence of their young mistress among them might dispel and destroy his own authority over them, and even result in some form of action entirely different from the line he wished them to take.

In his own secret consciousness Bonaventura was more upset than he had been for years. "I must," he told himself, "adopt some powerful course of action with this accurst runaway from Picardy, who evidently is a lecherous pick-up of Lilith's. I must frighten him in some sort of way."

Meanwhile Petrus had commenced in dead silence conveying his wishes to "Little Pretty".

"We must *will* him to lift up first one of his legs and then the other," he told her, articulating his intention very definitely and moving her head, still pressed against his skin, so that it should point straight at Bonaventura's skull. "First one and then the other, my treasure!" he repeated.

And behold! it actually happened; yes! it happened just exactly as our scientific student of magnetism had indicated to his precious magnet. Up went one leg of the General of the Grey Friars, while he made a shuffling movement with the foot still on the ground.

"Now make him lift the other, my sweet!" And down came Bonaventura's left leg and up went his right. "Make the old sod dance a proper jig now, pretty one. We'll learn him to be a Legate!"

And to the absolute amazement of a couple of Lost Towers men who had turned to look back while the rest of the crew were following Lilith into the Forest, and to the even greater astonishment of Friar Roger's cousin from London, the enterprising Perspicax, who having been invited the night before to take his breakfast with Tilton and young John and possibly even with their parents too, if the Baron got back in time from his morning jaunt, now stood at Peter Peregrinus' elbow.

"Is that a new kind of penance?" enquired the commander of the King's Men.

"Do you know, Capitaine, I really do believe that it is!" replied Maître Pierre de Maricourt. "And the odd thing is," he continued, twisting "Little Pretty" around against his own body so that her head pointed straight at the centre of the intruder's not very high forehead, "the odd thing is that this particular penance is infectious! I even feel like joining it myself!" And he shuffled a little with the toes and heels of his sandals in the long grass.

To the commander of the King's Men this untimely dance was indeed infectious. He raised his well-armoured knees in this grotesque jig even higher than the stately personage before them was lifting his grey robe; and he even went so far, for he had a daring and reckless spirit under his military restraint, as to stretch out his right hand and seize, much to this latter's discomfiture, Bonaventura's left hand.

This crazy dance, which might well have been, so Petrus grimly assured himself as he watched them, a dance in honour of an East-Indian idol, performed at Karakorum before the Khan, went on without a pause till the last of the red-brown bandits, together with their "leukolenian" or white-armed princess, had disappeared, and until a little group of highly amused but somewhat puzzled King's Men had come up from the camp and arranged themselves in a line, evidently waiting for the morning's proper business to begin.

It was from sheer exhaustion that both these dancers, Bonaventura in his noble grey garments and Perspicax in his by no means ignoble royal colours, finally and simultaneously sank, side by side, upon the moss and small ferns and woodgrass and ground-lichen beneath a half-circle of the massive trunks of five majestic pines. Mingled with an infernal satisfaction which distorted his face and made his tongue cleave to the roof of his mouth—and of course all chroniclers of Peter Peregrinus who neglect the physical motions of his tongue are dodging something essential—was a totally unexpected pity for the prostrate Perspicax.

What brought this pity into the erratic heart of our traveller was the simple pride which his humiliated victim had taken in being a soldier. This pride brought back to him his own childhood, and suggested to his mind the behaviour of the stately officials of the castle at Maricourt, and he couldn't help muttering aloud a familiar tag of Homeric Greek that he had learnt as a boy in a monastic school: "Ephane mega seema!" "There appeared a great sign!"

And indeed as he watched the King's Men lift up their commander and carry him off to their camp, and as he himself was assisting Bonaventura to his feet, there appeared, coming from between those enormous pine-trees, whose branchless trunks enhanced the romance of every event that occurred beneath them, no less a couple of celebrities than Albertus Magnus of Cologne and Friar Roger Bacon!

It was clear in a second to the wielder of "Little Pretty" that the great Dominican, who looked indeed a rampart of strength in his singular head-dress and peat-black raiment, had compelled the Prior of Bumset to liberate his captive, at least for a time.

"Whither were they bent now?" he thought. "Who could say? They must have started at dawn from the Priory! The Cologne man must have stayed the night there; perhaps in the very chamber of Roger Bacon, with whom he may have been arguing and discussing all night. There's simply no limit," thus Peter Peregrinus' thoughts ran on, "to these learned idiots' powers of disputation."

Curiously enough in the agitating look-skirmish and gesture-drama that ensued between these four men—with "Little Pretty", the deadly lodestone, pressed against the skin of Master Peter—the one who conducted himself with the greatest ease and the most successful assurance was Bonaventura.

Master Peter, as you can well imagine, didn't miss this fact; his agile mind kept turning it over and over, and even as he hurried to be the first to speak, he decided that this superiority in social self-possession came from the fact of Bonaventura's much wider experience of the contemporary world and more intimate knowledge of the royal courts of Europe than Friar Bacon could possibly have—or Albertus either, in spite of his two years as a Bishop.

"You will pardon me, your Reverence, I trust, for addressing you without your permission. But I am a student of scientific magnetism—a most complicated subject—and I was anxious to visit this famous inventor of the Brazen Head whom I now find in your company."

At this point Friar Bacon, who, to Peter's discerning black eyes, was far the most embarrassed of all the four, spoke out strongly, though Petrus could almost see his heart beating under his grey robe and his pulses throbbing under his grey sleeves.

"What we must all do now, and you with us, Master——"

"Petrus of Maricourt in Picardy!" interposed Bonaventura with a nod and a smile.

"And you with us, Master Petrus," went on Friar Bacon, "is to take advantage of my cousin Perspicax having a body of King's Men from London with him, and go straight to Lost Towers and possess ourselves of it in the King's name. King Henry, though very ill, is still alive, and we all know what his son, Lord Edward, would do if he were with us today! He would make short work of this stronghold of bandits, who have for some many years troubled the lives of quiet people in this part of our land! So the first thing we must do—and I trust you will accompany us, Maître Pierre de Maricourt—is to go to the camp and tell my Cousin Perspicax to assemble his men at once and follow us to Lost Towers."

Petrus told himself as he looked from this Friar in grey to the courtly Bonaventura, also in grey, and from them both to the black raiment and incredible headgear of Albert the Great, that what he really needed at this crisis in his life was one clear and definite and decisive word from the Devil Himself—for He alone could really help him at such an amazing concatenation as this—telling him by what word, what blow, what death-dance, he, Petrus, ought to make it clear to the whole lot of them that the long-predicted Antichrist was at last really among them, and that the hour had come for the crashing down, once for all, of the whole shaky edifice of the Christian faith.

"It is extraordinary," Petrus told himself, as he followed the two grey figures and the one black figure in the direction in which the King's Men had just conveyed their exhausted commander, "how a weak, timid, nervous, hermit of philosophy like this Roger Bacon can suddenly take the lead, and without any 'Little Pretty' pressed against his skin, can dominate—can dare to *try* to dominate—two such figures as this Grey One and this Black One, not to mention Antichrist himself, who in the shape of a lodestone-bearer has come among them!

"But it shows one thing. It shows that when a man is quiet and peaceful and timid and philosophical, and scared of both God and the Devil, and longs to live entirely for his own lonely sensations and for his fine points of learning and for the mystery of words, there may come a moment when he suddenly finds himself with a power of plunging into action and of abandoning himself to reckless and desperate moves, such as much stronger characters and much more formidable wills would never dare to display."

The four singular visitors were not long in discovering that, although he had so recently been down in the very depths of impotence, Friar Roger's cousin from Ilchester was now perfectly ready to retake complete command of the bulk of his men. And so without more ado, they set out through the forest and actually found themselves in less than a couple of hours at the entrance to Lost Towers.

They were, however, certainly not prepared for what they found when they reached those gates. Instead of riding for pure pleasure that morning, far less engaging in any boar-hunt or any wolf-hunt, the Lord of the Manor of Roque had left his bed while it was still quite dark, and had taken with him, completely unknown to Lady Val or Lil-Umbra or either of his two sons, the whole force of all the best Fortress-fighters who were available, and had hurried off with them to Cone Castle, where he obtained an interview with Lady Ulanda and her son. As for Baron Boncor himself, he had heard about the squadron of King's Men arriving by forced marches into Wessex and had foreseen that Friar Bacon and his Brazen Head

314

were bound to be included in the local trouble which the arrival of this royal force was sure to bring with it. And so, knowing that nothing would stop Lady Ulanda from rushing openly and shamelessly into the fray as long as there was the faintest chance that it might lead to the destruction of the inventor of the Head, he had already taken his own sensible counsel and nobody else's.

Having for once been able to slip out of their mutual bed without waking his infatuated lady, he had gone bare-footed to his cousin Raymond's chamber and communicated his intention to him. Raymond de Laon did exactly what his friend wanted him to do. He dressed with incredible speed, picked up a long hunting-spear with which, by climbing upon a particular buttress, he could tap on Lil-Umbra's window-sill at the Fortress, and glided, more like a beneficent spirit than an enamoured young man, out of Cone Castle and clear away from its precincts.

"Yes," he promised his cousin, "I'll hang around in the forest, clear of Perspicax's camp, till it's light enough for a talk at her window. So you get away, while the going's good. Don't give me a thought!"

So after ordering the obstreperous Turgo on no account to leave the Castle till his return, Boncor set off with only one attendant, namely a certain Bob Talirag, who had an aunt who worked there, and hurried through the forest by the first light of dawn to Bumset Priory. He felt he must see Roger Bacon and discuss the whole matter with him, not even excluding, if the Friar proved friendly, Lady Ulanda's prejudice and the unfortunate misunderstanding that had given birth to this prejudice.

But, as happens so often in our complicated world, this sensible course of action, taken by the only really wise and good ruler in that part of Wessex, was taken too late. The only person to be got hold of at that hour in Bumset Priory was Lay-Brother Tuck, who with some difficulty was roused from a drunken sleep. This was achieved by Bob Talirag, who obtained an entrance by climbing into the window of his Aunt Moll, an aged scullery-maid.

Brother Tuck, wrapt up against the chill of dawn in all his bedclothes, was soon seated on the top step of the Priory

315

entrance, with the door open behind him. "The truth is, my Lord," murmured the dishevelled and perspiring Tuck, "I wake up slowly."

"Are we to enter without further parley, my Lord?" enquired Bob Talirag, who, having been brave enough to disturb his respected and formidable Aunt Moll, felt ready for anything.

But before Boncor could reply, above the muffled head of Brother Tuck, who was fully prepared to go to sleep again, appeared the already quite decently attired figure of Bob Talirag's aunt.

"I am sorry, my lord, to have to say such a thing—be quiet Bob! I'm not talking to you!—but the truth is, my lord, his Reverence the Prior is still fast asleep. And when his Reverence the Prior is asleep"—and Bob Talirag's aunt gave vent to a high-pitched chuckle of an experienced jackdaw who has already educated more than one brood of open-mouthed ignoramuses in the ways of the world—"nobody can see nobody".

"Could this young friend of yours, my dear Dame," enquired Boncor quietly, "run upstairs to ask Friar Bacon if I could come up to give him a word of warning?"

"One minute, my Lord," replied the lady, and disappeared; while Brother Tuck, who had roused himself to consciousness again under his perambulated bed-clothes, went on more obscurely than before:

"The question I asked King Stephen in my dream was the simple question: who was the giant who had so many wives that in the end they turned him into a puppy-dog and wouldn't let him do his business in his own palace? And do you know what King Stephen answered? He said the giant's name was *Boncor*! And when he uttered that name, *your* name, my lord, do you know what I heard? I heard a choir of angels singing in a great purple cloud, and do you know, my lord, what words they sang? They sang a song my granny taught me when I was young. It went something . . . something like this:

> "If you're only good,
> When you feel your heart prick,
> In the depths of the wood
> You will hear a Tick-Tick.

316

If you're only bad,
When you feel your heart burst,
You'll go howling mad
And take best for worst!

With the end of your rod
Mix honey and gall,
So that neither God
Nor the Devil gets all!

A drop of the worst
Is the way to the best:
Let the Devil take the first:
And let God have the rest!"

Bob Talirag could see that to the Baron of Cone this blasphemous jingle was by no means unpleasing; but the news brought by Auntie Moll, when the old lady returned from the interior of Bumset, was so startling that it drove away all other impressions.

It appeared that Albert the Great of Cologne had spent the night with Friar Bacon, and then, before any one in the Priory save Brother Tuck, who was too drunk to know his head from his tail, was awake, had carried the Friar off with him, no one knew whither. Bob Talirag's aunt was pretty certain that it was to the camp of the King's Men from London that the two of them had gone, but she wouldn't swear to this.

"Well, Mistress," said Boncor, "that's where we must go! And please accept this small token of our gratitude for your information."

Saying this he must have handed her a golden coin; for the final impression Bob Talirag had of his Aunt Moll was of her supporting Lay-Brother Tuck, bed-clothes and all, with one arm, as they went in under the curved archway, while with the other she shook her clenched fist, containing the coin she had received, in an ecstasy of exultation.

XXII

THE ORACLE

If the visit of Baron Boncor of Cone to the Priory of Bumset was too late to achieve anything to the easing of the tension in Wessex, the visit of Sir Mort to Boncor's wife Ulanda and her extremely ingenuous son was, from Sir Mort's point of view, a triumphant success. He found Lady Ulanda in more than harmony with his project, and it proved easy enough, with the assistance of the lively Colin and the resolute Clamp, not to speak of the youthful Sir William, who might himself have well been called a "King's Man", to add the toughest of the Cone retainers to his own stalwarts.

"I'll come with you! I'll come with you! I'll come with you!" cried Lady Ulanda; and then to her son: "No! Never mind where your Father's gone! It's a grand chance for you to show your metal as a true knight of our King, who is a nephew of Richard the Lion-hearted! Besides, I'm coming myself! Yes! my child, your mother herself is coming! I've not got the blood of Rursuk and King Stephen for nothing; Sir Mort here agrees with me that we don't need Brazen Heads, or Grey Friars either, to guard our shores!

"Farewell good Turgo! Greet your master when he comes back, and say I told you to tell him that I shall be very angry indeed if he follows us! Tell him that, till his shoulder is entirely healed, he *must*, he *must* behave as a wounded man. Where the devil he's gone to now, only God knows! He has a way of climbing high hills before breakfast! I've never known him eat a morsel till he's been to the ridiculous top of some silly hill! I can't cure him of this madness. Yes! He's up there!"—and the besotted lady pointed solemnly to four

318

visible uplands, one on the north, one on the south, one on the east, and one on the west, and gazed so reverently at each of these small eminences, that Sir Mort, accustomed to Lady Val's very different attitude to himself, began to wonder whether this formidable woman wouldn't have benefited by the advice, when she was a child, of Nurse Rampant or even of somebody like Mother Guggery.

She had an expression on her face as she raised it to those four uplands as if her husband had been a divine personage rather than a human one.

But Sir Mort kept saying to himself: "Remember this, my good friend. The greatest worries in life come from the heads of these Orders of fanatical men, whatever they call themselves, and it's worth while being a little rough, even with the elements you worship, if you can give a crack or two to these same bloody heads! There's this head of the Franciscans trying to make the thieves of Lost Towers into heroic crusaders, if they'll smash the Brazen Head along with its maker's head! And now here's this Cologne fellow, who's head of the Black Friars, and who's bound to be savagely hostile to every Grey Friar in the land, whether he's a Head-maker or a Head-breaker!"

In such terms did what we have been taught to call "thought" pass in and out of Sir Mort's skull. And meanwhile the whole party, made up of the best fighters of both the Fortress and Cone Castle, didn't take long in reaching the outskirts of the former. There quite suddenly and without giving the lovers time to move, they came upon Peleg and Ghosta embracing each other beneath an oak tree.

After a hurried glance at Lady Ulanda—but that pathetically infatuated devotee of her lawful mate was so occupied with hill-tops that she had no eye for the roots of oaks—Sir Mort addressed the lovers in his most friendly and direct manner. He wasn't even humorous at their expense. He took the whole thing naturally and, as some historian would have put it, "in his stride".

"I tell you what you two might do for me," he told them. "You might run into the armoury and bring out the Brazen Head. You could carry it, couldn't you, Peleg? And *you* wouldn't mind putting a hand on it, would you, lady, if the thing tottered a bit on his shoulders? You see, don't you, that if we're to finish off these devils by the help of the King's Men, we mustn't leave any hostages behind?''

It can be imagined how quickly the lovers obeyed him; and this daring worshipper of the elements was not to prod the earth, splash the rain-water in a hollow elder-stump, wave his spear in the air and brandish it towards the only star still visible, before the Mongolian Jew-giant, accompanied by Ghosta with one long white arm raised to the Thing on her friend's shoulder, rejoined the weirdly heterogeneous group that, with Ulanda in its centre blazing with love and hate, now appeared at the entrance to Lost Towers.

Lilith was already there, and Perspicax with his King's Men was already there. Never since he first fabricated his demonic lodestone, after a much longer time spent upon it than Friar Roger ever spent on the Brazen Head, had Petrus Peregrinus felt more excited than he felt at this supreme hour of his life.

He had had to earn his living under terribly heavy handicaps so as to get the leisure to study, whereas Bacon's family after the defeat of Simon de Montfort had at least recovered something, though not very much, of their considerable manorial property. Not that Friar Roger had kept one silver piece of his private inheritance. The amount he had spent—"squandered", some would say, "given back to the Devil", was a more common opinion—on his scientific labours, was really startling. But it had all gone, and now he had nothing but what he could get, as a begging Friar, from the imaginative, the pious, and the charitable.

But here they were! Yes, here was the imprisoned Friar, and here was the wandering native of Maricourt, the one watching his Brazen Head swaying to and fro on the shoulder of a Jewish giant, and the other pressing his precious lodestone against his own body as he awaited his chance, not only to prove that in his person Antichrist had actually come, but to do something with "Little Pretty" in the presence of all men, that would show the world—even if he died while showing it—that by magnetism, and by magnetism alone, did the stars move on their courses, and Suns and Moons wax and wane!

It was Albertus Magnus, and he alone, who caught the full significance of this strange conclave, which was partly a human council of war against the caprices of Nature, and partly a parliament of primitive superstitious tribes instinctively fearful of being tricked into mystic slavery to some crafty Khan of Karakorum!

The red-brown jerkins and tunics and breeches, and the red-brown caps with short brown-and-white feathers sticking out in a queerly insolent and defiant manner, either above the wearer's left ear or above his right ear, according to his individual taste, were drawn up in thick battalions on the two stony ridges in front of the main entrance to Lost Towers.

They were armed with the most deadly-looking weapons, like broad double-edged Roman sword-blades fixed into the massive handles of ordinary hunting spears. It seemed to Albertus that the King's Men under Perspicax would not have a chance of victory, even though assisted by the wilder and less disciplined retainers from Cone Castle and the Fortress.

But the Cologne teacher had hardly reached this conclusion, with which without doubt most of his efficient and practical friends in that great centre of learning would have entirely agreed, when the sort of unexpected confusion arose such as probably only that particular portion of England in the whole western half of the entire world could have evoked.

The Lord and Lady of Lost Towers were evidently quarrelling between themselves; for the man's voice and the woman's voice were clearly audible above the general hoarse murmur and the general jarring chatter.

Presently both their figures, each pushed forward, evidently by their immediate attendants, hers female, and his male, were projected through the red-black lines with their alarming weapons and forced to come forward, though it was evident to everybody that the real force of the emotional feelings of those two was directed, not against the King's men and not against the mass of men from the Fortress and from Cone, but solely against each other.

But something less personal and much more far-reaching was now beginning to happen. This dangerous disturbance did not—so it seemed to Albertus—have any connection with the quarrel between their Lord and their Lady. It sprang from among a group of serfs, who were clearly setting out to do some autumnal job in the harvest-field and had just been met by similar groups from both the manors of Cone and Roque, who had joined the free followers of their respective lords of the manor out of curiosity rather than local patriotism.

Among these were old Dod Pole, that natural-born rebel, and several of his family, including not only little Bet, his great-granddaughter, but also his granddaughter Oona, or Una as many people called her, with whom—at least so we overheard the impulsive young John declare—his brother Tilton was in love.

These serfs, tagging along with the Fortress and Cone people, had quickly become the noisiest among their whole dramatic crowd, and talking earnestly among them by this time was none other than the outlandish figure of Spardo, mounted on his horse Cheiron, at the sight of whom, as it may be well believed, the father of Tilton and young John felt some rather odd feelings!

And not only at the sight of *that* pair was it Sir Mort's destiny, that fine morning, to suffer curious sensations; for lo and behold! before his very eyes, only sufficiently far away for him not to have to undergo any immediate responsibility—and what in the devil's name had brought *them* here?—were all his own family except Lady Val herself! There they all were: John so dark and slight and eager, Tilton so massively tall and fair and impassive, yes! and even Lil-Umbra herself, on horseback as usual—how that wench *did* love riding!—and her wise and tactful knight from Laon on horseback at her side.

Thank the gods, yes! His daughter was certainly like himself and knew sound wood from rotten wood! Would he *never* be able to make Valentia more sensible? The egoism of Sir Mort was so profoundly self-centred that it never entered his head to ask of destiny the obvious question—how it was that, just on this critical day and at this crucial hour when the Master and the Mistress of Lost Towers, having exhausted their verbal artillery, had become a pair of motley antagonists, wrestling in the midst of their red-brown retainers, all the whole neighbourhood supported by the enterprising Perspicax with the King's Men should have appeared on the scene to witness the victory of defeat of one or other of these sad, mad, and absurdly fantastic persons!

But the really scrupulous historian of the reckless and quite crazy doings of all of us mortal men will have made a shrewd guess already as to the particular cause of this queer concatenation.

"O how wonderful," said Petrus Peregrinus to himself, "how wonderful, O how far beyond all I have ever hoped or imagined or dreamed could happen to me, to actually be selected by" —he was going to utter the word "Providence" but just stopped himself in time!—"by Destiny, to be the Antichrist himself, the real, actual, historic person predicted by every prophet who ever prophesied from the foundation of the world!"

Deep into the top-curve of the bony arch between his belly and his thighs, and just above his generative organs, Petrus had dug the blunt, thick, staring-eyed cranium of the demonic lodestone he persisted in calling "Little Pretty", and while he dug it into himself, he had summoned into his presence every living person old or young, male or female, he had ever met or ever heard of in that district.

"I'll have your false heart out of you!" cried the Lady of Lost Towers.

"I'll tear the devil's-dam tongue out of your hell's throat for you!" cried the Lord of Lost Towers.

And then, before either Bonaventura in his grey robe or Albertus in his black robe could force a passage through the red-brown mêlée, some devoted adherent of the mistress of the Castle smashed the master's skull with a heavy stone, and some furious armour-bearer of the murdered Maldung knelt on the lady and strangled her to death with his two hands, before his own head was severed from his crouching body and all three corpses were soaked in his blood.

For several seconds there was a ghastly hush after this, as if over that whole worked-up mass of human creatures an enormous dark feather had fallen from the Empyrean, a feather struck from the wing of the Eagle of Zeus by the lightning-swift descent of some falling star.

Then the whole company of serfs who were present—those who had been following old Dod Pole, their one revolutionary mouth-piece, as well as those who were on their way to their labour in the fields—moved instinctively forward, while Dod Pole himself, leaping up from their midst upon the marble pedestal of the broken and prostrate figure of some forgotten

Roman ruler, almost hidden now under yellow moss and white lichen and tiny ferns, began an exultant threnody over all the deaths of all the wrongful owners of a planet that should be owned in common by all mankind.

"I call upon you, my brothers and fellow workers," cried old Dod Pole, in that trumpet-toned voice which had made him the prophet of those Wessex serfs for the last half century, "I call upon you to let these manor-lords, with their reeves and their bailiffs and their priests and their prelates, know, once for all, how we, the people of the West Country, really regard them and hold them! We hold them in contempt! We hold them to be thieves and robbers who claim the hell-born and not heaven-born right to hand down their stolen property from generation to generation!

"Yes, my friends, it is we who plough and sow and plant and reap and gather the harvest and bake the bread and butcher the meat! It is we, the shepherds and the hedge-planters, we, the cattle-tenders and the swine-herders, who own this sacred and holy and God-given earth of ours! Did these manor-lords create the earth? Did these water-lords create the seas and the rivers and the lakes and the ponds? Did they create the beasts of the earth and the fishes of the sea? Was it at their command that the birds of the air first spread their wings?

"Come, my friends, my companions, my brothers, let us make haste to show to these land-robbers and sea-shore thieves what their true position on this earth really is! They are all the same, every one of them! Handing down they are what they've stolen, from father to son, and son to grandson; and all the good earth and all the precious sea-shore of which they have robbed us curses them as wicked thieves! Come let us show them what we think of them! *To your tents, O Israel!*"

There must have been some immemorial power in this final cry, uttered in a really terrifying voice by old Dod Pole; for a most striking result followed at once, followed with that thundering finality that mankind knows as the most awe-inspiring sound in all human experience—a reverberating echo.

"Off with ye! Off with ye!" were now the words that rose from that whole heaving mass of red-brown rascality; and what they all proceeded to do came with the shock of a long-predicted earthquake that has now come. They tore off their mud-coloured tunics and jerkins, yes! and even in some cases their breeches too; though it interested the half-mad intelligence of Sir Mort to note that they had the wit—and he smiled sympathetically as he observed this—to throw nothing away.

Warm though the sun was, there was quite enough of autumn already in the air to make this a natural gesture, especially as the marshes and swamps to the west of Lost Towers only ended at the sand-dunes of the channel.

What most of them did was to wrap their mud-coloured vestments round their necks, though some, it is true, made bundles of them which they carried under their arms or even on their heads. But it was to the beat of the reverberating echo of Dod Pole's "Off with ye!" that they vanished among the pine-trunks of the forest and the reedstalks of the swamp.

And so now, wholly devoid of any defence at all, the great gates of the ancient stronghold of Lost Towers stood wide open. And they stood open in front of the most fantastic conglomeration of people that had ever gathered together in that part of Wessex for any purpose, whether in the stone age, or in the bronze age, or in the age of King Arthur.

The whole company gazed in silence upon those open doors at the base of that huge tower; and it was as if their united will-power had called upon Lilith to appear. For there, before the whole lot of them, Lilith now defiantly stood; and it seemed as if, in her complete loneliness, she were uttering a contemptuous challenge to every event and every object and every earthly person and every super-earthly person in the entire multiverse.

And Petrus Peregrinus, as he watched her, felt an overpowering wave of emotion sweep over him. "Yes!" he thought. "*You*, and you alone, come what may, in this world or any other world, are my one true love, and with you at my side I shall feel myself to be the real and only real Antichrist, destined by the creative power of Nature herself to destroy once and for all this poisonous, this corrupt, this rotten, this suppurating, this decomposing, this infecting, this contaminatory, this fulsome, this fetid, this fatal farce of an explanation of life, based on a crazy belief in the Persons of the Trinity."

Rendered almost heroic, cruel coward as he was, by this wild resurgence of his love for Lilith, Petrus of Maricourt rushed up the slope, and leaping over the corpses and splashing through the blood, was on the point of ascending the stone pavement in the centre of which she stood, when between them, hot and perspiring with the effort he was making, appeared in grey and greedy stateliness, the figure of Bonaventura.

"O St. Francis, help your child now or never!" was what the man prayed; and with every nerve in his body he announced to himself, "This is my moment! I shall be the next Pope myself or the appointer of the next Pope! I *must* lay my hand, before this whole crowd, upon this girl's head!"

In the twinkling of an eye, yes! in the pulse-beat of the most incorrigible vein in his whole body, Petrus turned the blunt thickskulled cranium of his "Little Pretty" full upon this grey-garbed interloper. "Off you go, my stately friend!" he murmured in his heart as he kept the other end—the "tail" we might call it—of his deadly lodestone pressed tight against himself.

Nor was the response for a second in doubt.

"That girl is too great a temptation!" the appointer of Popes told himself. "I should do for myself if I touched the tip of her fingers! A person can't have it both ways! In a country of devils such as this England is, a natural-born Saint like me can make no headway. I have heard that even their famous Robert Grosseteste thought sometimes about making Brazen Images that could speak! No! Where there is any northern influence at all some sort of devilry's sure to enter.

"Yes, dear God, I hear you, dear God, you are the only one in the whole world who understands me, I hear you clearly! You are advising me to take ship at once for France, and when well across their channel of sea-devils to make my way to Dijon and then to Avignon. No! I'll be too dignified to bid anybody farewell. I expect they will listen all the better to that shallow orator from Cologne.

"They tell me that he, just like this Bacon from Ilchester, has long been promising all the boys who come to see him, especially if they come from Italy, grants from the Pope, for O! how he longs to put a little devilry from the north into the

326

mind of that pupil of his called Aquinas! But you won't succeed, you ugly great lecturer on the loves of bed-bugs and on the moral yearnings of will-o'-the-wisps! You won't succeed!

"No! No! The north will always breed new devils for the south to exorcize. Yes, I must be off at once to the nearest sea-port. Why! There is that funny horse with the swollen neck, and that crazy fellow who takes it about! God must have sent that pair especially to take me to the coast!"

With these words comforting his heart, Bonaventura strode off. He knew well that he, the great Franciscan Pope-maker, if not the next Pope, was simply running away. But he justified his precipitate flight on the sound rational ground—and the unprejudiced chronicler must recognize that this *was* an authentic justification—that to be defeated in single spiritual combat by Albertus would be a much more serious blow to his personal career than a swift strategic retreat, a retreat which could always be explained as a sudden imperative call from Rome.

With all these thoughts settling themselves in his mind he now strode with as much dignity and self-possession down the slope as he had done a few minutes earlier up the slope, and even Albertus himself couldn't resist observing with a sort of humorous self-derogatory admiration, that was almost like the feeling of a rival athlete, the way Bonaventura managed his feet and his steps under that grey robe as he descended, calling aloud in authoritative tones to Spardo, and, when at Cheiron's side, hesitating not a second to mount the animal, an effort which he carried through with dignified ease and even with a certain grace.

Spardo himself, it must be confessed, was not greatly pleased by being taken possession of in this wholesale manner. Even if his employment by Bonaventura turned out well as a matter of business, he was not the son of his father for nothing. There was something ignoble in forsaking this tragic drama at the crucial point. But what was the alternative?

Cheiron was responding with interest to the way Bonaventura managed the reins; and the best thing he himself could do now was to make an exit worthy of leaving Lost Towers to its fate. And a dramatic exit he did manage to make. He suddenly seized, as he followed Cheiron and Cheiron's stately rider, one of the massive pikestaves, which were really very dangerous weapons, carried by the King's Men.

The person whose weapon Spardo seized naturally refused to relinquish it, until Perspicax himself, who was only a few paces away and who wasn't at all anxious to start trouble, gave the man a nod to let him have the thing. Once in his possession none of the King's Men, nor any member of any conceivable body-guard of royal persons, could have handled this weapon, in which the piercingness of a spear is mingled in such appalling unity with the cleavingness of an axe, more professionally than Spardo.

"Bastard I may be," every swing and sweep of his feather-like beard seemed to chant to the hairy flanks of Cheiron and the flapping skirts of Bonaventura, "Bastard I may be, but my father was a King! Where is there a King here, among these petty baronies and manories and flanories? Kings of Bohemia are Kings indeed; and, as the song says, 'the heart of the laurel is in its seed'; but these scrabblement codfish blown in from the sea haven't got a King nearer than London; and the one they've got is a dying one, 'fed upon pap and sleeping on sap', as the song says."

To feel this terrific weapon in his hand, and to feel that with it he could destroy anyone he wished at any moment, gave Spardo such lively satisfaction that it reconciled him to following his horse and its stately rider, even though it meant his own departure from this memorable scene; but by keeping a firm hold with his free hand on the back of Cheiron's saddle he considerably reduced the pace of their retirement.

After using all his own magnetic will-power in addition to all the magnetism in his precious lodestone, to bring everybody to this particular spot, Petrus Peregrinus was beginning to find that it was easier to bring people together than to manage them when they were brought. Here certainly they all were!

But he knew only too well, as pressing "Little Pretty's" oblong cranium harder and harder against himself, he awaited the next move of chance or providence, that his own future was anything but assured.

Suddenly he became aware that, not only was the black-robed form of Albertus Magnus approaching him, but that the gigantic figure of Peleg, carrying the Brazen Head itself on his shoulder, with Ghosta at his side with one arm raised to help in supporting the thing's weight, was also, yard by yard, slowly ascending the slope.

What unluckily nobody had seen—or luckily perhaps, for who can tell from what horrors to be safely dead may save any of us—was that by the force of his scientific magnetism Petrus had drawn Heber Sygerius, the old ex-bailiff himself, out of Sir Mort's "Little Room", and dragged him all through the forest, and not by the easiest route either, till he sank absolutely exhausted, just where this particular trail ended, at the foot of the Lost Towers slope.

Old Heber knew exactly where he was; and the odd thing was that, though totally exhausted and unable to advance another step, he felt, as he stretched himself out on the warm, dead, dry, brown pine-needles, and allowed his whole body to relax and his whole being to sink down and down and down and down into a deep delicious bed of submission to the need for everlasting rest, a wave of greater happiness than he had ever known in all his long life.

It may well be that what gives to the wind along that Wessex coast its indescribable mixture of vague sorrow and wild obscure joy comes from its passing, on its unpredictable path, the floating hair of so many love-lorn maidens and the wild-tossed beards of so many desolate old men.

As it blew now across those forests and those swamps, it might have been suspected of taking a goblinish delight in switching and twitching and bewitching the crazy wisps that fluttered this way and that from Spardo's chin. Was its long-drawn wail made deeper, was its wild exultation made shriller, when it became the choric accompaniment to Spardo's careless killing of the one man in all that place who had prayed morning by morning and night by night for years that he might perish by just such a stroke and cross Acheron while he slept? For with the weapon he had snatched the Bohemian Bastard beheaded old Heber.

It must have been his awareness of the black-robed teacher from Cologne advancing so rapidly up the slope behind him that made Peter Peregrinus start running towards Lilith, as she stood defying all possible universes with her slender girlish back to the open doors of the absolutely empty and deserted

Lost Towers. When he was just beneath her and only a foot or so below her, he gazed passionately at her face. He not only felt an over-mastering longing to possess her, but a longing to possess her in complete solitude. And where could he find such solitude if not within the mysterious castle before him, at whose entrance she stood?

But as he gazed at her he saw to his dismay that there had come into her face a look of horror at him and of loathing of him and of contempt for him, such as he had never seen upon anyone's face before.

"All the same for that", as Homer puts it when he deals with these crises in human affairs, Petrus moved towards her. What drove him, what actuated him was clear enough. The difficult question for any chronicler to decide is the question as to whence within the almost closed circle of this strange man's consciousness he drew the strength, the energy, the spirit, to enable him to risk all, in this almost heroic manner? For *that he was risking all* was a truth he felt in himself, and of which he had not the slightest doubt.

And yet, cold-blooded, calculating, unscrupulous egoist as he was, he could not have been blind to the fact that there was no reason in the ordinary natural course of events why anyone, who so far had derived all sorts of thrilling feelings from being alone in life and being absolutely impervious to everything save his own private, uncommitted responses to life, should run a risk of this magnitude. Yes, from what region, or channel, or nerve in his being, did he derive the courage to take such a chance? Is it perhaps that in the lives of all human beings there come moments when some particular desire—in Peregrinus's case just now, what we call "the passion of love"—drives such a sharp wedge into the rocky substance of our animal nature that it goes clean through it, leaving a slit or crevice or crack in the mysterious thing that Grosseteste taught Roger Bacon to analyse very carefully, the thing which the theologians declared to be the vegetative soul of the foetus developing a nutritive soul, which is thus laid open for "Something", we can call it a rational soul, to enter from the limitless Outside when the infant is born.

Yes, he was risking his all and he knew it. And yet with this strength that came to him from somewhere outside himself, perhaps from the great "Outside" of all our planetary struggles, he still went forward, pressing the lodestone desperately against the fork of his body and repeating hoarsely in the depths of his being: "I am Antichrist! I am Antichrist!"

Lilith retreated till she was in the space between the two big doors; then seizing them both with outstretched arms, she tried to shut herself inside. But she was too late; and it was together, and with a combined effort, that they finally got the great doors shut and barred, leaving only their dark woodwork in the centre of that vast structure of stone as the target for all that crowd of onlookers.

Only one of the numerous people, whom the demonic power in Peter of Maricourt's lodestone had succeeded in gathering before those closed gates, gave any thought at that moment to what was happening behind those closed doors, and that one was Roger Bacon.

"It is like what went on," he told himself, "between the Devil and the first wife of Adam; the very same devil who a little later was present at the creation of Eve. If I weren't so tired I'd work out a clear map of these zodiacal revolutions in Time and Space."

It was indeed only natural that our Friar felt "tired" as he had not been out of his prison-chamber for more than a year. But he felt in good spirits and extremely interested in all he saw. So he seated himself on the mossy root of the oldest oak-tree in sight, a tree that might well have been an offshoot of the yet older one on which the bird rested who first brought to Britain the news of the death of Jesus; and from this secure position, as he contemplated the crowd and watched his own creation, the Brazen Head, balanced on the shoulder of Peleg and supported by what Homer would have called the "leukolenian" arm of the stately Ghosta, he allowed his mind to drift in a mood of fascinated wonder over the long eddies and aberrations of mankind's historic pilgrimage down the ages, pondering upon its pathetic, humorous, and tragical struggles with itself, with Nature, and with the innumerable false prophets and false gods who from the beginning have led us all astray.

But as he rested under that oak, half-awake and half-asleep and unusually happy, he suddenly became aware, by no very unnatural thought-transference, of the laboured approach to his side of none other than Lay-Brother Tuck from the Priory. The most hostile historian could have caught nothing but friendly amusement in the tone wherein this anticipator of all mankind's wildest inventions replied to this interruption when he heard himself greeted by Brother Tuck.

"Sit down, Brother," was all the Friar said. "So you've come for me, have you? Well, well! We shan't have any trouble except in our own legs as we go back. O no! I haven't the faintest intention of leaving my room in the Priory, my 'Prison' some call it, but you and I know better! We know how little I regard it as anything like that! What did I become a Friar for? Wasn't it for a quiet study to work in? You know *that*, Tuck old friend, as well as I do! Nobody but you, Tuck old rogue—Here! Sit you down here! You must be fairly done in after all that distance!—nobody but you knows what racy stories go round in our rollicking Bumset!

"Yes, and nobody but I know what a patient listener you are, my dear, to my irreverent gossip about the so-called 'makers of history', whose crazy ideas I have to describe to the Holy Father to prove I'm not idling away my time.

"Just look at all these people, Tuck! Just look at them! Do you know what got them here? I can't tell you exactly; but I can tell you this much. It has to do with a discovery in magnetism by this acquaintance of mine—I hesitate to call him a friend, as, to confess the truth, I'm rather scared of him and a bit nervous—I always *have* been since I first encountered the man *somewhere* abroad—I don't think it was in Paris—a bit nervous—you know how cowardly I am, Tuck old friend!—that he might start his magnetic experiments on me!

"But let him go. And by God, he has gone! He's behind those barred gates now, practising on young Mistress Lilith, who's just watched her parents murder each other, and seen all their people and all their serfs bolt after a speech by Dod Pole! Yes, that Lilith-girl watched her father and mother fight to the death; and then saw all her people, both bond and free, strip off their clothes and rush away into the woods and marshes!

"Old Dod Pole made one of those orations of his that every-one's been telling me about. And do you know, Tuck my friend, the old boy struck some note in my midriff that brought back to my mind a scene at Montacute when—but what on earth is that Dominican from Cologne, and a demi-semi bishop he is, too, preaching about now up there? Can you catch what he's saying?"

It was clear enough that Brother Tuck *had* caught very distinctly one point anyway in the Dominican's speech: "Well! I never thought I'd live to hear——" he now cried out.

Roger Bacon turned to him with the most lively interest. "Hear what? For God's sake, old friend, stop chuckling like an enamoured goblin and tell me what the fellow's saying! You've had lots of foreigners in your kitchen and ought to know their accent by now! My long walk to this confounded place and this wild wind and the whistling of those King's Men seem to have made me stone deaf."

Lay-Brother Tuck rose on his toes, for the angel who presided at his birth had decreed that, if he was to be the merriest of the sons of his mother, he must consent to be the shortest. He also seized a branch of the oak above the Friar's head and hoisted himself up a little, placing a screen of leaves between Roger Bacon and the astonishing spectacle before him.

But the Friar had trained himself too long to accept such crampings of vision to fall into a rage because he now couldn't see this black-robed figure at the gate of Lost Towers any better than he could hear him.

"He's got a thing on his head," announced Brother Tuck, "more like a turban than a mitre."

"Never mind what he's got on his head, Tuck. Tell me, for Jesus's sake, what the fellow's saying."

"He's offering to marry anybody who wants to be married."

"Nonsense, Tuck! Nonsense! No priest of our time, even if he were Archbishop of Ireland, would stand on a hill before the gates of Hell and offer marriage to the world!"

"But he is, he is! I tell you, Friar, he is! He's saying that the great evil of our time is that people don't marry early enough!"

"Not early enough, Tuck! God in Heaven! Haven't I been trying all my life to stop this curst habit of marrying little girls of twelve to old men of sixty? Not early enough! What will these doctors of theology want to do next? Marry babies to each other? Marry foetuses in separate wombs, on the chance that they turn out of opposite sexes?

"The truth must be that we monks and nuns and friars are finding our celibate life so indescribably tedious that we want to increase the number of these kicking, scratching, biting, beating, strangling couples, in order that we can at least feel thankful we're free from the claws of a mate! But shall we never see, O my turtle-dove of Tucks, that it's our mania for marriage itself that's spoiling our world? Nature can provide us with loyal and faithful mates without our having formally to create such monstrosities of scratching and clawing."

Friar Roger continued for several minutes this diatribe against marriage; but Lay-Brother Tuck was by this time far too fascinated by what was going on to pay his metaphysical friend any further attention.

Roger Bacon's own mind, however, was itself soon wandering from the problem of marriage. It was of astrology he was thinking now as he stared heavenward above the left buttock of Brother Tuck and through an impenetrable mass of oak-leaves. Thus it was not the mid-day sunshine beating down on the black robes and elaborate head-dress of the teacher of St. Thomas Aquinas that the inventor of the Brazen Head was now beholding, but the black abysses of the star-sprinkled midnight sky wherein he saw, although many of them would in reality when midnight came have been totally invisible, all the stars that were important as signs of the zodiac.

But something in the whole atmosphere of this particular spot on the earth's surface at this particular moment soon forced our great scientist's mind back upon the religious creed which from childhood he had been taught to take for granted.

He shut his eyes to both the blue sun-bright sky of reality and the black starlit sky of his imagination and began murmuring to himself:

"*Dicit ut audiat vocem Domini et vocem angelorum et videat angelos transfiguratos*—He says that he heard the voice of the Lord and the voice of angels and that he saw transfigured angels.

"*Christo vero habuit divinum testimonium, quod testimonium Deus*

334

Pater fecit ei—Christ truly had a divine testimony, namely the testimony which God the Father himself made on his behalf.

"*Hic est Filius Meus dilectus in quo mihti complacuit*. This is my Beloved Son in whom I am well pleased."

Had some observant passer-by, endowed, let us suppose, with the power of reading a person's thoughts, caught the drift of the Friar's murmured words, he might well have been astonished that so great a scientist, whose inventions were beginning to be the wonder of the whole intellectual world, should be muttering at a crisis like this sentences that were involved in the very foundation of the Christian faith. The truth was that Roger Bacon had taken Aristotle for granted with one side of his nature, and the New Testament equally for granted with the other side of his nature, and had never, as Albertus of Cologne did, brought them into logical opposition to each other and into logical relation with each other.

But, after all, Friar Roger's ways are the ways of Nature herself in regard to these abysmal matters. Out of the confusion which she seems to prefer to any orderly workshop, Nature seems anxious to thicken out the drama she has inaugurated by creating ironic commentaries upon her own doings, whose choruses are not so much the expression of approval or disapproval as of humorous recognition, and produce the effect of a faint orchestral accompaniment, an accompaniment that reaches us from extremely far away and possibly from a sphere totally different from our own.

If Friar Bacon had not been so absorbed in his interior vision of the signs of the zodiac and of the relation between Mercurius and Virgo and in the agitating conclusion he had reached—for to him by far the most interesting aspect of astronomy was astrology—about the perilous influence of our earthly satellite, the Moon—"Luna significat super-nigro-manciam et mendacium—The moon is significant of higher black magic and trickery"—he would have doubtless had some striking commentary to make upon what was now going on in front of those closed gates of Lost Towers.

All that morning Albertus Magnus had been saying to himself: "Whatever it was that brought all these people here and brought me on the top of them all, I'd be worse than the

335

self-conscious fool I am if I didn't take advantage of it in some way. That's what's the matter with me. I'm no good at creating situations. I just accept them and make the necessary plunges and darts and dives and gestures as seem called for.

"The one single act of my whole life"—so the great teacher's thoughts ran on, even after he had begun acting his part for today—"that I did entirely on my own and under no influence from outside was when I gave up that bishopric: aye!" and Albertus indulged in a grotesque dramatic shudder and wrinkled up all his malleable features; "aye! aye! but it was an appalling experience, those two years of being a bishop! But what on earth am I going to do with this chance the Lord has thrown in my path?"

And then the inspiration came to him.

"Sex is the maddest force there is. Why then not consecrate this madness? All the way down the history of our race—not to speak of certain beasts and birds—males and females have gone through curious ceremonies to celebrate this union. When we Christianize marriage, it is to demonstrate our share in Christ's own desperate and eternal act of faith that He was the Son of God. Sex is the greatest pleasure and the greatest pain in life; and the ceremonious consecration of the joining together of sex-mates has been the instinctive retort of all animal life to the insanity of sex from the beginning of the world."

Thus did the thoughts of Albertus Magnus run on, even while he began the quaint performance into which his "guardian angel", or, if you like, "his conscience"—although that word introduces just as many insoluble riddles—had now precipitated him.

"Come hither my son Tilton, sculptor and carver and builder of a shrine! Come hither my daughter Una, of the family of Pole, largest of all the families upon the said manor! If you Tilton take you Una to be your wedded wife, and if you Una take you Tilton to be your wedded husband, all the old deep rifts, between those who work on the land and those who own and fight for the land, will be healed!"

To the absolute amazement of Brother Tuck and of a good many others of those who were watching this queer scene, but not to the surprise of young John, who was now standing at

Sir Mort's side and explaining to him more things than Sir Mort could or would or can be imagined ever wanting to understand, both Tilton and Una now appeared hand-in-hand before Albertus Magnus.

So accustomed was Albertus to this particular ceremony, every word of which he knew by heart, that it was not long before this pair's union was consecrated, consecrated before men and before birds and beasts and angels and demons, consecrated as one flesh.

This had no sooner been done than bursting forth from the band of people who surrounded Sir Mort, and followed with obvious anxiety by both the Baron Boncor and his boy-knight Sir William, there emerged in a furious rush of frenzy like a shrieking Valkyrie the figure of Lady Ulanda, whose whole body—since to increase her speed, or perhaps deliberately to enhance the effect of her wrath, she kept tearing from her person one flimsy garment after another—was positively contorted with emotion.

It was purely against Friar Bacon that her anger was directed; for, by his cold refusal on that one fatal visit of hers to his room, to play the part of her dresser-up and devoted medico-magico, he had hurt that centre of a woman's life-illusion, a blow to which goes deeper into her essential being than if you cut off one of her arms at the wrist or one of her feet at the ankle.

When she reached the spot where the gigantic Peleg was standing, with Roger Bacon's Brazen Head upon his shoulder, to the pedestal of which—for the Head had nothing except that neck upon which Ghosta had confessed to have had, in complete nakedness, a mysterious sexual ecstasy—Ghosta's perfect white arms were now raised, Ulanda for one second stood still.

Then with a wild cry she flung herself, not only against the weird Object, alive and yet not alive, created by the Friar, but upon all three of them, clawing at Peleg's throat with one hand, seizing Ghosta's right arm with the other, and shaking them both so violently that the Brazen Head fell to the ground!

By what some would call Providence, others Chance, and yet others the protective power of the Devil, the Brazen Head descended to the earth the right way up, and indeed sank into a patch of grass so smoothly and easily that it rested there at once in complete quiescence, as if that little patch of greenery had risen to meet it out of the abyss as its destined home.

There was something about this startling event, whether you considered it an event in favour of the Head or against the interest of the Head, that affected everybody who was looking on. The person who was most affected was young John; for his link with Roger Bacon was so intimate and close that to see Roger's creation fall from the giant Peleg's shoulder clear to the ground was more than young John's heart could bear, and he acted as a child might have done.

He fell on his knees, covered his face with his hands, and burst into a fit of violent sobbing and weeping. Young John's sobs, however, since he knelt on the ground and pressed his hands to his face, were not loud enough to turn people's attention away from Albertus Magnus.

This simple-minded great man, who had become without knowing it the most important teacher in the world, having successfully married John's dear brother Tilton to the beautiful Una or Oona and thus having ended the feud between the old rebel Dod Pole and the bailiff-family of Sygerius, had evidently, in that energetic innocence and inspired foolhardiness that characterized him, decided to continue his marriage campaign and had summoned, loudly and clearly, Raymond de Laon and Lil-Umbra to come before him.

The sound of their names roused Sir Mort from the trance he'd fallen into, a trance, or a cessation of every bodily activity save breath and pulse and heart-beat, which was more familiar to his family than any other mood of his, but which covered in reality a much more consciously philosophical attitude to life than Lady Val or his three children realized.

Sir Mort was a queer mixture of a predatory animal with the sort of animal that predatory creatures, including men, are so addicted to hunting: and it now struck him that here was a supreme opportunity for an absolute escape from all those accompaniments of marriage that Lady Val would most certainly have insisted upon. It pleased him also to note that Lady Ulanda, who was now clinging to her husband's arm with an expression of abandoned and doting felicity, was evidently beside herself with satisfaction at having caused the collapse of Roger Bacon's Brazen Head, even if no further than to the ground.

It was a lucky thing for young John, this abrupt and unexpected summons of Lil-Umbra and her betrothed Raymond to this unpremeditated exchange of marriage vows; for Tilton and his bride had roused Sir Mort from his "hunter's trance," and were conversing eagerly with him, and there was no one immediately available to hold the horses of these new candidates for the marriage sacrament. So that it fell to the lot of young John to stand between these two horses, one of which was called "Rip" and the other "Strip", and get a tight hold on both pairs of reins.

The impetuously well-meaning Albertus was himself just then a little bit worried by a tickling at the back of one of his ears, which he erroneously fancied to be due to some mis-arrangement of his head-dress, but which really was caused by the fluttering of a midge. And it was this small annoyance that made him completely forget to use one rather important sentence in the course of the ceremony, a sentence the omission of which made no real difference but had an odd effect. But though the excited Lil-Umbra did not notice this lapse, her calmer companion stored it up in his mind as one of those humorous accidents that seem intentionally to disturb the dignity of our human life upon earth as a professional fool rattles his bells.

Although the accident to the Brazen Head had set John weeping like a child it now became necessary for him to take the two horses down the hill, where he tied them, with the help of Lay-Brother Tuck, to Friar Bacon's oak-tree.

It was a much less agitating meeting than he expected that young John had then with his adored master. The Friar treated him, he noticed, with deep pride and satisfaction, rather as a responsible fully grown-up man and as an equal, than as a pupil or disciple.

"You and I mustn't let ourselves," the Friar told him quietly, "get too agitated, whatever they do to our Brazen Head. We know he is, poor old dear, only about a fiftieth part of a real person. We've given him the power of calculation along certain lines; and I *hope*, though I am not quite sure about that, that in a great crisis he might even speak. But I am afraid the poor dear is still devoid of real life, for so far we haven't learnt the art of creating life, though we may learn it before we've done.

"But we must remember that all living creatures, even worms and insects and sea-shells, have a consciousness of being themselves and only themselves, and have the power of saying to themselves like Jehovah, *I am that I am.* I wish I could believe that our poor old Brazen Head, whom an angry woman just now threw to the ground, has the power of saying to itself: 'I am the Brazen Head, made by Roger Bacon. I am as much of a real conscious self as that daddy-long-legs now resting on my shoulder!'"

Young John couldn't even smile at this, for the occasion was too serious. Pressing his knuckles against his own cheek to prevent the flush he felt mounting up under his skin, he boldly asked him a very delicate and crucial question.

"I needn't tell you, Father," he said, "how you have always taken the place for me since I was a boy of all other human loves and devotions. When I think of embracing anyone or of being embraced and of the closest intimacies"—at this point, as he felt his cheeks begin to burn, he thought with relief that, in the burning sun-ray that poured between those branches, nothing of what he experienced beneath his skin could possibly be observed—"I seem never able to think of anybody but of you, my beloved master. Now that Tilton, my elder brother, has found a mate, it's not, I hope, my duty to marry anybody, or to have children by anybody. Nor, as long as I feel no special call to join a religious order, is it, I hope, my duty to become a monk or a friar? What I want to do, master most dear, is to serve you and help you, until I die. When you let me take that 'Opus' of yours abroad and place it where I knew it would reach the Holy Father, I felt happier than I'd ever been in my life before. You don't think, master, do you, that I'm shirking my duty by refusing to marry and have children?"

Friar Bacon only revealed by a very faint trembling in his voice how deeply he was affected by his pupil's words. What he said was emphatic and definite.

"As long as we are considerate to other people," he said,

"and as kind and sympathetic towards them as our circumstances permit, we have all got to live to ourselves, for ourselves, in ourselves and by ourselves. This is how, as Aristotle teaches, matter produces us out of itself, as a product to satisfy its deep 'privation', or its desperate yearning and craving to possess what it feels *could* proceed from it, but what, so far in its long history, has *not* proceeded from it!

"You, my son, have so far dedicated your whole life to learning. And as long as you feel thus impelled, I think you should so continue. But on the other hand if by fate or chance you met a girl you loved, and who loved you, I would say you had better marry and use your education to help this old world of ours out of its ignorance in some practical and active way.

"As long as I am alive I shall cling to your help and hold fast to your love as the most precious help and the most sacred love that life has allowed me to know. And when death divides us, remember this. The fruits of a learning that has been harder than slavery to acquire will be sweeter than the roses of Sharon to enjoy."

Ghosta had sunk down beside the Brazen Head the moment it was upon the ground, and she was still pressing the palms of her hands against its neck and against its shoulders and upon its implacably oracular chin. She wasn't weeping as John had wept, but she was evidently affected by some strong interior emotion.

And it would have been clear to anyone present at this unusual scene, whose interest had been aroused by these two immigrants from Palestine, that the gigantic Peleg, who was standing over her, was not a little disturbed by this emotion of hers.

"Have mercy upon me Almighty Jehovah, Lord God of Israel, Lord God of Sarah and Leah, of Rachel and Rebecca!" this proud, reserved, and most beautiful daughter of Israel prayed. And as she prayed, she reminded herself that in a certain sense she had quite deliberately mingled her virginal life in a weird erotic ecstasy with the sub-human, sub-animal, sub-vegetable life of this Brazen Head beside her.

"Is there," she allowed herself to whisper to the thing, "is there any way I can get rid of this mad terror I have of the passing of time?"

But Ghosta and Peleg weren't the only pair of lovers brought to that place by the magnetism of "Little Pretty."

"What is it my angel?" asked Raymond de Laon of Lil-Umbra, as in their new relation they descended the slope towards their horses. "Are you hurt? Are you afraid? Have you seen something? Have you thought of something?"

For the first time since they first met Raymond noticed that Lil-Umbra had difficulty in replying. But with an effort she spoke clearly and distinctly.

"Something terrible is going to happen! I feel it all through me. But not to us, Raymond; no, not to you or to me. But stop, Raymond. Turn and look at those closed doors!"

He gazed at her in silence, and they both swung round, her eyes wide and terrified, staring at the entrance to the Castle, but his still fixed on her face. But as so often happens in a human crisis, they were suddenly jerked out of their tension by a voice at Raymond's side; and there, close at his elbow, was none other than Lay-Brother Tuck!

"He's gone to sleep, my lord of Laon! He's gone to sleep, my lady of Leon! And I thought perhaps you'd take him back to the Priory on one of your horses and perhaps take me on the other! If you will agree to celebrate your union by this great charity before going to—to wherever you *are* going for your wedding-night—to the Fortress I expect—I can promise you not only my own special prayers, but the special prayers of the whole Priory of Bumset!

"The most lucky first night," Brother Tuck went on, "that a bride and bridegroom can possibly have for their first bed together is a great and sweet charity, such as it would be to both me and the Friar if you found it in you to do for us this gallant and beautiful deed!"

Lay-Brother Tuck now began to bob and babble and bubble and burble round them so buoyantly that the tender clasp with which Lil-Umbra was holding Raymond's hand became first an indignant pressure and then an angry clutch.

"Bridegroom with Bride you be!" he went on. "And I be a'begging of 'ee to let me's wone baby-self and Friar's man-mighty self sit astride of your 'osses while you makes 'em gallop. 'Gallopy up and gallopy to it! Gie her a sup and she'll let 'un do it!' Don't 'ee understand, O most elegant lord of far-away Leon, that if the blessed Friar be behind she, and me wone self be behind thee, it won't take long to be at Priory door; and a holy charity you'll have performed."

Lay-Brother Tuck kept bobbing round them so vigorously and making with his short bare arms so many effective if quite inaudible shoo-ings and shush-ings that, in their present dazed state, Lil-Umbra upset by her premonition of catastrophe, and Raymond wondering what Lady Val would say if they *did* follow Tuck's suggestion and spend their wedding night in the Fortress, they were rushed down the hill just as if they'd been a goose and a gander, until they actually reached the oak under which Friar Bacon, in complete abstraction from all immediate events, was composing one of his most comprehensive sentences as to the relation between astronomy and astrology; and before they really knew what had happened to them, they were cantering rapidly towards Bumset and towards an extremely bewildered reception by Prior Bog.

Albertus Magnus of Cologne, having finished what in the energetic and impulsive simplicity of his mind he had suddenly conceived to be the will of the Maker and Sustainer of our incomprehensible universe, came slowly down the slope towards the group of manorial lords and their families who now surrounded Tilton and his bride Una. To the end of that generation some sticklers for local tradition persisted in calling Una by the more romantic name of Oona; and in his desire to make his brother as poetical as he could, so that he might be as far as possible from his own scientific and philosophical ideal, young John always warmly and ardently supported the Oona side in the division of opinion as to this maiden's name.

Indeed it more than once crossed the mind of Lil-Umbra, when she noted Tilton's interest in this beautiful member of what might be called the revolutionary family of old Dod Pole, whose influence was so great among the serfs of the Manor of Roque, that there was really something more daring and unconventional about Tilton's unashamed attraction to a girl of this class than in all young John's free-thinking attitude towards the foundations of the Christian faith.

What on earth their mother would think, what on earth their mother would feel, what on earth their mother would do

343

and say, when Tilton and his bride, whether she was called Una or Oona, got home to the family hearth that night, she hardly dared to imagine.

"I mustn't, I *can't* wish this man from Cologne hadn't come among us," she said to herself. "But with Mother's excitable nerves where anything to do with marriage comes in, and her sensitiveness about noble blood and noble manners, she may be furious with Father for letting this Albertus marry us off like this, as calmly as a Spanish prince breeds Arabian horses!"

But it was not of Tilton's bride that Lil-Umbra was thinking as she accompanied Raymond in their wild ride to the Priory, carrying with them both the creator of the Brazen Head and the Priory court fool, Lay-Brother Tuck; it was about that premonitory shock she had suffered just before they began their ride through the forest.

What on earth had that meant, that vision she had suddenly seen of the whole of Lost Towers going up in fragments like the flaming scoriac lava from a bursting volcano, up, up, up, towards a black and thundering sky!

It was curious that both the great manor-lords, the father of Lil-Umbra and the devoted friend of Raymond, accepted without a murmur Albertus' high-handed meddling with the destiny of marriage. Yes, both the scrupulous Baron Boncor and the unscrupulous Sir Mort Abyssum, took with complete *sang froid* the startling events that now began to occur. These events which future chroniclers will, let us hope, describe as calmly as we are describing them now, were heralded by a singular fit, or seizure, or obsession, so odd that it would be difficult to account for it, on the part of young Sir William Boncor, who surely must have been the youngest of all knights who ever received the accolade.

It is a faithful chronicler's duty, not only to his sovereign lord but to his own lawful heirs and descendants, to record the queerest occurrences just as they occur without either obsequious or malicious exaggeration. And what Sir William did at this point was to dance a grotesque dance, a dance that had become popular at all the country fairs in Cornwall and had just spread into Wessex, a dance that was called "Jig it for Judy" and that had gestures in it that were more amusing than seemly.

Lady Ulanda at first pretended not to notice Sir William's whirligig arabesque, but when the stately figure of Albertus of Cologne in his Dominican weeds joined their group and looked askance at this inexplicable tom-foolery, she let go her hold on her husband's wrist and gave her son a shrewish cuff across his left ear-hole.

This maternal rebuke having successfully quieted her youthful knight-errant, Ulanda turned her attention to the Brazen Head, and with her hand once more caressing Baron Boncor's wrist, as if she had chosen him as her only true-love that very day, she set herself to wonder whether anything especially disconcerting would happen to her if she suddenly snatched up the flintiest of the stones that sprinkled the hillside, and rushing straight at that Brazen Head in defiance of the Jewish couple who appeared to be guarding it, gave it a few of the straight blows she burned and throbbed to give its human creator.

The sun was already well-past its meridian, and there was a queer dark cloud resembling the head of a giant just above the sea-ward horizon, when everyone heard far away to the north a distinct roll of thunder.

"What the devil are all these people waiting for?" Perspicax enquired of Colin and Clamp, who, from an instinctive feeling that when King's Men from London awaited events, events were sure to arrive, felt reluctant to depart.

"I *think* I saw old Dod Pole's Bet hurrying off home with Bailiff Randy's daughter Crumb," replied Colin rather wistfull; for he had a tender feeling for both these little maids, especially for the exquisite way Crumb's hair would float on the wind when there was wind on which it could float.

"I can tell you whither those little birds are flitting!" threw in the unequivocal Clamp. "They're off to take the news to Lady Val!"

The prediction of Clamp proved correct. At that familiar little postern, whence from her infancy, and before she had so much as heard of the formidable House of Abyssum, she had peered out into the forest, Lady Val was even now listening to the sound of horses' hooves growing first nearer and then further.

And well indeed might the lady listen to those hoof-beats, for the horses were bringing, not only Roger Bacon and

Brother Tuck to the gate of the Priory, but Lil-Umbra and Raymond de Laon to that very door.

"Don't 'ee cry, child! They will all be back soon!" whispered Nurse Rampant on her left hand.

"Not without having seen and having spoke to the girt Devil himself, every thumping one of them!" grunted old mother Guggery on her right hand.

Young John had remained standing alone after Lil-Umbra and Raymond had carried off Roger Bacon and Brother Tuck. He had heard that roll of thunder. He had seen that cloud like a giant's head. And he was now staring at the closed doors of Lost Towers. Why he was compelled to stare at them he could not have told a living soul, not even his master Roger Bacon, for whom his devoted love went beyond all reason.

But suddenly young John saw those doors open wide and two human forms holding each other by the hand come forth, the forms of Petrus Peregrinus of Maricourt and Lilith of Lost Towers. Young John had always dreaded certain particular mental images, and the worst of all among these was the image of something different from the male organ of generation being thrust into a female's womb. Another was the image of a fiery rod being thrust into a man's anus.

Both these terrifying images now rushed simultaneously into young John's mind and even seemed to incarnate themselves in the human figures of Petrus Peregrinus and Lilith.

But the moment Petrus Peregrinus began speaking, these horrible images vanished from young John's mind—vanished forever, nor, until his death long afterwards, ever returned to trouble him. They did not even dare—although horrible images of this sort clearly possess devilish intelligencies of their own—to come near him on his deathbed.

"*I am Antichrist!*" were the words that Petrus was now shouting, and shouting in a voice whose appallingly penetrating tone none who heard it that day ever forgot to the end of their lives.

It was as if some power, far beyond the reach of any wanderer from Picardy, had spoken out of a hiding-place as old as the world. What young John did in the depths of his mind to drive into silence, not only the insane voice of this Antichrist from Maricourt, but the much less insane and for that very reason the far more loathsome voices of the treacherous and hypocritical and meretricious champions of a Christ with whom they had less in common than had His most shameless enemy; what young John did in the depths of his mind to overwhelm both of these was a very singular thing.

He gathered up all those wild and strange speculations about microscopes and telescopes and air-vessels and sub-marine vessels, of which Friar Bacon was always talking to him, and made of them in his mind a great mechanical shield which was so convoluted in its metalwork that it could repel any sound in the whole universe; and the echo it threw back when that Antichrist cry reached it was at once so rocky and aerial and oceanic and fiery that, as it rolled into space, it carried away with it both the pious hypocrisy that had been pierced by the voice of Antichrist and its own heroic recalcitrance to them both. In fact it carried everything away.

But when the echo from that shield he had mentally created from all those metallic elements died down, young John saw to his astonishment Lilith fling one of her long white arms about her companion's shoulders and swing him round till they both faced the castle.

Then young John saw the girl raise up both her arms, and he noticed that she held in her hands a curious little object like an extra large pen or pencil or a leafless hog-weed-stalk or a small six-inches-long bull-rush.

This little object Lilith first lifted up towards the sky, and then, with an incredibly swift movement of her arm, turned it against the Castle. And at once, clear before John's eyes, and before the eyes of all who were present, the whole structure of Lost Towers went up into the air, went up with the swiftness of a falling star, only it was a star that in this case was not falling but rising, until it vanished from sight in the blue depths of the empyrean. Then both those two figures turned to each other, each of them with raised arms. And it became clear to John for one blinding second that all four hands were clasped round that strange little object.

"They are pointing it at their own bodies!" he said to himself. And his vision of what they were doing was indeed the truth. Both their bodies now burst into flame and became one single fiery ball; and as John watched it, this burning orb became so dazzling as to shine in his eyes with the blaze of a sapphire, and he perceived that it was moving fast through the air towards the Brazen Head. At that moment he heard the Head speak.

"Time *was*," it said. "Time *is*," it said. "And time *will*——"

But the burning meteor then fell upon it, and neither it nor what destroyed it was ever seen again.

A GLASTONBURY ROMANCE

A New Edition with a Preface by the Author

"This is a notable English literary event . . . all the qualities of compassion and breadth and cunning insight which we associate with genius are here." ANGUS WILSON (*Observer*).

"His prose has an organic life and beauty of a unique and keenly enjoyable kind; and the construction of his best novels attains the complexity and success which are achieved only in the unconscious of a major writer. I commend *A Glastonbury Romance* to those readers who are able to recognise genius that is not yet mentioned in textbooks. Mr. Powys, I believe, is one of the last survivors in the main stream of the English novel's vanishing greatness." GEORGE D. PAINTER (*New Statesman and Nation*).

"We have today no more consummate stylist than Mr. Powys. I know of no living writer with so vast a vocabulary at his command, nor anything like his mastery of the long sentence. The style is classically grand with cadences reminiscent of Sir Thomas Browne, and yet, somehow, also homely and colloquial; while every phrase bears the imprint of a unique personality." G. WILSON KNIGHT (*Yorkshire Post*).

"Really a tremendous book. It makes the competent little novels that week by week are hailed as 'masterpieces' look silly. In searching for comparison, one finds oneself using such names as Hardy or Hamsun. . . . In breadth, rhythm and intensity *A Glastonbury Romance* has something of the mighty pantheism of Rubens." SIR GERALD BARRY.

ATLANTIS

A Novel of Odysseus

"John Cowper Powys is one of our few contemporary novelists capable of writing in the grand manner. With him everything is conceived on an heroic scale, and his works are massive attempts to encompass the significance of every created thing. . . . *Atlantis* is an exuberant, splendidly comic novel." PATRICIA HODGART (*Manchester Guardian*).

"I can think of no living writer who has the same kind of stature as Mr. Powys. . . . Melville is the only writer in English with whom he can be compared." JOHN HEATH-STUBBS (*Time and Tide*).

"There is something of Rabelais and Dostoevsky in the hilarity and nervousness of this weird book. And something of Mr. Powys himself in the superb man Odysseus, with all of his lordliness, his cunning and his laughter." STEVIE SMITH (*Observer*).

"A tremendous imaginative essay, a vast pantomime of the old gods playing out their conflicts against the background of that 'multiverse' which is the author's favourite philosophic conception. The theme emerges as the continuity of those conflicts, here elaborated in terms of mythology, fable, and the gods' obscure genealogies. The Powys prose rolls and surges in a sea of imagery, by turns splendid, fantastic, nightmarish, and comic." *The Scotsman.*

"The subject is eminently suited to the erudition and enormous energy of one so attuned to the spirit of the lusty pagan world. Mr. Powys flings himself with gusto into the atmosphere of that distant time, endowing the figures of ancient mythology with as human and colloquial a life as his own contemporaries, and inventing with fertile originality these further adventures in the odyssey of his hero." MARGARET WILLY (*Birmingham Post*).

PORIUS

A Romance of the Dark Ages

"A major work by a genius." DANIEL GEORGE.

"Before such a work as *Porius*, standards of measurement are confounded. Its imaginative shape moves through time and space impelled, as it were, by eternal forces. The philosophical profundities of *Porius* and the vigorously romantic texture of the tale are parts of a whole conceived on a scale rare in modern letters." *The Scotsman*.

"Populous as a Shakespearian History . . . . There is true grandeur of ambition in this book." JOHN RUSSELL (*Listener*).

"Reading it is like wandering by a river . . . so much is packed into this book of character and incident. Mr. Powys, indeed, is like a river himself: his wandering, ever-thrusting, yet tractless mind gives one at once the feeling that though the book itself is finished and closed the writer himself has gone on, drawn as by an insatiable longing, towards some impenetrable sea. . . . What a powerfully evocative writer Mr. Powys is. . . . One remembers his *Wolf Solent* and *Glastonbury Romance*, which seemed to yield up the very spirit of English country, unequalled since Hardy." JAMES HANLEY (*Recorder*).

"Mr. Powys's new novel is, among the minnows of contemporary fiction, a whale." HUGH L'A. FAUSSET (*Manchester Guardian*).

"*Porius* is no meat for babes. It demands, as it will reward, an endurance of attention. . . . He conceives greatly and labours magnificently. To him the writing of fiction is a matter for the mind and soul of man; of the high quality of mind and profundity of soul which he brings to its exercise there can be no question." COLLIN BROOKS (*Truth*).

PORIUS is currently available in the limited edition of two hundred copies, signed by the author and hand-bound by Bayntun of Bath in half morocco leather, at Five Guineas.

VISIONS AND REVISIONS

With a Preface by the Author

A book of Literary Devotions in honour of Rabelais, Dante, Shakespeare, El Greco, Milton, Charles Lamb, Dickens, Goethe, Matthew Arnold, Shelley, Keats, Nietzsche, Thomas Hardy, Walter Pater, Dostoievsky, Edgar Allan Poe, and Walt Whitman.

"Mr. Powys loves books because he glories in life itself and because books can be a means to more abundant life . . . in an age when bookloving has become suspect, and literary criticism is so often a kind of Lenten fast, Mr. Powys's gargantuan capacity for enjoyment—of Arnold and Pater no less than of Rabelais and Dante—is a unique and welcome phenomenon." *Times Literary Supplement.*

"He believes that the most valuable books are those which 'create a certain mood, a certain temper—the mood, in fact, which is prepared for incredible surprises—the temper which no surprise can overpower'. In searching for this special quality in the writers whom he loves he again and again draws our attention to facets of genius which we had not noticed before." SIR HAROLD NICOLSON (*Observer*).

"I find myself wondering whether a single page of his incisive appreciations may not often outweigh a whole volume of 'practical criticism' . . . only a great writer, who knows how to sink phrase on piercing phrase into the soul of each in turn, could do so much so briefly, so vividly, so poignantly." G. WILSON KNIGHT.

"A timely and salutary book, recalling us to a proper respect for literature and gratitude to great authors." DANIEL GEORGE.

"He is a dynamic, creative critic who, instead of standing outside his subject and coolly assessing its merits and defects by comparing them with the achievements of other writers, digs deep down into his subject, identifies himself with him, illustrates him, interprets him, shows his aims and intentions and how he appeared to himself." L. P. HARTLEY (*B. B. C.*).